JULIE-ANN'S JOURNEY

A NOVEL

WILLIAM PANZARELLA

ISBN: 978-0-578-12611-1

Book design by Maureen Cutajar
www.gopublished.com

Chapter 1

Julie-Ann Dyanna Crown is young, beautiful, rich, and smart. She leads the life that most people only dream of and that many people would sell their souls for. Just twenty-five-years-old, she has the looks of a model, standing a slender, statuesque five-foot-ten with long, straight platinum blonde hair, glowing hazel eyes, and a flawless face. She has sex appeal and class. Whether wearing jeans and a t-shirt or a Valentino dress with Manolo pumps, Julie-Ann never left the house without looking her best.

Julie-Ann's father, James Crown, has a net worth of over four hundred million dollars. He is the CEO of Diamond & Russell, a global Fortune-500 investment firm, whose headquarters are in Midtown Manhattan. At forty-six, he was the youngest man ever to be appointed to the position in the firm's illustrious eighty-five-year history. Now CEO for six years, he and the company survived the market crash and mortgage crisis of 2007-2008 and are once again starting to thrive.

Julie-Ann's biological mother died in a car accident when she was only six-years-old. Two years later her father remarried. Julie-Ann had always gotten along with her stepmother, Theresa. Having no children of her own, she never treated Julie-Ann like a stepchild. In fact, only twelve years her senior, Theresa treated her like a best friend. The two would go shopping together, and even went on vacations without James as he was usually too busy to leave work for more than a couple of days.

Julie-Ann was born with a silver spoon in her mouth and was spoiled throughout her life, but she was more than just beauty and wealth. Julie-Ann had always been a brilliant student. After graduating high school, she was accepted into Brown University, where she completed her Bachelors degree in finance.

Julie-Ann graduated college in 2009 when financial jobs were extremely hard to come by due to the Great Recession. Being the CEO of Diamond & Russell, her father was easily able to get her a position at JP Morgan Chase. But even with her bloodline and degree, no one was going to let someone without any real-world experience walk in the door and start trading. So Julie-Ann started as an assistant trader. However, because of who she was, she was put on the desk with the top equity traders and everyone treated her with kid gloves. Wall Street traders are usually ruthless towards assistants, especially newbies. Whether you are male or female, profanity, tongue-lashing, and degradation are commonplace on the trading floor. But no one wanted to piss off a Wall Street CEO, even if he was a competitor. Wall Street is still a small circle. Of course, there were the male traders that were hoping to get into her pants. Julie-Ann was stunning. Also, being the son-in-law of James Crown had a nice ring to it.

Julie-Ann never really took a shine to her job and after several months she was ready to quit. She was discovering that it just wasn't her niche. It was still mostly a boys' club, besides, she just didn't feel the excitement or enthusiasm. The whole stimulation of trading was to make money, and she already had plenty of money. Julie-Ann worked hard in college, but she always found time to party with her friends. Now, she usually arrived at work before 6:00 a.m. and didn't leave until 6:00 p.m., sometimes even later. Julie-

Ann knew she couldn't start off on the top, but still, she did not see the grueling work being worth the reward. She was not adverse to work, she just wanted to find a job—or a cause—she could be passionate about.

Julie-Ann discussed her feelings with her father. James Crown had always spoiled his daughter, but he always wanted her to know what it meant to put in a hard day's work and earn a living. He wanted her to be successful in her own right. Julie-Ann explained that she didn't have a problem with working hard but maybe Wall Street was just not for her. Mr. Crown had always told his daughter that she could do whatever she wanted to do; be whatever she wanted to be, and he told her that again. He also drilled home the point that it wasn't wise to just throw her four-year degree in finance out the window. He urged her to give it a little more time. If she still felt the same way after five or six months, then maybe she could look at other options. Somewhat reluctantly, Julie-Ann agreed.

Unbeknownst to his daughter, James had dinner with the head of Julie-Ann's department and asked if there was any way to get her more involved. Julie-Ann's boss said he would see what he could do. Both men knew that meant yes. Favors are a way of life on Wall Street, and Julie-Ann's boss knew that his would be repaid upon request. In that regard—and others—Wall Street is, and always has been very similar to La Cosa Nostra.

Julie-Ann's boss moved her from being an assistant trader to his personal protégé. Julie-Ann was not stupid; she knew her father had to have been behind it. But she honestly didn't see anything wrong with it. After all, despite her own accomplishments, having someone pull some strings for her was how she was raised.

Julie-Ann's boss taught her the ropes and had her work on various projects. He also had her sit in on meetings, both internal and with clients. It was during one of these client meetings that she met Kenneth Fister. Ken used to be a portfolio manager at JP Morgan, but now headed his own hedge funds. In fact, at twenty-nine-years-old, Ken was one of the hottest, young stars on Wall Street.

His upstart hedge fund company, Fister Capital, was outperforming some of the heavyweights in the industry.

Ken looked like he was made for Wall Street. Standing 6'2", he was slender with a sculptured face and chiseled chin. His teeth were gleaming white, and it seemed that he practiced his wide smile. His short, thick, black hair was always perfectly glued in place. Ken dressed impeccably, wearing Brioni suits, three hundred dollar silk ties, and gold cufflinks with his initials on them. Ken didn't just look the part, he played it. When he wasn't driving around in his black, GranTurismo Maserati, he walked around like he owned the world. Always speaking with a loud, outgoing voice, he smiled and was gentlemanly to the "powerful people" and sneered at or gave no time, to everyone else.

At first, Julie-Ann was only exposed to Ken's charming side. The first time she met him she was immediately sucked in by his good looks, as were most women. He had a commanding presence but was polite and always smiling. After the meeting, her boss explained how brilliant Ken was and how the sky seemed to be the limit for him. Of course, this only added to Julie-Ann's infatuation.

Ken also took keen notice of Julie-Ann, as most men did when they first met her. It was only afterwards, when he called Julie-Ann's boss about a business matter and inquired about her did he learn that she was James Crown's daughter. For someone who was all about connections and status, this peaked his curiosity. From that point on, like mounting a trophy on his wall, he made it his personal mission to get her into bed.

Julie-Ann wanted to see Ken again to get to know him better. She couldn't ask her boss; she just had to hope that he would take her along to another meeting. She did not have to wait long. A few days later, her boss needed Ken to sign some original documents. Ken suggested that his assistant just bring them over. Of course, he meant Julie-Ann.

After talking to Julie-Ann for awhile and buttering her up, Ken said that there were a few "very minor details" that had to be worked out for the deal and that the two of them could discuss it over lunch the next day. Julie-Ann said that she would have to run it by her boss, but Ken assured her that it would not be a problem. Her boss knew what Ken was up to, but truth be told, he just wanted to make Ken happy. His hedge funds were a very important relationship.

Within a few weeks, Julie-Ann and Ken were dating. It was the worst kept secret at both their firms. That kind of thing happens all the time on Wall Street. However, her father did not find out about the relationship until nearly a month later, when Julie-Ann told him. Although James Crown had never personally met Ken, he knew of him. He knew Ken had to be arrogant, but he also understood that he was bright, ambitious, and only moving up in the world. As long as Julie-Ann said Ken was treating her right, he approved of the relationship.

It was only a matter of time before Julie-Ann introduced Ken to her father. Ken pulled out all his charm, and the two seemed to hit it off. Of course, one being a titan of Wall Street and the other, a rapidly rising star, it did not take long until they started talking business and eventually had some dealings together.

Only seven months after they had started seeing each other, Ken proposed to Julie-Ann during a trip to Maui. She accepted. Her father gave them his blessing. Ken had his own money and was a go-getter. His stock was only rising. He also seemed to take loving care of Julie-Ann, and she was clearly in love with him. However, Mr. Crown was disappointed when his daughter explained that she was planning on quitting her job to become a fulltime housewife and to have a baby right away. He had nothing against being a grandfather, but he didn't want Julie-Ann to quit her job. He always told her to be her own woman, to never have to depend on a man. James reiterated his feelings to Julie-Ann, but her mind was made up. Eventually, Mr. Crown got over it. Besides, in reality, Julie-Ann would never have to depend on anyone financially.

The wedding was set for that August, of 2011. It was to be an elaborate event, with the reception at Cipriani. They had already sent invitations to over 250 guests. Julie-Ann's father insisted on paying for the wedding.

Though Julie-Ann often spent the night at Ken's apartment overlooking Central Park, she still lived with her father and Theresa, at their four-bedroom Midtown penthouse (Mr. Crown also had a house in the Hamptons). She and Ken had started looking at houses together and hoped to move into one by the time of their wedding. Ken wanted to be close to Manhattan because of his work, so they were searching in Scarsdale, one of the most affluent neighborhoods in New York.

Chapter 2

April 27, 2011. It was a little over three months away from Julie-Ann's wedding. Having already quit her job, she was flying to Miami for several days with her best friend, Amber. From there, she was going to fly to the Cayman Islands to meet up with Ken, who would be there on business. Because of the lax financial laws and tax breaks, many hedge funds do business in the Cayman Islands.

Early that morning, a personal limousine took Julie-Ann from her Midtown penthouse to John F. Kennedy International Airport, where a private jet was waiting for her.

It was a cold and dreary morning in New York, and as Julie-Ann gazed out the limousine's window at the gray sky, she took comfort in the fact that by the afternoon, she would be lying on the sun-soaked sand of South Beach. She called Amber to make sure she was also on her way to the airport. She was, and although they would see each other in about twenty minutes, the two friends giddily talked about what a fantastic trip it was going to be and all the things they were going to do.

Both twenty-five-years-old, Julie-Ann and Amber had been friends since they were fourteen. Like Julie-Ann, Amber was also beautiful and born into privilege. Her father, John Harlan, was a financial advisor to the stars. Though he worked with some famous actors, producers, and business moguls, he had found a niche advising some of the biggest names in the music industry. John had known James Crown from back when he used to work for Diamond & Russell. Like their fathers, the daughters became friends and even went to the same private school together. However, as Julie-Ann and Amber stayed close friends, John and James drifted apart. There was no bad blood between them. It was just that with their respective demanding positions and schedules, it was hard for them to find the time to hang out together. Still, they would sometimes talk on the phone, and once in a blue moon, would meet for lunch or dinner.

Amber's father had his own private plane, but today the girls would be flying on James Crown's Gulfstream G650, a high-speed, long-range jet and the flagship of the Gulfstream fleet. The pilot, a young, tall, handsome man dressed in a perfectly pressed captain's suit, met Julie-Ann and Amber on the tarmac, in front of the spotless white jet. The area was away from the commercial traffic of the airport. As the pilot greeted the girls and detailed their flying time and conditions, a luggage handler loaded their plethora of bags onto the plane. Just as the girls were about to board, the co-pilot, who routinely visually inspects the outside of the craft, came over and said hello.

Adorned in white leather and high-gloss cherry wood, the cabin exuded opulence. Able to carry ten passengers comfortably, there were seven, large swivel chairs, a long couch, three small but elegant tables, a wet bar, and several flat panel television sets. Everything was spotless and looked brand new.

"We should start taxiing in about ten minutes or so," the pilot said. "So if you ladies want to just take a seat."

Julie-Ann and Amber sat down in side-by-side seats, facing forward.

As the pilot went into the cockpit, the co-pilot came over to the girls remarking, "As you might have realized, Paul and I will be the only crew flying with you today. But if you need anything, please just let me know."

"Thank you," Amber said in a flirtatious voice as she flashed him her big, brown eyes.

The co-pilot looked at his watch. "We still have a few minutes. Can I get you ladies a drink?"

Julie-Ann smiled. "That's okay, but…"

Before Julie-Ann could finish her sentence, Amber interrupted. "Yes actually." She then turned to her friend. "Doesn't a mimosa sound good?"

Just then, the pilot called out for his partner from the cockpit, which had its door open.

"I'm sorry ladies. I have to go. I guess we're going to be taking off. But as soon as we reach cruising altitude, I'll make you those mimosas. Now if you would please, buckle up."

"No problem," Julie-Ann replied.

"We'll be waiting," Amber added in a coy voice.

As the co-pilot climbed into the cockpit and closed the door, Amber grabbed her friend's arm. "He is so hot. God, I'd like to get a piece of that."

Julie-Ann smiled. "He is pretty cute."

The pilot made an announcement over the intercom that they were beginning to taxi and that there were only two planes ahead of them before takeoff.

"Hey, have you ever had sex on the plane before?" Amber asked with a devilish grin.

"No. Where the hell am I supposed to do that? On the couch?" Julie-Ann pointed to the leather couch right behind the cockpit and visible to the rest of the cabin. "Besides, I'm usually with Theresa or my father." Julie-Ann paused. "Wait, you've done it on your father's jet before?"

"Well, you know his plane has that small sleeping compartment that you can close and lock the door. One time it was just me and Federico. You remember him, right?"

Julie-Ann nodded her head.

"Well, we went back there and had wild sex. In fact, we had to calm it down because the whole plane started shaking."

Julie-Ann laughed.

"Let me tell you something girl, you've gotta join the mile high club at least once in your life."

"Well, I will be flying back from Cayman with Ken. Maybe that'll be the perfect opportunity."

"So, you nervous about the wedding yet?"

Julie-Ann sighed. "Not nervous about getting married. There's just so much to do. I mean we have a fantastic wedding planner, but there's still so many things to decide on. It's a lot of pressure."

Amber patted her friend on the leg. "Don't stress, everything will work out fine."

Julie-Ann smiled. "Thank you. I'm so glad that you're going to be my Maid of Honor."

"Are you kidding me? I'm so excited."

The captain announced that they were next for takeoff. The girls paused from their conversation and checked their seatbelts. Amber clutched the armrest with her right hand. She was a frequent flier and was fine once in the air, but she still tensed up on takeoffs. Julie-Ann knew this, so she took hold of her friend's hand.

As soon as they reached their cruising altitude as promised, the co-pilot came into the cabin and made Julie-Ann and Amber their mimosas—using Dom Perignon—and poured them into Waterford Crystal flutes. Afterwards, he was ready to return to the cockpit, but Amber insisted on chatting him up, asking various questions about his life. Truth be told, he found it flattering and was eating it up. After about fifteen minutes, he poured the girls another mimosa each and explained that he actually needed to get back into the cockpit. Amber reluctantly let him go.

With the co-pilot gone, Amber and Julie-Ann resumed talking about the upcoming wedding.

"I still can't believe you got your father to get *Four to Go* to play at the reception," Julie-Ann said with excitement, referring to a hot new band.

"Well their manager loves my father. I think my father made him more money over the years than *Four to Go* did."

"Still."

Amber took a sip of her mimosa. "Well, wait to see what I have planned for your bridal shower and bachelorette party."

Julie-Ann smiled. "You're such a good friend. I can't believe everything you're doing. And here I am bitching to you."

Amber waved her hand at Julie-Ann. "Please Jules. Besides, what are BFFs for?"

Julie-Ann began to tear up. "Amber, you're gonna make me cry."

"Stop it. You'll ruin your mascara."

Julie-Ann daintily wiped her eyes. She then raised her flute. "Well here's to the best friend anyone could ever have."

Amber raised her glass. "Same here." With that, they gently touched flutes and then each took a drink.

After talking for about another thirty minutes, and finishing their second mimosa, Julie-Ann turned on the nearest television. While she was flipping through the channels, Amber fell asleep. Julie-Ann finally settled on TMZ, but after watching for only ten minutes, she also fell asleep.

The girls were awoken by the captain's announcement that they were beginning their approach into Miami International Airport. Within fifteen minutes, the plane was on the ground.

The Gulfstream taxied to a small terminal, away from the main commuter traffic. As Julie-Ann and Amber walked down the staircase onto the tarmac, under a bright, azure Miami sky, they were met by a heavyset man in a chauffeur's suit.

"Ms. Crown, Ms. Harlan, my name is Hector, and I will be your driver."

The girls said a fleeting hello as he led them to the white, stretch limousine and opened the door. Once they were inside, Hector helped an airport attendant with their bags.

As soon as they were in the limo, Amber opened up the small refrigerator which was stocked with Pellegrino water, juice, Heineken, Amstel Light, and various miniature bottles of liquor. She grabbed two Heineken bottles. "Time to party girl! We're in Miami! Hey look, there's a bottle of Dom on ice in the bucket. You wanna open that or do you want a Heineken?"

There was no answer.

Amber turned to Julie-Ann, who was rubbing her head and had a grimacing face. "Jules, what's wrong?"

"I just have this bad headache all of a sudden."

Amber opened a Heineken with an opener that was on the wet bar and went to hand it to Julie-Ann. "Well have a beer and drink it off. Or better yet, do you want a Vicodin? I have some. Or you could have both."

Julie-Ann continued to grimace. "No, that's okay."

"It hurts that bad?" Amber asked in a concerned voice.

"I never used to get headaches, but then all of a sudden, over the past month, I've been getting them a couple times a week. They seem to be getting worse. Maybe I should go to the doctor, but I figure they're just headaches. I mean everyone gets headaches, right?"

Amber put her beer in a placeholder and put her hand on Julie-Ann's leg. "Don't you see, Jules, it's just the wedding. You're getting all stressed out about it."

Just then, the driver's voice came over the intercom. "I'm sorry ladies, but I just want to make sure, we're going to the Fontainebleau, right?"

Amber pressed the talk button. "Yes," she replied in a visibly annoyed voice. She then turned her attention back to Julie-Ann. "Everything thing's under control. You have a fabulous wedding planner *and* Ken's a terrific guy!"

"Maybe you're right. Maybe it is the wedding."

"It's okay to be a little nervous, but don't let it overwhelm you. C'mon, when was the last time that just the two of us went away—no guys, just the girls? We're gonna have a marvelous time?"

Julie-Ann smiled. "You're right. We should be enjoying ourselves. I feel a little better already. Thank you."

"You're welcome," Amber replied as she handed Julie-Ann a beer. "Now chug-a-lug!"

Julie-Ann still had a headache, but it was getting better and she didn't want to seem like a downer. So she grabbed the beer, clanked it with Amber's bottle, and took a chug.

Amber turned on the XM Radio. The last thing Julie-Ann needed was to be in a confined space with blaring music, but once again, she did not want to seem whiney. So trying to completely cure her headache, she downed her beer as fast as possible. As soon as it was finished she tossed it in the trash. "Can you crack me open another one?"

"You go girl! Look at you. You leave me in the dust." With that, Amber opened another bottle of Heineken and handed it to her friend. She then started chugging hers to catch up.

As the limousine stopped at a red light, Amber noticed two teenage boys riding bicycles on the sidewalk. She rolled down her window. "Hey boys, you want a blowjob," she yelled at them.

"Amber!"

One of the boys looked over at the limo. With her head out the window and beer in her hand, she yelled the same thing again. The teens, which were now no more than fifteen feet away, dropped their jaws, not believing what they were seeing or hearing. As one of them continued to stare speechlessly at Amber, he totally took his eyes off where he was going and plowed into his friend, who was also looking over. The two of them crashed to the ground in a tangled web of bicycles. Amber thought it was hysterical.

As the light turned green and the limo pulled away, Julie-Ann playfully hit her friend. "Amber! That's awful," she said, though trying not to laugh.

"Oh, come on, they didn't get hurt. They were barely even pedaling. I probably made their day."

Julie-Ann couldn't hold her laughter back anymore.

As the limo approached the bridge to South Beach, Amber turned down the radio. "Oh my God, do you see that?" She said pointing out her still opened window.

Julie-Ann looked to see a makeshift tent-city of homeless people living adjacent to, and under, the beginning of the bridge. "Oh my God, are they living there?"

"Oh, how disgusting! That's so gross. Can't they go somewhere else?" Amber stuck her head out the window. "Go find a fuckin' job," she yelled at the top of her lungs.

"You don't have a job," Julie-Ann jokingly pointed out.

Amber looked at her best friend. Then, after a second of silence, without exchanging any other words, they broke out in laughter.

"Really though, that's so nasty," Amber added. "I better not see any homeless people in South Beach."

Just then, Amber's cell phone rang. It was her boyfriend, Tyler. She picked it up and started talking to him. Julie-Ann used the time to check her own phone. She returned some texts and then looked at her Facebook page.

The limo pulled up to the front of the Fontainebleau. The driver opened the back door for the girls as a porter came to help with their luggage. Her headache now entirely gone, and feeling a little buzzed, Julie-Ann tipped the driver twenty dollars. Then she and Amber walked into the sprawling resort and up to the check-in counter.

Although Julie-Ann and Amber were rich, they were not well known and didn't have to worry about paparazzi following them around. Still, they were VIPs—and treated as such. Both Julie-Ann and Amber had stayed at the Fontainebleau before, and Amber's father had also stayed there numerous times. In a resort that catered to the rich and famous, the Crown and Harlan names were royalty.

The woman at the front desk welcomed them back and asked how their trip had been. She then gave them VIP passes for the resort's club, LIV, one of the hottest clubs in Miami. She also let them know that they had a reserved cabana by the pool for their entire stay. Once she checked them in, which didn't take long, she personally walked them to their presidential suite.

On the top floor of the hotel, the suite was right out of the movies immaculate and sprawling, with white marble floors, exuding elegance. There were three large bedrooms, all with king size beds, 47" LCD TVs, and their own bathroom with whirlpool tubs. The master bedroom was enormous, with its own sound system, walk-in closet, wet bar, and sitting area with a couch. It also had its own balcony with tables and chairs that overlooked the ocean. The common area of the suite was comprised of two open living areas, a dining room, kitchen with a Sub-Zero refrigerator, and two bath-rooms. In one of the areas was a full-size bar, 57" LCD TV, and sound system. In the other living area were two white, leather couches, chairs, two small tables, and its own TV. The dining area had an ex-travagant, cherry wood dining table, large enough to seat twelve people.

"I know both of you have stayed here before," the woman said as she led them into the suite. "But just to let you know, we have chilled a complimentary bottle of Dom Perignon for you," she said pointing to the bar, on which was a polished, stainless steel bucket containing the bottle, along with two flutes. "Also, your gift baskets are on the table."

"Thank you," Julie-Ann replied.

"Now we were informed that you would not be in need of a butler or bartender on this stay, but if that changes, or if you need anything else, just dial 111 and as you know, you'll be connected to the VIP line. And your bags will be coming up shortly."

The girls thanked the woman, and Julie-Ann gave her a fifty-dollar bill.

As soon as the woman left, Amber ran over to the bar and popped open the bottle of Champagne. "It's time to party!" She yelled as white foam flowed from the bottle down her hands and onto the gleaming marble floor.

As Amber poured two glasses of Champagne, Julie-Ann opened the wide sliding glass door that led to the balcony. "I Love this view! Miami, here we are!"

The wrap-around balcony, which extended out seven feet, was as impressive as the inside of the suite. The main part directly over-looked the sprawling white sand beach and turquoise water. It had lounge chairs and small tables and on one side, a hot tub.

Amber brought out two glasses of Champagne. After toasting to having a good time, the best friends stood by the railing and gazed out into the ocean, a gentle breeze blowing through their hair.

Chapter 3

After drinking some Champagne, Julie-Ann and Amber changed into their bikinis and went down by the pool. As usual, it was a beautiful, hot, sunny late April day in South Florida. Being Friday, the resort's expansive pool area, which sat right next to the beach, was crowded. A hotel staff member showed the girls to their reserved cabana, right by the edge of the pool.

The covered cabana was equipped with four lounge chairs, a small couch, fan, stereo, refrigerator, and a flat panel TV. The young man said that he would alert their server and that he or she would be right over. With that, the girls set up camp. Julie-Ann put suntan lotion on her front, arms and legs, and asked Amber if she could put it on her back. The pool area, as well as the entire resort, was teeming with beautiful women, but that did not stop guys from peeking over, watching Amber rub lotion on Julie-Ann. Though some guys tried to be inconspicuous, Amber could see them looking over, so she hammed it up and unbeknownst to Julie-Ann, made faces of ecstasy as she slowly and methodically worked in the lotion.

While Julie-Ann was returning the favor and putting lotion on Amber's back, a tall, slender, dark-tanned young man dressed in pressed white shorts and a white polo shirt came over and announced, "Hello, my name is T.J., and I'll be your server today."

"Hello T.J.," Amber replied in a flirtatious voice. She would usually look down on people such as servers, but T.J. was handsome. "I have to tell you, we're gonna need a lot of attention." She probably would have said that to anyone the resort sent over, but the difference was now she said it in a playful tone.

The girls spent the next several hours by the pool. T.J. made sure they were always taken care of. With Pina Colada's in their hands, they laid on the lounge chairs, chatted, and looked at guys. Intermittently, they were both on their respective phones, texting or reading Facebook. After their first Pina Colada Amber talked Julie-Ann into going in the pool for a while. There, some guys tried to pick them up. They were not even up to snuff to flirt with so Amber instantly blew them off. Like circling sharks, two other guys saw their chances and went over. These two were better looking so the girls talked with them for a little bit, but that was it.

Between the drinks in the limo, champagne in the room and the Pina Coladas, the girls were drunk, and it was not even 2:00 p.m. Not having eaten all day they ordered some lunch, which they ate at the cabana. Then they continued drinking.

Two men, one with a slight beer belly, approached the cabana. "What are you looking at?" Amber snarled before they had a chance to even say anything. They just scampered off in defeat.

"Oh my God!" Amber said while looking at her phone.

"What is it?" Julie-Ann asked, before sucking some more Pina Colada through her straw.

"Mark Wesley just posted on Facebook that he's on his way to Miami. I know this is the only place he stays when he comes here."

Twenty-two-years-old, Mark Wesley was a singer and sensation of the day. His debut album, *I'm Here For You,* had just recently gone double platinum. His manager was a client of Amber's father and even talked Mark into investing with him as well. Through her father, Amber met Mark several months earlier, and the two actually went out and partied a few times.

Julie-Ann instantly perked up upon hearing the news that Mark Wesley would probably be in their hotel and knowing that Amber knew him. "He is so hot," she said in a dreamy voice.

"Yes he is."

"Do you think he'd actually hang out with us?"

Amber gave her friend a look. "Hell yes girl. Who is he? Saul created him," she said referring to his manager. "We'll still be filthy rich and beautiful long after he's yesterday's news. He needs people like us. Plus my father's made him a lot of money." Amber paused. "Besides, he's really cool. I'm going to text him right now."

Ten minutes later Amber received a text back from Mark. She read it to Julie-Ann: "That's great! Just landed in Miami. Call or text you once I'm all settled in at the hotel. Looking forward to hanging with you and your friend."

"Oh my God!" Julie-Ann said with jubilation. She had met plenty of famous people before, but at the moment, Mark Wesley was a big deal. He was also really cute.

After another drink the girls went back into the pool, and then Julie-Ann wanted to go to the beach. With fresh drinks in hand, they walked over to the crowded beach, which was pulsating with energy. They did some guy-watching and put their feet in the crystal clear water, but they did not stay long.

Returning to the cabana, after being up early, being in the sun, and having consumed plenty of alcohol, Julie-Ann and Amber both passed out on their respective lounge chairs.

Julie-Ann woke-up first. Still in a daze, she looked at her white, ceramic Chanel watch that was lying on the table. It was 4:24 p.m. She woke-up Amber and the two decided to head back to the room. Even with the nap, they were still exhausted.

In the elevator, Amber received a text from Mark. He had to go to an autograph signing at 7:00 p.m., but told her to stop by his suite beforehand. Amber and Julie-Ann looked at each other. They both looked stunning, but to themselves they looked and felt unkempt from being at the pool all day. In order to look presentable for Mark Wesley, they needed to take showers, do their hair, and put on make-up, which could take two hours. Neither of them wanted to say no to Mark or even tell him that they would catch-up later. So Amber text back that they would probably stop by in an hour. They rushed to their room and ran around like crazy trying to get ready.

As spacious and extravagant as Julie-Ann's and Amber's presidential suite was, it dwarfed in comparison to Mark's penthouse suite, which was two floors and had a regulation-size billiards table, a grand piano, and not to mention a private pool outside. Mark needed the space as he had an entourage with him.

Amber introduced Mark to Julie-Ann. Mark introduced the girls to the six other people in the room, including his publicist, his stylist, and his best friend, Justin. Justin looked to be in his early twenties. With crew-cut, black hair and a five o'clock shadow, Justin was wearing white pants and a beige unbuttoned short-sleeve shirt, which highlighted his tan six-pack abs. Both Amber and Julie-Ann certainly took notice.

Mark offered the girls some Champagne, which they accepted. They sat on one of the couches in the main room and chatted. Mark explained that he wanted to hang out, but his schedule for the rest of the night was hectic. He suggested that Julie-Ann and Amber hang out at South Beach with Justin and him the next day—just the four of them. It was music to the girls' ears. Not only did they like the sound of hanging out with Mark Wesley and his model-looking friend for a day, despite putting on a festive demeanor and sipping on Champagne, they were both shot and didn't have the energy to meet up later that night. Trying not to sound too excited, Amber accepted Mark's offer.

Not more than an hour after making it back to their suite, both Julie-Ann and Amber were out cold.

The next morning Julie-Ann received a call from her father. He asked how everything was going, but Julie-Ann, instinctively, could tell there was more to his call. She was right. He said that she would probably hear on the news on Monday that Diamond &

Russell was being investigated for overcharging active military members on their home mortgages.

"It's just an oversight," he went on to explain. "If someone in the military is deployed overseas the rates on their mortgages are supposed to lock and not be able to rise. Apparently, there was a glitch in our computer system and in a few isolated cases if they had adjustable mortgages, their rates went up."

Julie-Ann's demeanor instantly changed. "Is everything going to be okay Daddy?"

"Yes, yes," Mr. Crown tried to placate his daughter. "It was an honest mistake, and we're already dealing with it. You know the media—they try to make a mountain out of a molehill. And you know how people feel about the banking industry and Wall Street right now. It could get a little ugly. Don't pay it any mind," Mr. Crown paused, "and if anyone from the media tries to ask you anything, you know the routine."

"I'll just tell them the truth—that I don't know anything—and to contact your public relations office. I should just tell them to kiss my ass!"

Her father chuckled, "Jules."

"Well it's not fair! They don't see all the good you do. They're always just trying to make trouble."

"Well thank you. Please don't say anything and don't even bring this up to anyone. You know how the media is now—they're everywhere. They'll get someone to sit at the table next to you at dinner and eavesdrop on your conversation with Amber. Or maybe the maid overhears something and wants to make some money selling a story. Or..."

Julie-Ann cut her father off. "Don't worry Dad, I'm smarter than that. I know the drill."

With that, Mr. Crown told his daughter to enjoy her trip and not to worry about it.

Amber had overheard parts of the conversation and asked Julie-Ann what was wrong as soon as she hung-up the phone. Julie-Ann, who never hid anything from her friend, told her the truth.

"That's such bullshit," Amber ranted. "The media puts out all these lies and then everyone believes them. Don't they have anything better to do?"

"I know! They're vultures. Besides, people take out these mortgages and then companies are supposed to give them all these special exemptions and help them? I mean what's the point of signing a contract?"

Amber shook her head. "I know. Just because they're in the military. It's not like they were drafted; they volunteered. They knew what they were getting into."

The girls finished getting ready for their day with Mark and his friend.

As promised, Mark and Justin took the girls to South Beach, which was only three miles from the Fontainebleau. Mark's manager had arranged for him to rent a white, Maybach 57 convertible, which has a price tag over a million dollars. Mark drove and had Amber sit up front with him. Justin and Julie-Ann sat in the back. They cruised around Ocean Drive, Collins Avenue, and the Art Deco District. Mark reluctantly agreed to his manager's insistence that two security guards tail them in another car, mostly just in case his fans got out of control, or the paparazzi spotted him.

Driving a convertible, and with the slow moving traffic of South Beach, people did recognize Mark. Even though South Beach was accustomed to having the biggest named celebrities walk down its sidewalks and drive around its streets, Mark was red hot at the moment. A few times, while stopped at a traffic light, a crowd would gather around the car. Girls would tell him how much they loved him and asked for his autograph, which he managed to give if there was time. There was even the occasional marriage proposal shouted from the sidewalk.

From the backseat, Julie-Ann asked Mark how he was able to handle all the fans hoarding him all the time.

"Sometimes it can get to be a little too much, but I have the greatest fans in the world," he shouted back while driving. "Some of my fans would literally die for me. Really! If I told one of them to stab themselves, or kill someone, they would do it."

Mark asked the girls if they liked sushi, to which they both said yes. He then asked Justin to call his publicist and tell her to let Nobu know that they would be coming for lunch.

About twelve minutes later, Mark pulled up in front of the Shore Club, an exclusive, boutique hotel on Collins Avenue that housed the famed sushi restaurant. The valet let Mark park the Maybach right in front of the entranceway, under an awning. Mark's security detail pulled up in the back of him and escorted the group into the hotel. It is not unusual for at least some paparazzi to be camped out in front of South Beach hotspots, just hoping for someone famous to walk in or out. There happened to be one photographer in front of the Shore Club, who blurted some random questions to Mark and snapped as many pictures as he could. Mark was polite and smiled for the camera, but the two security guards kept the man at bay. Yet, curiosity spreads like wildfire and after a few flashes, a crowd of onlookers started to form.

Julie-Ann knew everyone was gathering for Mark and that no one would even know who she was, but still, she felt uncomfortable even getting her picture taken. She did not want anyone, especially her fiancé, Ken, looking at the photographs later and thinking that she was "with" Mark's friend.

Mark's private security, along with the hotel staff, whisked the group to Nobu, where they had a table waiting. They stayed there for about an hour and a half, sampling the chef's unique selection and drinking beer and expensive sake.

Julie-Ann was still hung-over from the day before, but after a few drinks she started feeling energetic again. Everyone was talking, laughing and having a fabulous time. The atmosphere was light. Julie-Ann could sense Justin trying to pick her up. So she started talking about Ken and her upcoming wedding. That cooled Justin down, but it did not stop him in his tracks.

After lunch, Mark announced that he had to get back to the hotel for a prior engagement but that the four of them should meet later on that evening and go to club LIV, in the Fontainebleau. Amber answered yes for both of them.

By the time they arrived back at the hotel, Julie-Ann and Amber both had a pleasant buzz going so they went up to their suite and continued drinking. First they started with beer, which was in the refrigerator, but when Amber came across the bottle of Gray Goose vodka that was in the bar she called the front desk and ordered triple sec, lime juice, and cranberry juice so she could make cosmopolitans.

Julie-Ann was not normally a big drinker, but she was on vacation with her best friend and went along with the flow. Besides, she knew if she stopped drinking after getting buzzed she would quickly lose steam, pass out and may be shot for the entire night.

Around 4:00 p.m., the girls started getting ready for their night out. Taking their time, they chatted and intermittently sipped on their drinks. Amber had put on some music.

At 7:30 p.m., dressed to kill, Julie-Ann and Amber went over to Mark's suite as planned. There were only twelve people in the room, but it seemed like more. Music was blaring, and the atmosphere was electric. A beautiful, scantily clad brunette was busy at work behind the bar. Mark introduced Amber and Julie-Ann to the few people they had not met the previous evening.

After doing the introductions, Mark yelled for everyone in the room to do a shot of Patron. A ruckus cheer erupted. The bartender started filling up shot glasses. Once all the shots were poured Mark held his up in the air. "Here's to tonight! Let's rock this place!"

Everyone cheered in unison before downing their tequila.

Julie-Ann had only met Mark the day before, but she had never seen him so boisterous. She figured he was probably drunk.

After about a half hour, Julie-Ann found herself talking to Mark's female publicist and two guys who he had introduced as friends. She noticed that Justin was sitting on the couch with his hands all over some blonde who looked to be no more than eighteen. Julie-Ann was just glad he wasn't making the moves on her.

At one point, Julie-Ann went to use the restroom. As she was walking down a short corridor, she heard someone calling her. She looked around and then finally glanced up to see Amber at the top of the stairs.

"C'mere," Amber said in a loud whisper as she motioned her friend to come upstairs.

Not thinking too much into it and forgetting all about the restroom, Julie-Ann went up the stairs. Amber grabbed her wrist and led her into a master bedroom and then closed the door behind them. Before Julie-Ann could ask what was going on she saw Mark sitting on a small couch, crouched over a table and snorting a line.

"Oh, no," Julie-Ann said to Amber.

"Come on, just one line. It's just coke. We've been drinking all day, and we're going to the club later. You don't want to be passed out before you even get there."

Julie-Ann had done cocaine before, but only a little here and there and she had not done any in over two years.

Mark wiped his nose and turned to the girls. "It's okay, she doesn't have to do any. I mean I hardly ever do it myself."

As Mark was talking, Amber gave her best friend a look as if to say: *Don't do this to me in front of Mark. Just be cool.*

At this point, Julie-Ann was drunk, and she knew she would probably be a mess or passed out by the time they got to the club. Maybe Amber was right, she thought. Maybe one small line of cocaine would straighten her out for a while, give her a second wind. "You know what, maybe you're right," she said to Amber's pleasure.

"You sure?" Mark asked.

"Yeah, I've been drinking since lunch. I need a little pep-me-up. But just a short line."

Julie-Ann held back her long, flowing blonde hair and snorted the line that Mark had chopped up for her. Mark and Amber then did another line each. The three then went downstairs and joined the rest of the party.

Mark's publicist and a few other people left for the night, but the remaining crowd was getting more boisterous. People were yelling and doing shots. Different people were going into the bathroom together to do lines. But it was all just an appetizer.

At 10:30 p.m., the entourage made its way down to the club. Onlookers gawked and took pictures with their phones as the group was led past the waiting line and through the red VIP ropes. Once inside, they were given a large, round table on the second floor. Two tall, hulking security guards, dressed in black suits, stood guard near the table, deterring anyone from getting too close.

By the time 11:00 p.m. rolled around Julie-Ann was feeling wasted. She actually asked Amber if they could do another line. Amber smiled and took her into the VIP ladies room. Mark had given her a small vial of cocaine in case she wanted to do some more at the club. With the paparazzi around, and people with cellphone cameras, he did not want to get caught doing blow or going into the bathroom with a girl. Once in the ladies room, Amber led Julie-Ann into a stall. She then broke out the vile and sprinkled some cocaine on the fat of her hand and Julie-Ann snorted it.

Julie-Ann woke up covered in sweat, half dressed, the covers tossed off the king-size bed. Her mouth was as dry as a desert, and her head throbbed with pain. She looked around the clock on the nightstand; it was 1:27 p.m. Julie-Ann tried but didn't even remember coming back to the suite. Through a murky haze, the last thing she remembered was going into the ladies room with Amber. Julie-Ann put her hand on her head, which felt like it was going to explode. Then, after summing up the strength, she arduously climbed off of the bed and lumbered into the main part of the suite. It was still clean, and there was no one lying around, so she figured that they had not come back there and partied. Feeling like she had sand in her mouth, Julie-Ann grabbed an unopened bottle of water that was on top of the bar, opened it, and took several large gulps. She then called out for Amber in a hoarse voice, but there was no answer. So she went into Amber's bedroom. However, Amber was not there, and her bed was still made.

Just then, Julie-Ann heard the main door to the suite open. "Can you come back," she yelled out. "I'm not dressed." She could hear the door close.

"It's only me," replied Amber in a hoarse voice.

Amber's hair was a wreck and she was wearing the same clothes as the night before. Yet she had a glow on her face.

"Amber, where did you spend the night?"

Amber smiled widely. "With Mark."

For the moment, Julie-Ann forgot about the pain she was in. "You heathen. I can't believe you."

"Oh Jules, it was amazing. It was so hot. We…"

Julie-Ann cut her off. "But what about Tyler," she asked referring to Amber's longtime boyfriend.

"Oh, come on Jules, I love Tyler, but we're talking about Mark Wesley. I had to do it. Besides, it's just a one-time thing, and Tyler will never find out about it." Amber grabbed the water bottle that was still in Julie-Ann's hand and took a drink. "I thought you were going to hook up with that Steve, the Calvin Klein model. He was so hot."

"What are you talking about?" Julie-Ann fired back. "I'm engaged. I'm getting married in a few months. And I love Ken." She paused. "Wait, I…I didn't…I mean…"

Amber had a devilish grin. "You mean you don't remember when we went back to Mark's suite, and you and Steve were making out on the couch?"

Julie-Ann's jaw dropped as dread flowed through her entire body. "Oh my God," she said putting her hand over her mouth.

Amber started laughing. "I'm just fucking with you. Nothing happened. You were a good girl."

Julie-Ann punched her friend in the arm. "You bitch! You almost gave me a heart attack."

Amber couldn't stop laughing. "I'm sorry Jules. But you should've seen your face. My God, what's the big deal anyway?"

"Are you serious? Did I just mention that I'm getting married?"

"It's just sex. It's not cheating if no one finds out. Besides, relax, like I said, nothing happened."

Julie-Ann and Amber spent the rest of the day holed-up in their suite, nursing their hangovers. Julie-Ann felt so sick at one point that she took a half of one of Amber's Vicodin and passed out for an hour. She promised herself that she would never do cocaine again and would never even drink that much again.

That night the girls ordered room service and stayed in their suite. Over a movie, they ate and chatted about their plans. Amber's father was coming to Miami in two days for business, so Amber was going to stay and wait for him. They were going to spend that weekend in Marathon at the house of one of her father's business associates. Julie-Ann was leaving the next morning for Grand Cayman, where she was rendezvousing with Ken, who was already there on business.

Chapter 4

The next morning, Julie-Ann boarded her father's private jet for the one hour and forty-five minute flight to Grand Cayman. Though she was feeling much better than the day before, when she was bedridden, she was still groggy from Saturday. So not to upset her stomach, she just had a fruit cup and juice before leaving the hotel at 7:00 a.m.

It was a quiet, smooth flight. Sitting alone in the cabin, Julie-Ann had hoped she would doze off, but instead gazed out the window as her mind wandered. Julie-Ann loved Amber, but she was happy to leave the crapulousness of Miami. She was looking forward to spending quality time with Ken, going out to dinner, and lying on the beach with him. She was looking forward to making love to him.

Julie-Ann could not help thinking about Amber sleeping with Mark and the cavalier way that she talked about it. Amber might not have been married or engaged, but she and Tyler had been going out for two years and were in a serious relationship. She would never do that to Ken—and she totally trusted that Ken would never cheat on her.

At the Grand Cayman's Owen Roberts International Airport, Ken was waiting for Julie-Ann on the tarmac as she de-boarded the plane. He was wearing white dress pants and a silk, pink short sleeve shirt. As always, his thick black hair was perfectly combed, even in the slight breeze.

Walking down the steps, Julie-Ann immediately saw him and smiled. "Ken," she said in a spirited voice as she scurried over to him.

"Hey baby."

The two then kissed.

"How was Miami?"

Julie-Ann sighed. "It was good, but sometimes it can be too much. You know, with all the partying and nightlife. But we did hang out with Mark Wesley. He was in town, and Amber's father knows him and his manager."

"Oh, that must have been cool. I'm glad you had a good time." Ken paused. "I hope you were a good girl though," he said pointing his finger at her in a half-joking manner.

Julie-Ann smiled. "Always." She then gave him another, quick kiss on the lips.

After the driver helped the airport attendant put Julie-Ann's luggage in the awaiting black Mercedes sedan, they were off to their hotel, The Ritz Carlton.

From the side cubbyhole on the back door, Ken pulled out a small, rectangular gift-wrapped box with a red bow on it. "I got you something while I was here," he said as he handed it to her.

Julie-Ann smiled. "Ken, you shouldn't have."

"Come on, go on and open it."

With her face glowing, Julie-Ann delicately peeled of the wrapping paper and opened up the velvet box. It was a pearl necklace. "Oh my God Ken, it's beautiful. Thank you so much," she said before giving him a passionate kiss. Julie-Ann already had a pearl necklace, but it's hard to shop for the girl who has everything.

The Ritz Carlton, which Julie-Ann had been to before with Ken, emanated affluence and elegance. But at the same time it was adorned by a Caribbean feel and pulchritude. In the grand foyer, Ken and Julie-Ann were met by a woman holding a tray of complimentary Champagne. Julie-Ann politely declined a drink.

After going up to their suite Ken suggested that they have an early lunch. He had not had breakfast and had a meeting at 1:30 p.m. Having only had a small cup of fruit, Julie-Ann was also hungry.

Julie-Ann and Ken went down to one of the hotel's casual restaurants, which overlooked the ocean. It was hot in Grand Cayman, but there was a constant, soothing breeze, so they sat outside. Over lunch, Julie-Ann asked about Ken's business trip thus far, and in particular, the seminar he had attended and was one of the presenters. It was more obligatory than anything else. Though Julie-Ann had a decent understanding of trading and finance, Ken rarely talked about his business and she was perfectly fine with that, finding it all rather boring. Without going into any details, Ken said that everything had gone well, and he was able to make some new contacts. He added that they had dinner reservations the following evening with a business associate and his wife. Ken then asked Julie-Ann more about Miami.

Julie-Ann glossed over it. She did, however, mention the conversation with her father. "He said the story would probably break today, but I haven't seen the news yet. Did you see anything?"

Ken was taken off guard, having not heard anything about the story. "No, I haven't. I mean I've seen the news and gone through the wires, but didn't see anything about that. What exactly did your father say? Did he sound worried?"

Julie-Ann went over again what her father had told her, adding that he didn't think it was going to be a big deal in the end.

"I'm sure he's right. Worst-case scenario is they might have to pay a small fine and get some unwelcomed publicity for a few days. I wouldn't worry about it." Ken was playing cool, but internally he was frothing over the inside information. In fact, a part of him wondered if James had purposely told his daughter, knowing she would share the information with him.

Ken didn't know any of the details, but knew there was little chance for such an investigation to have a long-term catastrophic effect on a firm the size of Diamond & Russell. However, when the news did break, shareholders could panic, and there could be a short-term drop in the stock. Ken had Diamond & Russell in some of his portfolios and certainly didn't want to lose money. He was more interested in making money on the news, perhaps heavily shorting the stock. First he had to learn more about the story. How bad was it? Was the SEC or FINRA looking into any other allegations? He *had* to find out before the information—or even the rumors—went public.

Ken explained, again, that he had a business meeting to go to after lunch. He suggested that Julie-Ann go down and lie on the beach. After he finished, he would meet her there. Julie-Ann liked the idea.

Ken did have a business meeting at 1:30 p.m. However, as soon as he heard about the news on Diamond & Russell, he sent an email to the person he was supposed to meet saying he had to reschedule it. He didn't tell Julie-Ann, and she didn't suspect anything because he was always on his Blackberry.

After lunch, Ken went up to the room, grabbed his briefcase with his laptop, and told Julie-Ann that he would see her down at the beach in an hour or so. He then found a small vacant conference room in the hotel, set-up shop and began working his contacts, trying to find out the whole story. He berated his head employee back in New York for not knowing about it. Within twenty minutes, Ken confirmed that the SEC, in conjunction with the Department of Justice was, in fact, investigating Diamond & Russell—and other firms—for fraud, for charging substantial mortgage fees to military members and their families that were unallowable under the recently enacted Interest Rate Reduction Refinancing Loans Program.

Rumors were already circulating, though only in the exclusive circles on Wall Street. News of the investigation went public later that day, after the close of the bell, but not before Ken shorted several hundred thousand shares. He spread-out the orders through eight different accounts, hoping not to arouse suspicion.

In the following days, Diamond & Russell's stock would drop five percent. After two weeks, with news of a settlement on the horizon, the stock rebounded. However, Ken was able to make more than five million dollars shorting the stock. As for the Diamond & Russell stock he already held, not wanting to wave a red flag, he had decided not to dump it right before the original story went public. He held onto to it, and once the stock rebounded, it would cover any losses. Ken never told Julie-Ann about using the inside information she had naively provided him. As for Diamond & Russell itself, after the original story about the investigation broke, the mainstream media paid little attention to it, reporting only when a settlement was at hand and then eventually reached. The firm wound up paying a fine equivalent to a slap on the wrist and did not suffer any long-term damage caused by the bad publicity.

As Ken worked vigorously to profit from her father's firm's problem, Julie-Ann went down to lie out on the beach. The Ritz sat on a seven-mile stretch of white sand beach that caressed tranquil, clear turquoise water. Besides the sporadic yacht or ship passing in the nearby distance, nothing could be seen except the seemingly infinite ocean and blue sky. There was no boardwalk or bars on the beach, just palm trees, lounge chairs, and cabanas.

Feeling better than she had earlier that morning, Julie-Ann laid in a lounge chair under an umbrella, just relaxing. When a server came over, she ordered a mango smoothie—without alcohol. After a while, Julie-Ann started reading her People magazine, which she had brought with her. She was amused to find an article in it about Mark Wesley and his clean-boy image.

Time slipped away unnoticed as it often does lying on a tropical beach. Julie-Ann never looked at her watch, but after an hour and a half Ken came down dressed in swimming shorts and carrying two Piña Coladas. Julie-Ann certainly didn't feel like drinking, but politely took hers and nursed it.

After about fifteen minutes, Ken talked Julie-Ann into going into the ocean. They found a spot on the beach where no one was lying and through the velvet soft sand, they walked into the calm, clear water. It was the perfect temperature, not cold, yet not too warm. Ken grabbed hold of Julie-Ann's slender wrist and slowly led her further until the water was halfway up to her chest.

"This feels so good," Julie-Ann proclaimed in a fading voice.

"It does," Ken replied as he let go of her wrist and then plunged his head under the water. He came up and slicked back his thick wet hair with his hand. "Aren't you going to go all the way in?"

"I don't want to mess up my hair."

Ken laughed. "You're at the beach. Besides, I think you look sexy with wet hair."

Julie-Ann smiled. Then she dipped her head into the water. After coming up, she brushed back her hair.

As small, gentle waves lapped the crystal clear water, Ken put his hands on Julie-Ann's waist and pulled her closer, so their faces were an inch apart. "I was right, you look so beautiful."

"Oh, Ken," Julie-Ann said in a low, seductive voice as she moved her lips towards Ken's.

Their mouths met each other's in a slow kiss. Ken then brought his hands up and put them on Julie-Ann's wet neck and chin. For a second, he pulled her away, but just as a tease as their lips once again glided along each other's and their tongues intertwined. Ken moved his left hand towards the back of her neck and then grabbed hold of her long wet hair and pulled it down so her head tilted up. At the same time, his right hand dropped below the water and onto Julie-Ann's firm behind. As they continued to kiss, his fingers slid beneath her bikini bottom and along her walls until his index finger slid inside her.

With her heartbeat accelerating, Julie-Ann pried her lips from Ken's. "Oh Ken," she whispered into his ear. "That feels so good. I want you so bad." Then, while slowly kissing the side of his neck, her hand went down and over his bathing suit, grabbed him. "You're already hard."

"You make me so hard," he whispered back to her. "I want to be inside you."

"I want you inside of me so bad," she said as her heart began to beat even faster. Julie-Ann then lifted her head from his neck and looked around. They were not that far from the shore, and though there was no one in their immediate area, there were plenty of people on the beach. "Let's go up to the room. I can't take this anymore."

Ken once again took Julie-Ann by the wrist and led her through the water. This time they moved at a much quicker pace.

With towels wrapped around them, Ken and Julie-Ann made their way through the hotel and into the elevator. They were the only ones on the elevator. Although their suite was only on the third floor, they could not keep their hands off of each other. While locked in a feverish kiss, Julie-Ann slid her hand down Ken's bathing suit and took hold of manhood. Before they could go any further, the elevator reached their floor. Just as they had separated, the doors opened and there was a family standing there, waiting for the elevator. Julie-Ann and Ken tried not to laugh or smile as they said hello and walked passed them.

As soon as they stepped into the room, using her foot, Julie-Ann shut the door behind her. Without saying a word, she whipped off Ken's towel, went to her knees, and pulled down his shorts. As Ken let out a deep breath of ecstasy, she put him inside her mouth.

"Oh God, that feels so good," he moaned as Julie-Ann slid him in and out, to the front of her lips, then to the back of her throat. After a few minutes, he announced in elation that he was about to come.

Julie-Ann took him out of her mouth. "No, please don't come," she said as she stood up. "Not yet. You taste so good, but I need you inside of me. I need you to fuck me."

Ken picked Julie-Ann up and brought her to the nearby couch. As soon as he placed her down, he pulled off her bikini bottom and thrust himself inside her.

"Oh Ken," she groaned. "Oh yes. Fuck me."

As he moved in and out, Ken tore off Julie-Ann's top and grabbed her firm breasts. With her legs over his shoulders, he then rubbed her hard nipples. "How does this feel?"

"It feels so good," she uttered between bated breaths. "Don't stop. Please don't stop!" She cried out as her entire body pulsated.

Ken tried and tried. He staved it off for as long as he could, but it was too much and he eventually climaxed inside of her.

That evening, they ordered room service and stayed in, cuddling on the couch as they watched a movie. Before going to sleep, they had sex again. For Julie-Ann, it had been a perfect ending and the crushing hangover she had the previous day was already long forgotten.

The next morning Ken said that he had to go to another business meeting. In reality, it was the meeting he had rescheduled. He gave Julie-Ann a stack of hundreds and told her to go into town and do some shopping.

Julie-Ann woke-up in a great mood and feeling energized. But while she was taking a shower, from out of nowhere, the back of her head was overcome with a sharp, stabbing pain. Grimacing in agony, she put her hand over her head, praying that it would pass. It did not. Julie-Ann turned off the water, wrapped a towel around her and went into her cosmetic bag for a bottle of Tylenol. With shaking hands, she popped two capsules and washed them down with a gulp of sink water. The pain felt worse than it ever had before. As she dried herself off, all of a sudden everything became blurry as if she was looking through a smeared lens. Julie-Ann began to panic, and her heart started to race.

With no depth perception, and using her hands to guide her, Julie-Ann put on her robe and went out into the bedroom. Ken had already left for his meeting. Trying not to bang into something, she made her way to the bed and lay down; hoping that either the Tylenol would quickly kick in, or the pain would go away by itself. For the moment, all she could do was lie there and endure it. After ten minutes, as the pain continued to stab at her head and resonate through her whole body, Julie-Ann started to cry in distress.

After about twenty minutes, the pain slowly started to subside, and as it did, her vision began to return to normal until everything was clear again. This episode had left Julie-Ann understandably shaken. Still lying on the bed, it took her a while to calm down. She promised herself to make a doctor's appointment as soon as she returned to New York, but in the meantime, try not to read too much into it. *It's probably just a bad migraine* she tried to convince herself.

Julie-Ann was eventually able to regain her composure, but she was afraid to go into town, fearing that it might happen again while she was out and about. Instead, she finished getting ready and just walked around the resort.

When Julie-Ann returned to the room it was 12:15 p.m. and Ken was there on his laptop. Ken asked if she had gone into town. Julie-Ann explained that she had decided to just walk around the Ritz. With the pain now gone for a while, she saw no point in complaining and telling Ken.

Ken suggested that they go into town to have lunch. He said he found a lovely, little French bistro. Having only eaten a banana in the room earlier, Julie-Ann was famished. Feeling better, she was no longer worried about leaving the resort, especially now that she was with Ken.

The restaurant was quaint but upscale. Ken asked if Julie-Ann wanted to order a bottle of wine, but she politely declined. Over escargot, Ken reminded his fiancée that they had dinner reservations at 7:00 p.m. with a business associate and his wife. Ken also made a point of explaining that it was an "extremely important" business associate.

Julie-Ann took offense to Ken's comment. "Why did you have to say that?"

Ken looked puzzled. "What do you mean?"

"That they're very important, so I should be on my best behavior and not embarrass you?"

Ken was taken aback. "I didn't say…"

Julie-Ann did not let him finish. "That makes it seem like I'm usually boorish or aloof."

Ken reached across the table and gently took hold of Julie-Ann's hand. "Whoa, where did all of that come from?" He asked in a calm voice. "You're the opposite of all those things. You're the smartest, most interesting, most elegant woman I've ever met. I didn't mean it that way. I'm sorry. I was…I was just saying…just pointing out that he and I are going to have an important business relationship going forward, that's all. I'm sorry."

Julie-Ann smiled. "No, I'm sorry. I don't know why I…you really think I'm elegant?"

"Jackie-O in her heyday never had a thing on you."

Now Julie-Ann started to blush.

They continued their lunch in a more light-hearted atmosphere. Now interested, Julie-Ann asked about this business associate. Ken explained that they would be starting a new hedge fund together, outside the umbrella of Ken's fund management company. "Charles is well known in the hedge fund circles," Ken went on, "and I'm lucky to be doing business with him. He also happens to be a lawyer and knows Cayman Island law—that's certainly an added bonus."

After lunch, Julie-Ann asked Ken if they could walk around town. She wanted to buy a new evening dress for their dinner. Ken made it clear that there was no need but that if she wanted to, they could go shopping.

It was another beautiful day in paradise, and the couple walked hand-in-hand down the bustling sidewalks of George Town. Two cruise ships happened to be in port that day, so the town was alive. The unmistakable sound of steel pans and congas echoed down the corridors of pastel colored shops and restaurants. On one street, a group of Caribbean dancers, adorned in bright, grandiose headdress and clothing worked their magic to a crowd of onlookers. Pulling Ken along, Julie-Ann made her way to the edge of the sidewalk and gleefully watched them dance to the loud rhythm of drums.

Julie-Ann was now feeling energetic and having a great time soaking up the sights and sounds. However, she was unable to find a clothing store with anything worthwhile. Finally, in one store, a woman suggested that she try Market Street at Camana Bay, which was actually next to the Ritz. So they grabbed a cab and headed over.

At Camana Bay, Julie-Ann was able to find several high-end retailers and after forty-minutes, picked out a graceful black, cocktail dress and matching shoes. Julie-Ann, of course, had her own money, but as he always did, Ken insisted on paying.

By the time they arrived back at the suite, it was 2:48 p.m. As she was brushing her teeth, from out of nowhere, her head started hurting again. It was not as painful as before, but she feared that it would soon escalate. Clutching the back of her head, she went out to the living area where Ken was sitting on the couch, working on his laptop. Julie-Ann told him about her headache, as well as the earlier episode

"Did you take some aspirin?"

"Yes," she replied in an anguished voice. "I'm telling you Ken, this morning it was so bad that my vision went blurry."

Ken didn't doubt that Julie-Ann was in distress, but thought maybe she was exaggerating. "Do you want me to make you a drink?"

"No, I don't want a drink!" Julie-Ann groaned in pain.

Ken stood up and walked over to her. "Did you get your period today? Is that it?"

"No, it's not PMS," Julie-Ann angrily shot back. "I've started getting them a few weeks ago, but they come and they go. But they seem to be getting progressively worse each time."

Ken put his hands on her shoulders. "Why don't you sit down, Jules? I'll get a damp cloth to put on your head and then I'll give you a shoulder rub."

Julie-Ann took Ken's advice and sat down on the couch. He then went into the bathroom and came back out with a damp face towel that she put on her head.

"Here, just try and relax," Ken said in a soothing voice as he began rubbing her shoulders.

"Thank you. That feels good." Julie-Ann paused. "Hopefully it will just pass. It's not as bad as this morning. Oh, Ken, that hurt so much it was like someone driving a knife through my skull."

"Why didn't you tell me you've been having these headaches for a few weeks now?"

Julie-Ann let out a deep breath, trying to relax. "I didn't want to alarm you. I figured they were just migraines. I'd just never had them before."

"Well they probably are just migraines," Ken replied while continuing to work on Julie-Ann's shoulders. "But when we get back to New York we'll make you a doctor's appointment anyway, just to be sure."

"Thank you for being so understanding. I'm starting to feel a little better already. I'll tell you if it was as bad as earlier today there'd be no way I could've made dinner."

Ken abruptly stood up. "Jules, is that what this is all about? I told you this dinner is very important to me. I told you in the restaurant you took what I said…"

Now Julie-Ann shot up. "This isn't about you or your stupid, little dinner! God, I can't believe how selfish you are!" With that, Julie-Ann stormed into the bedroom and locked the door.

"Oh, come on Jules," Ken whined through the closed door. "I'm sorry. Come on, let me in. I'm just under a lot of stress trying to put this new venture together."

After about five minutes, Julie-Ann finally opened the door and let Ken in. He continued to apologize and say how much he loved her. She apologized as well. Ken asked if there was something he could get her or do for her. She said no. The two then sat on the edge of the bed and watched some television. As they did, Ken continued to massage Julie-Ann's shoulders.

"Are you feeling any better?"

"Yes I am, thank you," she replied. Julie-Ann was feeling better. Her headache was almost gone, and it never escalated to the point of where it had been in the morning. "Actually, I feel quite relaxed now. In fact, I might take a little nap."

Ken asked if it would be okay if he went down to the gym to work out for a little while. Julie-Ann said to go and assured him that she would be fine.

By the time that Ken had changed into his workout clothes, Julie-Ann had already fallen asleep, lying comfortably on the made bed.

Ken worked out for forty minutes and then hit the sauna. When he arrived back at the suite it was 5:15 p.m. Julie-Ann had still been sleeping, but was awakened by the sound of Ken entering the room. He asked how she was feeling, to which she replied much better. Ken then said he was going to take a shower.

While Ken was in the shower, his phone, which he had placed on the dresser, vibrated. Julie-Ann was not a nosy person, but she happened to be right there and looked down at it. It was a text message: *I had a great time Sunday. I'll see you back in New York*. There was no name assigned to the text, only a number with a New York area code. A cold feeling washed over Julie-Ann. She went into Ken's messages, something she never did, to see if there were any more texts from that number. If there had been any, Ken had already erased them. However, she did notice that the same phone number appeared multiple times in his call log. Julie-Ann began breathing heavy. For a second, she thought about calling the number, but didn't.

As soon as Julie-Ann heard the shower turn off, she went into the bathroom with the phone. "Someone sent you a text," she said as Ken dried himself off.

He could tell instantly by her tone that something was amiss. "What did it say? Who was it from?"

Julie-Ann told him the number. "Who's number is that?" She asked without telling him what the text said, hoping to trip him up.

"I don't know. You know how many people I have calling me every day."

Julie-Ann put the phone up to Ken's face. "Nice try. It said 'I had a great time Sunday, I'll see you back in New York'".

Still standing in the shower and holding a towel around his waist, Ken took the phone. "Let me see."

"Let you see! How many people were you with on Sunday? Oh God, you're having an affair, aren't you," she blurted in a panic-stricken voice.

"What? Are you crazy? First of all, I was doing a seminar at the hotel on Sunday, and you know that." Ken then held up the phone. "This is from this girl, Vicky. She coordinated the seminar for me. She's new at the firm. She flew out with me, Friday and flew back to New York Monday morning. And she stayed in her own room."

Julie-Ann's initial panic turned to anger. "I've never heard of this Vicky. Why didn't you say you were flying down here with some girl?"

Still wet and with a towel around his waist, Ken finally stepped out of the shower. "I told you, she's new. She's only been with me for less than two weeks. If you would've come by the office, you probably would've seen her. You know I always need someone with me when I do these seminars, to assist me. It's a big job. She helped me with the PowerPoint, handed out the pamphlets, made sure everything was running smoothly, and took care of the partic-ipants. She was just thanking me because she's trying to kiss my ass—not literally," he said jokingly with a smile. "I think she's gun-ning for Carl's job."

"Then why didn't she just say 'thank you for the opportunity', or 'I enjoyed the seminar'?" Julie-Ann asked in a calmer tone.

"Jules, you're reading too much into a few words. All she said was that she had a good time and that she'll see me back in New York. It's not like she said 'I'll never forget the other night', or 'I love you', or 'I miss you.'" Ken could see Julie-Ann ease up. He put his hands gently on her face and looked straight into her eyes. "I love you, and I would never cheat on you. I thought you trusted me?"

"I did. I do. I just…when I saw…I'm sorry."

Again, Ken professed his love for Julie-Ann and swore that he would never betray her.

At 6:50 p.m. they went downstairs to meet Ken's new business associate and his wife at The Ritz's premier restaurant, and probably the most exquisite restaurant on the island, Blue by Eric Ripert. Ken was dressed in a perfectly fit suit and designer tie. Julie-Ann looked dashing, with her new black dress and diamond earrings and necklace, her long, blonde hair flowing down her shoulders.

Julie-Ann had believed Ken's story, but there was still a residual doubt that she could not shake. Nevertheless, she put on a blithe front for their guests and was charming.

Ken had told Charles all about Julie-Ann, and Charles had told his wife, Linda. Over appetizers in lighthearted conversation, Linda asked her about her time at JP Morgan.

"It was a great experience," Julie-Ann replied in a casual tone. "I worked with some really good people."

"Whom did you report to over there?" Charles asked.

Julie-Ann was ready to answer, but drew a blank. She thought about it for a second, but for the life of her, could not remember.

For the first time, there was an awkward pause at the table. "You probably worked for Walter Gasper's group," said Charles.

"Oh, oh yes," Julie-Ann replied. "He was the head of…" she was going to say which trading desk he was the head of, but again, she could not remember. She couldn't believe it. She was drawing a blank on the exact department for which she used to work. "He was the desk head," she went on, trying to cover herself. "As you know, at any large firm, you usually have several bosses and people you report to."

Charles chuckled. "Yes, that certainly is true."

The dinner went smoothly, but for the rest of the evening, Julie-Ann tried to remember her direct boss at JP Morgan, the person with whom she had spent so much time. Finally, by dessert, she remembered his name but kept it to herself. She did not want to blurt out that it suddenly came to her as if she had been trying to remember the name of a song.

After dinner the couples exchanged pleasantries and went their separate ways. Charles said that he would give Ken a call in a couple of days.

After Charles and Linda had left, Ken asked Julie-Ann if she wanted to have a drink at the hotel bar. She had a glass of wine at dinner and wasn't ready to retire for the night, so she agreed. Sitting at the bar, Ken thanked her for being so supportive. "Charles and Linda loved you," he said with a smile. "You were great."

"Well, they were really nice people," she replied.

Julie-Ann and Ken had a couple of drinks at the bar and talked for a while. There was no discussion about the text message. The conversation was light and even sprinkled with laughter.

Once back in the suite, they made love again. Afterwards, they cuddled on the bed and watched TV. For Julie-Ann, it was a welcomed ending to a long day that had started off so wrong, and for a while, looked like it would be catastrophic.

Chapter 5

The next morning Julie-Ann and Ken headed back to New York. Julie-Ann's father was using his jet, but Ken had access to his own private plane. It was not as spacious and luxurious as Mr. Crown's G650, but it was still a private jet. It also carried enough fuel to make the trip to New York nonstop.

Julie-Ann woke up feeling refreshed, and her head felt clear. In fact, she was sad to be leaving Grand Cayman, wanting to lay out on the beach at least one more day.

Julie-Ann and Ken ordered breakfast up to the room as they did some last-minute packing and readied themselves. By 10:00 a.m. they were at the airport and boarding the plane. The captain let them know that the flying time would be four hours and that they might encounter some turbulence once they approached the east coast but that it shouldn't be too bad. Both experienced fliers, neither Julie-Ann nor Ken fretted over it.

Once they were at cruising altitude, Ken pulled out his laptop and started working on some spreadsheets. Julie-Ann put in a DVD and watched it on the small television screen that pulled down from the ceiling. So as not to disturb Ken, she put on headphones. They had not yet hit any turbulence and Julie-Ann was relaxing, enjoying her movie. However, about forty minutes into the flight, the pain in the back of her head returned. It started off as a dull ache, but after a few minutes morphed into a sharp stab.

Ken noticed Julie-Ann taking off her headphones and grabbing the back of her head, obviously in distress. "Your head again? Do you have any aspirin?"

"Yeah," she said in a shaky, strained voice. "It's in my purse, over there. Can you get it for me?"

Ken grabbed her purse from under the seat and fiddled through it until he found a container of Tylenol. He poured two capsules into his hand and gave them to Julie-Ann. He then handed her a bottle of water that was in the seat pocket.

Julie-Ann swallowed the two capsules, knowing that they never seemed to work. The pain was now getting worse by the second and overtaking her entire body. "Arrrhh," she moaned in agony. "Ken, it really hurts."

All Ken could do was comfort his fiancé and hope the pain would pass. "It'll be okay," he said in a soothing voice as he stroked her shoulder.

It only seemed to be getting worse. Now Julie-Ann's whole head felt like it was literally going to explode. The pressure was unbearable. Crouched over in her seat, with Ken rubbing her shoulder, she prayed it would stop. But after another few minutes a new alarming, symptom arose. "Oh my God Ken, my arms…both my arms are going numb."

"What?" Now Ken was beginning to really worry, though he tried to remain calm for Julie-Ann's sake.

"My arms are tingling, and I can't feel my hands," she cried, with her arms now by her side. "Wha…what's happening to me? Am I having a heart attack?" Julie-Ann's heart was racing. "Ken," she said with bated breath, "I think I'm having a heart attack."

Ken thought about it for a second. "If you were having a heart attack, just your left arm would feel numb. You're probably just panicking. Just try to slow down your breathing."

Tears of fear were now streaming down Julie-Ann's face. "I…I can't. I'm having a heart attack. Or a stroke. Ken, I…I have to go to the hospital," she whispered between rapid breaths.

"Okay, just wait here. I'll be right back."

Ken went into the cockpit and let the pilot know about the situation. The co-pilot went out to the cabin. Julie-Ann was in full-fledged panic mode and begged him to make an emergency landing. He explained that nearest airport was in St. Petersburg, Florida, which was about twenty minutes away. Ken told him not to waste any time and request permission to land there.

Just as the co-pilot went back to the cockpit, the plane started to hit turbulence. A minute later, the pilot came over the intercom. "Okay, I told St. Pete we have a medical emergency, and they've given us priority clearance to land. So buckle up. It's going to be a bumpy ride from here on out."

Ken put on Julie-Ann's seatbelt, then his own. By this time, the small jet was bouncing all around. Julie-Ann was crying in pain and fighting to breathe. Then, she announced that her legs were going numb.

"Oh Ken, I don't want to die," she wailed.

Ken was strapped in next to Julie-Ann and holding her. "You're not going to die, baby," he said in a distressed voice, no longer able to hide his anxiety.

As the plane began to descend into a wall of dark, gray clouds, the turbulence increased. Even seat belted in, they were being jostled from left to right, forward and then back into their seats. Though still worried about Julie-Ann, Ken now began to also worry about the landing.

The plane was able to land unscathed, though it was an extremely rough touchdown. After turning off the runway, an ambulance was waiting on the tarmac. The paramedics strapped Julie-Ann onto a gurney and put her in the ambulance. They let Ken ride along in the back. As a paramedic administered some tests and asked Julie-Ann questions, Ken held onto her hand.

Once in the emergency room, more tests were administered and blood was drawn. She was also given some Demerol to calm her down. After about a half hour, Ken was allowed back to see her. She was hooked up to a heart monitor, had an IV in her arm, and a small, oxygen tube in her nose. She was cognizant and not in any pain.

Right after Ken arrived, a doctor walked in carrying a clipboard. "Okay Ms. Crown, you definitely didn't have a heart attack—or a stroke. In fact, your blood work came back perfectly normal. Have you ever had a panic attack before?"

"No," she replied in a sedated voice.

"Well, what about the pain in her head?" Asked Ken. "She's been having it on and off for several weeks now."

"Yes, well you are going to be taken shortly for an MRI, just to make sure everything's okay." The doctor then glanced at his chart. "Are you sure you haven't suffered any head trauma lately, maybe a car accident? You may not have felt a lot of pain in your head when it happened."

Julie-Ann assured the doctor that she had not been in any car accidents or had any other mishaps recently. The doctor then told her that someone would be by soon to take her for an MRI.

As the doctor left, Ken followed him, telling Julie-Ann that he would be right back. Then, in the corridor, he confronted the doctor, asking him if there was something he had not told them. Visibly annoyed, the young doctor reiterated that all the tests they had taken came back normal and that they would know more after the MRI. When Ken went back to the curtained-off section where Julie-Ann was being kept, he was met by an orderly, ready to take her for her tests. He kissed her on the forehead and told her he would be nearby in the waiting room. But before leaving, Ken added that he was going to call her father. Julie-Ann just nodded.

In the waiting room, Ken called Mr. Crown. His assistant said that he was in a meeting, which was not uncommon. Ken, who was familiar with the assistant, explained that it was important; she could tell by his voice that it was.

Less than a minute later, Julie-Ann's father picked up.

"James, everything's okay, but we're in St. Petersburg. Julie-Ann's in the hospital. She…"

"What?" Mr. Crown said in understandable alarm. "What happened? Why are you in Florida?"

Ken took a deep breath. "I guess Julie-Ann's been having these really severe headaches for a couple of weeks. She only told me about it yesterday. Anyway, she started having one while we were flying home. I guess it was real bad, and I think it might've caused her to have a panic attack. She thought maybe she was having a heart attack, but she wasn't. All her blood work came back completely normal. But they're taking her for an MRI now just to make sure—and probably to find out why she's been having these headaches."

"Okay, let me know the minute you find out about the MRI."

When Mr. Crown hung up the phone, he was not sure what to do. His daughter was never one to complain about pain or not feeling well, and he never remembered her having headaches before. Though he was grateful that nothing serious appeared to be wrong at this point, he feared that something might show up on the MRI. He decided to have his plane readied just in case. He called in his assistant and told her to make arrangements.

His long-time assistant rarely saw him rattled. "Is everything okay, Mr. Crown?"

He told her the truth.

Obviously, she knew Julie-Ann and felt terrible and worried. She told him that she would have the jet prepared.

Back in Florida, Ken impatiently waited for any news. Once Julie-Ann returned from getting her MRI, he went back to be with her. Ken told her that he had called her father.

In no more pain and with some time to think about it, Julie-Ann was now feeling embarrassed by the whole episode. What if it was just a crummy headache and she had worked herself into a panic attack? She made the pilot make an emergency landing, she freaked out Ken, and now she probably had her father worried sick. Her blood work had come back perfectly normal. What was the chance that the MRI was going to show anything? Julie-Ann told Ken how she felt, apologizing for making a scene and being a burden.

"Don't be crazy," he told her. "It's probably nothing serious and thank God for that. But it's not like you made the whole thing up. Migraines, if it turns out to be that, are no little thing, especially if you've never had them before. It can cripple you with pain and blur your vision. And my cousin Jenny used to get panic attacks. She said it felt just like having a heart attack. It's a scary thing."

Julie-Ann took hold of Ken's hand. "I'm so lucky to have you, Ken. You're so understanding and caring."

Ken reached over and kissed her on the forehead. "Anything for my girl."

Ken knew how long things could take in a hospital, especially the emergency room, but after forty-five minutes, he went to search for Julie-Ann's doctor. At the same time, Julie-Ann's father called him to see what was going on. Ken explained that he was trying to find the doctor and would call him back as soon as he found out anything. After looking and asking around, a nurse told Ken that the doctor was tending to a stabbing victim just brought in.

Julie-Ann's father trusted that Ken would call with any news, but he could no longer sit around on his hands. He called the hospital, trying to use his VIP status, but was just given the runaround. Now he was worried and pissed-off.

Another forty minutes passed. At one point, Ken went out again looking for the doctor, or anyone that could give him some news. He also fielded another call from Mr. Crown.

Julie-Ann began convincing herself that if anything bad had shown up on the MRI, they would have told her by now, so it was probably good news. Still, she felt like she had been in the emergency room forever and just wanted to leave the hospital. Then Ken came back and told her that the nurse said the doctor was still waiting to read her MRI.

Julie-Ann couldn't believe it. "This is ridiculous! They took me up to that stupid thing two hours ago. It's not like they have to wait for the film to develop. I mean they get the image instantaneously, right?"

"Yes," Ken replied in a deflated voice. "But they have to wait for the doctor to look at it. Believe me, I raised hell."

About twenty minutes later, Julie-Ann's ER doctor returned, along with another doctor. "This is Dr. Rubin, he's a neurosurgeon," he explained. "I wanted him to have a look at your MRI results. That's why it took so long."

A cold, uneasy feeling flowed through Julie-Ann's body. Why did he want a neurosurgeon to look at it? And why was the neurosurgeon standing in front of her?

"Ms. Crown," Dr. Rubin spoke in a matter-of-fact tone, "a spot showed up on your MRI in an area of the brain called the meninges. After looking at it, I have no doubt that it's a tumor."

It was as if someone had sucked the breath from Julie-Ann's lungs. She no longer felt her body and the room around her disappeared. All she could see was Dr. Rubin's face and all she could hear was that word: Tumor. "You…you mean…I…I have a brain tumor?" She said with utter fear in her voice.

"It's called a meningioma."

"Oh my God. Am I going to die?" Tears began swelling in Julie-Ann's eyes.

Dr. Rubin put his hand on her arm. "I don't want you to get too alarmed. There's a good chance the tumor is benign. Meningioma is not all that uncommon, though it does usually affect women who are more in their middle ages. In fact, some people have meningioma and may never even realize they have it. But it's just that yours is pressing up against some receptors. That's why you were getting the headaches and blurred vision."

"So you're going to have to go in and take it out?" Asked Ken.

"Well in this case, because the size and placement of the tumor, and because she's been having increased symptoms, I think surgery would be appropriate."

Understandably, Julie-Ann began to panic. "Oh my God! I need brain surgery."

"Well it's not something that has to be done right now, but I would strongly recommend having it done within the next few weeks. But I do want you to stay here overnight for observation, just to be sure."

"Someone will be around shortly to move you up to another room," added the other doctor.

Dr. Rubin assured Julie-Ann and Ken that it was not a death sentence, and there was a very strong chance she would recover from surgery and lead a perfectly normal life. He then told them to talk it over and left with the other doctor.

Despite Dr. Rubin's optimistic view, it was still a brain tumor, and Julie-Ann could not help but fear the worse. She cried into Ken's arm as he held and consoled her. He echoed Dr. Rubin's sentiment, that they would go in, take out the tumor, and she would lead a perfectly normal life. She would also not have to deal with any more painful headaches.

"Oh Ken, my father. Someone needs to tell him what's going on."

Ken took a deep breath. "It's okay, I'll call him. I'll let him know."

It was a call Ken was dreading to make, but it had to be done. He left Julie-Ann and walked all the way outside, in front of the hospital. After pacing in a circle a few times, mentally preparing himself, he dialed the number. Her father immediately answered. "James, I…well…"

Julie-Ann's father could tell that something was terribly wrong. "What is it Ken?"

There was no other way to say it, besides just putting it out there. "It turns out Julie-Ann has a tumor in her brain."

James Crown's world came to a standstill. He may have been tough as nails, swam with sharks, and made billion dollar deals, but in the end, he was a father and hearing that his little girl had a brain tumor was nothing he could have ever prepared for. "Wha…what do you mean? Is she…Ken, what the hell are you talking about?"

Ken explained everything the doctor had said. He also added that although they weren't going to operate right away, they were keeping Julie-Ann overnight for observation.

Mr. Crown told Ken not to have Julie-Ann sign anything or let them operate. He was flying to Florida and would be there as soon as possible.

James then told his assistant to have the jet prepared and have his driver ready. He then called his wife, Theresa. He had already told her that Julie-Ann was in the hospital but that it was probably nothing serious. Now he had to call and tell her that she had a brain tumor. Theresa treated and loved Julie-Ann like her own daughter and was shocked and devastated by the news. She told James she would meet him at the airport and left no room for debate.

On the way to the airport, Julie-Ann's father called a friend of his that was a surgeon, for insight and advice. He wanted to know more about meningioma and find out what he should do. Dr. Paul Olivera, who was a top cardiologist in New York, knew James well and had met Julie-Ann several times through the years. He explained his knowledge of meningioma and how most tumors turn out to be benign. Paul promised his friend that he would make some calls and make sure Julie-Ann received the best care.

James and Theresa landed in St. Petersburg at 7:17 p.m. As soon as they landed James checked his phone and saw that Dr. Olivera had sent him an email telling him to check Julie-Ann out in the morning and fly her back to New York. He was able to get her an appointment with a top neurosurgeon he knew that was affiliated with Memorial Sloan-Kettering, one of the country's premiere cancer centers and hospitals for brain surgery. He sent Paul an email back thanking him and told Theresa.

The Crowns went straight to the hospital. In the lobby, they were greeted by Ken, who looked exhausted. He then brought them up to Julie-Ann's room. He waited outside, letting Mr. Crown and Theresa have some time alone with her. Julie-Ann was sleeping, and her father did not want to wake her. He just stood over his daughter and his heart sank, seeing her lying there on a hospital bed, attached to monitors and an IV. It's something no father should have to see.

Of course, it was also difficult for Theresa, who loved Julie-Ann with every fiber of her being. Seeing her there, wondering what was going to happen, brought tears to her eyes. Without saying anything, she took hold of her husband's hand.

For what seemed like fifteen minutes, but in reality was only three, James and Theresa just stood there looking down at Julie-Ann. Then, James bent over and gave his daughter a kiss on the forehead.

He did not mean to wake her up, but Julie-Ann groggily opened her eyes. "Daddy."

"Hey sweetie," he said in a soft voice, with a smile.

"Theresa," she said in a weakened voice. "You came, too."

Theresa tried to fight back her tears. "Of course."

Julie-Ann grabbed her father's hand. "Daddy, I'm scared."

Mr. Crown could feel his heart breaking into pieces. It was not just her words, but seeing the fear in her eyes and hearing it in her trembling voice. He felt like bawling, but knew he had to be strong for his daughter. "It's going to be okay sweetie. Tomorrow morning we're all going to fly back to New York together and you're going to see one of the top neurosurgeons in the country at Sloan-Kettering. And from everything that I've learned, what you have, it's highly treatable."

Julie-Ann smiled. "I know. The doctor here said the same thing. But it's still so scary."

"I know sweetie," her father replied.

"You're going to have the best care and best doctors anyone could have looking after you," added Theresa.

The three talked for another fifteen minutes or so. Julie-Ann told them about her headaches and how she thought she was having a heart attack on the plane. Her father wished she had said something before about her headaches, wondering if her condition could have been more easily treatable if detected earlier. But this was not the time to lecture his daughter.

Her father and Theresa said they would see her in the morning and assured her once again that everything would work out. Mr.

Crown then tried to get a hold of the neurosurgeon that had seen Julie-Ann, but he had left for the day and was supposedly unreachable. After a while, he was able to track down the original ER doctor.

The doctor sat in a small waiting room with Mr. Crown, Theresa, and Ken. James explained that he was checking his daughter out in the morning and taking her to Sloan-Kettering. The doctor said that was their prerogative, and he would write a prescription for a painkiller because the pressurized cabin in the plane could aggravate Julie-Ann's symptoms. However, the doctor urged Mr. Crown to talk with the neurosurgeon before checking Julie-Ann out. Her father explained that he had been trying to get a hold of him, but had been unsuccessful. The doctor said he would try and took down James' cell phone number. He then wished the family luck and went off to another crisis.

Ten minutes later, while Mr. Crown, Theresa, and Ken were still in the waiting room conversing, James' cell phone rang. It was the neurosurgeon. He explained what Ken had already told him that the tumor was most likely benign. But that they could not know for sure without going in and doing a biopsy and that the tumor should be removed anyway because Julie-Ann had been experiencing escalating symptoms, which meant the tumor was probably growing.

After talking to the surgeon, and knowing that Julie-Ann was not in any imminent danger, James suggested checking into a local hotel for the night.

Just after 11:00 p.m., they checked into a nearby Marriott. Ken had his own room. James told him that they would leave the hotel at 8:00 a.m. to go to the hospital. He and Theresa were both mentally exhausted, but neither of them could go to sleep. Restless, James took a shower and shaved. Afterwards, he went on to his laptop and went through his countless emails. Finally, around 1:00 a.m. Theresa was able to go to sleep, but James worked on his computer for another two hours.

Chapter 6

The next morning, Julie-Ann checked herself out of the hospital. The doctor had written her a prescription for Percocet for the plane ride, as well as for any pain she might experience before going to her next appointment. Though she was understandably worried and scared about what lay ahead, Julie-Ann was happy to be going back to New York. She wanted to be at home and sleep in her own bed.

Julie-Ann took two Percocet on the way to the airport, and a half hour into the flight fell asleep. Thankfully, she did not have to endure any headaches during the trip.

When they touched down in New York, Ken told Julie-Ann that he was going to his apartment and then had to check in at the office, but would see her later on. She thanked him for everything and said she would be fine.

It was 1:12 p.m. and Julie-Ann's appointment was for 2:30 p.m., so they did not have much time. She told her father that she wanted to go home to change and freshen up. After all, she had not taken a shower in more than twenty-four hours and had on the same clothes she was wearing when she left Grand Cayman. On the way from the airport, Julie-Ann checked her phone. She had two missed calls from Amber. She made a mental note to call her back later that evening.

Despite having slept in the hospital and on the plane, by the time they arrived at Sloan-Kettering, Julie-Ann was mentally exhausted. She was also starving, having only nibbled on some hospital food since the day before. More than anything, she was nervous. She knew she would get the best care money could buy, and so far the prognosis sounded promising, but it was still a brain tumor. She still was not certain if it was cancerous, and if so, if the cancer had spread.

James, Theresa, and Julie-Ann were met at Sloan-Kettering by Dr. Henrique Libowitz. His main office was a few blocks away, but he also had access to an office in the hospital. A tall, fettle man with short, balding gray hair, Dr. Libowitz looked to be in his mid to late fifties. In a calm welcoming manner, he led the Crowns into the office and had them sit down. Then, from behind a large desk, he explained that he had already talked with the neurosurgeon in Florida and had seen Julie-Ann's MRI results, via email. He turned a large computer monitor that was on the desk so that they could see as he brought up one of the images. Now standing, he showed them the tumor, which appeared in the form of an oblong spot.

Dr. Libowitz explained that there were three main grades of meningioma: Grade I, benign; Grade II, atypical; and Grade III, malignant or anaplastic. He went on to say that the good news was that the vast majority of the tumors turn out to be benign, which meant non-cancerous and usually easily treated. Atypical means that the cells do not appear normal. They are not malignant, but in some cases may later turn malignant. He explained that atypical tumors also have a higher probability of reoccurring than benign if they are surgically removed. Malignant tumors were the worst-case scenario. They are cancerous and are likely to invade other parts of the brain. Dr. Libowitz told the Crowns that it was also the rarest form of meningioma. He went on to say that the increased headaches and other symptoms Julie-Ann had experienced were due to the placement and size of the tumor on the brain and did not reflect the grade of the tumor.

"I think the prognosis is very good," the doctor went on. "But it is important to understand that with any surgery, especially brain surgery, there are risks, and there could be complications."

Nervously, Julie-Ann looked at her father.

"But again," Dr. Libowitz said, "it's my opinion that in this case, I believe surgery is the best option."

"When can you do it?" Julie-Ann asked in an understandably strained voice.

"Well I've already looked at my schedule, and we can do it next Thursday, May tenth. That's a week away."

"Let's do it," exclaimed Julie-Ann.

James looked at his daughter and then back at Dr. Libowitz and simply nodded his head in agreement.

"Okay then, the tenth it is. But I'm going to need you to come back to the hospital, probably Monday. They can make the ap-pointment for you outside. I know you had blood work done in Florida, but we're going to have to do another round of blood work and some other tests just to make sure you're ready for surgery—that you don't have any infections or anything else that might make us want to push the date back." Dr. Libowitz paused. "It should only take an hour or so. And at that time they will let you know exactly how to prepare for surgery, as far as fasting and things like that."

The Crowns thanked Dr. Libowitz. The four of them then went outside to the receptionist who made them an appointment for Monday morning for lab work, as well as penciled in the surgery. Dr. Libowitz also wrote Julie-Ann a prescription for Percocet for any pain she might encounter before the surgery, but instructed her not to take any the morning of her tests. She only had two pills left from the Florida doctor, so she did not even mention getting the previous prescription.

As they left the hospital, Julie-Ann said she was starving and asked if they could stop and eat somewhere.

Her father realized that he had only eaten a candy bar and a banana since the previous afternoon. Theresa had barely eaten either in the past twenty-four hours. "Of course," he said in a drained voice. "I think we all need to eat. How is Palm?"

"Sounds great," replied Julie-Ann. "I could go for a big steak."

James had the driver take them to the restaurant about three miles away. It was 3:57 p.m. and the streets of Manhattan were already congested with the beginning of rush hour. James took the time to call his assistant and check in. Julie-Ann checked her own phone. Amber had called again and also sent two texts. Julie-Ann text her back that she would call in a few hours—and they she had a story to tell. Ken had also text he asking if everything went well with the doctor. She replied "yes", that they were going out to eat and that she could call him afterwards.

When they arrived at Palms' Steakhouse it was before dinner, and after lunch, but it did not matter anyway. Mr. Crown was a regular and a VIP. The maître d' greeted them with a warm smile and asked how Mr. Crown was doing. He lied and said well. The maître d' then escorted them to a large, round table in the back. Famished, James, Theresa, and Julie-Ann all looked over the menu as soon as they sat down.

After ordering, Mr. Crown started talking about Dr. Libowitz and what he had said about the surgery.

"Dad," Julie-Ann said in a rare sheepish voice, "do you think we can talk about something else, anything else? What's going on with the whole SEC investigation?"

"Okay. It finally broke on the news, but we're handling it. It's just a big misunderstanding." James understood his daughter being overloaded by her condition and not wanting to talk about it for at least a half hour, but the truth was he didn't truly want to talk about his firm's scandal either.

Theresa stepped in to change the conversation in a more light-hearted direction asking Julie-Ann how the weather was in Grand

Cayman. Julie-Ann happily obliged by saying it was beautiful and talked about the beach and the town. She then told Theresa and her father about meeting Mark Wesley in Miami.

As they waited for dessert, her father asked Julie-Ann if she wanted to be dropped off at Ken's for the night.

"No. You know what? I'd like to spend the night at home tonight," she answered.

On the way back to their penthouse, Julie-Ann called Ken and told him that she was spending the night at home, but would see him the next day. He said that might be for the best because he had to work late anyway. He then asked how she was feeling, to which she answered "much better."

The first thing Julie-Ann did once she was home was take a long, hot shower. Afterwards, she finally called Amber and told her about what happened and her condition.

Amber was floored. She knew Julie-Ann had been suffering from sporadic headaches lately, but never in her wildest dream could she have imagined that it was a brain tumor. Julie-Ann tried to be stoic and told her best friend that the doctor had assured her that the surgery would be successful, and she would be able to live a normal, healthy life. But Amber wasn't born yesterday. She knew that even if the prognosis was very good, there was no such thing as routine brain surgery. She was devastated for Julie-Ann, whom she considered a sister. Like Julie-Ann did for her, she tried to be positive and supportive, saying that everything would work out. She also asked Julie-Ann if there was anything she could do. It was a gesture from the heart. Unfortunately, they both knew there was nothing anyone, besides the surgeon and the hospital staff could do.

After getting off the phone, Amber went on her computer and Googled meningioma.

That night, Julie-Ann lay in bed with the television off. She was exhausted, yet a thousand thoughts raced through her head. With tears swelling in her eyes, for the first time in her life, Julie-Ann thought long and hard about her own mortality. What if the tumor was cancerous? What if they could not remove it? What if something happened during the surgery and she died on the operating table? She was only twenty-five-years-old. She thought about her life and the future she was supposed to live. She thought about Ken, about the wedding, about the house in Scarsdale they were supposed to buy. Was any of that going to happen? With the weight of life and death on her weakened shoulders, Julie-Ann finally cried herself to sleep.

Julie-Ann didn't wake up until 10:30 a.m. the next morning. She was hoping the previous two days had just been an awful dream— but it was real. She went downstairs to the living room and was greeted by Theresa, who asked how she was feeling.

"I'm okay," she replied in a tired voice.

"I'll have Rita make you some breakfast. An egg white omelet with mushrooms and spinach, with a fruit salad?" She knew it was Julie-Ann's usual morning breakfast.

"Okay," Julie-Ann replied with a smile. "Thank you, that'll be great."

Theresa then called out for Rita, who doubled as a maid and cook, and was usually there Monday thru Friday, from 8:00 a.m. – 6:00 p.m. Rita had been working for the Crowns for three years, after their previous maid, Svetlana, had to go back to Russia for family reasons. Rita, a forty-six-year-old Panamanian immigrant with an affable personality had become close to the family, and especially liked Julie-Ann.

As Rita prepared breakfast, Julie-Ann and Theresa sat at the dining room table. "You know, we really should tell Rita about me," Julie-Ann said in a whisper as she leaned across the table.

Theresa sighed. "You know, I haven't even really thought about it, but I guess you're right. I mean she's probably going to find out anyway."

Just then, Rita brought over a platter with the omelet, bowl of fresh, mixed fruits, and a glass of orange juice. "You sure I can't get you anything Mrs. Crown," she asked Theresa with a smile.

"No, thank you Rita." Just as she was about to walk away, Theresa stopped her. "Rita."

"Yes." As soon as the word left her mouth, Rita looked at Theresa's face and knew something was wrong. She had already surmised that something was up when Theresa told her that she and Mr. Crown were going to Florida. They never went on an impromptu trip together and that they were gone for only one day and returned with Julie-Ann made it even more suspicious. But it was not her place to pry.

"Well, I don't know how…well…"

Julie-Ann could tell her stepmother was trying to find an easy way to break the news. "I have something called meningioma," she blurted out. "It's a brain tumor."

Rita put her hand over her mouth. "What?" Her eyes were already tearing. "Oh Jules, what…I'm so…oh, my God."

Julia-Ann didn't want to upset Rita, but was touched by her heartfelt concern. She explained what it meant, how she found out, the pending surgery, and the prognosis.

With tears now streaming down her face, Rita took hold of Julie-Ann's hand. "I will go to church and pray for you. I'm sure the surgery will be a success."

Now Julie-Ann was beginning to tear-up. "Thank you Rita, that means a lot."

After Rita left the room, Julie-Ann looked down at her breakfast, no longer really hungry.

That afternoon, Julie-Ann took a car to Ken's apartment to spend the weekend. It was Friday and usually the two would go out. Under the circumstances, they decided to stay in, order Chinese food, and watch a movie.

The next day, Julie-Ann was feeling cooped-up and asked Ken if they could do something. It was a mild, sunny early-May day, so they decided to walk around Central Park, which Ken's apartment overlooked.

It was in the mid-seventies, and there was no forecast of rain. It was a Saturday, so the park was bustling. People were walking down the paths, leisurely hanging out on the grass, playing Frisbee. They walked past a small group of people practicing yoga, which was not uncommon. Side-by-side Julie-Ann and Ken strolled down the winding path, surrounded by grass, sporadic hills and rocks, and a variety of towering trees.

Julie-Ann was dressed casually, wearing white capris, a t-shirt, and sunglasses, and her long, blonde hair in a ponytail. Through the corner of her eye, she could see different guys turn to check her out as she passed by—and it made her feel good.

At one point, they were walking past the fenced-in dog park. Julie-Ann pulled on Ken's arm. "Oh, can we go see the doggies?"

"Sure," Ken replied with a smile.

Like a little kid eyeing a mall Santa, Julie-Ann scurried over to the enclosure. All different types of dogs were separated in little packs, happily playing and running around. Julie-Ann stood at the small, wire fence and watched with glee. She had always loved dogs, but growing up in the city, she was never allowed to have one. "Look at that little yellow lab puppy," she excitedly said to Ken, who was now standing by her side. "Oh Ken, can we get a dog when we move into our house? Maybe a lab?"

Ken laughed. "We already had this conversation, remember? You already talked me into saying yes."

Julie-Ann had no recollection of any such conversation. Dr. Libowitz had explained that sporadic, temporary memory loss was sometimes a symptom of meningioma. That was probably why she could not remember the name of her former boss when she was in the Cayman Islands. "Yes, of course, I remember," she said with a forced smile. "I was just testing you, making sure you haven't changed your mind."

"Of course not." Ken did not connect the dots.

They looked at the dogs for another few minutes and then continued on their way. Dr. Libowitz had said that once the tumor was removed the memory loss and other symptoms should go away.

Still, it understandably rattled Julie-Ann. Yet she saw no point in alarming Ken, so she just tried to push it to the side.

After another ten minutes or so, they came to the path leading to the Central Park Zoo. From seemingly out of nowhere, Julie-Ann vividly remembered the time when her father took her there as a child. She was watching the monkeys when one of them jumped from its tree and onto the fence, right in front of her and snarled. She was terrified and screamed. For at least a year after that, she would have intermittent nightmares about being chased by monkeys. Being able to vividly recall the memory put a smile on Julie-Ann's face. She even shared the story with Ken, who thought it was hilarious. Afterwards, she thought about the strange and unpredictable way the mind works, being able to forget a memory that happened two months ago, but remember another one that happened nearly two decades ago. It all seemed so random.

Both in great shape, Julie-Ann and Ken could have walked all day, yet after forty minutes they were getting hungry. It was almost noon, and both only had a bowl of cereal for breakfast. So they decided to walk out of the park and to go somewhere for lunch.

Familiar with the area, they walked to a small, Mediterranean café about four blocks west of Central Park. Right after ordering, a dreadful, familiar pain spiked through Julie-Ann's head. Instantly, she crouched over in distress.

Seeing her hold her head, Ken knew exactly what was going on. "Are you okay?" He asked out of reflex. "I thought the doctor gave you something for pain."

"He did," she moaned. "But it's back at the apartment."

Ken saw Julie-Ann grimace and could tell it was only getting worse. "It's okay, we'll take a cab back." Ken then called for the waiter and said they had to leave, and gave him a fifty-dollar bill.

Luckily, Ken was able to flag a taxi down right away. On the short ride back to the apartment, Julie-Ann's condition was escalating. The constant, driving pain was now accompanied by blurred vision.

After getting out of the cab, Ken helped Julie-Ann walk, propping her up by slinging her arm around his neck and holding onto her waist. In immense pain and scared, Julie-Ann was also starting to panic. While they were on the elevator, with a trembling voice, she told Ken where the Percocet was. As soon as they entered the apartment, Ken laid her down on the couch. He then went into the bedroom bathroom and retrieved the bottle of pills. She quickly swallowed a Percocet. Ken steadied her trembling hands as she washed it down with a glass of water. Her hands were shaking too badly to hold it. Then, Julie-Ann lay back down and prayed for the medication to work its magic quickly.

After about ten minutes, the pain began to subside, but her vision was still fuzzy. Ken said for her to go into the bedroom and lay down on the bed, but she did not even want to move. Then, after another twenty minutes, Julie-Ann faded to a deep sleep.

When Julie-Ann woke-up it was already 6:17 p.m. She was groggy from her long nap. Thankfully, her head no longer hurt, , and her vision had returned to normal. She and Ken just hung out in the living room for the rest of the evening, watching television.

Julie-Ann never had problems sleeping, but that night, because she had already slept for nearly six hours earlier, she lay wide-awake in bed. Long after Ken had already fallen asleep, she laid in silent darkness, watching the minutes of the clock slowly drip by like molasses. She thought about putting on the TV, but did not want to wake-up Ken. Once again, her head could not help but fill with anxiety and thoughts about her situation. By 2:00 a.m. she had almost worked herself into a panic. She thought about taking another Percocet just so she could relax and go to sleep, but she decided not to. Finally, somewhere before 3:00 a.m. she was able to doze off.

The next day, Sunday, Julie-Ann sat around the apartment. She felt fine, but was afraid that if she went out, she would have another episode. At least if she was at the apartment when it happened, she could take a pill and lie down. In the afternoon, however, Ken did go out to the store, but only after making sure Julie-Ann was okay staying by herself.

Julie-Ann took the time to call Amber back, who had left a message earlier that morning. She wanted to see how Julie-Ann was feeling. Her father also called to check in on her, and Theresa got on the phone as well. Julie-Ann was pleased that they were all so concerned and that she had such loving people in her life. She told Amber about what happened at the Café, but she did not tell her father or stepmother.

Ken returned with some groceries and sushi. As they ate, Julie-Ann talked about her appointment at the hospital in the morning.

"Again, what time it is your appointment?"

Julie-Ann finished swallowing her piece of sushi. "It's for nine o'clock."

"Okay, I'll take you. I have a meeting with someone at the head of derivatives at Goldman Sachs at ten, but I'll just have to cancel."

"Don't be silly," Julie-Ann said in a casual tone. "I'll take a car. It's no big deal. They're just going to draw blood and give me some other routine tests. I'm not going to find out anything. The doctor who's doing my operation won't even be there."

Ken hesitated before answering. "Are you sure?" He asked in a skeptical voice.

"Yes, I'm sure. Really."

That evening, Theresa called Julie-Ann again, this time to remind her about her appointment. Julie-Ann explained that Ken had an important meeting, and she was just going to go by herself. "Nonsense," said Theresa. She insisted that she would go with her. Julie-Ann thanked her. After thinking about it for a few seconds, she told Theresa that she would just spend the night at home, to make it easier. Theresa said there was no need, but Julie-Ann's mind was already made up. After getting off the phone, she told Ken of her plans and called a cab.

Chapter 7

The next morning, Theresa and Julie-Ann had James' personal driver take them to Sloan Kettering. Mr. Crown was already at work.

As they sat in the waiting room of the hospital, Julie-Ann turned to Theresa. "I really appreciate you coming with me, being here for me."

Theresa smiled. "Don't be silly. You know I'm always here for you."

"I know," Julie-Ann replied in a soft voice. "You've been a great mother to me."

Theresa was moved. She and Julie-Ann had always been close, and she had no doubt that Julie-Ann loved her, but she had never before referred to Theresa as mother. "Oh Jules," she said, fighting back tears, "that means so much to me. It really does. And you know I couldn't consider you more of a daughter if I had given birth to you. And I would do anything for you."

Now Julie-Ann could feel her eyes tearing-up. "I know," she replied with a smile. "I know."

Sitting in the waiting room, the two then embraced.

The tests did not take long. Julie-Ann just had to provide a blood and urine sample, and had an EKG test. The nurse said that the results would be sent to Dr. Libowitz by the next morning.

Julie-Ann was done by 10:50 a.m. She was not able to eat anything before the tests, so she asked if Theresa wanted go out and have an early lunch. Theresa was more than happy to spend more time with Julie-Ann. Besides, she had not eaten any breakfast either and was starving.

They found a café in Midtown. The conversation was kept light. Theresa wanted to try and give Julie-Ann a break from dwelling on her situation and the upcoming surgery, plus Julie-Ann needed the break. Still, at one point, Julie-Ann thanked her once again for taking her to the appointment. As they finished their lunch, Julie-Ann said that afterwards she was going to walk over to Ken's office, which was only a few blocks away, to surprise him. Theresa asked if she wanted a ride—their private car and the driver was waiting outside—but Julie-Ann felt like walking.

After lunch, the women parted with a hug and kiss on the cheek. Julie-Ann said she was probably going to stay the night at Ken's.

Early May in New York is hit and miss. It can easily be in the low sixties, windy, cloudy, and rainy, or you might get a bright, sunny, seventy-five-degree day. This day was the latter, a clear, blue sky adorned in warmth, with a slight soothing breeze. As Julie-Ann strolled down the busy city sidewalk, the breeze combed through her hair and felt refreshing on her face. Taking in a deep breath, she looked around at the engulfing metropolis. The sun's rays shined down through the corridors of towering buildings. Lines of yellow cabs and other cars and trucks trudged down the straight streets, stopping and going, honking their horns. The scents of various foods being cooked by street vendors wafted through the air. But what Julie-Ann noticed the most was the seemingly endless stream of people hurriedly walking down the sidewalks.

Julie-Ann lived in Manhattan and thus certainly was no stranger to crowds. In fact, she usually walked down the streets in her own little world, oblivious to the hordes of pedestrians along side her—just as most New Yorkers do. On this day, however, she looked at their passing faces and wondered the stories each of them had to tell. Where were they all going? What secrets did they hide? Did any of them have a tumor or some other medical condition? As she passed a young woman that looked to be her age, Julie-Ann wondered if the woman would even be alive in a year's time. Would their paths ever cross again? As Julie-Ann gazed at the strangers that she had previously never paid mind to, she realized that it was the thought of her own mortality that made her attune to the lives of others.

But as Julie-Ann came upon Ken's building, she was snapped out of her deep thoughts. Excited to see Ken and surprise him, she entered the lobby and went up to the security desk and checked in by showing her driver's license.

Ken's firm was located on the forty-third floor. Although handling hundreds of millions of dollars of other people's money, as well as their own assets, Fister Capital had less than ten employees. This is actually not uncommon for hedge fund companies. Some hedge funds firms consist of no more than two people.

Julie-Ann exited the elevator and opened one of the two glass doors that led into Ken's company. With a smile and bounce in her step, she walked up to the spotless, oak receptionists desk. "Hi Cheryl."

Cheryl, who Julie-Ann had met on numerous occasions, seemed taken aback. "Oh, hi Jules."

"I know, he wasn't expecting me, but I was in the area and figured I'd just pop in to see him."

"Oh, well actually you just missed him."

Usually Cheryl greeted Julie-Ann with a smile and was overly friendly. But now she seemed standoffish. Julie-Ann wondered if Ken had told Cheryl about her tumor and she just didn't know what to say or how to act. Julie-Ann didn't feel like getting into it, or even worse, bringing it up if Cheryl had something altogether different on her mind. "Well, where did he go?" She asked.

Cheryl hesitated before answering. "I'm not quite sure. I think just somewhere around here. He just left about ten minutes ago."

Julie-Ann found the answer a bit odd. Usually Ken never left the office during the day without telling Cheryl where he was going. "Well, I guess I'll just call him then."

"Okay. When he comes back I'll tell him you were here anyway, just in case you can't reach him—if he's having lunch with a business associate and doesn't answer his phone."

Julie-Ann thanked her and said goodbye.

"Well, it was good seeing you," Cheryl said with a smile. "Even if it was just for a minute. I'm sure I'll see you again soon. Enjoy the rest of your day."

Cheryl now sounded more like her regular self, and as Julie-Ann waited for the elevator, she thought perhaps she had just read too much into nothing. Once down in the lobby, Julie-Ann pulled out her phone to call Ken. But for some reason, she decided instead of calling him to stop by his favorite place to have lunch, Bobby Van's, which was on the same block. Nestled on the outside of Grand Central Station, Bobby Vans is a popular place for the financial crowd to sit down and have lunch, whether to broker a deal, schmooze, or for just some time away from the office.

As men with suits and ties and well-dressed women walked up to the maître d, Julie-Ann peeked through the restaurant's glass façade. Scanning the crowded tables and booths, it did not take long for her to find Ken, sitting at a small table in the corner—with a woman. A cold sensation overcame Julie-Ann as she watched Ken's posture, leaning forward and laughing with the pretty, young brunette, who didn't look a day over twenty-three. The girl was giggling back and playing with her long, straight hair. They both had a glass of wine in front of them. Now oblivious to everything else going on around her, Julie-Ann stood frozen by the entrance-way, locked-in to every move that Ken and his mystery guest were making, wondering what they were talking about.

As Julie-Ann watched with Argus-eyes, Ken turned his head, probably to look for the waiter. As he did, he caught Julie-Ann standing there. His face, which had just adorned a smitten smile a second before, instantly morphed into the look of a deer caught in headlights. He quickly put on an awkward smile and waved Julie-Ann over. After taking a deep breath and trying to compose herself, she slowly walked into the restaurant and over to them. As she did, she watched as Ken said something to the mystery woman. Julie-Ann tried to read his lips, but could not. The woman then turned and looked her way. Surprise was written all over her face.

As Julie-Ann came upon the table, Ken stood up. "Honey, what are you doing here?"

"I dropped by your office, and they said you were out to lunch, so I came here," Julie-Ann answered in a sharp tone.

"Oh, well...sit...sit down," he said while still standing. "This is Vicky, the new employee I had told you about. We were just having lunch and talking over some business." He then turned to Vicky. "Vicky, this is my wife, Jules."

Vicky stood up, revealing her short, but slender frame, and large breasts that were popping out from her tight, low-cut blouse. "Hi, it's a pleasure to meet you," she said with a smile as she extended her hand.

Julie-Ann wanted to slap her right there, but she refrained. "Hello," she replied in a drab voice as she loosely shook her hand.

"Please, sit down," Ken asked again. "We already ordered, but I'll call over the waiter."

"No, that's okay," she replied as she finally sat down at the table. "I already had lunch with Theresa."

"Oh yes, how did your tests go?"

Vicky finished taking a drink of wine and put down her glass. "Yes, Ken told me about your tumor. I'm so sorry. It must be horrible. I can't even imagine."

Julie-Ann's blood, which was simmering, escalated into a full boil. She caught Ken shooting Vicky a quick stare. "Yes Vicky, it is horrible," she replied in a clear sarcastic tone. "You know, maybe I should go. I don't want to disturb anything."

"Don't be silly." Ken tried to be relaxed and diffuse the situation. "We were just talking about a new client we are bringing on."

"Excuse me, I have to use the ladies room." With that, Vicky slowly left the table.

Ken leaned over to Julie-Ann. "What's the matter? Was there a problem with the tests?"

"No, Ken. It has nothing to do with that."

Ken let out a forced laugh. "Oh come on, it's not that I'm having lunch with Vicky? She works for me. I told you, we were just talking business. I go out to lunch with Cooper, too and James. You're being paranoid." Just then, Ken's phone, which was resting in front of him on the table, came to life with an incoming call. Ken made a face. "Shit, I'm sorry, I have to take this. I've been waiting for this guy's call all day." With that, he picked up the phone and began talking.

Julie-Ann was just about to get up and leave when she happened to notice that Vicky had left her purse on the floor by her chair. It was open, and Julie-Ann could see her cellphone resting on top. Instantly, she thought about being able to look through the phone to see if there were any texts or emails to or from Ken. It was a split-second decision, one that just happened to present itself. She then glanced back at Ken, who was lost in his phone conversation and looking in the other direction. With her heart racing, Julie-Ann looked around for Vicky. Not seeing her, she bent over and pretended to fumble through her own purse. But instead, she quickly snatched Vicky's phone. Oblivious, Ken didn't notice a thing.

As soon as Julie-Ann took the phone, she began to panic. *What if there's nothing incriminating on it? What if Vicky comes back to the table and goes right for her phone? She's going to know I took it. Oh my God, what if it rings while we're all sitting here? I hope it's on vibrate. I can't believe I stole her phone! I've never stolen anything!* Then, Julie-Ann looked over at Ken's half-empty glass of wine and was glad she took the phone.

Just then, the waiter came to the table with Ken's and Vicky's lunch. He asked if Julie-Ann wanted to order anything, to which she replied "no thank you". Right as the waiter was leaving, Vicky returned and sat down. "He's on some business call," explained Julie-Ann.

Ken put up his index finger, signaling he would be just another minute.

"Are you sure you don't want any lunch?" Vicky asked.

"No, thank you. In fact, I think I'm going to be leaving. I'll leave you two to finish your business. Please tell Ken that I'll call him later."

When Ken saw Julie-Ann stand up, purse in hand, he politely asked the person on the other end if he could hold on, and put his hand over the phone. "Jules, wait, I'm sorry. I have to take…this is the client that we came here to discuss."

"That's fine. I was just stopping by. I'll call you later. It's no big deal. Conduct your business," she said in a calm voice. Then, as she was about to walk away, she turned back to both Ken and Vicky and added: "And enjoy your wine."

Julie-Ann didn't give Ken a chance to stop her. She quickly scurried out of the restaurant and into Grand Central Station. Her heart was still beating out of her chest, both from her suspicions about Ken and Vicky, and stealing Vicky's phone. For the next few minutes, she just slowly walked, taking deep breaths, trying to compose herself.

Aimlessly, she had walked to the other end of the station and out the door, back outside. Her nervousness had now turned back to anger. *Just talking business,* she bemoaned to herself. *I saw the way they were looking at each other, giggling like two teenagers. And drinking wine. And they were in the Cayman Islands together! And how dare he talk to her about my tumor! It makes me sick!* Not paying attention to where she was walking, Julie-Ann inadvertently bumped into a middle-aged man.

"Oh, I'm sorry," he said, even though it was her fault.

Julie-Ann just snarled at him and kept moving. All the people that she had less than an hour ago found so enthralling now were nothing more than nuisances, getting in her way, taking up her space.

Walking to nowhere in particular, full of adrenaline, she began thinking about the phone. On one hand, she wanted to look through it as soon as possible, her curiosity killing her. But, on the other hand, she was afraid to look at it. Was she prepared to see what she might find? But the first hand won out. She didn't steal this girl's phone and then wasn't going to go through it. Plus, she tried to convince herself, she was prepared for anything.

Julie-Ann was ready, even chomping at the bit, to look through the phone. But where? She didn't want to thumb through it while walking down the street. There were no parks around where she was. Just then she walked past one of countless of pubs that lined Manhattan. Julie-Ann stopped and looked in through the façade of windows. Though it was still lunchtime, it was not too crowded. She figured it was as good a place as any. She went inside, walked up to the bar, and ordered a Grey Goose and cranberry. She then took it over to one of the several small, tall round tables that were next to the bar, facing the street.

Julie-Ann took a swig of her drink and then, almost ceremoniously, went into her purse and pulled out Vicky's cellphone, placing it on the table in front of her. While staring at it, she took another drink. Then, after a deep breath, she picked it up and went straight for the texts. Luckily for Julie-Ann, Vicky did not have a pass-lock on her phone. With anxious trepidation, Julie-Ann scrolled down the list of conversations, searching for Ken's name or his phone number. She found neither. She was about to look through the emails when a new text came in. It was from someone named Vinny: *I'll see you tonight at Mario's. I have a room for later. Can't wait to touch that sexy ass body.*

Intrigued, Julie-Ann found previous texts between Vicky and Vinny and started to scan through them. There was a lot of sexting, some quite detailed and graphic, but one text in particular caught her eye. It was from Vicky to Vinny: *I should have never told you that. It was nothing, just a one-time thing. We were at a business function, and I was drunk. Really. Won't happen again.*

Julie-Ann scrolled down to the previous text, which was from

Vinny. *I know we're not exclusive, but I do get jealous when I think of you with another man. Especially that jerk-off boss of yours.* Julie-Ann's stomach sank. With trembling hands, she put the phone down. Tears were already beginning to swell in her eyes. After a minute of trying to gain her composure, she finished her drink in one swig and then picked the phone back up and went through the rest of their texts. There were no more mentions about her "boss". Still shaking, she put the phone down and wiped her eyes.

Julie-Ann was not finished with the phone. She still had the emails to go through. But first, she needed another drink. She went up to the bar and ordered another Grey Goose and Cranberry and then returned to her table. Oblivious to the world around her, she took a gulp and then went into Vicky's emails. There were two accounts that showed up: her work account with Ken's firm's name—which infuriated her—and a Gmail account. Julie-Ann went straight for the Gmail account. The first few emails were brief exchanges with what appeared to be friends, but of no interest. After scanning through six emails, Julie-Ann took another dink, thinking that she was not going to find anything incriminating. The next email immediately changed everything. It was from an unknown email address, but it would become brutally clear to whom it belonged. It read: *I would like that. You always make me feel better. And it's been too long for me, too. Cayman already feels like weeks ago. God, you know how to blow my mind!*

Trembling and with her heart palpitating, Julie-Ann dreadfully read the previous email, which was from Vicky. *So sorry to hear about your wife. That must be so tough for you. I can't imagine. But I am here for you. I promise I will do everything to make you feel better. I'll let you do whatever you want.*

Instantly, Julie-Ann went to throw-up. Her cheeks puffed out, and she put her hand over her mouth, but she was able to keep it down. She quickly grabbed the phone and her purse and ran to the ladies room. She went into a stall, locked the door behind her, knelt down, and vomited. Julie-Ann could not believe what she had just read. It went beyond Ken just having an affair. It was as if he didn't care a scintilla about her, as if she didn't even know him, as if the life she had been living with him and the future they had planned was all a lie. It was nothing but lies. Still kneeling on the dirty bathroom floor and holding up her hair, she threw-up again.

"Are you okay in there?" Asked a hesitant female voice.

Julie-Ann spit into the bowl. "Yes," she replied in a weak and embarrassed voice. "Yes, thank you, but I'm fine. It's just my stomach. I'm okay."

"Okay, I was just checking."

Julie-Ann waited until she heard the woman leave the restroom and gingerly stood up and flushed the bowl. She then peeked outside the stall to make sure no one was else was there. Realizing the coast was clear she went over to the sink, rinsed her mouth out with some tap water and washed her hands. Once finished, Julie-Ann looked at herself in the mirror. She was a mess. Thick streaks of black mascara and tears stained her usually effervescent face. Her hair was all out of place. Not wanting anyone to come in and see her that way, she hurried to finish cleaning herself up.

As she left the bathroom and walked back into the bar, Julie-Ann felt as though everyone was looking at her. Having already paid for her drink and left a tip, she kept walking, straight out onto the busy sidewalk.

Her knees weak and heart racing, Julie-Ann aimlessly went with the congested flow of pedestrians. Feeling like the bright daylight was burning, she reached into her purse and put on a pair of dark sunglasses, which totally covered her eyes. *Okay, compose yourself. Take a deep breath.* But her heart would not stop racing. And her legs felt like they could give out at any time. *What am I going to do? Where am I going? Maybe I'll go sit somewhere and try to calm down. Maybe another drink will calm my nerves.* With that, Julie-Ann walked into the next tavern, which was right across the street.

Still wearing her sunglasses, Julie-Ann grabbed a stool at the end of the bar where no one was sitting and ordered a Grey Goose on the rocks with a splash of lime. Still shaking, she used both hands to bring the glass up to her mouth and take a drink. Then, before she could put the glass down on the bar, she took another drink. After a few more deep breaths, she began to calm down a little. At least she didn't feel like she was going to pass out any-more. She thought about what she was going to do. She thought about going through some more of Vicky's emails, but then decid-ed against it, at least for the moment.

Her shock was now turning to outrage, her panic to anger. *I'm going to call that son-of-a-bitch right now!* Julie-Ann went into her purse and pulled out her phone. She was just about to call Ken at work and go off on him when she realized she had seven new texts. Distracted for a second, she realized that three of them were from Amber, asking how her tests went. Amber! It was like a light went on. More than anything, what Julie-Ann needed most at the moment was a friend—her best friend.

She text Amber back. *Just found out that Ken has been cheating on me with his bimbo employee. No doubt. Took her phone and went through her texts and emails.* As she typed, she could feel herself starting to cry again. Trying to be as inconspicuous as possible, she quickly lifted her sunglasses and wiped her eyes.

As Julie-Ann waited for a response, she took another drink. Less than a minute later her phone rang. It was Amber.

"Oh my God Jules, what happened? What are you talking about?"

"It's a long story. I can't really talk on the phone now. I'm in some bar," she said softly, fighting back more tears.

"Where, what bar?"

Julie-Ann told her the name and location of the bar.

"Just stay there. I'll be right over. I'm on Fifty-seventh Street at the Burberry store. But I'm leaving right now. Don't worry, I'll be there as fast as I can."

As Julie-Ann hung up the phone, she took solace in the fact that she had such a good friend. At least she was not alone. But the second of comfort was shattered when the phone, still in her hand came alive with her personalized ringtone. It was Ken, calling from his office. Although Julie-Ann was ready to call him only two minutes before, she now decided not to answer it.

About fifteen minutes later, Amber showed up. They greeted each other with a tight hug.

"Oh Amber, I can't believe it," she sobbed into Amber's shoulder. "It's all been a lie. A big fuckin' lie!"

"I'm so sorry Jules," she replied in a whisper. Then, Amber suggested they get a booth, so they could talk in more privacy.

Julie-Ann left the bartender a tip and the two then had the hostess show them to a secluded booth near the back. As soon as they sat down, Julie-Ann tried to order drinks from the hostess, but she explained that the waitress would be right over.

"How many drink have you already had?" Amber asked, picking up on Julie-Ann's already slurred speech.

Julie-Ann paused to think about it. "I don't know, four or something."

Just then, the waitress came over. Julie-Ann went back to the Grey Goose and cranberry and Amber ordered a Cosmopolitan.

"So Jules, what the hell happened?"

Julie-Ann told her the whole story. As she did, tears freely flowed. Amber just listened in disgust. The waitress came back with their drinks and was going to ask if they wanted to order anything to eat, but could tell they were in a heavy conversation and left them alone. At one point, Julie-Ann even pulled out Vicky's phone and showed Amber the emails.

"That motherfucker! And that bitch! She has the audacity to bring up your condition! She should be run over! And he should have his balls cut off!"

Julie-Ann wiped her eyes and cheeks. "And to think they probably had sex the night before in the same room—the same bed— that I stayed in."

Amber didn't instantly connect the dots. "What room?"

"You know, when I met him in…at…" All of a sudden, Julie-Ann could not remember the name of the hotel. "When…after we went to Florida."

"Oh, when you met him in the Cayman Islands."

"Yes, thank you," she replied through her sobs. "I couldn't even remember the name of the hotel. That's another thing I have to worry about—losing my memory because of this stupid fucking tumor! Maybe soon I won't even remember my name. Ken, a brain tumor—why is all this happening to me? Why me? Why does God hate me so much? What did I ever do to deserve this? It's too much Amber. Maybe it's better if I don't make it through the operation."

Amber reached across the table and firmly grabbed her friend's arm. "Don't you ever say that! You hear me! You have people that love you." Now Amber was in tears. "Fuck that jerk. He's the devil. I'm talking about me, your father, Theresa. Oh Jules, if anything ever happened to you I don't know what I would do."

Julie-Ann looked at Amber and smiled. "I don't know what I would do without you," she replied before wiping her face with a napkin. She then leaned across the table and took hold of Amber's hands. "Don't cry. I'm sorry. I'm just really upset now. I'm not going anywhere. Best friends forever."

"Best friends forever. Don't be sorry. I can only imagine how hard all of this is for you. But I'm here for you."

"I know."

Julie-Ann and Amber took turns going into the bathroom and cleaning themselves up. Afterwards, they ordered some appetizers and another round of drinks. Over the next hour and a half they sat in the booth, eating and drinking, talking about Ken and then guys in general. At times they would find themselves laughing, then Julie-Ann would start crying again.

At one point, a phone rang with an unfamiliar ringtone. Amber and Julie-Ann looked at each other. Then it came to Julie-Ann. "Oh my God, it must be her phone. What if it's her trying to call her cell?" She reached in her purse and fished out Vicky's phone. "It says Dan."

Amber reached out her hand. "Here give it to me. Let me answer."

Drunk, Julie-Ann was game. She handed Amber the phone.

"Hello," Amber said in a straightforward voice. "Your little skank can't come to the phone right now. She's busy giving some guy a blowjob in the bathroom." Before giving the shocked person on the other end a chance to reply, Amber hung up the phone.

Julie-Ann and Amber busted out in laughter as if they were two high school girls who had just pulled the ultimate prank. "I can't believe you did that. What if that was her brother or something?"

"So." Suddenly a giant smile formed on Amber's face. "Hey, I've got a great idea, let's call everyone in her phone directory and tell them what a whore she is."

"You are so bad. Should we?"

Just then, Vicky's phone rang again. It was Dan again. Amber and Julie-Ann just giggled.

The girls ordered another round of drinks. Then, Amber started going through Vicky's phone directory and calling random people. Most of the time she would just say that Vicky is a slut and a whore and then quickly hang-up. Other times there was a brief, heated exchange, and then she would hang up. People started calling back right away. Sometimes she would answer it, other times not. Amber and Julie-Ann thought it was hysterical. Amber did, however, hold back from calling "Mom" and "Dad".

After about six calls, the novelty was wearing off. Amber paid for the tab and then suggested they go to another, more happening bar. She pointed out that it would soon be happy hour and knew of a great place. So for the moment, giggling and having a good time, they piled into a cab and made the two-mile ride.

At the new bar, the drinking continued. Just as Amber had predicted, as soon as 4:30 p.m. rolled around the place started to fill up.

Ken had text and called Julie-Ann several times, and she finally responded with a text. *I know all about your little whore Vicky. Just try denying it. You fucking disgust me!*

By this time, some of the friends and family members that had received Amber's crank calls had phoned Vicky at work to tell her about it and ask what was going on. It did not take her long to put two-and-two together and surmise that Julie-Ann had somehow stolen her phone. She was fuming. She ran into Ken's office and told him about it. That set him into panic mode. He asked if there could be anything incriminating on the phone that would prove they were having an affair. Vicky pointed out that she had erased any texts between them after Ken told her about Julie-Ann seeing the one text in Grand Cayman. He then asked about emails. Ken knew they had exchanged indicting emails—even though he used an account Julie-Ann wasn't aware of that didn't have his name—but hoped Vicky had deleted them once they were read. In the heat of the moment Vicky did not remember if she had erased all of his emails or not, but told him that she had.

When Ken received the text from Julie-Ann he prayed that she had no real evidence and was just guessing. He sent another text denying everything and told Julie-Ann to call him.

She responded with a text. *I stole your little whore's phone, and I saw the emails. How could you! Talking about how fucking her would take your mind off my medical problems. I don't even know you! I'm just glad I found out before we got married. OMG, just the thought of being with you now repulses me. Whatever I have in your apartment you can keep. I never want to see you again! I hope you and your little slut bitch have a miserable life together!*

After trying to conjure up some far-fetched story, Ken tried calling Julie-Ann, but she didn't answer. He then sent another text, which she did respond to with more diatribes. As she was typing her second text, she began to cry again. Amber told her to leave it be, that he was not even worth a response, but Julie-Ann was in a zone.

Amber was feeling drunk, but Julie-Ann was downright plastered and a mess. She was crying, and then yelling loudly in the bar about how all men were scum, then crying again. She was causing a scene. Amber realized that it was time for Julie-Ann to call it a night—even if it was only 5:30 p.m.

At first Julie-Ann didn't want to leave, causing an even bigger scene. When Amber finally got her outside, Julie-Ann pleaded to go to another bar. Finally, Amber was able to convince her friend to go back to Amber's place. She bribed Julie-Ann by saying they could hang out there for a while and then go to another specific bar that didn't become happening until later. But really Amber prayed that Julie-Ann would just run out of steam and pass out.

During the cab ride, Amber had Julie-Ann text Theresa to say she was going to spend the night at Amber's. It was not that unusual. Amber had her own, large apartment in SoHo.

As Amber had hoped, not long after they arrived at her place while sitting on the couch watching TV, Julie-Ann passed out and even began to snore. Amber put a pillow under her head and put a blanket over her. Julie-Ann slept right through the night.

Chapter 8

Julie-Ann woke-up the next morning at 8:15 a.m. She had slept for over thirteen hours straight. Still, her head was in throbbing pain. She could not tell if it was because of her tumor or the buckets of alcohol she had consumed—or a combination of both. Still in a daze, she looked around. Julie-Ann knew she was in Amber's apartment, but had no recollection of getting there.

Amber was still asleep, and the loft was dead quiet. Her mouth and throat feeling like it was full of dry concrete, Julie-Ann gingerly climbed off the couch and went into the kitchen in search for water. She grabbed a bottle of Poland Springs out of the refrigerator and drank half of it down right away. She then made her way back to the couch. Her purse was on a corner table next to it.

As sometimes happens, she decided to check her phone log hoping to piece together the rest of the night. There were several unread texts from Ken. Just seeing his name brought back all the angst of the previous day. Nevertheless, after taking a deep breath, she read the texts. The first two were him saying how sorry he was and how much he really loved her. He had just been under a lot of stress lately (that part made her especially furious). The next one was blaming Vicky, how she seduced him and promising that it was over between them and how he would get rid of her right away. The last text was him saying that Vicky really needed her phone back and that she was making a huge deal about it and threatening to call the police and say Julie-Ann had stolen it. Suddenly, Julie-Ann recalled all the crank calls Amber had made with Vicky's phone. Julie-Ann started to panic. She certainly didn't want to get in trouble with the police. She text Ken back saying that she would return the phone and that it was childish to take it. Then she added: *But I still never want to see or talk to you again!*

Julie-Ann also saw that she had several voice messages. *What if one of them is the police,* she dreaded. But none of them were. One was from Ken with more apologies. Another was from one of her friends. The last one was from her father asking how she was feeling and that he would really like if she spent the night at home Wednesday, the day before the operation.

It was not long before Amber woke-up. She also had an intense hangover. She ordered them breakfast from a nearby café. The café didn't usually deliver, but for esteemed customers like Amber they made an exception.

Julie-Ann expressed to Amber her fear of getting in trouble over Vicky's phone. Amber knew her friend had enough on her mind with Ken and her upcoming surgery. She told Julie-Ann that if it came to it, she would take full responsibility for taking the phone. Julie-Ann appreciated the gesture, but was not going to let Amber take the rap, not to mention that Amber never had the opportunity to steal the phone.

Later that afternoon, Julie-Ann went back home. Amber made her leave Vicky's phone with her, promising that she would make sure it was returned. Amber kept her promise, giving it to a courier that delivered it to Vicky's work that day.

On the car ride back home, Julie-Ann went on Facebook. She had been going back-and-forth contemplating whether or not to post anything about her condition and upcoming surgery. But now, out of pure despondency she posted the following: *Life isn't fair. In fact, it sucks! Found out I have something called meningioma—basically, a brain tumor. Having surgery Thursday to remove it. I know, shocking isn't it?* She did not mention anything about Ken.

When Julie-Ann arrived at the penthouse, Theresa was there. Julie-Ann looked terrible, and Theresa could clearly see that she was troubled. She imagined that it was merely the overbearing weight of the pending operation.

"Are you okay honey?" Theresa asked in a concerned voice. She then walked over and gave her stepdaughter a hug. "I know it's a lot to think about. But it will work out. Still, it's okay to be scared."

Julie-Ann took a deep breath. "It's not just the operation."

"What, what is it? Did you have another episode? You don't look so well."

"It's not that," Julie-Ann said as she walked passed Theresa, towards a couch in the living room. "It's Ken," she continued as she sat down. "He's been cheating on me with one of his employees, some new girl—and that's just what I know about. God knows who else he's been sleeping with."

Theresa put her hand over her mouth in disbelief. "Oh honey," she said as she walked over and sat beside Julie-Ann. "Are you sure?"

Julie-Ann shook her head as she once again could feel her eyes swelling with tears. "I'm sure. I found some emails between them," she said, not wanting to get into all the details about the phone. "He tried to deny it at first, but he finally fessed up to it. It wasn't a one-time thing either. In fact, he was with her with the night before I met him in the Cayman Islands—probably had sex in the same bed as I slept in."

As Julie-Ann began to cry freely, Theresa put her arm around her and pulled her close. "Oh, Jules, I'm so sorry. That son-of-a-bitch!"

"And to think I was going to marry him," Julie-Ann sobbed.

"Just be glad you found out before the wedding."

"I know." Julie-Ann wiped away some tears. "But please don't tell my father, at least not until after the surgery. It's just..." Julie-Ann never finished the sentence.

"Okay honey. Don't worry."

Theresa was outraged at Ken and felt terrible for Julie-Ann. She wondered how much one young woman could go through. Here she was, just finding out of the blue that she had a brain tumor, and they would have to operate to try and remove it. If that wasn't bad enough, she now finds out, three months before her wedding, that her fiancée is having an affair. As Theresa held Julie-Ann in her arms, she wished there was something she could do to take away all of her pain and worries. All she could do was be there and offer support.

That afternoon the hospital called with the test results. The surgery was a go.

It was Wednesday, May 9, the day before Julie-Ann's surgery. From the moment she woke-up, Julie-Ann was overcome with nerves and sick to her stomach. She was unable to eat breakfast and at one point, had to go into the bathroom to throw-up. Finally, she took a Percocet, just to calm herself down. At first, being on an empty stomach, all it did was made her feel even sicker. After forcing down a piece of toast, it eventually kicked in.

After a light lunch, Theresa asked if she wanted to watch a movie on demand. Wanting to think about anything but reality, she took Theresa up on the offer. The two huddled on the couch in the middle of the afternoon and watched a funny movie. They were even able to laugh.

Mr. Crown came home early, at 3:30 p.m., which he never did. He had planned on having Julie-Ann's favorite dinner, rack of lamb, prepared, but then remembered that she was not supposed to eat the night before the surgery. Nevertheless, he wanted the three of them to spend time together. Though he obviously hoped and prayed for the best, a part of him realized that there was a chance that something could go wrong in the surgery, and he might never be able spend time with his daughter again. That thought crippled him.

That night Julie-Ann laid in her bed dwelling on the gravity of the next morning. For the first time since finding out, she did not think about Ken or her called-off wedding. She dwelled on something even more important—life and death.

She thought about her childhood, most were treasured memories. So many memories flashing before her mind's eye in a phantasmagoria sequence. She saw herself riding a pony when she was six-years-old, her birth mother standing by the side, smiling and clapping. Then she remembered vividly the day she learned that her mother had died. She watched as if seeing a film, her father and Theresa's wedding. She watched as various vacations and outings flashed before her eyes; the time they went to Hawaii, being in Europe, playfully running up and down the deck of a cruise ship. She thought of the time when her father and Theresa took her and Amber to Disneyland. She looked back on her first kiss, in sixth grade, with Peter Winstead, behind the school bleachers. She thought about the several trips she and Theresa took together; the time when she was seventeen, they went to Cabo San Lucas and Julie-Ann had a fling with a boy she met there. She flashed through her college years and saw herself on graduation day, so happy and full of life.

When Julie-Ann tried to envision her future she saw nothing. Would there even be a future? Or had she already lived her full life. Was this how it was going to end, at the young age of twenty-five? And what if she did survive the operation, only to find out that the tumor was cancerous? What if she was faced with a slow, painful, drawn-out death? Or what if something went wrong in the operation and she woke-up an invalid? All these harrowing thoughts swirled through her mind. It was all too much to comprehend. One day she was a young, healthy woman with the whole world in the palm of her hands and a future as bright as any star. The next day, she's contemplating death or living out her days as a vegetable.

That night, Julie-Ann did something she had not done since she was a little child—she knelt beside her bed, clasped her hands together, and prayed. She prayed for God to spare her life and for the operation to be a success. Like many people do when they ask God for something, she tried to bargain, promising God that if her prayers were answered she would live a righteous life and help others.

Around 2:00 a.m. Julie-Ann was finally able to fall asleep. However, she woke-up three hours later. Having to be at the hospital by 8:00 a.m., she saw no use in even trying to go back to sleep. Instead, in the silence of her darkened room, she grabbed a pen and a notepad and wrote a note to her father and Theresa.

Dear Dad and Mom,

First, I know I always call you Theresa, but you are as much of a mother to me if you had given birth to me. I appreciate everything you've done for me over the years. You've been a great mother. And Dad, to say thank you and I love you seems so understated. But there are no words to convey how much you have done for me and how much I appreciate it. You have always been there for me. You both have always been there for me.

I write this letter the morning of my operation, fully expecting and hoping that everything will turn out all right. But if it does not, if God forbid something should go wrong and I do not make it, please take solace in the fact that you have both given me a blessed life, despite what may have happened at the end. And know that I loved you both dearly and we will meet again some day.

Love your daughter,

Julie-Ann

Before they went to the hospital, Julie-Ann pulled her father aside. "Dad, I want you to take this," she said in a hesitant voice as she handed him a white envelope.

He was taken aback. "What is it?"

"If anything should go wrong during the operation…"

"Oh, Jules, don't…"

Julie-Ann cut her father off. "Please Dad, don't make this harder than it already is," she said, fighting back tears. "I'm sure everything is going to work out, and I'll be fine, but if it doesn't…just…this is for you and Theresa. But only if…"

James could feel his heart breaking. He took hold of his daughter and pulled her towards his chest. "I will take it sweetie. But I'm going to give it back to you after you recover. And I don't want you thinking any negative thoughts, you hear me."

"Okay Dad."

Julie-Ann, her father, and Theresa were met at the hospital by James' older brother, Larry. James was wondering where Ken was, but figured he would show-up soon.

Julie-Ann was almost immediately taken to be prepped for surgery. The nurse assured the family that they would get to see her again before she went into the operating room. After about fifteen minutes, Dr. Libowitz came out into the waiting room and went over the procedure with James, Theresa, and Larry. He explained that it was difficult to estimate how long it would take until he was actually inside. Before leaving, he said once again that there was a high likelihood of success.

Not long after Dr. Libowitz left, the nurse came in and said Julie-Ann was about to be led into the operating room and now was their chance to see her. Larry loved his niece and was worried sick about her, but he let his brother and Theresa have a moment alone with her and stayed in the waiting room.

There was Julie-Ann, sitting in a wheelchair, her head shaved, adorned in a hospital gown, an IV in her arm. Both James and Theresa were nervous wrecks, but they tried their hardest to put on a strong front for Julie-Ann's sake. For her part, Julie-Ann smiled and said she would see them in a few hours and not to worry. As they were about to part ways, she could not pretend any longer. She clutched her father's hand. "Daddy, I'm scared."

Fighting back tears with all his might, Mr. Crown bent over and gave his daughter a kiss on the head. "I know sweetie. But everything is going to work out. I know it is."

"I love you, Dad."

"I love you too, sweetie."

Sitting in the wheelchair, Julie-Ann then turned her head to Theresa. "And I love you, too—mom."

"I love you too. With every fiber of my being. And like your father said, everything is going to work out."

Julie-Ann just smiled in response before an orderly wheeled her away. Less than a minute later she entered the operating room. It was just as she had seen in countless movies and television shows. She was brought over to the awaiting operating table, where Dr. Libowitz and four others were doing some preparations. Dr. Libowitz stopped what he was doing and greeted Julie-Ann. She was then hoisted onto the table, along with her IV.

As she looked up, a man's face appeared in front of the several blinding overhead lights. "Hello Julie-Ann, my name is Peter, and I'm going to be your anesthesiologist today. Now I want you to relax. In a minute, you're going to feel a slight prick in your arm. When I tell you, I want you to take a few deep breaths. That's it. The next thing you'll remember is waking up in the recovery room."

With that, the man disappeared into the background, leaving only the beaming overhead lights. Julie-Ann turned her head to see what was going on. She saw Dr. Libowitz talking to yet another person, with what appeared to be a miniature saw in his hands. Frightened by the sight, she looked straight back up. Then, she felt the sting of a needle being plunged into her arm.

"Okay," the anesthesiologist's voice floated through the room, "I want you to take a few deep breaths."

Julie-Ann quickly prayed again to God that she make it through the operation and for it be a success. She then took a deep breath. Instantly a warm feeling flowed through her entire body and everything started to blur to white. Just as she took her second breath, an image seemed to appear over her head. It was a long, vacant highway surrounded by a soft white cloud. Rather than scare her, it set her mind at ease. It looked so peaceful. "Go," a deep, soothing voice echoed in her head. Then, there was nothing, Julie-Ann was out.

Back in the waiting room, James was wondering aloud where was his daughter's fiancée. "I don't understand. She's having surgery and he's not here? I don't care if he had a business meeting with God himself scheduled. You don't think she wanted to see him before she went in? You don't think she was wondering where the hell he was? When is he going to get here—when it's over?" He pulled out his phone. "That's it, I'm going to call him."

Theresa couldn't sit silently any longer. She stood up and grabbed her husband's arm. "James no, you can't call him."

He looked at Theresa. "What do you mean 'can't'? What's going on?"

Theresa looked around the waiting room. There was another couple and what appeared to be their teenage son. "Let's take a walk outside." She then turned to James' brother. She did not have to say anything.

"I'll wait here just in case the nurse comes in," Larry said. "It's okay."

"Thank you," replied Theresa.

Agitatedly curious, James followed Theresa downstairs and outside. She then told him about Ken. Understandably, James blew-up. "That no good…I'm gonna…how could he? And even after he found out about her tumor?"

Theresa hesitantly nodded her head. "That's what Julie-Ann said. And she said he confessed to it."

"I'm going to break his neck!" He pulled out his phone again. "I'm going to call him right now!"

Theresa grabbed his hand. "James, please, not now. Now's not the time. Julie-Ann's up there being operated on. We need to just focus on that right now. Please."

He took a deep breath. "I guess you are right," he said, putting away the phone. "But after she recovers, I'm going to give him a piece of my mind."

With that, they went back upstairs to the waiting room.

About twenty minutes later Amber walked into the waiting room, accompanied by her father. After learning about Julie-Ann's tumor, John had called his old friend to give his support and ask if there was anything he could do. James certainly appreciated the gesture.

Neither James nor Theresa knew that John and Amber were coming to the hospital, but were touched that they showed up. They thanked them for coming and James introduced his brother. He then explained that they had not yet heard any news.

The men sat together. Amber sat next to Theresa few chairs down.

"I'm scared."

Theresa took hold of Amber's hand. "I know. You're a good friend. You've always been." She then paused. "I'm scared, too, but I'm sure the surgery will be a success."

"I know. Still, it's just not fair. Julie-Ann never did anything to anybody. Now all this is happening to her. The tumor, Ken." As soon as the word left her mouth, Amber wanted to recant it, not knowing if Theresa knew about Ken cheating. "I…I shouldn't…"

"It's okay, Julie-Ann told me what happened with Ken."

Amber shook her head in disgust. "Can you imagine that scumbag? How could he do that? I mean not just cheating on her, but still doing it after he learned about her tumor, knowing what she's going through."

Theresa sighed. "Yeah. Though I'm sure it didn't help her finding out right before having surgery, at least she found out before getting married to him."

"That's certainly true."

An hour passed without any news. Then another. James tried to find out how the procedure was going, but to no avail. There was not even a hint if things were proceeding successfully or if it was worse than they had expected. All they knew was that she was still in the operating room. Everyone was on pins and needles.

At one point, James and Theresa went into the hospital chapel, and each said their own prayer. They had both been raised Catholics, but James had not been to church since his first wife was alive; Theresa had not gone since she was a child. Now, they needed God to answer their prayers like never before.

Finally, over four hours after the surgery began, Dr. Libowitz walked into the waiting room. Immediately, everyone circled around.

"Julie-Ann is resting peacefully in the recovery room. You should be able to see her in an hour or so." Dr. Libowitz paused. "While I was doing the operation I had a piece of the tumor sent to the pathologist. It turns out that it is atypical."

There was a collective gasp. James could feel his legs buckle.

"But the good news is that we were able to remove the entire tumor without affecting any of the surrounding area."

"Oh, thank God," proclaimed a shaken Theresa.

"She will have to undergo some radiation."

"Radiation treatment?" James asked in a distressed voice.

Dr. Libowitz put up his hands. "Nothing long lasting. In fact, she may just need three or four sessions. Just as a follow-up."

"So as far as her brain functions, her memory, her…"

"There weren't any complications. Of course, with the brain we always have to monitor for a few days and watch for swelling or some other unforeseen development, but I would say she's going to be perfectly fine. There shouldn't be any more headaches or memory loss. As I told you before, atypical tumors do have a chance of reoccurring, but usually not for at least five years—and sometimes not at all. Julie-Ann will just have to come in for an MRI from time to time to monitor her."

James and Theresa thanked Dr. Libowitz. He reiterated that all in all it was good news. He said they would talk more soon and went on his way.

After Dr. Libowitz left, James turned to his brother, John, and Amber. "I know you guys all want to see Julie-Ann, but they'll probably only let *us* see her today."

John put his hand on his daughter's shoulder. "He's right. She needs her rest today. We can come back tomorrow and visit her."

Amber just shook her head.

"Come on, we'll walk you guys out. I can use some fresh air anyway. I feel like I've been in this room for days."

Just as the group was walking towards the exit, the glass doors slid open and in walked Ken, holding a vase with a dozen red roses. Everyone saw him; he was right in front of them.

"You son-of-a-bitch!" James shouted while pointing his finger.

Theresa grabbed his other arm. "James, don't."

Everyone in the foyer was now looking.

"James, please, I just came here to see Julie-Ann."

"You can take those flowers and shove them up your ass! My daughter's been through enough without having to see you."

Larry got in between his brother and Ken. "Whoa, James, what's going on?"

"Ask him!" He shouted vehemently, spit flying from his mouth.

"You know what, I don't need this." With that, Ken turned around and left, flowers in hand.

After he left, James begrudgingly told them that Ken had cheated on Julie-Ann and the wedding was off. Unbeknownst to James or Theresa, Amber had already told her father. But it floored Larry, and he wanted to run after Ken and kick his ass.

Chapter 9

Julie-Ann was in the hospital for five days, mostly for monitoring. There were no complications. At first, she was understandably shaken when she heard that the tumor was atypical. But then after having time to digest everything she felt lucky. She had not only cheated death, but was expected to make a complete recovery and to live a long, healthy, normal life.

Naturally, her father and Theresa came to the hospital every day. Whereas, James still had a company to run and was in and out of the office, Theresa stayed by Julie-Ann's side for hours at a time. Amber also came to visit and would stay with her friend for a while. Julie-Ann's friend Michelle, as well as some other family also came by. Ken did not come back, but he did send flowers and tried to call; Julie-Ann did not accept either the flowers or the apology.

Even with all the visitors, there was plenty of time when Julie-Ann was alone. She had her own private room. She would sleep a lot and watch TV. Sometimes she would just lie in her hospital bed thinking. She had remembered the vision of the highway just before she went under for surgery. She also remembered it being accompanied by what appeared to be an omnipresent voice saying the word "go". Not able to shake it, Julie-Ann tried to decipher its meaning—if there was any. Was the voice that of God? If so, where was he telling her to go? She discounted that the road was to heaven or the afterlife because she did not die. Also, the road was not ascending; it was a flat, straight, normal, albeit deserted highway.

It was not just the vision of the highway that weighed on her mind. The second night in the hospital, Julie-Ann had a dream that she was walking through what appeared to be a county fair. She was walking hand-in-hand with someone, but the face was blurred. The dream in itself was not overly strange, but Julie-Ann almost never remembered her dreams. Yet this one stuck with her. Besides the blurred face of the person she was with, everything else about the dream was so vivid—the blades of green grass, the various booths and rides of the fair, the blue sky lightly brushed with sporadic thin clouds. However, it was not just the visual aspect; there was this unexplainable feeling attached to it.

Julie-Ann was not contemplating dreams or anything deep, the morning of May 15th. The time had come for her to go home, and she could not have been happier. She felt as though she had been in her hospital room for a month. Of course, she was also overjoyed that she was deemed healthy enough to go home.

Julie-Ann knew her recovery was not yet over. She would have to undergo several rounds of radiation. She was naturally worried about its side effects. Dr. Libowitz explained that radiation treatment affected people differently. Some people may experience no side effects and others might. However, he assured her that the dose she was going to receive, at worst she might feel nauseous, lethargic, and possibly have a slight redness near the area of the treatment but that any symptoms would quickly fade. Dr. Libowitz also explained that throughout her life, she would periodically have to have tests done to make sure the tumor had not returned. At the moment, she did not even want to think about radiation or the chance of the tumor returning. All she wanted to do was go home and sleep in her own bed.

As soon as they arrived home, Julie-Ann was met by Rita, who gave her a big hug. "Oh, Miss Julie-Ann, I am so glad you are all right," she said with tears in her eyes. "I prayed for you and the Good Lord answered."

Julie-Ann was moved. "Thank you, Rita. That means a lot. It really does. I'm happy to be home."

Next, Theresa took Julie-Ann into her bedroom and presented her with four different wigs she had bought. "Hopefully you like one of them. It's just something until we can go and get you professionally fitted."

Julie-Ann smiled. "Yes, of course. Thank you so much." She then gave Theresa a tight hug.

For Julie-Ann's first night home, Mr. Crown had hired a personal chef that he used from time to time to cook dinner. Tonight's fare included a rack of lamb, Julie-Ann's favorite. Before they ate, as they sat at the dining room table, Theresa had something to say.

"I know we've never done this before, but I think under the circumstances, we should say grace."

James was surprised but agreed.

Theresa took a deep breath before beginning. "Dear Lord, thank you for making Julie-Ann's operation a success and allowing us to be together as a family. Thank you for answering our prayers." Theresa paused. "That's it. Amen," she said with a smile.

"Well said," replied James.

Julie-Ann put her hand on top of Theresa's. "Thank you. That was beautiful."

Over the delicious meal, the conversation was more lighthearted. They talked about the last time they had a rack of lamb, at a restaurant in Atlantic City. Julie-Ann joked about the awful hospital food. Then she asked her father about how things were going at work. Not wanting to burden his daughter he simply replied that business was going really well. He then shared a joke someone had told him the previous day. Theresa and Julie-Ann laughed.

Over dessert, James suggested that they spend the weekend at their summer home in the Hamptons. Both Julie-Ann and Theresa loved the idea. Though James owned the house, none of them had been there since early October.

After dinner, Julie-Ann went on her computer and checked her Facebook page for the first time since she had posted about having to have surgery. There were a plethora of well wishes and various messages. Everyone was shocked. Some people said they would pray for her. Most people that had left an original message posted a second one asking how the surgery went. Though no one wrote it, after hearing no news a few days after the surgery, some feared the worse. Julie-Ann was touched by all the messages. She posted an update. *Thank you all for your kind and touching wishes and prayers. I am happy to report that the surgery was a success. They were able to remove the entire tumor without affecting any part of the brain. I should have a full and complete recovery.*

That night, while lying in her own bed, Julie-Ann thought about Theresa's words during grace. After all she had been through, she did feel fortunate and she thanked God for answering her prayers as well. Her feelings of gratitude and blessedness would soon be put to the test.

The next morning Julie-Ann headed back to Sloan-Kettering for her first radiation appointment. Theresa went with her. Julie-Ann was not too worried. Dr. Libowitz had said that she would only need four sessions and that there was a chance that she would not suffer any side effects and if she did, they would be short lived. Still, she began to get nervous. On the car ride home, Julie-Ann threw up in a bag that the nurse had provided for just in case. After vomiting, she still felt nauseous.

Right when they arrived back at the penthouse, Theresa laid Julie-Ann down in bed. As soon as she did, Julie-Ann said that she was going to throw-up again. Theresa ran into the bathroom and retrieved a wastebasket, which Julie-Ann vomited in.

"Oh, Theresa, I feel so sick," Julie-Ann moaned.

"I know honey. I'm sorry. But you only have three more sessions, then it's over."

Rita brought a damp washcloth and placed it on Julie-Ann's forehead. She also brought her some water.

Julie-Ann stayed in bed for the rest of the day. Theresa and Rita intermittently came to check on her. At one point, Rita brought her some soup and bread and said that she needed to eat. Julie-Ann took it and was able to swallow a little soup, but that was it.

Julie-Ann tried to sleep, but couldn't. Then she watched some television for distraction, which only worked for about an hour. Julie-Ann felt physically ill, but after a while, it also started affecting her mental state. Lying in bed, weak and uncomfortable, she started thinking about Ken and what he had done. Then she started thinking about the wedding they had been planning and the picture-perfect future they were supposed to have. What was she going to do now, she wondered? What was she going to do with her life? Her feelings of fortune and gratitude were now not even an afterthought. Julie-Ann was back to asking "why me?"

Julie-Ann's self-pity continued into the next day. She would look into the mirror from time to time, staring at her bald head and pale face and tell herself how ugly she looked. Then, one time she went on Facebook she saw a posting by one of her friends that her boyfriend had taken her to Spain and proposed. That made Julie-Ann feel jealous and bitter.

Julie-Ann also started dwelling on the possibility of her tumor returning, and even becoming cancerous. *What if I finally find a man, get married and have a family and the tumor returns and becomes malignant? It's like having the Grim Reaper always lurking in the shadows. I don't care if it's a one-in-a-million chance, with my luck, I'll be the one.*

Thursday afternoon she was watching entertainment news on TV when they started talking about a famous actress that was in a car accident. The actress wound up having a broken arm and a black eye and the news anchor was going on about how unfortunate it was and that she was going to have to halt work on her new movie for a couple of weeks.

Julie-Ann stood up. "Oh, we're supposed to feel sorry for her," she yelled aloud at the TV. "A broken arm and a black eye! That's it! You wanna trade places with me? Try living my life!"

Theresa could tell that Julie-Ann was depressed and tried to cheer her up. She asked if she wanted to see a movie and if she wanted to go shopping for a fitted wig. But Julie-Ann politely declined any offers. Amber could also tell Julie-Ann was down in the dumps from talking to her on the phone, so on Thursday she paid her a visit. At first, they just watched some TV. But after a while, Julie-Ann started with the woe is me. Amber tried to get her to look on the bright side.

"I know it's been hard Jules, and I can't even imagine, but think of how it could have turned out. I mean you had a brain tumor and survived. Not only survived, but you're not even going to have any lasting effects, like memory loss or speech impediment. You're not going to have any more of those horrible headaches." Amber stood up. "And as far as Ken goes, just imagine if you got married and then found out. And Jules, you're gorgeous. You can have any pick of guys."

Julie-Ann was not budging. "I know you're just trying to cheer me up, and I appreciate it, but forgive me if I don't feel lucky. I just had brain surgery. I have to go through radiation that makes me sick. I'm completely bald. There's no guarantee that one day my tumor won't return. And on top of it all, the man I was in love with and was planning on marrying and getting a house with has been fucking his tramp employee—and God knows who else." Julie-Ann paused. "And I'm anything but gorgeous. In fact, I feel hideous."

Friday morning, Julie-Ann went for her second radiation session. Once again, Theresa accompanied her. Julie-Ann walked into the waiting room with great trepidation. She didn't want to spend another day throwing up and bedridden. It was not the end of the world, but she had worked herself up into a panic. She did not convey her feelings to Theresa—she just didn't see the point. In fact, Julie-Ann did hardly any talking that morning.

At one point, Theresa excused herself to go to the ladies room. Julie-Ann just nodded her head and then picked up a magazine to help distract her. But then she noticed a girl, about ten-years-old, who was with her mother in the waiting room, and she was walking towards Julie-Ann. The girl, who was bald, sat in the seat right next to her.

"Hello. My name is Allie," she said with a smile, in the squeaky, innocent voice of a child.

Julie-Ann forced a smile. "My name is Julie-Ann."

"Is this your first time?"

It took Julie-Ann a second before she realized what Allie meant. "No, it's going to be my second session."

"Don't be scared."

"Wha…what makes you think I'm scared?"

Allie looked up at Julie-Ann. "I can tell. It's okay. It's no fun being sick I know, but we have to appreciate the time we have. The time we get to spend with our family and friends. It's a gift. We can't use it to sit around and be scared and feel sorry for ourselves."

Julie-Ann was taken aback. She could not believe such words were coming from this little girl. "I guess you're right. Is that you mother over there?"

"Yes. She's the greatest mom in the whole world. I just feel bad that she has to go through this. It's hard on her. But I always tell her 'mom, it's okay, God will take care of me.'"

Just then, a nurse came into the waiting room. "Allie, you're up."

"Well it was a pleasure meeting you Julie-Ann."

Julie-Ann smiled. "It was a pleasure meeting you Allie." She then shook her hand.

Before Allie went with the nurse, she ran over to her mother and gave her a kiss on the cheek. Her mother then waved and watched as her daughter was led away, talking to the nurse in an upbeat tone. Julie-Ann looked at the mother. She could not have been older than thirty-three.

Theresa reappeared and sat back down next to Julie-Ann. Julie-Ann was still fixated on the mother. "Excuse me," she said to Theresa, before walking over to the young woman.

"I'm sorry if she was bothering you," the woman said before Julie-Ann had a chance to speak. "She's very talkative."

Julie-Ann could see the woman trying to keep from crying. "Oh no, not at all. She was just...I mean it's fine. I was just...my name is Julie-Ann."

The mother extended her hand and smiled. "I'm Melissa," she said before shaking Julie-Ann's hand.

"Do you mind if I sit down?"

"Oh no, please." She then patted the seat next to her.

"I hope I'm not out of line and please tell me if I am. But do you mind me asking about her prognosis? She seems so upbeat and positive."

Melissa let out an uneasy laugh. "That's Allie. She's always more concerned about everyone else. She's always worried about me and her father, telling us to cheer up." Melissa paused and her face grew taut. "Talking to her, you would never know she may only have a year or so left."

Julie-Ann put her hand over her mouth as tears instantly began to swell in her eyes. "Oh, I'm...I'm so sorry. I didn't..."

Melissa wiped her own eyes before patting Julie-Ann on the leg. "It's okay. If she were here, she would tell you that everything will be all right or that everything happens for a reason. Nevertheless, she knows her situation. She has Leukemia. Found out when she was six. She has had two surgeries and endless radiation and chemotherapy. At this point, the doctor's say the best they can do is try to prolong her life a year or two. Sometimes I feel like stopping the treatment. It makes her so sick, but she hardly ever complains. I don't know where she gets it from. I mean she's only eleven-years-old. She has more strength and benevolence than anyone I've ever met." Melissa looked at Julie-Ann. "I'm sorry. I'm just rambling on. I didn't mean to..."

"Oh no, please." Julie-Ann put her hand on Melissa's shoulder. "I'm just so sorry. It's just not right. But you have a special girl, very special."

Just then a nurse came out and called Julie-Ann's name.

"Well it was nice meeting you Melissa. And Allie. I hope the best for you both."

Melissa wiped her eyes. "Thank you and I hope the best for you as well."

"Thank you." With that, Julie-Ann followed the nurse.

The whole time Julie-Ann was undergoing her treatment she could not stop thinking about Allie and her mother. She felt so bad for them. She also felt guilty and ashamed. Here she was, cancer free, with a bright prognosis, and having to go through four measly radiation sessions and she had been acting like it was torture. Here she was, wallowing in self-pity, asking why God had been so unfair to her. Then there was Allie, who had known nothing but hospitals, chemotherapy and radiation, and sickness in her short life, and who probably wouldn't see her thirteenth birthday. Life had handed her the rawest of deals, the cruelest of fates. Yet there she was, refusing to let it bring her down, instead, trying to be positive, worried more about her family than herself. At twenty-five-years-old, Julie-Ann wished she could be half the woman that littlie Allie was.

As soon as Julie-Ann and Theresa arrived back home, Julie-Ann threw-up. As nauseous as she felt, she could not help but think of what Allie had to endure and told herself that it paled in comparison. She was not about to complain or feel sorry for herself.

Not long after Julie-Ann came home her father called to ask how she was feeling. Since she had felt so nauseas after her first treatment, he said that maybe that weekend would not be the best time to go to the Hamptons. However, she told her father that she was a little nauseous but was up to the ride. In fact, she said she was looking forward to it.

Mr. Crown came home at 1:30 p.m. and he, Theresa, and Julie-Ann took a limousine out to the Hamptons. It was at least a three-hour drive, depending on traffic. Julie-Ann was still feeling a little queasy, but not as bad as she did after her first radiation session. Instead of the motion of the car making her feel sicker, she rolled down one of the windows and the fresh air actually helped.

It was not until the car ride that Theresa asked about the woman Julie-Ann had conversed with in the hospital waiting room. Julie-Ann told her and her father about Melissa and Allie. She explained Allie's condition and her amazing positive outlook.

"Here I've been bitching and moaning, acting like a baby and feeling so sorry for myself," she went on. "I feel so guilty and I'm sorry about the way I've been acting."

Mr. Crown put his hand on his daughter's knee. "Don't be absurd. You don't have to apologize. You've been through a lot."

"Nothing compared to that little girl and her mother. Or a lot of other people. Everyone was right before, I am lucky the way things turned out. And believe me, I'm done complaining and feeling sorry for myself!"

The family arrived at the summer home at 4:45 p.m. Located right on the water, the colonial-looking house had two floors, four bedrooms, a massive kitchen, two fireplaces, a wine cellar, pool, and hot tub. The dining room looked like something out of a movie, with its crystal chandelier and long, wood table and chairs. Everything in the house sparkled with elegance and wealth. Nothing was out of place or cluttered.

James had called ahead for a personal chef, as well as a maid service to clean the house once a day while they were there. Sometimes he had a full-time servant while they stayed at the house, but did not bother for this trip.

That evening they stayed in for dinner. Their personal chef prepared broiled stuffed lobster tail and wine braised short ribs. Before the main course, they indulged in oysters Rockefeller and caviar.

James opened a bottle of 1972 Chateau Margaux and poured three glasses. He then stood up from his seat at the head of the dining room table. "I would like to make a toast."

Julie-Ann and Theresa raised their glasses.

"Here is to Julie-Ann's health and the three of us being out here together."

The three of them gently touched their glasses together before taking a drink.

Julie-Ann was still feeling a little off, but was able to eat most of her dinner. She even had a couple of bites of her crème brulee, which was one of her favorite desserts. She only had half of her glass of wine.

After dinner, James suggested they all sit on the deck outside, but it had been a long day and Julie-Ann was exhausted and politely declined. Her father and Theresa went out back by themselves, with what was left of the bottle of wine.

The next morning Julie-Ann woke-up feeling well rested. She was happy to find that she did not feel nauseous at all. After a light breakfast, she and Theresa decided to go into town. James stayed behind to take care of some business. It might have been Saturday, but being the CEO of an investment firm, there were always phone calls and emails which to tend.

There was a professional wig shop in town and Julie-Ann decided to finally take Theresa up on the offer of going to get a fitted wig. It was a mostly sunny day and there was not any rain in the forecast. In the mid-70s, without any humidity, the weather was perfectly comfortable. It was a beautiful day for a stroll. Being a Saturday and nearing summer, the streets and sidewalks of quaint South Hampton were buzzing.

Theresa and Julie-Ann made their way to the small, but elegant wig store. Julie-Ann said she would like something as close as possible to her natural hair before it was cut off and then described it. After showing her five wigs, Julie-Ann finally found the one she liked most. It had straight bright blonde hair that went about an inch past her shoulders. Once she put it on, Julie-Ann looked in the mirror and a big smile grew on her face. She felt whole again.

After the wig shop, Theresa said she wanted to stop in a specific jewelry store a few blocks away. Julie-Ann was just happy to be out and about, enjoying some fresh air.

Theresa already had plenty of expensive jewelry, but she seemed to always be looking for another piece. She tried on several gold tennis bracelets, asking Julie-Ann's opinion about each one.

"Are you sure you don't want to look for something for yourself?" Theresa asked Julie-Ann. "A woman can never have too much jewelry."

"No thank you," Julie-Ann replied with a smile. "I'm good."

As Theresa's attention turned back to the salesman, Julie-Ann noticed two teenage girls looking at necklaces in an adjacent display. They both looked about fifteen. "Okay, I'll take this one," Julie-Ann overheard one the girls tell the saleswoman.

"Don't you already have one like that?" Her friend asked.

"Not exactly," she replied as she handed the saleswoman a platinum Amex card. She then excitedly clapped her hands like a child. "Oh, getting new jewelry makes me so happy."

Julie-Ann turned her attention back to Theresa.

Theresa finally settled on a bracelet. As they left the shop, Julie-Ann noticed an AT&T store across the street. "Do you mind if we stop at the AT&T store?" She asked Theresa. "I need to get a new pair of headphones. I forgot to bring mine with me and I don't think there's a Best Buy or anything around here."

"Sure."

They went into the store and Julie-Ann went straight for their small selection of headphones. As she was checking some out, her attention was drawn to a mother and son. The boy looked no more than thirteen-years-old.

"We just got you an iPhone not even six months ago," said the woman.

"But this is the new iPhone mom," the boy whined. "All my friends already have it."

"I still don't see what's so different about it."

The boy stomped his foot. "Why'd you even bring me here? I can't believe you mom. This is important. You just bought a new Mercedes and..."

"Okay, okay. I was just asking. I'll get you the phone."

Just then a salesperson walked over to Julie-Ann and asked if she needed any help.

"Oh, oh no, that's okay. Thank you." Julie-Ann then chose a pair of headphones and paid for them.

By this time it was already noon. Theresa suggested that they walk around a little more, maybe stop in a few other stores and then go to lunch. Julie-Ann said it sounded like a good idea. They then wandered into an antique store. They browsed together, commenting on different pieces, but did not buy anything. Next, they stopped in a clothing boutique that was next door. There, Theresa wound up buying a pair of sandals. Afterwards, she called James to see if he wanted to meet them for lunch. He said he was still working and for them to go without him, to have a good time and that he would see them back at the house.

Theresa and Julie-Ann decided to go to one of their favorite eateries in town. It was a posh bistro that served seafood and French cuisine. Since it was such a beautiful day they sat outside.

As they waited for their meals, Theresa sipped on a glass of wine; Julie-Ann had sparkling water. Theresa asked how Julie-Ann was feeling, to which she replied fine. They then reminisced about the time they were in the Hamptons with Amber and she was hit by a wave and lost her bikini top. They both laughed talking about it. Then, suddenly, their lighthearted conversation was broken by an outburst from a woman sitting at the table next to them.

"I can't believe you! What is wrong with you?" The young woman, who was with a male companion, was berating a female server.

"I'm so sorry ma'am," the young server said in a shaken voice. "It was an accident."

"This is a Versace! Thank God it was only water!"

Just then a waiter came over and asked what had happened.

"This girl spilled almost a full glass of water on me," the woman continued to rant as her companion just sat there. "Do you know how much this dress cost? I mean really, what kind of service do you have here?"

"I am so sorry ma'am," said the waiter as he handed her a cloth napkin. "I will send over a bottle of wine on the house." The older waiter then pulled the young server aside and whispered something to her. She looked like she was about to cry.

Julie-Ann wanted to say something to the woman at the table—that is was only water and it was an honest accident—but refrained. Instead, she just turned away in disgust as the situation died down. But it bothered her the whole time they were at lunch. Most of all, she wondered what was going to happen to the server. She would probably be yelled at some more by the manager. The bottle of "complimentary" wine would also probably come out of her already small paycheck. Or was it something she could be fired over?

After lunch, while walking back to the house, Theresa could tell that something was bothering Julie-Ann. She asked her what was wrong.

"I just can't stop thinking about that woman at the restaurant. Making a scene over a little spilt water. It's not like that server did it on purpose. The poor girl was embarrassed in front of everybody. And for what?" Julie-Ann paused. "That spoiled kid at the AT&T store whining about his phone. And that girl at the jewelry store."

"What girl at the jewelry store?"

Julie-Ann shook her head. "Just some teenager saying how jewelry made her so happy. I mean it's only jewelry."

"Okay, maybe that woman in the restaurant was a little over the top, but you can't blame some kids for getting excited about a piece of jewelry or new gadget. It doesn't make them bad. I mean you always like to have the newest things. Besides, you can't go around worrying yourself over other people."

"I guess you're right." Julie-Ann said it just to appease Theresa. She pretended like she was no longer bothered, but she was. In fact, now she was fixated on what Theresa had said about her always wanting and getting the newest gadget or expensive jewelry. She knew Theresa did not mean it in a bad way and she was not upset with her. But it was true. Maybe Julie-Ann didn't whine like the kid in the phone store, but she never had to. Ever since she was born, Julie-Ann had everything handed to her on a silver platter: the best clothes, the finest jewelry, exotic vacations, luxury cars, and anything else that she ever wanted. When it came to money and objects, she had never heard the word "no".

Later that day, back at the house, Julie-Ann sat alone outside on the deck. Sitting on an oversized wooden chair, she stared out into the infinite ocean and pondered life. She looked back through the years and realized that so many things that she had believed to be important now appeared trivial. She thought about the time when the hairdresser messed-up her hair; she was furious and depressed for days, or the time when she lost her cell phone.

Gazing out into the ocean and the way it melded into the sky's horizon, her own life felt insignificant. It made her realize that long after she was gone, life would go on. The world did not revolve around Julie-Ann. In fact, it did not revolve around any one person. Everyone was just guests on planet Earth, living on borrowed time.

Julie-Ann's father came out through the sliding glass doors. "Hey sweetie," he said in a soft voice, "what are you doing?"

Julie-Ann looked up at him and smiled. "Nothing. Just thinking about things."

Mr. Crown sat down in a chair next to his daughter. "What kind of things?"

"I was just admiring the ocean, how grand it is and how small we all really are—like specks of sand on that beach. I don't mean that in a bad way. I just mean that…well, it just makes you think about what's really important."

"Yes it does." Just then Mr. Crown's cell phone rang. He looked to see who it was. "I'm sorry sweetie, I have to take this." He quickly answered the phone and got up. "I told you, we have to have this figured out by Monday morning," he spoke sternly to the person on the other end. "This is extremely important," he continued as he walked back into the house.

The next day, Sunday, Julie-Ann took a long walk along the beach. It was a cloudy May day, still too cold to lie out or to go into the water. Besides the occasional passersby doing the same thing, she had the beach to herself. Instead of being filled with philosophical thoughts, Julie-Ann used the time alone to clear her head. It was liberating. For the first time since finding out she had meningioma, she wasn't thinking about anything in particular. She just felt content, breathing in the fresh air, feeling the coarse sand on her bare feet, feeling alive.

Mr. Crown had to get back to New York that night, because he had to be in the office early in the morning. He proposed that Theresa and Julie-Ann should stay in the Hamptons until Tuesday (Julie-Ann's next radiation appointment was Wednesday morning). He would send a car to drive them home. Theresa and Julie-Ann discussed it amongst themselves and decided to stay.

As it turned out, it rained most of Monday forcing Theresa and Julie-Ann to stay inside. Making the most of it, they ordered a couple of movies on demand and watched them together. Julie-Ann even made popcorn. It was nice and relaxing. They didn't talk about anything serious and there were no unwanted interruptions. It was just the two of them spending fun, but quality time together.

Early the next afternoon, Theresa and Julie-Ann piled into the limousine that had come to take them back to the city. Because of the time and it being a weekday, there was not the usual congested, Hamptons' traffic.

About forty minutes into the drive, Theresa fell asleep. When she did, Julie-Ann rolled down the window and gazed outside at the passing scenery. It was a straight wall of tall, thick green trees, a world removed from the skyscrapers, asphalt, congestion, and noise of the city. Breathing in the exhilarating rushing air, Julie-Ann thought to herself she could be anywhere. About fifteen minutes later, still staring out the window, there was a break in the tree line as they passed the town of Shirley. Julie-Ann peered at the town from a distance as it rolled by. She had never stepped foot there before or even driven through it. She wondered what kind of people lived there, what they did for a living, what they did for fun? She wondered about all the stories they could tell—stories that the rest of the world would never know.

Chapter 10

Wednesday morning, Julie-Ann went to her radiation appointment. She was hoping to see Allie there, but did not. As she had promised herself, Julie-Ann took her treatment in stride. She was nauseous and tired for most of the day, but did not complain or feel bad for herself. She just lay in bed and watched some television.

In the late afternoon, Julie-Ann was still lying in bed when Rita brought her soup and a sandwich on a tray. She placed it right on the bed. Julie-Ann thanked her. But before Rita could leave, Julie-Ann stopped her. "Rita, can I ask you something?" She said as she turned off the TV with the remote control.

"Certainly."

"Do you like your job?" Julie-Ann could see Rita's face instantly grow weary. "No, no. Don't worry, it's nothing like that. You do a great job and we all love you. I was…I was just wondering that's all."

Relieved that she wasn't about to get fired or in trouble, Rita took a step towards the bed. "Well yes, I like it very much."

"But I mean don't you get tired of waiting on us, cleaning up after us?"

"No," Rita quickly replied. "You and Mr. Crown and Mrs. Crown have always treated me very well. Mr. Crown pays me well. In fact, I feel very grateful to have this job, especially now when so many other people are out of work."

Julie-Ann gave the obligatory nod of the head. She was not yet finished with Rita. "What was it like when you were growing up? I mean what kind of childhood did you have?"

Rita was taken aback. Julie-Ann had always been kind to her, but had never before asked about her personal life. Feeling comfortable around Julie-Ann, Rita took a seat beside her on the bed. "I had a good childhood. I grew up in Panama, in a small town by the water. It was a simple place but the area was beautiful. Me and my sisters used to go down to the beach."

"How many sisters do you have?"

"I have three older sisters—well one passed away two years ago—and a younger brother."

"I'm so sorry about your sister."

Rita smiled. "Thank you."

"What was her name?"

"Margaret. My other sisters are Alana and Juanita. My brother's name is Alex."

Julie-Ann could see Rita's face light up when she mentioned her siblings' names. "You were a close family growing up?"

"Oh yes. Unless my father was working late we all sat down and had dinner together every night and on the weekends we would go to the beach together or into town. We might have been four girls, but my father would teach us how to play baseball. I had great parents." Rita's face suddenly changed and became sullen. "But then when I was thirteen my father died in an accident at work. It was a very hard time for us. My mother went to work to support the family, so did two of my sisters. And we were able to make ends meet. When I was fourteen, my sister Alana, who was sixteen at the time, decided to move to America. We had an uncle in Santa Fe who a successful restaurant. He offered my sister a job and to stay at his house with his wife and son. And I wound up going along."

"What about your other sisters and your brother?"

Rita took a deep breath. "My two other sisters were working and helping to support my mother—even though she was also working—and my brother. At first, I didn't want to go and leave them behind. But Alana, who I was closest to, talked my Uncle into taking me too, and convinced me that living in America was a golden opportunity that I could not pass up." Rita paused. "It was a hard decision, but I wound up going with my sister."

"It must have been tough being away from your mother, brother and other sisters."

Rita shook her head. "Yes. Yes it was, but Alana was right, it was an opportunity that I could not pass up. It was like suddenly everything seemed possible. Growing up in Panama, you always heard about the American Dream. Now I was able to live it. By the time I was seventeen I was supporting myself and living in an apartment with a roommate. Then, when I was twenty-five I finally got my citizenship. I was ecstatic. It was one of the happiest days of my life—besides, of course, the birth of my children."

Julie-Ann knew Rita had a son and a daughter because she had mentioned them before and had taken a few days off here and there to visit them. Yet she didn't know anything about them, including their names. "Oh yes, you have two kids right?"

"Yes. Mary is twenty-three. She is married and lives in Albuquerque. Alex is twenty. He lives in New Jersey. He's a sous-chef right now, but he's going to culinary school. He's going to be a very successful chef one day."

"You must be very proud."

Rita's face beamed with pride. "Oh yes. They are very good kids. Kids—they're adults now. Their father left when Alex was just six-years-old. He literally left one day and never came back. He didn't even leave a note. He called a few weeks later to say he was sorry and that it wasn't our fault, but he never came back or supported the kids. Anyway, I was always working and wasn't able to spend as much time with Mary and Alex as I should have, but they hardly ever complained. They always did well in school and stayed out of trouble. Mary always looked after her brother. And now they're both doing well." Rita paused as a smile grew on her face. "Yes, I've been blessed with them both."

Julie-Ann asked Rita a few more questions about her background and her kids and listened intently to her story. For her part, Rita was happy to share it with her.

After Rita left, Julie-Ann was glad that she took the opportunity to find out more about Rita. However, she was also embarrassed that she had never before inquired. Rita had been a mainstay at their house for three years and Julie-Ann had never before even knew the names of her children, or what they did, or that she had siblings. As she nibbled on her soup and sandwich, Julie-Ann wondered all the other things she did not know about Rita.

The next morning, Julie-Ann woke up feeling restless. It was supposed to be a beautiful day and she did not want to spend it inside. After a banana and some toast, Julie-Ann jumped in the shower. After getting out, she felt a little queasy, probably from the radiation, but it did not deter her. She put on her new blonde wig, a pair of shorts, a t-shirt, and sneakers. She put on minimal make-up. Her appearance still mattered to her, but she no longer stressed over trying to look perfect.

The city sidewalks and streets were bustling as always. Though most people were already at work, there were still plenty of pedestrians going to and fro. Julie-Ann had no destination. She was just glad to be outside and the fresh air made her slight queasiness disappear.

Julie-Ann was not a big coffee drinker, but after walking several blocks she decided to go into a Starbucks just for something to do. She tried to figure out what to get while waiting in the line. Even though there seemed to be a Starbucks on every corner of Manhattan, each one still always had at least a short line; during lunch some of the lines were out the door. As Julie-Ann looked at the drink menu board overhead, a woman, who looked to be in her late twenties, and wearing business attire, started going off on the girl behind the counter. "I told you I wanted a Mocha Frappuccino, not a Carmel Frappuccino," she ranted so everyone in the store could hear. "Does Mocha sound like Carmel?"

This time Julie-Ann, who was three people behind the woman, could not bite her tongue. "Relax, it's only coffee."

The woman heard the comment and turned around, but did not realize who said it. She just shot everyone in the line a disgruntled look and then turned her attention back to the cashier who had already yelled for someone to get her a new coffee.

Julie-Ann ordered a tall Vanilla Frappuccino and took a seat at the counter facing the street. Sipping on her drink, she gazed at all the people passing by. They all seemed to be in a hurry. Then, across the street, she noticed a yellow cab and a town car in what appeared to be a fender-bender. The drivers of both cars were in the street yelling at each other, waving their hands and pointing their fingers.

Julie-Ann sat there until she finished her drink, watching through the window façade the spectacle that was city life. Of course, it was nothing new to her, but she began to question it. *This is normal to me? It's controlled chaos and it's not even rush hour. Look at them all, like rats in a maze, running for the cheese. It's like everyone's wound up so tight they don't even have time to stop and breathe. They're all ready to explode or lash out at any time. Is that living?*

After finishing her coffee, Julie-Ann decided to walk to Central Park, hoping that she could find some serenity there. As soon as she left, she happened to walk alongside a slender, tall middle-aged businessman, dressed in a fitted, blue suit and tie. He had slicked-back black hair and was attractive. Julie-Ann mostly noticed the man because he was on his Bluetooth, talking loudly, oblivious to the world around him.

"I think we got the deal. I took him and his partner out last night to Sparks and then to the strip club and got 'em wasted," the man blared. "The fat bastard was in the Champagne Room for about half an hour. I footed the whole bill, put it on the company card. By the end of the night he probably would've signed over his daughter."

Julie-Ann listened to the conversation, which wasn't hard to do since he was advertising it to the whole world.

After a pause to listen to whomever he was talking with he continued, "No, of course he didn't sign the papers last night but don't worry, he will. I'm not letting his fat ass get away. I don't care if I have to send him two Russian prostitutes. We just have to seal the deal before Linda and her team gets their hook in him. I don't trust her. All she has to do is let him feel her up and he'll probably cave."

As the businessman turned in another direction Julie-Ann just shook her head. There was nothing shocking about what he said. Julie-Ann was not naïve; she had been around the offices and boardrooms and knew how the wheel was turned. Yet like everything else, it seemed she now looked at it through different colored glasses.

Julie-Ann continued to Central Park. Amongst the trees and grassy knolls, she felt far away from the hustle and bustle of the city streets, even though it was a short walk away. It was a warm day and Julie-Ann had been walking for about twenty-five minutes straight and was beginning to sweat. She decided to rest on a vacant park bench. There, she watched as a man played Frisbee with a boy in a field across from her. They looked like they were having so much fun. Her eyes then caught two young lovers lying on a blanket on the slope of a small hill. They were laughing and smiling. Next, two women, each pushing a baby stroller passed by, engaged in some placid conversation. Julie-Ann took a deep breath and took solace in knowing that she could find peace and quiet in the city.

Just then a young, fit, pretty woman with her long, black hair in a ponytail came jogging up. She stopped right before Julie-Ann and retrieved a cellphone from her fanny-pack. After wiping sweat from her brow, she answered the phone. "Hello. Yes." There was a pause. "Well can't you get us first class? I hate flying coach. It's too crammed and it makes me not feel right." There was another pause as she listened to the person on the other end. "Good. Okay. And remember to make sure to get the suite right on the beach. It's just more romantic."

Julie-Ann was listening, but pretended to be watching something else.

"Okay then, I've got to go. I'm out jogging." The woman hung up the phone and put it back in her pouch. She then turned directly to Julie-Ann. "You believe this guy? I agreed to go away with him. I'm at least getting first class and a nice suite out of this deal. I'm not staying in some standard room. I mean we don't come cheap, am I right?"

Julie-Ann just replied with a crooked smile and nod. With that, the jogger continued on down the path.

As soon as she was gone, Julie-Ann shook her head. She couldn't believe how superficial the woman was. Then Julie-Ann quickly remembered that she usually flew on private jets and only stayed in the best hotels and suites. *I'm no different than her,* she told herself. *In fact, I'm worse. I've never gone out with a guy that didn't have money. I never paid my own way or even chipped in. I always wanted to be pampered and treated like a princess.*

Julie-Ann stayed on the park bench for a little while longer, deep in introspection, before deciding to head back home.

When Julie-Ann arrived at her building the doorman said he had a package for her. It was from Ken. Once upstairs, she opened the small box. It was a ruby-encrusted bracelet. And it came with a note:

Dear Julie-Ann,

> *I've tried stopping by, but you won't see me. I've called, but you won't come to the phone. I'm so sorry about what happened. But I swear to you on my life that it was only a few times and it didn't mean anything. Let's not throw away our*

*entire future on a few stupid, meaningless indiscretions. I love
you so much and I know that deep down you love me too. We
were meant to be together.*

*I hope you are feeling well. I want to be there for you so
much. Please, at least tell me how you are doing. I can't even
sleep, thinking about you, wondering how your recovery is going and just wanting to be with you.*

Love,

Ken

After reading it, Julie-Ann crumpled it up into a ball and tossed it
into the trashcan. She did not forgive Ken, she knew she never
would, but nevertheless, there was a void now in her life. There was
also an uncertain future. She fought back tears, telling herself that
she was stronger than that and she was not going to feel sorry for
herself.

Just then the phone rang. Julie-Ann looked on the caller-ID. It
was Amber so she picked it up. She was calling to say that Tyler
was taking her to Paris.

"That's great Amber, I know how much you love Paris."

"I know. I haven't been there in over a year. We're leaving next
week, just for five days."

They talked some more about Paris and Amber asked how Julie-Ann was feeling. Before getting off the phone Amber suggested
that they hang out tomorrow.

"That'd be great," Julie-Ann replied, "Maybe we could go out to
lunch or something."

"Whatever. I'm free the whole day. Just text me in the morning."

With that, the best friends said their goodbyes for the night.

Later that evening, Julie-Ann was lying in bed watching TV. She
was flipping through the channels when she stopped on a show
about people traveling across the country in RVs. Her curiosity
whet, she sat back and watched as an older couple told of their
experience.

"I was a corporate lawyer in Chicago for thirty years," said the man. "It got to a point where I just needed to get away from the grind—for good. A friend of mine had recently bought an RV and was always going on about how great it was. So I told my wife that I was selling the practice and we were going to travel the country in a motor home."

"I thought he was crazy," his wife replied. "I mean we had a nice home, roots in the community. Our son Jimmy and our grandchildren lived not too far away. But now, I wouldn't trade it for the world. It's been an unbelievable experience."

Julie-Ann turned up the volume and sat straight up in bed.

The man, who looked to be in his sixties but appeared in good shape, continued. "We've got to go to places that we probably would've never otherwise seen. There's so many great towns out there and great people."

"So many great people," his wife added. "We've made so many friends. It's just fascinating hearing their stories, learning about their own journeys."

Enthralled, Julie-Ann watched the rest of the show. As she did, she thought of her dream about the county fair and the vision of the highway before she went under for the surgery. By the time the show was finished she knew what she had to do.

The next afternoon Julie-Ann met Amber for lunch. Amber immediately started talking about the new bathing suit she had just bought for Paris. Julie-Ann mostly listened as Amber went on about her pending trip. But then, while they were waiting for their food, she made an announcement of her own.

"So I've decided to drive across America," Julie-Ann said nonchalantly. "But not just drive straight through. Take a few months and explore; stop in different little towns."

It took Amber a few seconds to digest what Julie-Ann had said. "Are you serious? Where did this come from?"

"I've just been thinking about things lately. I feel like I just have to get away. I mean the tumor, Ken, it's all been a wake-up call for me.

But I don't mean that in a bad way. It's like I've been given a second chance and I don't want to waste it. I want to see what's out there, meet different people, experience new things—have total freedom."

"Have you told your father and Theresa about your plan?"

Julie-Ann smiled. "No. I'm going to tell them tonight. I have one more radiation session tomorrow and I plan on leaving next week."

"I don't know Jules. I mean a vacation or road trip is one thing, but driving across the country by yourself, especially stopping in some crazy little town, it seems dangerous. Haven't you ever seen Deliverance?"

Julie-Ann laughed. "You watch too many movies. Besides, I'll have a cellphone and email."

Amber could tell that Julie-Ann had made up her mind and was not going to change it. "You know what, you're right. It does sound kind of fun. Wait for when I get back from Paris and I'll go with you. It'll be a blast. Just the two of us. But I don't know about a month or…"

Julie-Ann reached across the table and put her hands on Amber's arms. "Amber you know I love you and I appreciate you wanting to come with me, but this is something I need to do on my own."

Amber was taken aback—and a little offended. "But I don't understand. You don't want me to go with you?"

"It has nothing to do with you. Like I said, it's just something I need to do on my own. It's hard to explain."

After lunch the best friends parted ways, but agreed that they would get together again that weekend. Afterwards, Julie-Ann called her father and asked if he would be home for dinner. She said she had something to talk to him and Theresa about. She promised it was nothing bad.

Even though Julie-Ann said it was nothing bad, Mr. Crown was leery. His daughter usually didn't call him at work so he knew it could not be anything trivial if she wanted to tell him and Theresa at the same time. He said he would make sure to be home by 6:00 p.m. The rest of the day, he tried to figure out what the news could be. He hoped it was not to say that she was getting back together with Ken.

That evening, the family gathered around the dining room table. Theresa had ordered Chinese food. Before they could eat, both James and Theresa were chomping at the bit to know what was so important that Julie-Ann had called a family meeting.

"I didn't mean to worry you guys," Julie-Ann said, sitting at the table. "But I just wanted to tell you both at the same time. I've decided to take a month or two and travel around the country."

It was certainly not what her father had been expecting. "What? What do you mean—by yourself?"

"Yes. I've been doing a lot of evaluating lately, evaluating my life, what's important. And I've had an amazing life. Thanks to you I've been all around the world, stayed in the best resorts. But I realized I've never really explored my own country."

"What do you mean?" Her father asked. "You've been to Florida, California, Las Vegas, Chicago."

"Yes, but everywhere I've been I've always stayed at an exclusive resort or private beach house. I want to get out there and see small towns, the heartland. I want to meet 'real people', see how the other half lives. And I don't want anyone to know that I'm rich or treat me special."

Her father combed his hand through his thick, graying hair. "Listen sweetie, I know you've been through a lot—the surgery, Ken—and I understand you are looking at things a little differently now. And I'm not saying that's a bad thing. But a twenty-five-year-old beautiful girl wandering across the country by herself trying to meet complete strangers can be very dangerous."

"I have to agree with your father," Theresa chimed in. "Anything can happen. There's a lot of crazy people out there Jules. How about you and I go on a vacation somewhere? We can go to Arizona or Texas. I have a cousin that lives in San Antonio."

"Besides, you're in no condition to be driving cross country," added her father.

"I feel fine. Tomorrow is my last radiation treatment and Dr.

Libowitz said that I probably wouldn't need a follow-up MRI for three months." Julie-Ann took a deep breath. "Look, I know you're both worried about me and I appreciate that, but this isn't some fleeting fascination. I've given it a lot of thought and this is something I *need* to do. It isn't just about finding what's out there—it's about finding myself."

James looked across the table at his daughter. A month earlier she was a happy-go-lucky twenty-five-year-old planning her dream wedding and looking at houses with her fiancé. Her biggest worries were if the right flowers were going to show up at the reception or if someone was going to complain about the seating arrangements. Then, like a bomb falling out of a clear blue sky she had to deal with a brain tumor, the surgery, and the cancellation of her wedding, all in one cruel swoop. It was a one-two punch that would have broken a weaker person. As Mr. Crown looked into his daughter's eyes, he did not see defeat or self-pity; he saw purpose and life.

"Are you sure this is something you want to do?" He asked in a calm, but direct voice.

"Yes. It's something I want to do. It's something I need to do. And I promise I'll be safe and I'll be okay."

"James." Theresa was surprised by her husband's reaction.

He put his hand on Theresa's arm. "She's had to deal with a lot tougher situation than driving cross country."

Julie-Ann smiled.

"If this is what you need to do," he continued, "then how can I tell you no, or not support you."

"Thank you, Dad." Julie-Ann then turned to Theresa.

Theresa nodded. "We're just worried about you. You've never done anything like this before. But you have been through a lot and if this is what you think you need to do then…well…you just be safe, you hear."

Over Chinese food, James and Theresa asked Julie-Ann more about her plan. It became clear that she didn't have many details. However, as she put it: "That's the whole point, to just get out there on the road and play it by ear."

Her father did suggest that it was not a good idea to drive around in her convertible Mercedes Cabriolet. "You don't want to draw attention to yourself and announce to the world that you have money."

"Yeah, I guess you're right."

"We'll get you a reasonable car, something that's safe and reliable, but that doesn't stick out. Nothing too flashy."

"Thanks Dad. Maybe we can go look at cars together this weekend. That would be fun."

That night, in the privacy of their bedroom, James talked more about Julie-Ann's plan with Theresa. Though still worried about her safety, he explained that maybe it wasn't such a bad idea and that after a week she would probably get bored and head home. Theresa agreed.

In her own bedroom, Julie-Ann flipped through the channels, looking for a travel show on America. She even scanned the news to see if there were any stories about some small, unfamiliar town or city. She had no luck.

The next morning Theresa accompanied Julie-Ann to her last radiation session. Once again, Julie-Ann was hoping to run into Allie and her mother, but they were not there. She wondered if she would ever see them again. She hoped so, that their paths would somehow cross again in the future. Then, in a moment of silence, she asked God to look over little Allie and send her a miracle.

Chapter 11

On Saturday, Julie-Ann and her father went looking for cars. Theresa wanted him to have some time alone with his daughter, so she stayed behind. James wanted Julie-Ann to get a conservative-looking sedan. Instead, she instantly fell in love with the new Camaro convertible. She loved convertibles. Her father argued that although not a luxury car, it was still flashy and might draw attention to her. She pointed out that plenty of young adults, and even teenagers had Camaros and that she would actually blend in more with the car. He explained that the trunk was small and there was not a lot of room for her to put her luggage. Usually, when Julie-Ann went on a weekend trip she brought three pieces of luggage. This did give her pause. After all, she was planning to be gone at least a month. The salesman showed them some sedans and even a couple SUVs. Julie-Ann kept coming back to the Camaro. In the end, she got her way.

Her father did insist that the car have built-in GPS and OnStar. The salesman explained that they had a white convertible in stock that fit the bill. While Julie-Ann filled out some paperwork, James called his insurance company to cover her. When he gave the salesman his Amex Black card to pay for the car, the salesman wondered what he was doing at the GM dealership, or at least why he wasn't buying a Cadillac or Corvette. Once everything was complete, Julie-Ann drove the car back to the garage adjacent to their building, where they kept all their cars.

At the dealership, Julie-Ann was still feeling a little sick and lethargic from the radiation treatment she had the previous day. She tried her hardest to hide it from her father. She knew it would pass and after being home for a while, lying on her bed, it did.

On Sunday, Julie-Ann met Amber for appetizers and a drink. Concerned for her safety and well-being, Amber had hoped that Julie-Ann had changed her mind about the journey, but she had not. Amber then tried to get Julie-Ann to let her go along. She was even willing to cancel her Paris trip.

"I can go to Paris any time."

Julie-Ann was touched by her friend's offer and concern. But she reiterated that it was something she needed to do by herself.

Amber made Julie-Ann promise that she would at least email her everyday to say how she was doing. She also told her to call any time (whenever out of the country, Amber had an international calling plan). Julie-Ann agreed.

That Tuesday, James and Theresa accompanied Julie-Ann to a follow-up appointment with Dr. Libowitz. Mr. Crown had made his daughter promise that she would not go on her journey if the doctor did not give the green light. Julie-Ann had agreed to the condition to appease her father, thinking there was no reason why the doctor would say she could not go. But on the way to his office, for the first time, she started worrying what if, for whatever reason, he did not think she was up to it.

As soon as they sat down with Dr. Libowitz Julie-Ann immediately went on about how great she was feeling. James then told him about his daughter's plan. Dr. Libowitz chewed on it for a bit while he read over her chart.

"Well, if you feel you are up to it," he said. "I would like you to have a follow-up MRI in two months, but other than that I don't see why you can't travel or continue with your normal activities. Now if you feel overly fatigued, have any blurred vision, or you start having bad headaches, I want you to immediately go to a hospital. Just tell them your history and have them call me."

Julie-Ann promised Dr. Libowitz, her father, and Theresa that if she started noticing any of the symptoms the doctor had laid out, or if she was just feeling sick, she would seek immediate medical attention and cut her trip short. Dr. Libowitz gave her the green light.

The rest of the week, Julie-Ann spent getting her things together and packing. It was at this time that she thought maybe her father had been right about getting a sedan with a larger trunk to accommodate all her belongings, but it was too late. Luckily, it was the beginning of June and Julie-Ann would not need jackets and thick winter clothes that would take up a lot of space. Also, she did not have to pack dress clothes and evening wear as she was not planning on going clubbing or attending any galas.

James realized there was no turning back and didn't try to talk his daughter out of going. However, the more he thought about it, the more he began to worry. Not only was she traveling around the country by herself, but there was this idea she had about wanting to meet people. He knew his daughter was smart, but also knew that there was a lot of cunning conmen and predators out there. Julie-Ann was simply not used to being on her own and dealing with strangers. She may have been bright, but in some ways, when it came to street smart, she was naïve. He asked her to at least follow a plotted course and suggested she visit tourist destinations and landmarks.

"You should go to Boston, D.C., Nashville. You can see the National Mall, Graceland. You've never been to the Alamo."

"I would like to see the Alamo," she replied. "And I haven't been to D.C. since I was twelve or something. I guess if I'm going to be traveling across America, our country's capital would be a good starting off point."

Julie-Ann did like the idea, but she was also saying it to appease her father. Her main goal was still to put the map away, visit random towns, and meet the locals.

Anxious to get on the road, Julie-Ann planned on leaving that Friday. Rita was not going to be around Friday so Julie-Ann said goodbye to her Thursday afternoon. Julie-Ann had already told her all about her plans.

Though Rita was concerned for Julie-Ann's safety and health, she thought the journey was a good idea. She loved Julie-Ann and thought the world of her, but knew all too well that she had grown up in a crystal tower and until the tumor, had never known any real adversity, or had to go without anything. She believed traveling through the heartland, seeing how the other half lives would be a healthy, life-learning experience.

Rita reached into her pocket and pulled out a Rosary. "I want you to have this," she said with a smile. "It will keep you safe on your journey."

"Rita, thank you, but I can't take this from you."

"It's okay, I have another one. Really. Keep it with you."

Julie-Ann took the rosary and gave Rita a hug. "Thank you."

"Be safe. And I hope you find what you're looking for."

Julie-Ann let go off Rita and smiled. "So do I," she replied in a soft voice. "So do I."

Friday morning Julie-Ann woke up at 7:00 am. After taking a shower and getting dressed she updated her Facebook page. *Starting my journey across the country this morning. I will periodically check in with updates and some pictures.*

Theresa called Julie-Ann into the kitchen. It was extremely rare that she cooked, but she wanted Julie-Ann to have a full stomach for the trip and Rita was not around. She had made some pancakes and bacon. James, wanting to have breakfast with his daughter and say goodbye, planned on going into the office late.

After breakfast, Julie-Ann retrieved the Camaro from the garage and parked it in front of their building. Her father helped her bring down her several suitcases. Julie-Ann left behind all of her expensive jewelry and high-end watches. Her goal was to blend in.

On the sidewalk, in front of their building, the family said their goodbyes for the time being.

"You have your ATM card and your credit cards?" Asked her father.

Julie-Ann let out a chuckle. "Of course, Dad."

"What about your AAA card and your health insurance card?" Asked Theresa.

"Yes," Julie-Ann replied with a smile, "and my cell phone and my charger and my laptop and everything else I need."

Theresa gave her a hug and a kiss on the cheek. "Well you take care of yourself and make sure to call us everyday."

"I will. And I'll let you know every time I arrive somewhere new. You can always get a hold of me—phone, text, email. So please don't worry."

Next it was James' turn to hug his daughter. "Take care of yourself sweetie."

"I will Dad."

With that, Julie-Ann climbed into the driver's seat and punched the address of the hotel she had reserved in D.C. into the GPS. She then waved goodbye and started her journey.

It was a beautiful, sun soaked, early June morning. Julie-Ann had the driver's window halfway down, but after a few blocks thought what was the point of having a convertible if she was not going to use it on such a splendid day? So she found a spot to pull over, hit the button on the dash, and retracted the top. She did worry though, about her wig flying off, but the saleswoman had assured her it would stay on. Nevertheless, she firmly put on a Yankees' baseball cap.

As Julie-Ann trudged through the congested, noisy streets of Manhattan, stopping and going, being cut-off by the overflow of taxis, she could not wait to get on the open road. She could not wait to be free from the city.

It was not until Julie-Ann hit the Jersey Turnpike that she had reached the open road. There were plenty of other vehicles, but no congestion. There were several lanes and everyone was spread far enough apart and moving fast. Julie-Ann turned on the XM radio and pressed harder on the gas. It was invigorating—the top down, the wind whipping over the windshield and along the sides of the car, the blue sky above, the long, straight stretch of highway, the whole day still ahead. Julie-Ann could not help but smile. Her plan was to stay the first two nights in Washington D.C., but really, she could go anywhere. She could turn off at any exit, follow any highway sign, turn off the GPS and just drive. Inhaling and then exhaling a deep breath, she felt as though the world was her own.

After stopping once to use the restroom and fill up the tank, Julie-Ann arrived in the nation's capital at 2:00 p.m. She went straight to the hotel, which was in downtown, not far from the National Mall. As freeing as the open road felt, she was happy to get out of the car. She was not used to traveling so long in a car, let alone driving. She was sure it was something she would get used to as her journey progressed. But for now, it felt good to stretch her legs and put away the keys for the day.

Even after her big breakfast, by the time Julie-Ann arrived at the hotel she was hungry. She checked-in, went up to her room and freshened up. She text her father and Theresa saying that she had gotten to the hotel safely and that she would call them later. She then went down to one of the hotel's two restaurants.

It was a casual restaurant and not crowded, still Julie-Ann felt weird sitting there eating lunch by herself. She wanted someone to talk to, to eat with.

After lunch it was only 3:30 p.m. It was still a beautiful day and Julie-Ann did not want to spend the rest of it just sitting by herself in a hotel room. So she decided to walk around the National Mall. It was Friday and June, so there were a good amount of tourists milling about. Julie-Ann took her time, strolling around the park. While doing so, she text Amber saying that she was in D.C. and hoped things were going well in Paris.

Julie-Ann walked by the Washington Monument. Figuring it was a good time to start her photo album of her journey, she retrieved the camera from her purse and snapped some pictures. Then, she asked two women, each with baby strollers and other kids, if one of them would mind taking a picture of her in front of the monument. One of the women gladly obliged.

Julie-Ann then made her way to the National Museum of American History and went inside. There, she leisurely looked at the exhibits and took some more pictures.

By the time Julie-Ann finished walking through the museum it was 5:15 p.m. and she was exhausted. It had been a long day. She decided to go back to the hotel. The walk back seemed to take forever.

The first thing Julie-Ann did once she returned to her room was take a long shower. The water pressure was strong and for a while she just stood in place and let the streams of hot water rain down on the back of her head and shoulders. The steam opened her pores and taking deep breaths, expanded soothingly in her lungs. By the time she was finished, Julie-Ann felt completely relaxed and clean. Not planning on going anywhere else the rest of the day, she didn't even bother getting dressed, putting on only panties and a terrycloth robe that the hotel provided.

Julie-Ann retrieved her laptop and sat on the couch, putting the computer on the small, rectangular table in front of her. There, she checked her emails and replied to some of them. She also uploaded the picture of her in front of the Washington Monument onto Facebook.

She then called home. Theresa answered the phone. They talked for a little while. Theresa was happy that Julie-Ann was in good spirits and everything was going well so far. Theresa explained that her father was at a business dinner. Julie-Ann, not wanting to bother him, told Theresa to say she was fine and that she would try him the next day.

Julie-Ann spent the rest of the evening lounging around and watching TV. She ordered a shrimp cocktail, salad, and soup from room service. By 9:30 p.m., exhausted from the long day of driving and walking around, she was asleep.

Julie-Ann was able to sleep right through the night; she woke-up at 6:15 a.m. She lay in bed watching some TV, flipping through the channels for a half hour or so before getting up. After stretching, she peered through the bedroom window. It looked like the start to another bright sunny day. Not checking out until the following morning, she planned to spend the day sightseeing.

After taking her time getting ready, Julie-Ann figured she should have a hearty breakfast for all the energy she would need walking around D.C. She went down to the hotel restaurant and ordered eggs benedict with hash browns. The eatery was crowded and as Julie-Ann looked around she noticed that she was the only one sitting by herself. She did not care what anyone else thought (not that they would even notice). It was just a lonely feeling. Once again, she pushed it to the side and enjoyed her breakfast.

It was a warm, sunny Saturday and although it was early in the morning, the National Mall was already abuzz with tourists and locals alike. Julie-Ann's first stop was the National Air and Space Museum. She was fascinated by all the massive and rare exhibits. From time to time she would pull out her camera and take some pictures. She spent at least an hour there, slowly moving from display to display.

Next, Julie-Ann ventured to the National Museum of Natural History. Once there, she started to long for someone to share the experience with and discuss the exhibits. She looked around and saw parents with children, couples looking at the displays and reading the plaques together, even small tour groups.

After the museum, Julie-Ann went online on her phone to see what time it was in Paris; it was 5:50 p.m. She called Amber's cell and was excited when she answered. Amber asked how everything was going with Julie-Ann's trip. Not mentioning that she was feeling lonely, Julie-Ann played it up like she was having the time of her life. She then asked about Amber's vacation. Amber went on in detail about what a great time she was having with Tyler. Though Julie-Ann hid it well, she was jealous—not of Amber's boyfriend—but that Amber had someone to share her time and experiences with and she did not. Nevertheless, Julie-Ann was genuinely happy for her friend and actually felt guilty for being jealous. Before hanging up, Amber asked her friend to send her some pictures of her journey and to stay in close contact.

After getting off the phone with Amber, still walking around the Mall, Julie-Ann called her father on his cellphone. Once again, she concealed her growing loneliness. She told him about the museums and specific exhibits. Knowing that she was planning on leaving Washington the next morning, he asked if she had decided where her next destination would be. She said she did not know, but implored him not to worry and promised to call again.

After talking with her father, with a full day still ahead, Julie-Ann decided to visit the U.S. Holocaust Memorial Museum. From the very first exhibit, she forgot all about feeling alone and was completely captivated by the graphic pictures, artifacts, and stories of the holocaust. Of course, Julie-Ann knew about the holocaust, but its horrors had never before been brought to life like they were in that museum. Moved nearly to tears, she solemnly read individual accounts of the atrocities and stared at black and white photographs of bodies piled like cordwood ten feet in the air and others of skeleton-like prisoners just waiting to die.

After the Holocaust Museum, Julie-Ann sauntered around the National Mall. For a while, she could not stop thinking about the atrocities of the Nazis. After a while of walking, noticing families and couples together, her loneliness started to seep back. It was only 1:30 p.m. and she wondered what to do with the rest of the day. She had already been to three museums. Feeling worn out, but not wanting to go back and sit in a hotel room by herself, she decided to get some lunch. She passed a couple eateries, but they both seemed so crowded with tourists. She didn't want to wait in line and then be the only one in the restaurant sitting alone. Julie-Ann noticed a taco truck. It had a long line, so she figured it would be good. She ordered two chicken tacos and a drink and then sat down on a park bench. There, she took her time eating and people watching. After her lunch Julie-Ann checked her texts and emails. She also went through the comments that various people had left on her Facebook, under the picture she had posted the previous day.

Afterwards, Julie-Ann started walking again, but she was losing steam. She headed back to the hotel. Going through the lobby, she noticed a floor sign in front of the hotel bar, which read: Happy Hour Today 3 – 6. She made a mental note.

Once back in the room, Julie-Ann flipped on the TV. At first, it felt good to be relaxing and not walking around. After about forty minutes she was starting to get bored. There it was again—that feeling of isolation. She looked at the clock on the corner table, it was 4:05 p.m. Julie-Ann knew that if she sat in the room by herself until bedtime, she would go stir crazy. That's when she remembered the happy hour sign. As most women, Julie-Ann was not one to go to a bar by herself, but this was a little different. It was a hotel bar and there would probably be all kinds of people mingling. It was not uncommon for people to drink by themselves in a hotel bar, either waiting for someone or just to pass the time. Besides, if she didn't like it, she could just go back up to the room.

Like a teenager with a place to go, Julie-Ann eagerly freshened up and changed into one of the few dresses she had brought with her. She re-did her makeup and made sure her wig was on perfectly.

By 5:00 p.m. Julie-Ann found her way down to the bar. It was not a club, yet it was a large bar for a hotel, with almost a dozen tables and large screen television sets. By the time Julie-Ann arrived, it was already abuzz with various people, their conversations all melding together into a floating white noise. Some people were in shorts and t-shirts, others already dressed for a night out. Typical for a hotel lobby bar, it seemed a pit stop, a meeting place for a few drinks.

Julie-Ann looked through the open entranceway to the long bar. There were only two open stools and both were tightly in the middle of other people. Not wanting to sit down at a table by herself, Julie-Ann thought about leaving. Maybe she could walk down the block and find another bar. As she was standing there, she saw a group of three people leave the bar. Quickly, but trying to be inconspicuous, she went up and grabbed one of the vacant stools before they were taken by someone else. Once the bartender came over, she ordered a cranberry and vodka.

It did not take long before Julie-Ann was approached. Before she could even get her drink, a pudgy, middle-aged man sitting one stool over started in with some small talk.

"How are you doing this evening?"

Julie-Ann looked over at the man, who was balding and dressed in designer jeans and an un-tucked, button-down shirt that accentuated his potbelly. She had come down to the bar hoping for some conversation, but now she felt a little uncomfortable. "I'm okay. I just came down for a drink before meeting my friends." She opened her mouth and the words just came out, as if by reflex.

With perfect timing, the bartender brought Julie-Ann her drink.

"So, are you staying at the hotel?" The stranger asked.

At first, she did not know what to say. Though he probably meant it innocently, just trying to start a conversation, what if he was some predator, she wondered. "I'm staying here with a couple of friends. Just for the night."

"Are they as beautiful as you?"

Julie-Ann smiled, but her uneasiness was growing.

Breathing a sigh of relief when another man walked up to the guy sitting by her and patted him on the back, "Hey Tom you ready to go? Larry's waiting for us at the White Horse Pub."

The stranger took some money out of the pile he had in front of him and left the rest as a tip. He turned to Julie-Ann. "Well it was nice meeting you. Have a good time with your friends."

Now Julie-Ann felt stupid. He was just some harmless guy trying to hit on her. "Take care. It was nice meeting you," she replied with a smile.

As the two men walked away, she could hear one of them say: "You were talking to that hottie?"

The bartender came over to Julie-Ann. "Was he bothering you?"

"Oh no. It's okay."

"He's been staying at the hotel since Thursday. He comes in here at least twice a day and tries to hit on any girl who's by herself. Needless to say, he hasn't had any luck."

Instead of feeling scared of the guy, now Julie-Ann felt a little sorry for him.

Julie-Ann sipped her drink and picked up on a few of the various conversations going on around her. Shortly, two well-dressed men, who both looked to be in their early to mid thirties, walked over to her.

"Excuse me, is this seat taken?" Asked the taller, more attractive one.

Julie-Ann noticed how white his teeth were. "Oh no, please."

The man pulled out the stool, but stopped before he could sit down. "You were waiting in line at the taco truck this afternoon weren't you?" He asked with a million-dollar smile.

Julie-Ann could not help but smile back. "Yes. Yes I was."

"Whoever knew you could get such good tacos out of a truck."

"Yes, they were pretty good," she replied.

"You should try their tamales. Amazing. Best tamales east of New Mexico." The stranger then extended his hand. "My name is Bret."

"Jules," she said while shaking his firm hand.

Bret then introduced his friend, Josh. They sat down next to Julie-Ann and Bret ordered two beers. He then asked Julie-Ann if he could buy her a drink.

She looked down at hers; it was still a quarter filled. "I'm good right now, but thank you."

"So, are you here on business or pleasure?"

Julie-Ann thought about it for a second before answering. "Just getting away for the weekend. What about you?"

"Well I used to spend a lot of time here on business. I'm a corporate lawyer in New York. But right now we're just here with our wives, a little weekend getaway, like you."

Julie-Ann thought it was odd that he would offer to buy her a drink if he was there with his wife.

"So Jules, you also from New York?" Asked Josh.

Julie-Ann chuckled. "Is it that easy to tell?"

"Well I mean it's not a bad thing. You don't have a New York accent or anything. You don't have a southern accent either and you just seem sophisticated."

"Sophisticated?" Julie-Ann said with a laugh.

Just then the bartender brought over their beers.

Bret immediately took a big swig. "So Jules, what is it you do in New York?"

She was not prepared for the question. She didn't want to say anything. She certainly didn't want to say that she was James Crown's daughter. "I work at JP Morgan."

"Ah, JP Morgan. I have quite a few friends that work there. What do you do?"

Julie-Ann finished off her drink. "I work on the equities desk. But to tell you the truth it gets so stressful sometimes that when I'm not at work I don't like to talk about it."

Bret laughed. "I know what you mean." He took another swig of his beer and then noticed Julie-Ann's empty glass. "Can I get you that drink now?"

Julie-Ann smiled. "What about your wife?"

"Hey, whoa. It's just a drink. I was just trying to be a gentleman."

Julie-Ann thought about it. "Well, if that's the case then I guess I'll have a cranberry and vodka."

Bret ordered the drink and told the bartender to put it on his tab. He then asked Julie-Ann what she had done so far since being in D.C. She told him and Josh about the museums she had visited.

Bret was just about to order another round of beers when Josh stopped him. "The girls are here," he said motioning with his head towards the entrance of the bar.

Julie-Ann looked over at the two women. They were both attractive and dressed for a night out on the town.

"Josh, do me a favor—go over and tell them that I'm paying the tab and I'll be right out."

"Sure." Josh then waved to the wives and went to meet them by the entrance.

Bret looked at the bill, which the bartender had placed inside an empty glass on the bar. As he did, he inconspicuously looked over to where Josh and his wife were standing. "Well it's been a pleasure meeting you," he said while retrieving money from his pants pocket.

"Likewise."

Bret laid a twenty and a ten on the bar. Then, while looking straight ahead, he put a small piece of paper down by Julie-Ann's hand. It was his business card. "Give me a call on my cell tomorrow if you're still around," he said without turning towards Julie-Ann. "I'll be free from one to four." With that, he nonchalantly left.

Julie-Ann looked down at his business card and could not believe he basically propositioned her with his wife standing twenty feet away. She was both disgusted and outraged. Julie-Ann turned around and saw him walk up to his wife and give her a kiss. She wanted to march over and say something, tell his wife what a snake he was yet she did nothing.

Julie-Ann finished her drink, thinking about Bret. That of course made her think about Ken and then men in general. Were they all cheating assholes, she wondered? Then she laughed as she thought about the first guy who tried to pick her up. *He was probably actually a nice guy,* she told herself.

Her encounter with Bret made her think of Ken. The atmosphere in the bar and the buzz from the two drinks energized her. In fact, she felt like going out. But there she was again, by herself. So instead, she decided to go back up to the room. It was only 5:45 p.m.

After changing into pajama shorts and a t-shirt, she spread out on the couch and watched some TV. After a half hour she ordered some room service. By 8:00 p.m. Julie-Ann adjourned to bed. She still had the TV on, but was no longer paying attention to it. Instead, she dwelled on her loneliness. It was not just having anyone to talk with, but for the first time since Ken had left, she realized it had been over a month since she had sex. Lying there alone in that hotel bed, it felt like even longer. She wanted to feel a man's touch, to make love, to wake-up with someone lying beside her. Instead, she pulled down her shorts and panties and pleasured herself.

Still wide-awake, Julie-Ann decided to pull out her laptop and try and figure out her next destination. She was scheduled to check out in the morning, although she could easily stay another night or two, she saw no point. After all, this was supposed to be a trip through the heartland, stopping at cities and towns off the beaten path. She looked at Google Maps and some other sites, but soon grew discouraged. For the first time, Julie-Ann asked herself what she was doing. She wanted to meet people, but how? Was she just going to drive around the country, park her car, walk down the sidewalk and start introducing herself to people who passed by? For the first time, she realized that she hadn't really given much thought to the details. Feeling dispirited, she turned her attention back to the TV.

Chapter 12

Julie-Ann woke up Sunday morning at 7:30 am. She decided to put her reservations of the previous night behind her. *It's hasn't even been three days,* she said to herself. *And I've only made it to D.C. I can't get discouraged now. This is what I'm supposed to be doing. I told everyone that. How would it look if I turned around now? How would I feel about myself? It's just going to take a little time. I'll meet people; see places I've never seen before. I'd be lonely at home anyway. I'm just going to get in my car and drive.*

After a quick breakfast, Julie-Ann checked out of the hotel and had the valet retrieve her car. She did not put any destination into the GPS. She remembered seeing an interstate sign not too far away and figured she would just get on it heading west and drive. The morning was partly cloudy, so she left the top on the car.

Julie-Ann wound up on I-66 heading west. She had on the XM Radio and was back to not having a care in the world. The road was open and that feeling of liberation had returned.

After about seventy miles, Julie-Ann turned onto I-81 heading south through Virginia. It was not a conscious decision, but more of an accident. She just went with the flow. After another ten miles or so she stopped at a service area, where she filled up the tank, used the restroom, and bought some snacks.

The sky had been gradually darkening and by the time Julie-Ann returned to the car it had started to drizzle. Still having no idea where she was going, she continued south. After about twenty minutes, the drizzle turned into a steady rain. Julie-Ann turned down the radio so she could concentrate more on the road. For a while, the rain made her nervous, but after a half hour she was used to it and turned back on the radio. She no longer had the energized feeling of liberation. After nearly three hours of driving, the open road had turned into just a long road. Once again, she wished she had someone with her. *Maybe I should have waited and had Amber come along,* she wondered. *That would be great if she was here.*

Julie-Ann felt like she had been driving all day, but it was only 12:45 p.m. Unfortunately, there didn't appear to be too many places to stop on her route. All she could see along the interstate was forest. So she pressed on. After being on the road for five hours, finally, Julie-Ann saw a sign for Blacksburg, five miles ahead. Tired and wanting out of the car, she decided to check it out.

Though home to Virginia Tech, Julie-Ann didn't know anything about Blacksburg. At first, she just drove through town, taking in the sights. Spread-out across a vast valley, Blacksburg is nestled between the Blue Ridge and Allegheny mountain ranges, making for a majestic background. With its abundance of trees and most of its buildings no more than three floors, it is a far cry from Manhattan, or even D.C. But neither is it some small, backwoods town. Not only home to Virginia Tech, but it also has plenty of stores and restaurants.

Julie-Ann decided that this was where she would spend the night. Stopped at a red light, she looked for nearby hotels on the GPS. There was a Marriott Courtyard only a mile away, so that's where she went.

Julie-Ann checked into a King Suite for two nights. As soon as she entered the room, she went over to the bed and threw herself on it, spreading out. It felt good not to be driving anymore. For ten minutes or so she just laid there. Then, taking her time, she started to unpack.

Having only snacked on some potato chips since breakfast, Julie-Ann was hungry. She didn't feel like going anywhere, so she ordered up some room service. While she waited, she took the time to call Theresa and let her know where she was. She also checked her texts and emails and updated her Facebook page saying she was in Blacksburg, Virginia.

By 6:00 p.m., Julie-Ann was bored and feeling restless. She wanted to walk around town, but it had started raining again and hard. Figuring she would explore the area in the morning, she looked through a book of local attractions that was provided by the hotel.

That night, as Julie-Ann laid alone in yet another hotel room, she started thinking again how much better it would be if she had Amber with her and began to contemplate asking Amber to meet her once she came back from Paris, but then she realized that it wouldn't be fair to Amber, having her go on some endless road trip right after getting back from Europe. Besides, this was something that she was supposed to do on her own. Julie-Ann just had not taken into account how lonely it would be.

Julie-Ann then started thinking about Ken. She did not want him back, but at the same time, she missed him. She missed romantic companionship. She missed being coddled and touched, having the warmth of a body against her. She could not help but wonder how long it would be until she was with another man.

Julie-Ann woke-up the next morning ready to go out and explore Blacksburg. She did not want to spend another hour in her hotel room. She did not care if it was raining or even if there was a storm. Luckily, it was a beautiful morning.

After getting ready, Julie-Ann headed out. A block away she found a small café, where she stopped in to have a juice, a banana, and corn muffin. She ate her food outside at a small table. Wearing sunglasses, she scanned the landscape. It was picturesque. Everything seemed so open and vivid. Nothing was cluttered or congested. The mountains formed a majestic backdrop under the clear, sun-swept sky. It was not just the sights; the air was so crisp that it seemed to melt in her lungs. Though in a commercial area, there were no sounds of horns or sirens. In fact, Julie-Ann honed in on the singing of nearby birds. People walked by, but all at a leisurely pace. No one, not even the cars, seemed to be in a rush.

After taking her time eating, Julie-Ann started walking. She had no destination. She just figured she would explore the area. With a bounce in her step, she strolled around town, stopping to look in various store windows. Wearing shorts and a t-shirt, the warmth felt comforting on her legs and arms, and the fresh air soothing to breathe. Content, she forgot about feeling lonely and just enjoyed the jaunt.

Julie-Ann wandered into a sporting store. While she was looking around, a young salesman came over and asked if she needed any help. She said she was just browsing, but the salesman started up a conversation, asking if she was new to the area. Julie-Ann explained that she was just passing through to her way out west. She inquired about the local attractions and activities. Among other places of interest, he told her that there was a hiking trail nearby. He explained that it was a safe and easy trail and was frequented by families.

Julie-Ann bought some hiking shoes and thanked the salesman for his help. After stopping at another store for some bottled water, she headed out on the trail.

It was a Monday, so not many people were out, but she passed a few. As the salesman had assured her, the path was easy to follow and not too arduous, the scenery was beautiful. In between rows of towering pine trees and seemingly endless forest, Julie-Ann felt as though she had wandered miles away from civilization. Only the sound of birds and the transient chatter of occasional passersby broke the quiet of the trail. At certain points the path would bend and a break in the trees would showcase the vast mountains that soared in the nearby distance.

After about two miles, Julie-Ann decided to turn around and head back. The path, though dirt, was well defined and sporadically marked, but she was still leery of traveling too far and getting lost. After all, she knew nothing about the area.

Julie-Ann enjoyed her hike. It cleared her mind and put her at ease. Walking peacefully back to town, she noticed it was only just after noon. Her legs were tired, but she did not want to go back to the hotel and sit in the room. Wondering where she could go and get off her feet for a little while, she noticed a bar across the street, nestled in a small strip mall. She decided to go check it out.

From the outside, Molly's Tavern looked almost like a storefront, except for two neon beer signs hanging in the small windows. The front door was propped open and Julie-Ann took a peek inside. There were no customers, just a woman behind the bar. She saw Julie-Ann. "Come on in, we're open."

Julie-Ann walked in. The place was dark and narrow with only a few small tables towards the rear, where a lone pool table stood. Some Southern rock song was playing low on the stereo. Julie-Ann bellied up to the long bar, which took up most of the establishment.

The barmaid came over. She looked to be in her late twenties or early thirties. Thin, with short, blonde hair, her tank top revealed several tattoos on her shoulder and arms. She had a pretty, effervescent face with big, brown eyes. "So what'll it be?" She asked in a pleasant voice, with a southern Virginian accent.

"I'll have a…" Julie-Ann was going to order her usual cranberry and vodka, but it didn't seem apropos. "You know what, what kind of beer do you have on tap?"

"I have Bud, Bud Light, Miller Lite, Sam Adams Lager, and we just got in Harpoon IPA."

Julie-Ann thought about it for a second. "I'll have the Sam please."

The barmaid pulled out a glass and started to pour. "So, you picking someone up from the college?"

"Wha…oh, no. I'm just passing through. I'm on my way to Arizona to live with my sister and decided to stop in Blacksburg for a few days." Julie-Ann had prepared the story after realizing the question of what she was doing in a particular town might come up again. She didn't like lying, but it just felt strange to say she was on some aimless journey across the country.

The barmaid gave Julie-Ann her beer. "Oh, well Blacksburg is a nice town. A little boring to live here, but nice to visit. Most people that come up here are just visiting Virginia Tech."

"You get a lot of college kids in here?"

"Here, no. We're far enough away. We get more of the locals in here. I mean the college kids would bring more business, but they can also bring more headaches if you know what I mean. But I'm sorry, what am I saying, you look like you could still be in college."

Julie-Ann let out a fleeting laugh. "No."

"Well I'm Krista," she said, extending her hand.

"Jules." Julie-Ann shook her hand. "I like your tattoos. Who is that on your arm?" She asked, pointing to a large, black ink tattoo on her left upper arm of a man walking away, wearing a long overcoat and carrying a guitar case.

Krista smiled. "That's Johnny Cash." She then lifted her arm and on the inside of her bicep, in big, black block letters was the word: CASH. "I love Johnny Cash. But really it's a tribute to my father. He used to be crazy about him. He was the one that turned me on to his music."

As Julie-Ann drank her beer, she and Krista talked. Krista asked how long she was in town and where she was from. Julie-Ann asked more about Blacksburg. Then, the phone at the bar rang.

"Excuse me," Krista said as she went to the end of the bar to answer it.

Julie-Ann did not mean to eavesdrop on Krista's conversation, but it was impossible not to overhear. There was no one else in the bar, the music was low, and Krista was only about ten feet away. She also started talking loudly and angrily.

"Connie, everything's already set up. I thought you said he was going to be okay with it." There was a pause as she listened to the person on the other end. "I understand, but it's beyond that now.

You have to try something." There was another, longer pause. "Well every little bit helps and you tell him that we're going to have it whether he's on board or not."

Krista hung up the phone in anger and walked back to Julie-Ann and apologized.

"Oh no, please. Don't apologize. I just hope everything's okay."

"That was my sister. Her house is getting foreclosed on."

"That's terrible. I'm sorry."

Krista nodded. "Yeah. And she and her husband have three kids too. We're supposed to hold a charity event here Wednesday to try and raise some money. I mean a lot of people are hurting here too, but like I told her, every little bit counts. We're going to have some raffles and some people are donating different things that we're going to try and auction off. I mean even if we raise enough just so they can fend off the bank for another month or two so they can maybe work something out."

"But your sister's husband doesn't want you to do it? I'm sorry, I couldn't help but overhear."

"That's okay. Yeah. I mean I understand where he's coming from. He's a very proud guy and worked hard his whole life. He was a project manager for a local construction company. He did real well, provided for my sister and the kids. They bought a nice four-bedroom house. But shortly after the economy took a shit the construction company he worked for went out of business. He collected unemployment for a while, but who can live on that? He tried to find another job, but there are no jobs out there these days. They tried borrowing money but no bank would lend it to them. Finally, my sister got a job as a secretary and he stayed home with the kids. But that still isn't enough to pay the mortgage. I mean it must be hard on him, but…" Krista paused and looked at Julie-Ann. "I'm sorry, I don't mean to be laying all of this on you."

"Oh no, please. It's okay. It just seems so unfair. Aren't there programs to help homeowners that are underwater? Have they tried to work something out with the bank?"

Krista let out a sarcastic laugh. "Oh yeah. I can't tell you how many times they've been to the bank and been on the phone with different people and agencies. You hear about these programs but it's all bullshit. The banks, they don't care. And the government certainly doesn't care." Krista's voice started to rise with frustration. "I mean they give hundreds of billions of dollars to the people on Wall Street who put us in this mess in the first place, but where's the bailout for the people? I'm not talking about helping out freeloaders. People like my brother-in-law, hardworking people who pay their taxes and make an honest living and got completely screwed through no fault of their own. Where's their help?"

Just then, someone walked in through the open front door. About six foot, with thick, black-and-gray peppered hair and a full goatee, wearing jeans and t-shirt, he looked to be in his late forties. "Hey Krista," he said in a hoarse voice.

"Hey Tommy."

Tommy sat two barstools down to the left of Julie-Ann. "What's wrong?" He asked Krista, sensing a strain in her facial expression.

"Oh nothing. We were just talking about Connie and Frank."

"You still having the benefit for them on Wednesday?"

"Yes, but Frank's giving Connie a hard time about it. You know, it's a pride thing. But I told her the kids come before pride."

As Krista opened a bottle of Budweiser and placed it on the bar, Tommy turned to Julie-Ann. "It's not fair. Guy worked hard his whole life, made an honest living, did things the right way, provided for his family, and what does he get for it? A bunch of rich con-men on Wall Street wreck the economy and now there's millions of people out of a job, losing their homes and livelihoods. It's called collateral damage."

"Yeah, we were just talking about that exact thing," Krista replied. "By the way, this is Jules."

Tommy extended his weathered hand. "Tommy. Pleased to meet you."

"Nice to meet you," Julie-Ann said with a smile.

"You know what, enough of this depressing talk," Krista said in a more upbeat tone. "Lets all do a shot—on me. And you need another beer?" She said to Julie-Ann.

Julie-Ann inconspicuously glanced at her watch. It was only 1:47 p.m., but she went with the flow. Krista and Tommy had a shot of Jameson's, and Julie-Ann a shot of tequila. She then quickly washed it down with a gulp of her fresh beer. Having not eaten since the morning, she was already feeling buzzed, but she was also enjoying the conversation. Both Krista and Tommy were friendly and made Julie-Ann feel as though she already knew them. They were different than many of the people she encountered—in a good way. They were down to Earth and "real".

Changing the subject to more lighthearted matters, Tommy, who was a local mechanic, told a funny story about one of his customers that happened the other day. Julie-Ann and Krista laughed. Then Krista told a funny story of her own about a drunken patron who passed out in the men's bathroom a few nights earlier.

At one point, Tommy innocently asked Julie-Ann what she did for a living. She certainly didn't want to say anything related to Wall Street after what Krista and Tommy had said earlier. So she said she worked for a small publishing company in New York. It was just the first thing that popped into her mind.

Soon another customer wandered into the bar. Krista introduced him to Julie-Ann. He also seemed friendly and jumped right into the conversation.

Julie-Ann was having a good time, but by her third beer—plus the shot—she was starting to feel drunk. She knew she should eat something. As much as Julie-Ann was enjoying the conversation and companionship, after finishing the beer, she announced that she had to leave. Tommy and the other man said goodbye and wished her well. Krista told her to stop by again before leaving Blacksburg. Julie-Ann said she definitely would.

Once outside, Julie-Ann realized she had no idea of where she was or how to get back to the hotel. So she pulled out her iPhone to get walking directions. Once she did, she saw that there was a text from Amber, Theresa, two other people, a missed call, and multiple Facebook notifications. She decided to reply later. Her first order of business was walking back towards the hotel and getting something to eat.

A block from the hotel, Julie-Ann passed a pizzeria. Wanting something fast, she decided to go in. She ordered two regular slices and sat down at a table. The pizza was awful. *Well, I guess some things are better in New York,* she said to herself as she laughed.

Julie-Ann walked back to the hotel, but didn't want to just sit alone in the room. So instead, still in the drinking mood, she stopped by the hotel bar. It was a Monday afternoon, and Blacksburg was not a big tourist attraction anyway, so there was only a young couple in the bar, engrossed in their own conversation. Over a beer, Julie-Ann started talking to the bartender, who appeared to be in his early thirties. She asked him about the area and told him about the hike she had gone on. He recommended a hike around the Falls Ridge Preserve, which was more picturesque and had a waterfall. He said it was just southeast of Blacksburg and was easy to drive to and safe.

Julie-Ann drank her beer slowly and once the other couple at the bar left, had the bartender all to herself. He was attractive, but she was more enjoying just having someone to converse with. Besides talking about hiking, he asked her where she was from and what she did for a living. She decided to stick with the story of working for a small publishing company.

As much as Julie-Ann appreciated the conversation, after her second beer she felt a little strange—and somewhat desperate—sitting at the bar by herself and taking up all of the bartender's time. Just as someone else came into the bar, Julie-Ann polished off her beer. She asked the bartender for her tab and said it was a pleasure meeting him. Sorry to see her go, he hoped to see her again before she left town.

After the bar, Julie-Ann went up to the front desk and asked if it was possible to extend her stay for three more days, which was no problem.

Once back in the room, Julie-Ann replied to her texts. She also returned Theresa's call. She told her about her hike and meeting Krista. Theresa could hear the excitement in Julie-Ann's voice, but was leery about her meeting strangers in a bar. She told Julie-Ann to please be careful and not to drink too much. Julie-Ann appreciated Theresa's concern, but assured her that she would be fine. She also said that she was staying in Blacksburg until Friday.

After getting off the phone with Theresa, Julie-Ann went on Facebook. She replied to several messages and wrote a new post. *In Blacksburg, VA. People here are really nice and down to earth. Also had a great hike and going on another one tomorrow.*

Later that evening, Julie-Ann started thinking about Krista's sister and brother-in-law. She knew the economy was still recovering from the mortgage collapse. Though she realized that there had been people responsible for grandiose scams, like Bernie Madoff, and even smaller conmen, Julie-Ann had always protected people like her father and Wall Street as a whole. She had always been of the opinion that, at least the mortgage crisis, was mainly due to people taking loans that they knew they could not afford. In fact, she saw many of the people asking the government for help and protesting Wall Street as freeloaders.

Julie-Ann thought about what Krista said about her brother-in-law, how he had always been an honest, hard working man. Of course, she didn't know him, but had no reason to think Krista was lying or even exaggerating. It wasn't his fault he lost his job; his entire company went out of business. Julie-Ann did know that even in big cities construction had come to a standstill. She could just imagine how it was in Blacksburg. How many other career opportunities were there in Blacksburg she wondered? Julie-Ann also thought about the three kids that she had never met. Were they going to get kicked out of their home? It was a sad situation.

The next morning, Julie-Ann woke-up early and after getting ready and having a hearty breakfast, drove out to Falls Ridge Preserve. It was a slightly overcast day, but with no rain in the forecast. It was supposed to make it up to eighty degrees, but it was already feeling muggy. Julie-Ann had packed several bottles of water and some power bars in her small backpack.

Julie-Ann took her time hiking and exploring. Just as the bartender had promised, it was a beautiful area lush with various towering trees and vegetation. Streams and creeks snaked through its valleys and hills. Freshness permeated the air, as the singing and fluttering of birds echoed through the trees. There was a well-defined dirt path, but Julie-Ann could not go far without stopping at a clearing or cliff and just taking in the pulchritude. She would take deeps breaths of clean air and then take out her phone and snap a picture or two.

Also as the bartender had told her, there were other people enjoying the preserve. It was not crowded, which Julie-Ann appreciated, but a person or small group was never too far away. Sometimes when someone would pass they would say hello and smile and she would reciprocate. Hiking through the preserve, Julie-Ann felt so content, her mind so clear and free. *How could anyone be in a bad mood walking through such a beautiful place,* she pondered.

After about a half hour, Julie-Ann came to the base of a waterfall. Standing by the river's edge, she looked up, enthralled by the roar of the water rushing from the hilltop, hitting various rock cliffs on its way down. It seemed so powerful, yet so peaceful. She was close enough that a fine mist gently caressed her face. It felt revitalizing. After a few minutes of just standing there, taking it in, Julie-Ann backed up and took out her phone to take a picture. As she did, she realized that a young woman was a few yards to her right, also enjoying the scene.

After taking a few pictures, Julie-Ann went over to the slender woman, who looked no older than her. "Excuse me, would you mind taking a picture of me in front of the waterfall?"

The young woman, who had her long, black hair in a ponytail and was wearing a baseball cap, smiled. "Of course not."

Julie-Ann gave her the phone and then went as close to the river's edge and the base of the fall as she could get. The stranger snapped a few photos, making sure to get a good picture.

"Thank you."

"No problem," she replied as she handed Julie-Ann back her phone. "Actually, do you think you could take a picture of me now?"

Julie-Ann smiled. "Of course."

She pulled a digital camera from her cargo shorts' pocket and handed it to Julie-Ann. Then she went to the same spot where she had taken a picture of Julie-Ann.

After taking the picture, Julie-Ann handed her back the camera. The young woman thanked her and introduced herself as Michelle. Julie-Ann introduced herself.

"So, you live in Blacksburg?" Asked Julie-Ann.

"No." Michelle paused and her facial expression changed. "I used to go to Virginia Tech. I was actually there for the shooting in 2007."

"Oh my God. That must have been awful."

Michelle let out a deep breath. "Yeah. I was in my second year. I heard people screaming and then heard what sounded like firecrackers. At first, I thought it was some kind of prank—I mean who thinks something like that is going to happen—but after a few seconds I saw people running and saying that someone one was shooting people."

"So, you were that close?"

Michelle nodded. "Yeah," she replied in a fading voice. "I wasn't injured, but my roommate was killed."

Julie-Ann gasped. "Oh my God. I'm so sorry."

"Yeah, it was pretty devastating. She was a sophomore just like me—only twenty-years-old." Michelle paused. "After classes resumed I tried going back, but I just couldn't be on the campus anymore. It was just too much. I moved back home to North Carolina. It affected me for a while. I had nightmares and…" Her sentence trailed off. "But I started going to a therapist and after a while things got better. I mean you never forget something like that, but I was finally able to move on. In fact, last year I came back to Blacksburg for the first time. It was hard walking around the campus, but afterwards, I came here to the preserve. It's a great place to clear your head. It's so peaceful and beautiful. Anyway, so I decided to come back to Blacksburg once a year—in remembrance and to pay homage. And maybe for my own healing. This is my second time and just like the first, I just felt compelled to come out to preserve. It's hard to be angry or sad when you walk around here."

"Yes, it is beautiful."

Michelle laughed. "I'm sorry. You just asked me if I was from here and I told you my whole life story."

"Oh no, please. I'm just so sorry about your friend. But I'm glad that you were able move on and find at least some closure."

Michelle smiled. "Thank you. Hey, I'm going up the trail towards the top of the fall. I don't know which way you were walking, but if you'd like to join me…"

"Oh yes, thank you. I wanted to see the top of the waterfall. And it'd be nice to have someone to walk with and talk to."

The two young women left the base of the waterfall and started slowly hiking back up the gradual trail. "So, Jules, you don't sound like you're from Blacksburg. Are you just visiting?"

For the first time since leaving New York, Julie-Ann opened up and told her real story. She explained about the tumor, what happened with Ken, and her decision to traverse the country. It felt therapeutic for her to get it off her chest, like a weight had been lifted from her shoulders.

Michelle listened intently. Julie-Ann's story was no doubt one of adversity and turmoil, but in the end, Michelle saw it as a tale of overcoming odds and perseverance. She loved the idea of Julie-Ann going on her journey, on a quest for some greater good and meaning.

Julie-Ann and Michelle seemed to share a common bond of trauma and healing. They were also the same age. Time ticked away unnoticed and they hiked through the preserve. Then, before separating, Julie-Ann asked Michelle, who said she was leaving the following morning, if she would like to have dinner with her. Michelle happily accepted the offer.

Later that evening Julie-Ann met Michelle at a Chili's, not far from her hotel. Michelle had suggested it, saying that there really weren't too many good restaurants around.

Over a drink and dinner the two talked about more mundane topics. Michelle, who had never before been to Manhattan, asked Julie-Ann what it was like living there. In return, Julie-Ann asked about Raleigh, Michelle's hometown. Michelle also talked about her new boyfriend, as well as working for her father as a hostess in his restaurant. The conversation flowed and the end of their dinner quickly crept up on them.

Before departing, the two exchanged numbers and email addresses and promised to stay in touch. In particular, Michelle asked Julie-Ann to update her on her journey and wished her luck.

Later that night, Theresa called to see how Julie-Ann was doing. Julie-Ann told her about Michelle and the story of her roommate being one of the victims of the Virginia Tech shooting.

After talking with Theresa, she talked for a while with her father. He was glad to hear that she appeared to be in good spirits and had not yet run into any problems.

After getting off the phone, Julie-Ann went on her laptop and checked her emails. She then went on Facebook and posted a picture of her by the waterfall with the following caption: *Falls Ridge Preserve, Blacksburg Virginia. It is a gorgeous, serene place and worth going to Blacksburg just to hike it. I also met a new friend today— Michelle. Just got back from having dinner and drinks with her. Really, hope to stay in touch.*

Chapter 13

The following evening, Julie-Ann decided to go back to Molly's Tavern to attend the benefit for Krista's sister and brother-in-law. She did not know when the benefit was supposed to start and arrived by 5:30 p.m. There was a half dozen people congregated at the bar. Krista saw Julie-Ann come in and waved her over.

"Hey, good to see you again," Krista said with a smile. "I didn't know if you were still in town."

"Yeah, I decided to stay until Friday. I remembered you said you were having a benefit tonight for your sister. I hope it's okay…"

"Yes, yes, of course. Most people won't be here until six or seven. Sit down, have a drink."

Julie-Ann took a seat at the bar next to two middle-aged, blue-collar looking men. Krista introduced them to Julie-Ann. They were polite, but they could not help looking Julie-Ann over—neither could the other guys at the other end of the bar.

Krista brought Julie-Ann her glass of Sam Adams Lager. "Don't worry, they're harmless," she said about the two men who were already trying to start up a conversation with Julie-Ann.

Julie-Ann reverted to her story about being a low-level editor from New York on her way to Arizona to move in with her sister. The two strangers had no reason to doubt her story or find it suspicious. Julie-Ann felt uncomfortable lying about herself and changed the conversation. She asked them if of them knew either Krista's sister or brother-in-law. They both did.

"It's a shame what the bank's doing to them," one of them said before taking a swig from his bottle of beer. "I mean the irony is that Frank is one of the most trustworthy people you'll ever meet. Never stole so much as a candy bar in his whole life. The guy would give you the shirt off his back to help you out—wouldn't matter if he knew you or not."

"He's always been a hard-working guy, ever since he was young," the other one added. "But when his company went under…I mean he looked for other work, but he was pulling down close to six figures as a project manager. It's just almost impossible to find that kind of salary around here in this economy. And all he's ever done is construction and right now, well you know, construction is basically at a standstill—not just here, but across the entire country."

Julie-Ann nodded in agreement. "Well it's nice of Krista to have this thing for them."

The man closest to Julie-Ann finished taking a drink of his beer. "Krista is a great girl. She has a huge heart and obviously wants to help her sister. Our friend Rich owns a guitar shop in town and he's donated a Les Paul to raffle. And there are some other items and people will give what they can. But in reality…I mean, come on…at best it's still going to be a drop in the bucket. At best we might raise enough money to get the bank off of their back for another month or two. But it's just delaying the inevitable. I mean no one here's rich."

"Hey, every little bit counts," his friend added.

Just then a man and a woman came over. After the four locals finished their greetings one of the men who Julie-Ann had been talking to introduced her to the newcomers.

Slowly the bar started to fill up. Though Julie-Ann was a stranger in a strange land, someone always introduced her to someone else and she was never left sitting by herself without conversation. In fact, she felt as though she had been welcomed into a private club with arms wide open.

Krista was splitting her time behind the bar with another bartender, and mingling with the crowd. At one point, she went over to Julie-Ann, who was engrossed in a conversation with another woman about the Virginia Tech shooting, and introduced her sister, Connie.

Connie looked different than Krista. Although they looked almost the same age, Connie didn't have any visible tattoos and was dressed conservatively. And unlike Krista's short hair, hers was long and flowing.

"It's nice to meet you," Julie-Ann said as she shook Connie's hand. She did not know what else to say. She did not want to introduce herself by saying *sorry to hear that you're losing your home. Hopefully, people can give you enough charity to help you out.*

Connie was polite, but seemed distracted, which under the circumstance was understandable. After the introduction, someone else came over and commanded Connie and Krista's attention. Julie-Ann turned back to the woman with whom she had been previously talking.

By 7:00 p.m., Molly's was bustling. Most everyone was local and there specifically for the benefit. Though it was a serious subject—trying to raise money for Connie and her family—the atmosphere was lively. People were laughing and the drinks were flowing. Every time someone left a big tip, which was all going to be part of the donations, Krista or the other bartender would ring a bell.

Julie-Ann was bouncing from group to group, sharing in different conversations. One guy in particular kept trying to pick up on her, but it was nothing she couldn't handle. Some of the older men looked after her.

"Is this guy bothering you," one of them said half-jokingly about one of the other locals. "You tell me if he gets fresh and we'll take him out back."

The fact was Julie-Ann felt very comfortable and let her guard down. She had already met and talked to half the people in the bar. She was having a good time listening to their stories and sharing a drink with them.

At one point, she could feel her phone vibrate in her jeans pocket. It was her father calling. Too noisy in the bar, she walked out front to answer it. But by the time she went outside she had missed the call, so she dialed him back.

"Hey sweetie. I just wanted to see how you were doing."

"I'm good Dad," replied Julie-Ann. "I'm actually at a benefit event right now. This woman that I met, her sister is having her house foreclosed and they're trying to raise some money to help them out."

There was a pause. "Jules, you have to be careful. You know how many scams there are out there? I don't want you..."

Julie-Ann cut her father off. "It's not a scam Dad. Not everything is a scam. These are real people. Hardworking people that just happened to lose their jobs and fell behind."

"Sweetie, you don't know these people. All I'm saying is don't get caught up in some sob story. Have they asked you for money?"

Julie-Ann sighed. "No Dad, no one's asked me for any money. And no one knows who I am or that I have money. In fact, I've told everyone that I work at some small publishing company. It was just somewhere to go, something to do. Don't worry."

"Well just be careful. If people find out that you're rich..."

She again cut her father off. "No one's going to find out. Please, everything is fine. There's no need to worry. I'll text you when I get back to the hotel."

Now her father sighed. "Okay. Just be careful."

"Okay Dad. Love you."

"Love you, too."

With that, Julie-Ann hung up the phone. She then realized that she had several unread texts and emails. As she stood a yard or so from the front door, checking them, she noticed Connie walking outside with another woman. Connie immediately pulled out a pack of cigarettes, put one in her mouth and handed one to her friend. They either didn't notice Julie-Ann or figured she was busy on her phone.

Though Julie-Ann was replying to an email, she could not help but overhear their conversation.

"So where's Frank?"

Connie lit her cigarette with a lighter and then used it to light her friend's. "He refused to come," she said with the cigarette dangling from her mouth. "I can't blame him. I mean my sister, God bless her, is just trying to help—and so is everyone else—but it's so embarrassing."

"It's nothing to be embarrassed about."

"Come on Lacey—asking for money from your friends and neighbors. I've turned into a charity case." Connie took a drag off her cigarette and shook her head in disgust. "How the hell did it come to this? Frank always had a good job. We never spent extravagantly—just went on a vacation now and then."

Lacey put her hand on Connie's shoulder. "You're not a charity case. And you did nothing wrong. It's the whole country. You know how many people lost their jobs and their houses? It's just the times we live in."

Julie-Ann peeked over and could see Connie as she started to cry.

"The other day Frank and I were arguing," Connie said as tears dripped from her eyes. "Lindsay overheard us and came over crying and said 'I'm sorry.' I said why are you sorry? She said because if we didn't buy her a bicycle for her birthday we would have more money. Then she offered to sell it. You know how that made me feel?"

"Geez, Con, I'm sorry."

"Then for some stupid reason Frank mentioned that if we have to move into an apartment we might not be able to take Buddy. Justin flipped out. I mean I love that dog too, we all do, but Justin was beside himself. He said he would run away with Buddy." Connie paused. "God, Lacey, he's only twelve. He doesn't understand."

Just then a couple approached the bar from the parking lot. Connie quickly wiped the tears from her face and tried to compose herself as she said hello. After exchanging a few words, Connie and

Lacey threw their cigarettes on the ground and the four of them went into the bar.

Julie-Ann could no longer concentrate on her emails or texts. She was heartbroken from overhearing Connie's story. After taking a few deep breaths, she also went back into the bar. She no longer felt like laughing and having a good time.

"Hey Jules, I thought you might've left."

Julie-Ann looked at the polar-bear looking man whom she had been talking to earlier. "No, I just had to use the phone," she said with a forced smile.

He tried to start up a conversation with her, but Julie-Ann wasn't really paying attention. It had nothing to do with him personally; she just couldn't stop thinking about Connie. As he was talking, she saw someone hand Krista a white envelope. She had already seen a few other people give her an envelope or check. Julie-Ann had planned on contributing to the cause, but hadn't really thought of an amount up to that point. After overhearing Connie and thinking about her kids, Julie-Ann felt the need to help out in some meaningful way.

Julie-Ann excused herself and went into the ladies room. There, in a stall, she opened up her purse, pulled out her checkbook and wrote a check. Earlier, Krista had made an announcement of Connie's full name so if anyone wanted to write a check they would know who to make it out to.

Afterwards, Julie-Ann sought out Krista. She was at the edge of the bar, talking to someone. As soon as Julie-Ann saw an opening, she grabbed Krista's ear. "I'm sorry, I know you're busy, but is there any way I can talk to you outside? It'll just take a minute."

Krista first thought was that one of the guys had gotten out of line with Julie-Ann. "Is everything okay?"

"Yes, yes. I just wanted to talk to you."

"Yeah, sure." Krista told the other bartender that she would be right back and then followed Julie-Ann outside, wondering what she wanted to tell her.

Julie-Ann walked down towards the end of the bar so they were not right by the entrance. She then pulled out the folded check from her front jeans pocket. "I wanted to give you this for Connie."

"Oh Jules, you don't have to give anything. Really. You don't even know Connie. I'm just glad you were able to come."

"This is something I want to do. Please."

Krista gently took the check from Julie-Ann's hand. "Well thank you. That's very kind of you."

"Just do me a favor—don't tell anyone else about it besides your sister. I don't want people thinking I have a bunch of money."

Krista was puzzled by Julie-Ann's comment. To be polite, she started to put the check in her pocket without looking at the amount in front of Julie-Ann. But now she unfolded it and took a peek. Krista gasped and read the check again. "Jules there must be some mistake," she said in a low, serious voice. "This check is for ten thousand dollars."

"No, it's not a mistake. I'm sure it's not all they need, but at least it should hold off the bank for a while."

Krista folded the check back up and went to hand it to Julie-Ann. "Jules, I think you should lay off on the shots. It's nice that you want to help but…"

"I'm not drunk. I've only had four beers."

"Jules, I appreciate it, really. But I can't take this from you. My sister can't take this from you."

Julie-Ann politely pushed Krista's hand away. "Listen, between you and me, I have the money. Trust me. Ten thousand dollars isn't going to put me in a hole. I just really want to help out Connie, Frank and especially their kids. It isn't right for them to have their house taken away."

"Are…are you sure you…"

"I'm positive," Julie-Ann replied with a smile. "Please, don't make a big deal out of it."

Krista laughed. "Don't make a big deal out of it? I don't know what to say. I mean…wait, stay here, please. I'll be right back."

Before Julie-Ann could even respond, Krista turned around and went back into the bar. A few minutes later she returned with Connie.

"Don't worry," she said lowly, "I didn't say anything to anyone besides my sister."

Tears were starting to swell in Connie's eyes. "Why are you doing this? You don't even know me."

"Listen," Julie-Ann said in a soft voice, "I've been very fortunate in my life. Growing up my family had money and I never had to worry about a thing. I still have it good. And I just want to be able to give a little back, to be able to help someone else out."

"I…I don't know what to say."

"You don't have to say anything. The only thing I ask is that you don't tell anyone else, at least not for tonight. I just don't want people thinking I have a bunch of money. It's just…"

Connie put her hand on Julie-Ann's arm. "Don't worry, no one here will know." Tears starting to freely flow down her face, Connie looked at Julie-Ann in the eyes for a few seconds. Then, she gave her a big hug. "Thank you so much."

Now Julie-Ann was fighting back tears. "Your welcome."

After Connie and Julie-Ann separated, Krista put a hand on each of their shoulders. "Now let's go back in the bar and celebrate. Drinks are on me."

Both Connie and Julie-Ann wiped their eyes and followed Krista back into the bar.

By 8:30 p.m. Molly's Tavern was raucous. The jukebox was blaring and people were yelling over it. Some customers were already smashed. But no one was getting out of line. Molly's didn't have a kitchen, but a local pizzeria donated pizzas and wings. The owner of the bar, Max, also put a Weber grill right outside the back door in the parking lot, which he used to cook hamburgers and hot dogs. Patrons spilled out back, eating and drinking.

The police did stop by once, but it was a good visit. One of the officers knew Connie's husband. He and his partner stopped by the bar to make a quick donation.

Julie-Ann was having a great time. Krista tried to keep filling her up with shots and beer. Everyone was talking to her. But unbeknownst to Julie-Ann, Krista had asked her cousin Bobby, who was 6'2" and a black belt, to look after her. However, he didn't need to set anyone straight. The worst that happened was some bad pickup lines.

By 10:30 p.m., after doing four shots of tequila, drinking six beers, and eating only a hamburger, Julie-Ann was wasted. Krista saw her stumbling around, getting more flirty, and decided it would be best if she called it a night. Julie-Ann didn't argue. She said she was going to walk back to the hotel, but Krista called her a cab. When it came, Krista and Connie walked her outside and thanked her once again. They also exchanged contact info.

In the cab, Julie-Ann text her father to say she was on her way back to the hotel and that she was fine. As drunk as she was, she did not tell him about writing Connie a $10,000 check. She was not worried that she had gone against his wishes. She knew he wouldn't understand. Besides, it was her own money. Julie-Ann had over $4,000,000 spread-out in several accounts in her own name. That was not counting stocks, bonds, trusts, and her inheritance. $10,000 was barely a drop in the bucket.

Julie-Ann woke-up with a throbbing headache and a dry throat. She gingerly lifted her head and turned to look at the clock on the nightstand. It was 11:08 a.m. "How many shots did I do last night?" She asked herself aloud as she rubbed her head.

After turning on the television and lying in bed for another ten minutes or so, she finally got up and went into the bathroom. After grabbing a half-empty bottle of water that was on a table, she went back to lie down.

It was a dreary, drizzling day outside—a fitting day to nurse a hangover. Julie-Ann ordered up some room service. She was craving some eggs and bacon, but the hotel stopped serving breakfast at 11:00 a.m.so instead, she ordered a chicken club sandwich.

Julie-Ann had finished her food and was just lounging around watching TV, when the hotel phone rang. Not thinking anything of it, she picked it up.

"Ms. Crown."

"Yes."

"This is the front desk. There is someone in the lobby for you."

Before Julie-Ann could ask who it was, the clerk handed off the phone. "Hi Jules, it's me, Connie. I'm so sorry to disturb you. I...I should've called first."

"It's okay. Is everything all right?"

"Oh yes, yes. I just stopped by with my husband and kids. They wanted to meet you, especially, Frank, and thank you. I don't want to intrude. It'll just take a minute. If you just want to come down to the lobby. We don't want to go upstairs."

Julie-Ann was certainly not expecting it. "Sure. Sure. Just give me a few minutes and I'll be down."

"Certainly. Take your time."

Julie-Ann was already wearing sweatpants and a t-shirt. She took off her shirt to put on a bra. She went into the bathroom and looked at herself in the mirror. That's when she realized that she did not have her wig on. Not wanting to keep Connie and her family waiting, she rushed to put it on and brushed her teeth. Julie-Ann appreciated Connie's gesture, but wished she had just done it over the phone, or at least called before showing up at the hotel.

Julie-Ann took about twelve minutes to get ready. She then took the elevator down to the lobby, where Connie was waiting with her family. Connie introduced them: her husband Frank; Justin, who was twelve; Trevor, who was ten; and Lindsay, who was eight-years-old.

Frank, who was about 6'1", slender, clean-shaven and wearing a polo shirt, extended his hand. "It's a pleasure to meet you. I really can't tell you how grateful we all are."

Julie-Ann felt embarrassed, but at the same time, also rewarded. "It's my pleasure. Like I told Connie yesterday, I've been blessed with a very good life and I'm just trying to pay my share, give a little back."

"Mommy, is this the lady who saved our house?" Lindsay asked, as she halfway hid behind her mother's leg.

"Yes honey."

"Thank you," Lindsay said in a sheepish voice. "I really like that house."

Julie-Ann chuckled, but was greatly moved. "You're welcome." She didn't know what else to say.

Justin, who had short black hair, and was wearing jeans and an un-tucked button-down shirt, went up to Julie-Ann. "Now we won't have to get rid of our dog, Buddy," he said with tears swelling in his eyes. "I wanted to bring him so you could see him, but mom and dad wouldn't let me."

As Julie-Ann looked at little Justin's face, she fought to keep from crying. "What kind of dog is Buddy?"

"He's a yellow lab. He's a great dog."

"Listen," Connie said with a smile, "we don't want to take up any more of your time. We just wanted to say thank you."

"Yes," added Frank. "For someone we've never met...I mean...you're like a guardian angel. Thank you."

Julie-Ann could feel tears seeping from her eyes. "Please, I'm no angel. I'm just glad I could pitch in a little. You have a beautiful family."

As Julie-Ann took the short elevator ride up to the third floor, she let her tears flow freely. They were not tears of sorrow, nor were they tears of joy. She was just so moved by the gratitude and also felt a sense of pride that she was able to help such people.

As she walked into her room, Julie-Ann forgot all about her hangover. She was thinking about what she had said to Connie and Frank, about having had a fortunate and blessed life and just wanting give a little back, to be able to help others. She started thinking back to the vision she had on the operating table of an open road, to the feeling like she had to travel. She also thought about Allie and how inspiring it was to see such a sick little girl care more about others than herself. As she put everything together, it was an epiphany. Julie-Ann knew right then and there that she was not supposed to just travel across the country and meet people. She was supposed to travel across the country and help people.

Julie-Ann was set to checkout of the hotel the following morning. She knew now what her purpose was, but did not know how to accomplish it. She had no idea where she was going next. After racking her brain, she finally decided that she would just get in the car and start driving. After all, that's how she found Connie. If wandering through the country to help people was truly her destiny then she figured God would lead her in the right direction. Unbeknownst to her, that direction would come sooner than she had imagined.

Later than evening, Julie-Ann was lying in bed watching Dateline when a segment came on about unemployed veterans and reservists. It talked about how difficult it was for troops returning from Iraq and Afghanistan to find work and how the unemployment rate among military members was much higher than their civilian counterparts. It was a revelation for Julie-Ann. She had not been aware that such a problem existed.

The segment highlighted that Indiana had one of the highest veteran unemployment rates. The host interviewed a Marine who had returned from Iraq four months earlier. With his wife by his side, the twenty-five-old explained his situation.

"I've looked everywhere for work. I can't tell you how many applications I've filled out and how many interviews I went on, but nothing. The few jobs that are out there, they want you to have specific experience. I went for an interview at a bank. The gentleman asked if I had any experience as a bank teller. Well for the last three years I was a heavy machine gunner. I told him I was a fast learner, but he didn't care."

"I think too, a lot of companies are leery about hiring people who saw action overseas," his wife added. "They hear about PTSD and think that everyone who returns home is a ticking time bomb. Also, they're worried about hiring someone and then that person being called to duty again."

The interviewer asked the man how they were holding up.

"It's difficult. We have a two-year-old son and the bills are piling up. We had to move back in with my parents," he said with a strained voice. "I'm not looking for any handouts. I'm a hard worker. I did three tours in Iraq. Now, I just want to be able to earn an honest living and provide for my family. I thank my parents for taking us in, but my wife and son deserve to live in their own house."

After the interview, the host added that there were many unemployed veterans in Anderson, the city where the marine resided.

By the time the segment finished, Julie-Ann knew her next destination: Anderson, Indiana. Though she was not sure what exactly she was going to do when she arrived there—if she was going to somehow seek out the marine in the interview or find someone else to help—there was something just telling her that's where she needed to go. Julie-Ann pulled out her laptop and went on MapQuest to see the distance between Blacksburg and Anderson; it was seven and a half hours.

Next, Julie-Ann went on Travelocity to find a place to stay. There were not many hotels in Anderson and they were all modest. There were no Hyatt's or Hilton's. Also, most of the hotels were close to each other, in a centralized area not far from the highway. After looking at some of the reviews, she settled on the Best Western. Julie-Ann booked four nights, figuring if she decided to stay longer it probably wouldn't be a problem and if she wanted to leave earlier, she would just forego the $78 a night.

Chapter 14

Julie-Ann woke-up early Friday morning. She had already done most of her packing the previous night. While getting ready, she ordered room service. Knowing that it would be a long day on the road, she wanted a hearty breakfast in her stomach.

Julie-Ann was checked out of the hotel and was on the road by 8:30 a.m. She figured that stopping once or twice for gas and a bathroom break, would put her into Anderson around 5:00 p.m.

It was a clear, sunny day and the temperature was already in the high seventies, so Julie-Ann decided to put the top down on the Camaro. She had on a long, blonde wig, which had a premade ponytail. So it would not blow away, she firmly put on a Virginia-Tech baseball cap, which she had bought in town, and threaded the ponytail through the back opening.

As she drove through Blacksburg, Julie-Ann felt melancholy about leaving. Not only would she miss the people she had met, but she would also miss the city itself. She had enjoyed walking through town and going on the hiking trails, taking in the picturesque landscape. As she hit the highway, Julie-Ann promised herself that she would one day return to Blacksburg.

Once she was on US-460 W, the GPS said that she would not have to turn again or exit for another forty-three miles. Julie-Ann turned up the radio, hit the gas, and took in the open road. The whipping, warm air felt rejuvenating on her face and bare arms, as the sunglass-tinted blue sky and mountainous backdrop reverberated with vividness and life. The world seemed to breathe the possibility that only a new day can bring, and for Julie-Ann, the unwritten page of a journey she had only started.

After an hour on the road, Julie-Ann saw a sign for an upcoming service station five miles ahead. She figured it would be a good chance to fill up with gas and use the bathroom.

Right off of I-77, it was a rather large rest stop, with all the obligatory amenities: a gas station, souvenir shop, newspaper stand, Burger King, Starbucks, and Cinnabon. Julie-Ann parked in the lot, which had over a dozen cars already in it. She knew she still had a long way to go, but it already felt good to get out of the car and stretch her legs. In no hurry to get back behind the wheel for another three or four hours without stopping, Julie-Ann took her time sauntering around the bustling station. After using the restroom, she browsed through the souvenir shop, bought some snacks for the road and stopped at Starbucks.

Once back outside, while sipping on her latte, Julie-Ann decided to check her phone. The ringer had been off and she had missed a call from her father. She called him back, but his assistant said he was in a meeting. So Julie-Ann called Theresa.

"Jules, how are you?"

"I'm good. I'm at a rest stop right now, on my way to Indiana."

There was a pause. "Indiana?" Theresa said in a puzzled voice. "What's in Indiana?"

Julie-Ann didn't want to get into the real reason she was going there. It just seemed too strange to explain. Julie-Ann also didn't want Theresa telling her father that she was on some crusade to help people and have him freaking out that she was going to get scammed.

"I'm stopping for a few days at this place called Anderson. I just saw a story about it on this show the other day and it seems like a real nice place." After saying it, Julie-Ann hoped that Theresa didn't happen to see the same story. "Then I might stop in Indianapolis and some other places around there," she spontaneously added, not really meaning it.

"Well…well, just be careful. So how are you doing?"

"I'm great. Listen Theresa, I know you and my dad are worried about me, but I'm telling you, I think this is just what I needed. I just needed to get away and clear my head—do my own thing. Don't worry, I'm being careful. I'm not going anywhere shady."

Theresa could hear the life and enthusiasm in Julie-Ann's voice. "Well I'm happy for you. I really am."

Out front of the service station, with a bag of snacks and her latte in one hand, Julie-Ann talked to Theresa for another five minutes or so.

"Okay, well be safe and call when you get to Anderson."

"I will."

"Love you."

Julie-Ann smiled. "I love you, too. And tell dad I tried calling him."

"Okay—oh and hey, send some pictures."

"Will do."

As soon as Julie-Ann hung up, she sent Theresa several pictures of Falls Ridge. That's when she noticed she had a new text. It was from Amber. *We decided to extend our stay for another 5 days. We r going to Belgium 2morrow for a couple nights. Hope u r doing well. Where r u now? It's 4:05 pm here now. Call me.*

Julie-Ann wanted to talk to Amber, but knew the call would last for a while and it was time for her to get back on the road. So she text Amber back saying that she would have to call her later or the next day.

With that, Julie-Ann went back to the car. It was getting more humid out so she decided to put the top up. After a stop at the gas station to fill up, it was back on the interstate.

After another hour of driving, the backdrop changed from picturesque mountain ranges, to endless, bland flatlands. The road no
longer felt liberating, it just felt long and monotonous. To break up
the monotony, she put in her Bluetooth earpiece and called Amber
back. Amber answered the phone, excited to hear from her best
friend.

"So, what are you doing? Where are you?"

"I'm actually on the highway right now. I'm heading to Indiana."

"Indiana? What's in Indiana?"

Julie-Ann wasn't sure if Amber would completely understand
what she was doing, but she had never kept anything from her and
tried to explain. She started with telling her about Connie and
Frank.

Amber could hear the excitement in Julie-Ann's voice as she told
the story. "Jules, it's great that you want to help people, but you have
to be careful—once people know that you have money…"

"I don't let anyone know that I have money. I don't wear any of
my expensive clothes or jewelry. And I've been telling people that I
work for a small publishing company."

"You just said that you wrote them a ten thousand dollar check.
How do you explain that you have ten thousand dollars just laying
around?"

Julie-Ann explained what she had told Connie and Frank.

Amber could tell that Julie-Ann was enthusiastic about what
she was doing and wanted to be supportive, but at the same time
she was genuinely worried about her friend. "Jules, if this is really
what you want to do and it's making you happy, then I'm happy for
you, but you have to be careful. Just because this Connie woman
turned out to be sincere, the next person you meet might be some
con artist. I mean what are you going to do? How are you going to
just find people to help? And what's in Indiana?"

"Well I was watching the news last night and…"

Just then, a semi-truck's air horn blared as if it was in the back
seat. Engrossed in her conversation, Julie-Ann had drifted into the
right lane. In a fraction of a second she looked through the corner

of her eye and saw an eighteen-wheeler inches away, swerving to avoid contact.

"Oh my God," Julie-Ann blurted in a panic as she turned the steering wheel to the left. But she did not look before doing so and there was a car in her blind spot. The driver blasted his horn and was able to cut to the median on his left. At the same time, Julie-Ann swerved back to her lane.

"Jules, are you okay?" Asked a frantic Amber.

An accident was adverted, but Julie-Ann's heart was pounding out of her chest.

The car that was to her left pulled alongside her with its passenger window down. "What's wrong with you, you crazy bitch! Learn how to drive!" Yelled the irate driver before speeding away.

"I just almost got in a major accident," Julie-Ann said with bated breath. "I'm okay, but I gotta go. I'll call you later." She didn't even wait for Amber to say goodbye. Still shaking, she took off her earpiece and threw it on the passenger seat.

The eighteen-wheeler once again thundered its horn. Petrified that she was about to crash again, Julie-Ann glanced over to her right to see the truck passing her, while its male driver flipped her the middle finger.

Her heart racing and nerves pulsating, Julie-Ann scanned for a place to pull over so she could try and compose herself but there was nowhere. So gripping the steering wheel like a vice and still trembling, she continued down the highway.

It took Julie-Ann a good fifteen minutes to calm down, but she was still hyper-vigilant. She did not put the radio back on for another hour.

Just after crossing into Indiana, with over eighty more miles still to go, Julie-Ann stopped at another service station where she topped off the tank and stretched her legs.

At 5:35 p.m., Julie-Ann finally reached the turn-off sign for Anderson. Feeling like she had been driving for days, she let out an exasperated sigh of relief. Though it was after five, it was still light out and the sky still blue. She scanned the landscape and saw it was as flat and open as what she had been driving through for hours. Happy to be able get out of the car for the rest of the day, Julie-Ann took the exit to Anderson. The exit ramp took her through a highway underpass. As she drove under it, she spotted what appeared to be about a half-dozen homeless people camped on the concrete. However, she was moving too fast to get a good look.

Less than two miles from the underpass, just off the highway, Julie-Ann arrived at the Best Western. Located next to several other motels, the area was drab and cold, consisting mostly of parking lots. There were no restaurants or stores in sight. Behind the hotel was a vast, dirt field. It was a far cry from picturesque Blacksburg, Julie-Ann thought. Nevertheless, she was relieved to finally be at her next destination.

The lot was half-empty and Julie-Ann was able to get a parking space right in front. Mentally and physically exhausted, she wheeled her suitcase into the lobby. There, a young, rather plump receptionist assisted her.

"Okay Ms. Crown," she said with a smile, "we have you reserved for four nights. And I see here that you already paid in advance, so all I'll need is a driver's license and a credit card just for incidentals—in case you charge something to the room or make a phone call."

"Sure," Julie-Ann replied as she went into her purse and retrieved her wallet.

"Thank you," said the receptionist, as Julie-Ann handed her the license and credit card.

"I'm sorry, but I couldn't help notice when I was driving in…the underpass by the highway…were those homeless people living there?"

The receptionist looked up from her computer. "Um, ah…yeah," she said in an uncomfortable, hesitant voice. "I'm sorry about that. But don't worry, they don't come around over here."

"Oh no, I wasn't worried about that," Julie-Ann quickly replied. "I was just…I just happened to see them and…It's just sad I guess."

The receptionist nodded in agreement. "Yeah, it is. But I guess unfortunately every town has its homeless population. I mean you must have some in New York, right?"

Julie-Ann didn't want the receptionist to think that she was trying to put down her town. "Oh yes, we have our share in New York, especially now with the economy."

"Yeah, we got hit pretty hard over here, too. A lot of people lost their jobs and houses. It's tough." She then handed Julie-Ann back her license and credit card. "And here's your room key."

Julie-Ann was surprised to see that it was an actual key.

"You're in room two-fifteen," she said before giving directions.

Julie-Ann thanked the receptionist and then went on her way.

The room was small and dated. The size of a box, it had a queen-size bed, two nightstands, small table and chair, dresser with a tube television set on it, closet, and bathroom. It appeared clean, but old. The wallpaper and furniture looked like they belonged in the seventies and had visible wear. Julie-Ann opened up the bathroom door. In a space smaller than any of her walk-in closets at home, there was a sink, small mirror, toilet, and stand-up shower. Like the rest of the room, it was clean, but diminutive. Julie-Ann had read reviews about the hotel online and had gone to their website. She knew the room was not going to be anything fancy, but it just seemed so much smaller in person. She also knew from the Internet that the Best Western was probably the best hotel in the area.

After getting situated, Julie-Ann changed into sweat-shorts and a t-shirt. She then lay on top of the bed, with her back propped up with all the pillows. Though in front of the TV, she checked her phone for messages, texts, and emails. She was happy to see that Michelle had sent her an email, asking how she was doing and if she was still in Blacksburg. Rather than reply on her phone, Julie-Ann took out her laptop and rested it across her legs. In response, she wrote about being in Anderson and why she had chosen it. She also told Michelle all about Connie and her family.

After replying to a few more, mundane emails, Julie-Ann realized she was hungry. By now, it was after six. She looked for a room service menu, but could not find one. So she called the front desk, only to find out that the hotel did not offer room service. In fact, other than a small breakfast buffet area, the hotel did not have any restaurant. However, the receptionist explained that there was a Cracker Barrel and several fast food eateries about a half-mile away. The last thing Julie-Ann wanted to do was hop back in the car, but she had to eat. So she threw on a pair of jeans and sandals and headed out. She returned to the hotel with a bag of Burger King, which she ate at the small, lone, round table in the room. In between bites, she flipped through the channels of the outdated tube television. She finally settled on a Hallmark movie and after eating and throwing away her trash, lay on the bed and watched it for another half hour until it ended.

Julie-Ann was already feeling claustrophobic in the room and she hadn't even been there for a night. Unlike Blacksburg, she could not just walk out of the hotel and stroll around town. Even where she bought her food, which was a half-mile away, it wasn't an area to wander around. So Julie-Ann once again took out her laptop, went on the Internet—the hotel did have Wi-Fi—and decided to find out more about Anderson. After a few searches, she Googled: *Anderson Indiana Veterans.* It brought up the address and site of a local VFW hall, American Legion, and office of veterans affairs. She then searched: *Anderson Indiana homeless.* The first result was for The Christian Center, a local shelter. Julie-Ann browsed through the site and decided that she would visit it the next day.

Just then Julie-Ann's cell phone rang. It was her father. She closed her laptop and answered it. He asked how she was doing and said that Theresa told him she was going to Indiana. Julie-Ann said that she was in Anderson, but did not go into the real reason she had come there. She knew she was going to tell him at some point, but was too tired to get into it right then. Instead, she tried to steer the conversation in a more lighthearted tone, telling her father that she was probably going to visit Indianapolis and talked about the drive.

By the time Julie-Ann got off the phone with her father it was 8:00 p.m.—but it felt much later. It had been a long day. Exhausted, she went into the bathroom and brushed her teeth, took off her wig, and removed the little bit of make-up that she had worn that day. She then changed back into her sweat shorts and crawled under the covers. Julie-Ann felt as though she could go to sleep, but knew if she passed out that early she would probably wake-up in the middle of the night. So, as the sound of heavy rain started to reverberate outside the window, she flipped through the channels. After some searching, she settled on an episode of CSI.

As Julie-Ann watched the show, the rain began to fall even harder, forming a constant droning rumble. Then, through the cracks in the curtains there was a flash of lightning. A few seconds later, as if on queue, came the distant, muffled roar of thunder. But through the next half hour, the lightning became more brilliant and the thunder louder. As it did, Julie-Ann began to feel like a scared little girl. *Come on, it's just a storm. What are you ten-years-old?* She said to herself. But then she would look around the small room and realize that she was all alone, nearly a thousand miles from home.

After a while, curiosity compelled Julie-Ann to get out of bed and peel back the thick curtains of the room's window to look outside. The dull glow of two lampposts eerily illuminated an otherwise darkened parking lot, as sheets of rain pounded the ground. Beyond the lot was only barren night. A chill ran down Julie-Ann's spine. Then, as she stood there peeking at the eldritch view, a brilliant spider web of light flashed down on the vacant field across the street. Less than a second later came the heavenly roar of thunder, so loud and close it seemed to shake the room. Julie-Ann quickly left the window and jumped back in bed.

It's just a storm. It's just lightning and thunder. Her heart racing, she flipped through the channels, trying to find something funny to watch, to hopefully, calm her nerves. She finally found a rerun of Seinfeld.

As a second episode started, the storm began to fade. Slowly, Julie-Ann began to relax, actually making fun of herself for being so scared. Then, after another half hour or so, with the TV still on, she fell asleep.

Chapter 15

Julie-Ann woke-up late the next morning, having a good night sleep and feeling fully rested. After stretching, she went to the window to see if it was raining; the sun was out. Not wanting to hang around in the room, she started getting ready.

The pressure in the shower was weak, but the water was hot and Julie-Ann stayed in their for a while. After getting out, she dried herself off and stood in front of the small, rectangular mirror. Her hair was already growing back, forming a thick, blonde crew cut. But she still decided to put on her favorite wig of straight, long, blonde hair. She then put on khaki cargo shorts and a t-shirt. She wore minimal make-up.

Once in the lobby, Julie-Ann asked the two receptionists if either could recommend a good place to have breakfast.

"The Empire Diner of Seventh Street," one of them said.

"Yeah, that's pretty good," the other agreed.

Julie-Ann thanked them and went on her way. Amidst the smell of freshly fallen rain and a new morning, she made the short walk to the car and put the name of the diner into the GPS. It came right up.

The diner was less than a ten-minute ride. Julie-Ann nestled into a booth and looked over the voluminous menu. Then, after ordering an egg white omelet with hash browns, she sat back and looked around the diner. It was almost full. Inconspicuously she took note of the other tables and booths. She wondered who they all were, what they all did, what stories they had to tell?

By the time Julie-Ann walked out of the diner it was 11:40 a.m. She figured she would visit The Christian Center. In the car, she put the address into the GPS; it was just over four miles away.

In a drab part of town, on a narrow, but main road, Julie-Ann approached her destination. There happened to be a parking lot right across the street, so she parked there. As she exited the car, Julie-Ann felt nervous. What was she doing there? Was she just going to go in and look around? After a deep breath, she slowly walked across the street.

She looked up at the weathered, three-story brick building. A large, wooden cross hung above the front, glass door. As she stood there, the door swung open and a thin elderly man wearing jeans and a sweater walked out. He glanced at Julie-Ann before walking down the block. It was at least eighty degrees and she thought it odd that he was wearing a sweater. She quickly re-focused her attention the entranceway. *Well you can't just stand here forever,* she told herself. *You came here for some reason.*

Julie-Ann apprehensively stepped inside. She was immediately surprised by how clean and well kept it looked. There were several people in the wide reception area, three of which were locked in conversation. A third person, a black, slender middle-aged woman, immediately walked over to her.

"Can I help you?" She asked in a pleasant voice.

Julie-Ann froze.

The three men looked over.

Julie-Ann felt as though a spotlight was on her. "Hi, yes, this is the homeless shelter, right?" She asked in a diminutive voice.

"Yes it is. Can I help you with something? Are you looking for someone?" The woman could sense Julie-Ann's nervousness. She stepped closer. "Do you need help?" She practically whispered.

"Oh…oh no. I'm…I'm sorry. I was just wondering, well, how I can help out…if I can maybe make a donation or something."

The woman smiled. "Well that's very kind of you. Step over here," she said, leading Julie-Ann to a small counter. "My name is Kendra," she continued while extending her hand.

"Nice to meet you. I'm Julie-Ann," she replied while shaking her hand.

Kendra went into an open doorway and behind the counter. "We certainly appreciate any donations. And just to let you know, of course, it's tax deductible. They just tell me to make sure I say that."

Julie-Ann went into her purse and retrieved her checkbook. "How many people do you house here?"

"Well we have twenty rooms here and some rooms have two people in them."

"All the rooms are full now?"

Kendra sighed and nodded. "Yes. Times are particularly tough now. Sadly, sometimes we have to turn people away. But we also have a food pantry, to help those who may have a place to live, but simply can't afford to eat."

Julie-Ann thought about it for a second—literally not having enough money to eat. It was surely something that she never had to contemplate in her lifetime. She opened up her checkbook. "Whom do I make it out to?"

"The Christian Center. And any amount makes a difference. We really appreciate your help. It's very kind of you."

"It's my pleasure," Julie-Ann replied as she wrote the check. "You know I saw this piece on Dateline the other night, specifically about veterans in Anderson—how a lot of them are not able to find employment and how some of them have actually been left homeless." Julie-Ann handed her the check.

"Oh yes, you saw that?" Kendra said as she took the check. She then looked at it and gasped. "This is for five-thousand dollars!" She practically shouted in disbelief.

Just then, one of the men who had been locked in conversation in the foyer came over. Looking to be in his mid fifties, he was about 6'2", slender, but muscular, with a cut chin and gray, crew cut hair. He was wearing blue jeans and a tucked-in polo shirt. Julie-Ann immediately thought that he looked too well manicured and in too good of shape to be homeless.

"Kendra," he said in a friendly, yet confident voice, "you sure you want to be announcing that to the world?"

Kendra put down the check. "Oh yeah. I was just taken by surprise." She turned her attention back to Julie-Ann. "Are you sure you meant to write five thousand?" She asked in a lowered voice.

Julie-Ann smiled. "Yes. Really, it's no big deal."

The man extended his hand to Julie-Ann, showing off his thick, defined forearms. "My name is Rory McAlister."

"Julie-Ann," she said while shaking his large hand. "But most people just call me Jules." His grip was firm and tight.

"I'm sorry, but I couldn't help but overhearing you ask about homeless veterans."

"Yes."

"Rory here volunteers at the shelter," added Kendra. "He's always here helping out and bringing food. He's been a godsend."

Julie-Ann explained to Rory that she had seen a segment about struggling veterans and how one of the interviewees was from Anderson. She went on to say that she was moved by the piece and just wanted to help in any way she could.

"Well that's very generous of you," Rory said, looking straight into Julie-Ann's eyes. "Lord knows the world can use more people like you." He then paused. "It was nice to see that someone finally talked about the hardships that our military men and women face when they come home from Iraq and Afghanistan. They go over there, give everything and then when they get home, no one wants to give them a job. And the mainstream media, they don't care."

Julie-Ann could see Rory was getting worked up.

One of the men Rory had been talking to came over. "Some guys are doing three, four, even five tours over there. Then when they come home and look for a job, employers want specific experience.

It's like, well 'sorry, for the last four years I was overseas protecting the country.' Employers should understand that even though these men and women may not have specific experience, because of their military background they're easily trainable. And they have courage, commitment, loyalty, ingenuity."

"And some employers are—well let's come out and say it— they're scared to hire someone that's seen combat, because they hear all about PTSD and are afraid that they're going to freak out." Rory stopped. "I'm sorry," he said with a smile. "I didn't mean to go off on a tangent. You're trying to help and here we are bombarding you."

"Oh no, that's okay," replied Julie-Ann. "How do you know so much about the military?"

Kendra and the other man looked at Rory.

"I come from a military family. My father fought in World War II. I joined the Marines, along with my brother, and served in Vietnam. My three kids are all in the service…well, I'm mean were. My son…" Rory choked up and struggled for words.

The other man put his hand on Rory's arm. "Rory's son, Danny, was killed in Iraq last year."

Julie-Ann gasped. "Oh, I'm so sorry. I…I don't…"

Rory fought to regain his composure. "It's okay. I mean, of course I think about it everyday and it's something you never get over. But I have another son and a daughter to think about. And two wonderful grandchildren." Rory took a deep breath. "Would you like me to show you around the shelter. I mean, if you have the time."

"Yes. Please. I would actually like that."

Rory led Julie-Ann out back to a large, fenced-in grass area with trees and picnic tables. There were several people congregated at two different tables. As Rory walked by each group, everyone said hello to him. At the second table, where two men were playing chess, one of them inquired about Julie-Ann. Rory introduced her and said that she had made a donation and he was taking her on a tour of the center. Both men thanked her for the donation.

Walking on, Rory told Julie-Ann the men at the tables were temporary residents, meaning they were homeless. "That's one of the things that's good about this shelter," he said in a peaceful, but straightforward voice. "They can come out to the courtyard and play board games, or just get some fresh air. They don't have to be cooped-up inside or walking the streets."

"It's a nice area," replied Julie-Ann. "Big."

"Yes, well the shelter also uses it to hold different fundraisers." Rory paused and stopped in his tracks. "That's how I originally became involved with the Christian Center. It was a few weeks after Danny had died. I heard that there was a fundraiser at the Christian Center to help homeless and hungry veterans. I was still very bitter over Danny's death, but I figured I could at least help others serving in the military—and I knew that's what Danny would've wanted me to do. So I went. I met a lot of great people that day and have been involved with the center ever since. They really do good work here…with the help of people like yourself."

"Oh, it's the least I can do. Again, I'm so sorry about your son."

Rory let out a deep breath. "Thank you. It's something you never get over, but like I said, I have another son and daughter to think about—even though they're grown."

Rory went to explain that his other son, Kevin, who was thirty-two, had served in the Marines, though he had not been deployed in either Iraq or Afghanistan. He currently lived in Chicago with his wife and two children, and worked as a sales rep for a major food distributor. Rory's daughter, Amanda, twenty-four-years-old, was in the Navy, and currently on duty with the USS Stennis, in the Persian Gulf.

"Wow. So you fought in Vietnam and all your children also enlisted in the military?"

Rory nodded. "Yep. And like I said before, my father fought in World War II, same with my uncle."

Julie-Ann turned and looked straight up at Rory. "I have to thank you for your family's service. It's quite a dedication to the country."

Rory smiled. "Thank you. I appreciate that."

Continuing the tour, Rory took Julie-Ann back inside and showed her the center's food pantry. It was a huge room with rows of tall, metal shelving that held various food items. There was also a walk-in refrigerator and freezer.

Rory pointed to the half-full shelves. "It's rough times for sure. A lot of people are out of work and have no money. But people still give what they can. It's a good community."

After the pantry, Rory showed Julie-Ann the small chapel, explaining that religion was a big part of the Christian Center. "Don't get me wrong, they accept people from any faith," he went on to explain. "They're not going to turn you away just because you're Jewish or Mormon. It's not so much about praying a certain way or adhering to a strict code. It's more about hope and redemption and giving yourself to a higher power."

From the chapel, Rory took Julie-Ann upstairs to the living quarters. Envisioning the filthy, derelict homeless shelters she had seen in movies, she was surprised how clean everything looked. Though none of the rooms had their own bathrooms, each floor had at least one communal bathroom with showers.

Rory explained that currently every room was occupied and there were plenty of people milling around upstairs. Rory introduced Julie-Ann to a few of them. They were all cordial and polite, but Julie-Ann could feel a few of them checking her out. It was not until then that she noticed that there were no other women around. As they were walking back downstairs, Julie-Ann asked Rory about not seeing any women. He explained that the shelter only housed men. She then asked him how many of the men were veterans.

Rory stopped at the foot of the stairs. "Too many," he said in a dejected voice. "I would say that a quarter of the men currently here served in Iraq or Afghanistan. It's a big problem."

"I don't get it," Julie-Ann said angrily. "We should be taking care of our men and women in uniform. How can we just abandon them?"

"Don't get me wrong, it's not like when I came home from Vietnam. We were spit on and called baby killers." Rory paused, as he relived a moment in time. "Today most Americans fully support our troops. They're able to separate their opinions of the wars from the brave men and women who fight them. Unfortunately, many people think that once they come home from overseas, it's just back to normal life for them. I think most civilians simply just don't even know that there is a problem with unemployment and homelessness amongst our vets."

"Why do you think that is? I mean I happened to see some small piece on Dateline, but why isn't this all over the news?"

Rory let out a sarcastic chuckle. "Have you seen the news lately? They care more about what that Snooki girl is doing or which celebrity is dating who. And if they're not showing that garbage they'll show a couple of pundits or politicians going after each other, trying to prove which side represents the American people. But they're all full of shit—none of them are looking out for the people. Those in power, all they care about is staying in power, and all the other side cares about is getting in power."

"Well that's ridiculous. We need to make sure our troops are taken care of."

As they reached the front entrance, Rory turned to face Julie-Ann. "It's nice that you care so much about our servicemen and women. Really, I mean it. But like I said, I think most people now really do feel the same way—which is great. It's just getting the word out and convincing employers to hire more veterans. That's the main thing, finding them jobs." He paused. "So I hoped you enjoyed your tour," he said with a smile.

"Oh yes, thank you very much."

"Again, it's really generous of you to donate so much. It will go a long way."

Julie-Ann almost felt guilty. Five thousand dollars was nothing to her; she had spent as much on a purse.

Rory opened the front door to a bright, blue sunny June day. "So, do you have family in town?" He asked as they walked onto the porch.

"No, I'm just passing through."

Rory let out a fleeting laugh. "Passing through Anderson?"

Rory had opened-up to Julie-Ann and had been gracious to her. She wanted to show him the same honest respect and not tell him some made up story about why she was in Anderson. Though she knew it was not his intention to pry, Julie-Ann started to explain her story—from her affluent background, to her tumor, to why she was in Anderson.

Rory listened, letting Julie-Ann talk, interrupting only with an occasional "wow", or "really". As she spoke of her quest to help people, he was moved.

"Well I'm glad they were able to remove the tumor and you're okay," he finally said once she was finished. "And I think it's amazing what you are doing. Really."

"Thank you. But as I said, I'm just trying to do a very small part in giving back. All my life I've been taking and receiving."

"There's nothing wrong with being rich or successful. It's not like you stole from anyone. You have nothing to feel sorry about. But it is great that you want to share with those less fortunate."

Just then, two men walked out of the center and said hello to Rory and Julie-Ann.

"So, where are you staying?" Rory asked.

"The Best Western."

"Well here, take my number. If you need anything don't hesitate to call me."

Julie-Ann put Rory's number into her cell. Before parting, they agreed to see each other again before Julie-Ann left. Rory said he would like to introduce her to his wife, Kathy.

As Julie-Ann walked slowly across the street to her car, she felt wholesome. She was glad she donated to the Christian Center, glad she took a tour and met some of the residents, and of course, glad she met Rory. It was what she set out to do—meeting new people, learning about their stories, and giving back.

Once she arrived at her car, Julie-Ann was brimming with energy. It was only 1:45 p.m. and the last thing she wanted to do was sit in that small hotel room for the rest of the day. So, she decided to just drive around and explore Anderson.

In no particular direction, she drove down the narrow streets. There didn't seem to be a centralized downtown to walk around, or even a main street lined with restaurants and stores. The area was spread-out and didn't seem to have any continuity or energy to it. It was clean, but old, as if she had taken a time machine back to the fifties or sixties. None of the small buildings looked modern. After driving around for about twenty minutes, she felt as though she had seen everything there was to see. Reluctantly, she started heading back towards the hotel.

Knowing there was no restaurant at the Best Western, or in the immediate area, Julie-Ann stopped at a café she noticed along the way. There, she sat by herself and ate a horrible turkey sandwich with stale bread.

Julie-Ann was back at the hotel by 3:00 p.m. She had no idea what to do with the rest of the day. The hotel did not even have a bar where she could sit and have a drink. So, she just went up to her room, lay on the bed, and watched TV.

After about an hour the room phone rang. Not having any idea who it could be, she reached over and picked it up. She was surprised to hear Rory on the other end.

"Hi, Jules, it's Rory. I'm sorry; I hope I'm not imposing or caught you at a bad time. I knew you were staying at the Best Western."

"Oh no, not at all. I don't know why I didn't give you my cell number. What's going on?"

"Well I told my wife about you, about how you donated at the center and your story. Anyway, we both feel that there's no need for you to stay in a hotel. We would like for you to stay with us. You would have your own room and you can come and go as you like."

Julie-Ann was taken aback by the offer. "Oh, Rory"—Julie-Ann had tried to call him Mr. McAlister before, but he insisted on her calling him by his first name—"that's very generous of both of you, really. But I don't want to impose."

"Listen, if you're uncomfortable, that's fine, but it's no imposition, really. We would love to have you. I know the Best Western and that area. There's no need for you to be crammed in a little room for your stay. And you can eat some real food. Kathy's a hell of a cook."

Julie-Ann immediately thought about the horrible sandwich she had for lunch. Then she looked around the tiny, gloomy room. *Besides*, she told herself, *isn't this what you wanted to do—meet people, see how they live?* Julie-Ann accepted Rory's gracious offer.

"Great. Listen, it's already four-o'clock. I don't want you to feel like you have to rush and pack. I don't know what you're doing now. So how about you come by tomorrow—say ten o'clock, if that works. Or if you want you can come tonight."

"Oh no, that's okay. Tomorrow morning would be great."

Rory gave her the address and Julie-Ann thanked him and his wife again.

As soon as Julie-Ann hung-up the phone she started having mixed thoughts. *That was so nice of them to let me stay at their house. They don't even know me. But isn't it going to be weird staying at some strangers' house? I'm going to feel totally uncomfortable. But isn't this what I wanted to do—get to know different people that I otherwise would never have met? But what if they're freaks or he's some serial killer? I just met him today. Don't be stupid, Jules. He's a family man and they're just being gracious. But how can I be sure? Wait, I'm getting carried away—everything will be fine.*

Julie-Ann eventually turned her attention back to the television. By 6:00 p.m. she was feeling restless and cooped-up. She took out her laptop, checked her emails and Facebook, and surfed the web. After a half hour of that she was back to feeling stir crazy. She knew her hotel didn't have a bar, but called the front desk to see if any of the adjacent hotels had one. At least she could go and have a drink or two and waste some time. The receptionist said that Hampton Inn across the road had a bar. So Julie-Ann put on some long pants, a different shirt and headed out.

As she walked, she felt weird, going to some bar by herself, but she couldn't spend the rest of the night just sitting in that room, with the walls closing in on her. She was not in the middle of town, where she could just go walking around.

From the outside, The Hampton Inn looked basically like the hotel she was staying at. With some hesitation, she walked inside and was immediately greeted by a woman behind the front desk.

"Hi, checking in?"

Through the corner of her eye, she spotted the bar, next to the lobby. "Oh no," she said with a forced smile, "I'm just going to the bar," she said, pointing to the small bar.

The lounge was tiny, just a short bar with five stools crammed together. There was not even a single table. And there was no one inside, besides a middle-aged bartender watching ESPN on the lone, small TV that hung above his head. Julie-Ann thought about just turning around and heading back, but the bartender noticed her.

"How you doing this evening?" He asked with a hoarse voice.

Julie-Ann slowly walked over and took a seat at the bar. "I'm okay. Can I have a Grey Goose and Cranberry please?"

"Sorry, we don't have Grey Goose. We do have Absolute."

"Okay, that's fine."

The bartender made Julie-Ann her drink and gave it to her. Then, just as she started sipping it, a man came into the bar and sat down next to her. Slender, with thick, slicked back black hair and a five o'clock shadow, he looked to be in his late twenties or early thirties. He was wearing cowboy boots, faded blue jeans and a black, button down short sleeve shirt. He ordered a Captain and coke with a boisterous voice. He then turned to Julie-Ann.

"How you doing tonight?"

Julie-Ann could smell alcohol already on his breath and he instantly gave off a creepy vibe. "I'm okay," she answered in a sheepish voice.

"My name's Carl," he said, extending his hand.

Julie-Ann felt as though she had to shake his hand. "I'm Julie-Ann."

"Julie-Ann," he said in a fading voice. "That's a pretty name."

"Oh, thank you."

"So, you staying at the hotel?"

"Ah, yes," she lied. "I'm here with my boyfriend."

The stranger smiled. "Now you wouldn't just be saying that, would you?"

Now Julie-Ann started feeling uncomfortable. She just wanted to finish her drink and get out of there. "No, I'm not just saying that," she said before taking a big gulp. "He just went to pick up his friend."

"All right."

Julie-Ann polished off her drink in another big gulp. She then left a few dollars on the bar for a tip. "Well it was nice meeting you," she said as she stood up.

The man loosely grabbed her wrist. "Where you going? At least let me buy you a drink. I promise, I won't get fresh."

Julie-Ann yanked her hand away as her heart began to race. She could see the bartender now looking over. "Sorry, I really have to go."

As she walked away, her thoughts started to run wild. *Wait, I just told him that I was staying at the hotel; what's going to happen when I walk out the front door? Who cares what I told him! But what if he follows me? Where else are you going to go? Just get out of here!*

Julie-Ann scurried out the front door, into a darkening parking lot. After a few feet, she looked behind her to see if he was following. He was not. As she hurried through the lot, she began to feel like someone was watching her. *You're just being paranoid,* she told herself as she darted across the street. *What if he's watching me go into my hotel? Then he'll know where I'm staying. What am I talking about—what am I going to do, just walk around?*

Her heart still racing, Julie-Ann went into the Best Western. As she did, she glanced behind her. Then, once inside, she gave a more thorough look through the glass at the parking lot and across the street. She saw no one.

As soon as Julie-Ann entered her room, she locked the door, secured the swing latch, and looked through the peephole. She then tried to calm down and turned on the TV to take her mind off of fear. Being alone in that small hotel room, in the middle of nowhere, didn't help. Then, all of a sudden, she remembered the rosary that Rita had given her. She fished it out of her purse and held onto it, praying that she would be safe for the night.

After about twenty minutes, Julie-Ann's nerves finally started to ease. She was more grateful than ever about Rory and his wife offering her to stay at their house.

After watching some television, Julie-Ann looked at the clock and saw that it was 8:00 p.m. She suddenly realized that she had not had any dinner. The hotel had no restaurant or room service and she was not about to go outside again, especially now that it was dark. She remembered seeing a snack vending machine down the hall. She told herself that it would have to do. Her dinner was a small bag of potato chips, Kit-Kats, and a coke.

Knowing that she wasn't going anywhere else that night, Julie-Ann got ready for bed. Wearing pajama shorts and a t-shirt, she went under the covers and watched TV. She had left all the lights on in the room. Julie-Ann was flipping through the channels when she hit the 10:00 p.m. news, just coming on. She decided to see what was happening in the world. The lead story was about Kim Kardashian breaking up with her boyfriend. Julie-Ann thought about what Rory had said earlier in the day about the media. Disgruntled, she changed the channel. Then the irony hit her—two months ago she would have been enthralled by a story about Kim Kardashian.

Chapter 16

The next morning, as Julie-Ann was getting ready, Rory called. He told her not to worry about eating, because Kathy was cooking breakfast. Julie-Ann didn't want to be an imposition, but was grateful, especially because of her junk food dinner and she was starving.

Julie-Ann started loading her bags into the car and checked out of the hotel. They said they would have to charge for the rest of her stay, because it was nonrefundable, but obviously, she didn't care.

After putting Rory's address into the GPS, Julie-Ann was on her way. It was only a twelve-minute drive. As she turned on his block she noticed that it was a nice community. Everyone's yard was manicured and the houses were larger than she had imagined. She pulled up to Rory's house. It was brick, two stories, with wide, tall bay windows. From the outside it looked well kept.

As she exited the car, a little bit of nervousness returned. She was contemplating whether or not she should leave her bags in the car for the time being when out came Rory.

"Hey Jules," he said with a booming, but welcoming voice as he came down his paved walkway towards her. "Did you find it all right?"

"Oh yes. Well I mean, I just put the directions in the GPS. It's hard for even me to screw that up."

Rory, who was now right by her, laughed. "Yeah, I know what you mean. Well here, let me help you with your bags."

"Oh, thank you."

With that, Rory carried Julie-Ann's two large suitcases and led her to the house. But before they could get to the open front door, out pranced a full-grown chocolate Labrador retriever. With tail wagging, he went right up to Julie-Ann and sniffed at her leg.

"Oh, this is Mickey. I'm sorry; I guess I should've mentioned him before. I hope you don't have a problem with dogs. He's real well behaved though. He just wants to say hi."

"Oh, no, I love dogs," Julie-Ann blithely replied, as she knelt down with a bag over her shoulder and petted the happy lab on the head.

As soon as they reached the front doorway, Julie-Ann was immediately hit by the embracing aroma of sautéing onions and peppers. Then, from an adjacent room, came a slender woman with thick, short light blonde hair.

"This is my wife, Kathy."

With a bright smile, Kathy extended her hand. "So nice to meet you Jules. We're glad you came. Welcome."

Julie-Ann shook her hand. "Oh, thank you so much for having me. It's really so generous of you."

Kathy looked like she might be a few years younger than Rory, and appeared in good shape. It was obvious that she took care of herself.

"Rory, why don't you show Jules to her room." She then turned her attention back to Julie-Ann. "I'm just finishing up breakfast. How do you like your eggs?"

"Oh, it doesn't matter."

"Oh, don't be shy now. I can make you an omelet, sunny side up, scrambled..."

"I'll just have whatever you two are having. Really."

"Well come on. I'll show you your room and then after breakfast we'll take you on a full tour of the house." Rory then led Julie-Ann up a wooden staircase, facing the front door.

"You have a very nice house."

"Oh, thank you."

Upstairs, there was a polished, hardwood floor hallway with Mojave-colored walls. Julie-Ann assumed the rooms on either side were the bedrooms. Rory walked into the last one on the left.

"Well here you are."

It was a modest-size room, but had a tall, queen bed, flat panel television set, chest of drawers, and a closet. And everything looked immaculate, not even the hint of dust on any surfaces.

As they walked back down, Rory pointed out the bathroom, which was two doors down. He also explained that he and Kathy had their own bathroom, so she didn't have to worry about inconveniencing them.

As soon as they hit the base of the stairs, Kathy announced that breakfast was ready. Julie-Ann walked into the kitchen to see Kathy laying out a complete spread—omelets, homemade hash browns, sausage, biscuits, and orange juice.

"Wow, I mean, I would've been good with just eggs. This is something. And it smells amazing."

"Thank you," Kathy replied as she put the finishing touches on the table and then sat down.

Julie-Ann thanked Rory and Kathy again for their hospitality. As they dug into their food, Kathy turned to Julie-Ann. "So Rory told me about your story. First, I just want to say thank the Lord that you're okay now. My sister just had a double mastectomy last year."

"Oh, I'm so sorry." Julie-Ann didn't know what else to say.

"Well thank you. She's doing fine now. But this cancer—it's such a horrible thing. I don't think anyone doesn't know at least one person that has had some kind of cancer."

Julie-Ann finished taking a drink of juice. "Yes. I consider myself very lucky. My tumor wasn't actually cancerous and they were able to remove it."

"Thank God," Kathy replied. "And I think it's a wonderful thing that you're doing, trying to help people. God bless you."

Julie-Ann felt somewhat embarrassed, almost not worthy of Kathy's accolade. "Well thank you. I mean to be honest with you; sadly, it's something that I had really not given much thought to until recently. But I guess going through certain things, it makes you think, it gives you a different perspective on life." Julie-Ann paused. "And really, I didn't actually start off on this journey with the goal of trying to help people. At first, I really just wanted to get out of my element, to travel across the country and meet different people, see how they lived, learn their stories."

Kathy smiled. "Well I think that's wonderful."

"Well speaking of meeting different people—I know you were very interested in our veterans—I sometimes volunteer at the veterans hospital in Indianapolis. I was thinking, if you're interested, we can go there today and I can introduce you to some very special people."

Julie-Ann nodded. "Yes, I would love that."

As they continued breakfast, Julie-Ann asked Rory and Kathy about their life. Though at first, she was reluctant to mention it, she felt the need to give her condolences to Kathy for her son Danny. She also thanked her for her family's military service.

Julie-Ann learned that Rory had been a deputy sheriff until 2002, when he retired. Kathy sold jewelry that she made over the Internet and at flea markets. Kathy also volunteered sometimes at the Christian Center and headed several fundraisers. Julie-Ann listened intently as they told their stories, some serious, some funny. But most of all, she was impressed by their community service and patriotism.

After breakfast, Julie-Ann tried her hardest to help Kathy clean up, but Kathy would not let her, saying that she was a guest. Instead, she went with Rory to Indianapolis to visit the veterans' hospital.

It was an hour and a half drive from Anderson to Indianapolis.

During the ride, Julie-Ann asked Rory about his experience in Vietnam. He shared that when he had first returned from combat, he did not talk about it to anyone who wasn't there, but with the separation of years, he now had no problem discussing it. He did, however, withhold the gory details.

In return, Rory asked Julie-Ann more about her background. She had already told him that she came from a wealthy family, but for the first time she divulged that her father was the CEO of a large investment firm—though she did not specify which one.

Julie-Ann did not know what to expect at the veteran's hospital. As they walked-in, a nurse and a receptionist greeted Rory. Julie-Ann was beginning to think that he knew everyone in the state of Indiana. He introduced Julie-Ann to the receptionist as a friend of the family and said that he wanted her to meet "some of the guys". With that, they took an elevator up to the second floor. Rory explained that they were going to the recreation room, where patients were able to congregate.

Once they walked into the open, noisy room, they were immediately met by a young man in a wheelchair. "Hey, Rory, what's going on? You bring any more of Kathy's brownies?"

"No, she can't make them fast enough for you guys."

Julie-Ann looked at the young man, who couldn't have been a day over twenty-five. He was missing both his legs, right below the kneecaps.

"Oh, Rich, this is Jules. She's a friend of the family."

With a wide smile, he extended his hand. "Please to meet you."

"Nice to meet you, too."

"Hey Rory," rang out a voice from across the room.

"Come on," Rory said, "I'll introduce you to some more of the guys."

As they walked across the room, Rich wheeled beside them. "John's won five hands in a row," he said. "Frank's lost thirty bucks."

They walked over to a round table, where three men were playing cards, the oldest of whom was maybe in his mid thirties. Julie-Ann noticed that one of them was missing an arm, which had been replaced by prosthesis. Another was in a wheelchair, though he appeared to have both his legs and had an eye patch and a bandage wrapped around his head. The third man didn't seem to have any obvious disabilities.

"Hey Rory," one of them said, "You believe this guy has won five straight hands. He better give me a chance to win my money back before they wheel him off to therapy."

"Hey, who is your beautiful friend?" Another asked.

"Guys, this is Jules. She's a friend of the family and is staying with us for a while." He bent over the table and pointed his finger at them. "Don't any of you get any ideas," he said in a half-joking manner.

Julie-Ann said hello and they all introduced themselves, but then Rory left them alone to their card game. He, Julie-Ann, and Rich went over to a nearby empty table.

"So Rich, how's physical therapy going?" Rory asked as he sat down.

Rich nodded. "Okay. You know, it takes time, but I won't let that discourage me." He turned to Julie-Ann. "I don't stay here. I just come in everyday for therapy. They're fitting me for prosthetic legs. It's some new design where the feet are actually these metal blades."

Julie-Ann was amazed how upbeat he sounded. She couldn't even fathom losing both her legs. She felt horrible for him. "I'm so sorry." She just opened her mouth and the words came out.

"Don't be," he replied with a smile. "I was one of the lucky ones. Our Humvee hit an IED in Kandahar. Our driver was killed instantly." His tone suddenly changed. "Then when we got out to get into another vehicle, our convoy came under fire. We wound up losing three men that day."

"I...I'm...I..." Julie-Ann was at a loss for words.

"Don't get me wrong, when I learned that I lost both my legs I was devastated. But then I thought about the guys that didn't make it. God had to have saved my life for some reason. It wasn't just to sit around and feel sorry for myself." Rich paused. "I don't care how long it takes—my goal is to run a marathon."

Just then a male orderly came over. "Okay Rich, you ready for your therapy?"

"Well it was a pleasure meeting you Jules."

"It was an honor meeting you," she replied with a smile.

After saying goodbye to Rory, the orderly went to push Rich away, but he would have none of it. "I can wheel myself."

After he was gone, Julie-Ann leaned across the table towards Rory. "I can't believe how upbeat he is. How strong."

Rory smiled. "Yeah, Rich is a real inspiration. It's amazing how strong-willed some of these young men are."

The man with one arm, who had been playing cards, came over to the table. "Mind if I take a seat?"

Rory motioned him to sit down, which he did. It was at that time that Julie-Ann noticed he also had a hearing aid and scar on the left side of his head.

"I'm not playing cards with John again," he said while shaking his head. "I don't know how, but he had to have cheated."

Rory chuckled. "Come on, Frank, you know he didn't cheat."

"I know," Frank said in a depleted voice. "But man, he was on a tear." Frank then turned his attention to Julie-Ann. "So, Jules, where are you from?"

"New York. I'm just staying in town for a few days."

Frank turned to Rory. "She's in town for a few days and you take her here?" He said with a fleeting laugh. "You should be downtown or at the bar. This is no place to hang out."

"Oh, no, I wanted to come. It's an honor to meet people like you, who served our country."

Frank's playful demeanor morphed into a more serious face. "Well thank you. It's great to know that people support us."

"Well, I've always had a high regard for our troops. But, I have to be honest with you, I've just been learning about the difficulties many of you face once you get home. Not just with injuries, but how hard it is for so many veterans to find jobs and the financial strain. It's not right."

Frank leaned back in his seat. "Well, I don't want to make it like what Rory and his buddies had to go through when they got back from Vietnam. I mean, the public has been great and really does support us. You see complete strangers at airports greeting our troops when they get off the plane. And even with such rough times, citizens still give to foundations like Wounded Warriors and the Fallen Heroes Fund." Frank took a breath. "Its really big companies that need to make a more concerted effort to hire those that have come back from Iraq and Afghanistan. You have some companies that actually prey on and take advantage of our servicemen and women. Like those bastards at JP Morgan and those other firms that got caught overcharging military families on their mortgages."

Rory knew that Julie-Ann's father was a CEO of an investment firm and didn't want her to feel uncomfortable. "Well, I'm sure they're not all crooks. You can't blame all of Wall Street for what a few firms did."

Frank gave Rory a look, surprised at his words. "They're all a bunch of criminals—you've said that yourself." Frank then turned back to Julie-Ann. "But that Jamie Dimon, and the heads of those other firms that were caught defrauding our servicemen and women, they should be locked up and have the keys thrown away." Frank leaned across the table towards Julie-Ann. "A buddy of mine, while he was on his third tour in Iraq, the bank increased his mortgage rate from five percent to six and a half. Now under the law, no matter what type of mortgage, they're not supposed to raise the rate while the person is deployed overseas. But they did it anyway."

"Didn't the bank correct it and put it back?"

Frank chuckled. "It's been four months now and they're still fighting it. Meanwhile their mortgage payment went up three hundred dollars a month. I know that doesn't sound like a lot, but his wife is barely scraping by working as a waitress and trying to take care of their two young kids. And his story is just one of a thousand. Some people actually lost their house over this. And how is the bank going to make it right for those people—buy them a new house? They're lucky if they get an apology."

"Now Frank, don't get all worked up," Rory said in a calm voice. "It's not Jules' fault."

Frank took a deep breath. "I know. I'm sorry. I didn't mean to go off on a tirade. It just gets me so upset."

"You have every right to be upset," replied Julie-Ann. "Our troops are the last people that anyone should be taking advantage of."

Frank stayed at the table for another ten minutes or so, talking about less heated subjects, like his son just learning how to ride a bicycle and the new dog they picked out from the pound. Before leaving, he told Julie-Ann that it was a pleasure meeting her to which she responded in kind.

As soon as Frank left, Rory apologized for his diatribe about Wall Street. Julie-Ann reiterated that he had every right to be upset and that it was egregious for any firm to take advantage of military families—even if it was by accident.

Just then, one of the other men who had been playing cards came up to their table in a wheelchair. He had legs, but obviously could not walk for some reason. He also had an eye patch on his left eye and a bandage around his head. Rory introduced him as Sergeant Ralph Francisco.

The sergeant, who looked to be in his mid thirties, reached across the table to shake Julie-Ann's hand. "Pleased to me you," he said with slow, impaired speech.

They chatted for a little while. Ralph asked how things were going at the Christian Center. He then asked about the coming Saturday's barbeque. Rory explained to Julie-Ann that they were having a barbeque in the courtyard of the shelter and that if she was still around she would have to come. Ralph praised all the volunteer work Rory and Kathy did to Julie-Ann. For his part, Rory downplayed it.

After the sergeant left, Rory told Julie-Ann about his story. While on his fourth tour in Afghanistan, his unit came under fire. While carrying one of his wounded men to safety, Ralph was shot in the head. Though his helmet absorbed some of the force, the bullet still went through it and lodged in his brain. He still managed to get his wounded man to safety inside a bombed-out house. Badly injured and barely able to see, he rushed back out to rescue yet another man that was lying on the ground. However, before he could get to him, Ralph was shot again, this time in the back. The first bullet wound up costing him his left eye and impairing his speech. The second bullet paralyzed him below the waist.

Julie-Ann's heart went out for Sergeant Francisco. She was also amazed by his heroism; heroism she found difficult to even comprehend.

Rory walked Julie-Ann around more of the hospital. As he did, they bumped into another patient that he knew. They also ran into a doctor, to whom he introduced Julie-Ann.

As they left the VA hospital, Julie-Ann thanked Rory for taking her there. She explained that she wanted to donate some money to the hospital.

Walking towards the front exit, Rory turned to Julie-Ann. "Listen Jules, I don't want you to get the wrong idea. I certainly didn't take you here with the hopes of getting money out of you. Believe me, it didn't even cross my mind. After talking to you yesterday, I just thought that you would want to visit."

"I know that's not why you took me here. But it really moved me, and I really want to donate."

Rory felt bad. On one hand, he always encouraged people to donate, but he was not trying to bilk Julie-Ann just because she was rich. "Listen, it's very admirable that you want to support our vets. And if you really want to give something that's fine. But don't go crazy. You've already given so much to the center." Rory paused as they walked through the automatic door to the outside. "And you can also support our troops by spreading the word and volunteering."

"It's just so amazing. I mean seeing them with missing limbs and unable to walk, hearing their stories. You think they should be so down, so bitter, but most of them are so upbeat." Julie-Ann paused. "It really gives you an appreciation of their bravery and service."

Rory nodded. "It certainly does."

Rory changed the subject by asking Julie-Ann if she wanted to look around downtown Indianapolis. She gladly accepted his offer. Rory suggested it was probably better for them to walk than drive around. Julie-Ann was all for that. It was a sun-drenched June afternoon, warm, but not too hot. They strolled around downtown for about forty minutes, as Rory pointed out different buildings and establishments and talked about the city.

On the drive back to Anderson, Julie-Ann asked more about the men at the veterans' hospital. She then asked Rory's opinion of the Iraq and Afghanistan wars.

"Well as you probably know, we're supposed to be withdrawing our last combat troops from Iraq by the end of this year."

Julie-Ann did not know and she felt embarrassed for not knowing.

"And personally, I think it's time to get out of Afghanistan, too. I mean, I understand why we went in. But we've been there for ten years."

"Wow. I guess we have," Julie-Ann said in a fading voice. "It's hard to believe."

With his eyes on the road, Rory nodded. "Yep. It is hard to believe that this September will be the ten-year anniversary of nine-eleven. Anyway, our brave young men and women have done everything they've been asked to do. It's time to bring them home. Many of these guys and girls have done multiple tours. And for what? Nation building? I don't remember that being the reason we went in there."

"I mean why *are* we still there? To stabilize the country? Do you think we can actually turn Afghanistan into a normal democracy?"

Rory gave a sarcastic chuckle. "If you ask me, whether we leave tomorrow, a year from now, or ten years from now, as soon as we leave the end result will be the same—the country's going to descend into chaos. It's all tribes and sects. They don't want our democracy. And you can't force democracy on someone. Not to mention that you have Iran, the Taliban, Pakistan, all trying to exert their control over the country. And in some ways Iraq is even worse."

"Yeah," Julie-Ann said in a deflated voice, "I don't think they'll ever be peace in the Middle East."

"Unfortunately, you're right about that."

By the time they arrived back at the house it was 4:15 p.m. Kathy greeted them and said she was cooking pot roast and potatoes. Julie-Ann asked if she could help with anything, but Kathy said that everything was already in the oven.

As Rory used the phone, Kathy asked Julie-Ann about their day. Julie-Ann talked enthusiastically about the people she had met and how awe-struck she was at their stories and attitudes. Kathy agreed. She had also met Frank and Ralph.

After talking for a while in the kitchen, Mickey came up to Julie-Ann, wagging his tail, with a tennis ball in his mouth.

"Oh, hi Mickey," Julie-Ann said with a smile as she bent down and petted him on the head.

"He loves that ball," said Kathy. "He wants you to play fetch with him."

"Oh, can I?"

"Of course. Watch this—Mickey, wanna go outside?"

With the ball still in his snout, Mickey started hopping up and down, his tail feverishly gyrating.

Julie-Ann took the lab out to the backyard and played fetch with him. He would retrieve the ball and then bring it back and lay it right by Julie-Ann's feet. She seemed to be having as much fun as the dog. Then, after about five minutes, her cellphone rang. She grabbed it from her front pocket and answered. It was her father.

"Hey sweetie, how are you doing? I haven't heard from you."

"Oh, hi Dad. I'm fine. I was just playing fetch with a dog. You should see him, he's great."

"Dog? Where'd you get a dog? Where are you? Aren't you still in Anderson?"

Julie-Ann thought about it for a second before answering. "Yes. But I'm not at the Best Western anymore. I met this really nice couple and they invited me to stay at their house."

There was a pause on the other end. "Julie-Ann, what are you doing? Who are these people? You're just staying at some strangers' house?"

Julie-Ann told her father about meeting Rory at the Christian Center, about his son that died, about having worked in the Sherriff's office, and his work in the community. She also told him about his wife, Kathy.

"Well they sound like very nice people, but you still have to be careful. And what is this fascination with homeless people? It's good to want to help out, but there's people out there just waiting to take advantage of someone like you."

Julie-Ann disregarded his remarks. "Dad, let me ask you something," she said in a calm tone. "That scandal that your firm was involved with regarding overcharging military members on their mortgages..."

Her father abruptly cut her off. "What about that? Did these people ask you about that? Did you tell these people who you are?" His voice became louder and sharper with each word.

"No one asked me about it," Julie-Ann snapped back. "I want to know for my own reasons. Was it really just a mistake?"

"Of course it was! I thought I already told you that. It was just an oversight."

Julie-Ann shooed away Mickey, who was jumping at her leg, trying to get her to throw the ball. "Well once you realized it happened, did you refund the people back right away? And if it was just a glitch, how come there were several firms involved."

"Julie-Ann I am your father," he barked. "I don't need this from you. I get enough of this from the press. What have these people done to you? Whose side are you on?"

"No one did anything to me. I'm just thinking about all those people who got screwed. These are people who are fighting for our country."

"That's it! Julie-Ann, I want you to come home. These yokels are trying to brainwash you."

Julie-Ann was livid. "I'm not coming home. And no one is trying to brainwash me. And these people aren't yokels! They've dedicated their whole lives to serving our country and helping other people."

"Listen, I've got to go. But I'm serious about you coming home."

Julie-Ann hung up on her father, something she had never before done.

After trying to gain her composure, Julie-Ann went back inside the house.

"Is everything okay?" Kathy asked. She had seen Julie-Ann arguing on the phone and could tell that she was upset.

Julie-Ann forced a smile. "Oh yeah. Just had to deal with something over the phone."

Kathy did not want to pry.

About a half hour later, Julie-Ann was sitting down for dinner with Rory and Kathy. Though not able to completely put the conversation with her father out of her mind, she was no longer agitated. Rory told Kathy that he had let Julie-Ann know about the upcoming barbeque.

"Oh yes, we would love you to go if you're still here," Kathy said with a smile. "I don't know if Rory told you, but what we usually do is have the barbeque over at the center and later, come back to the house with some people and continue the festivities."

Rory told a funny story about the last barbeque they had when they came back to the house. One of their neighbors got so drunk they found him passed out in the bushes. The three of them laughed. Kathy then told another funny story.

After dinner, Julie-Ann insisted on helping Kathy clean up. She also thanked her again for the dinner and said how delicious everything was.

Later that night, Julie-Ann lay in bed, watching television. She was happy not to be at the Best Western. Gone were any reservations about staying at someone's house. Rory and Kathy were so welcoming and down to Earth that they eliminated any awkwardness. Julie-Ann felt more like they were old friends or family than people she had just met. She also felt completely safe.

Chapter 17

The next day Julie-Ann spent hanging out with Kathy. They went shopping and out to lunch. They also stopped by the Christian Center and dropped off a couple cases of canned soup.

While at lunch, Kathy told Julie-Ann that she was trying to start a foundation to help women veterans find housing and employment. She explained that the number of homeless female veterans had more than doubled from 2006 to 2010.

"Most homeless centers aren't set up to house women, especially those who may have young children," Kathy went on. "Some simply don't accept women. Others just aren't safe. The VA Inspector General recently did a review of twenty-six facilities and found that a third of them didn't have adequate safety."

"A third? What do you mean by not safe?"

"Don't get me wrong, some shelters, like the Christian Center are safe places and they really take pride in monitoring what goes on. But other shelters can be pretty scary places, especially for women or children. The VA found numerous registered sex offenders living at the same facility as single mothers with their young kids. Some places didn't provide locks on the bedrooms—or bath-rooms."

Julie-Ann shook her head. "That's terrible. I mean I didn't even know such a problem existed."

Kathy let out a deflating sigh. "Yeah. It all goes back to employment. Did you realize that the jobless rate for females who served in the military since two-thousand-one is twelve-point-four percent?"

Kathy explained that the first thing she wanted to do was bring awareness to the epidemic, like Julie-Ann, most people didn't even realize it existed. She also wanted to put pressure on companies to hire female veterans and for shelters to provide safe housing. But as she put it: "The main thing is to keep them from becoming homeless in the first place."

Kathy was not trying to deliver a sales pitch to Julie-Ann. She was not trying to get her to donate because she knew Julie-Ann was wealthy. Rather, she was just passionate about the cause and Julie-Ann had shown such an interest in the welfare of veterans. Even though it was not her intent to sell the idea to Julie-Ann, she was sold. Julie-Ann thought it was a great cause and wanted to help. Though she did not offer Kathy money right then and there, she wanted to know all the details.

Over the next several days, Julie-Ann spent time with both Rory and Kathy. She volunteered at the shelter and also the VA hospital. She came to know some of the guys better. One of the men she particularly became close with was Sergeant Ralph Francisco. Sometimes, they would sit at a table in the rec room of the hospital and talk for a while.

Julie-Ann told him about her journey, wanting to help people, about her tumor, and that she was from New York. However, she never told him exactly who she was. Though Ralph didn't talk about his experiences in the war, he told Julie-Ann about his family and his background. He also talked about the tribulations many servicemen and women faced when they came back home. Julie-Ann already knew about the unemployment and homeless problems. He also informed her about the mountains of red tape and hurdles wounded servicemen and women had to traverse in order to get their proper benefits. He enlightened her about the Walter Reed scandal.

A few years earlier, an investigation uncovered abhorrent conditions at the Walter Reed Army Medical Center, where wounded troops were quartered in mold-filled, rat-infested rooms. Many areas were unfit for living by anyone, let alone those in need of medical attention. The center was also badly understaffed and gridlocked with bureaucracy. After the situation was brought to light, senior Army officials were fired and others resigned, and eventually Walter Reed was cleaned-up. Julie-Ann thought she remembered hearing something vague about it on the news, but was shocked as Sergeant Francisco told her the details.

Though proud of his service, and saying that he would do it all over again, the paralyzed sergeant was critical of the government's handling of the wars and the troops.

"And now you hear that they're looking to cut six-hundred-billion dollars from the defense budget," he told Julie-Ann during one of their sit downs. "How can you do that during a time of war? These guys—and women—are already stretched to the max, doing three, four tours and having their time in between tours cut short. You know, when people hear defense cuts they think okay, we're going to build less ships and planes. But the first thing that'll happen is they'll close military bases, cut the number of troops."

Julie-Ann listened, agreeing to what seemed like commonsense.

"Cut six-hundred-billion dollars from the military while we have troops fighting overseas," he went on. "This is the same government that gave nearly a trillion dollars to Wall Street—after they destroyed the economy. Now how the hell does that make sense?"

Julie-Ann was seeing things in a new light.

Back at the McAlisters', Julie-Ann helped out around the house. She helped Kathy go grocery shopping and prepare for the upcoming barbeque. Kathy let Julie-Ann do some laundry, which she was grateful for. Julie-Ann also forged a bond with Mickey, taking him out for walks and playing fetch with him.

Knowing that she was traveling across the country by herself, Rory gave Julie-Ann some self-defense courses. He gave her a kubaton, a thin, tubular handheld device that could fit on a key-chain, and taught her how to use it. The kubaton doesn't look menacing, but in the right hands, can be used to apply force to certain pressure points of the body, immediately disabling an attacker.

Rory and Kathy made Julie-Ann feel at home and they truly enjoyed her company. But Julie-Ann didn't want to overstay her welcome. Though Kathy had told her she could stay as long as she wanted, Julie-Ann knew that she could not stay there forever. She started thinking about the next stop on her journey, nothing really stuck out in her mind. She just hoped to receive some kind of sign, maybe see something on the news like she did that led her to Anderson.

During down time, Julie-Ann began using Face book, email, and even opened a Twitter account to help spread the word about the unemployment and homeless problem among veterans. She urged people to donate to the Christian Center and other reputable organizations. She also tried to shed light specifically on the problems female veterans faced, and wrote about the foundation Kathy was trying to establish.

Julie-Ann kept in touch with Michelle, Connie, and Krista, not so much to ask them to donate, but to tell them what she had been up to, the people she had met, and what she had learned. All three emailed her back expressing their encouragement and admiration for what Julie-Ann was trying to do. Michelle sent one email stating that she had just donated $50 to the Christian Center; Krista a similar email, donating $75 to the Fallen Heroes Fund.

Connie let Julie-Ann know that they were in the midst of working out a payment plan with their mortgage holder and said it would have never been possible without Julie-Ann's help.

Julie-Ann was beginning to feel part of a much bigger picture. It filled her with pride and meaning. She smiled every time she received a positive response on Facebook or Twitter, especially from someone saying they were going to donate. She also received a few messages from active and retired military members thanking her for the support and for shedding light on their plight.

She showed several of the messages to Rory and Kathy. Kathy told her husband that she believed that God had sent Julie-Ann to them. Unbeknownst to her, Julie-Ann felt the same way. Of all the places she could have ended up, all the people she could have run into, she wound up meeting Rory at the center. She didn't believe it was just randomness. She was also forever grateful to Rory and Kathy, not just for letting her into their home, but into their lives, and introducing her to equally amazing people. She had learned so much in less than a week—more than she had learned in twenty-five years. After meeting Connie and Frank, Julie-Ann felt that it was her purpose to help people, to give back to those in need. Now she knew it was not only about the money she could give, but also the ability to spread the word and hopefully convince others to help as well.

Julie-Ann had still not talked to her father since their argument. But she had talked to her stepmother. Theresa was a little more understanding of what Julie-Ann was doing, but still tried to make Julie-Ann see her father's point of view, and tried to play the peacemaker.

It was Saturday morning, the day of the barbeque at the Christian Center. Luckily, the forecast was for clear, dry, sunny skies. Rory's friend came to the house to help bring the supplies to the center. By 10:30 a.m. they were setting up outside in the courtyard. Julie-Ann did what she could do to help.

An hour later food was being served; burgers, hotdogs, chicken, corn on the cob, and Kathy's homemade potato salad. Other volunteers brought other types of salads and one person even brought sausage. There was plenty to go around. There were two grills going and a table with serving trays of other foods. The courtyard was bustling. Even some people that were not staying at the center, but were hungry and had no food, stopped by.

The mood was rather light. There was joking and laughter. No one was arguing—possibly in part due to the fact that there was no alcohol allowed. People congregated in groups, standing around the courtyard and at the wooden benches.

At one point, after helping to serve for a while, Julie-Ann found herself sitting at a table with an African-American gentleman who was staying at the center. She had met Lester before, but only briefly. Looking to be in his late fifties or early sixties, he was thin, with gray curly hair, and weathered skin. As he ate his hamburger and corn, he thanked Julie-Ann for volunteering and how grateful he was for the barbeque.

"It's good to know that there's still good people in the world," he said in gentlemanly tone.

Julie-Ann nodded with a smile. "Lester, do you mind if I ask you a question?"

"Sure. What is it?"

"What's your story? I mean, how did you get here? You seem like a well-educated man, very polite and nice mannered." Julie-Ann paused. "I'm sorry. I don't mean to be too personal. I didn't..."

"That's okay," Lester said with a half smile. He then leaned back and let out a deep breath, as if preparing himself to tell his story. "I used to own a florist shop here in Anderson," he said with pride. "It was a great little shop. For a while, it did very well, customers every day. The people knew me, trusted me. I had the same customers for years." Suddenly, Lester's face turned sullen. "Then when the economy collapsed, business fell off a cliff. I mean it was like it went from booming to dead overnight."

"That fast? You weren't able to weather the storm?"

Lester paused before answering. "I had always been responsible with my money and saved some up. I thought it would be enough to live on for the rest of my life. But in two-thousand-nine my wife, Edith, had a stroke."

"I'm so sorry."

Lester nodded. "Yes. She was a great woman. The stroke didn't kill her, but it was bad enough to basically turn her into a vegetable."

Julie-Ann could see that Lester was fighting not to cry.

"Well, I mean she wasn't brain dead, but she had to be taken care of twenty-four hours a day. She had to be hooked up to monitors. Well, if you've ever been in a hospital, you know how much it costs for even one day."

Of course, Julie-Ann had stayed in a hospital for several days and had a major operation. But the truth was she had no idea what any of it cost. She never paid a cent out of her pocket. If anything was owed after insurance, her father must have paid for it.

"By this time I had already closed my shop," Lester went on. "Health insurance was so expensive, but Edith said we had to have insurance. We were both in good health and hardly ever even got sick, so I got what I thought was a sufficient policy. But after she had the stroke, it only covered about sixty percent of the hospital care. The bills quickly piled up. Within a few weeks I owed over a hundred-thousand dollars."

Julie-Ann gasped. "Oh my God."

"Yep. That burned through my life's savings. But as the bills kept coming in, even that wasn't enough. Then, after a nearly a month of being in the hospital, Edith suffered another stroke and died."

"I'm so sorry."

"I used every last cent I had for the funeral. But I still owed about seventy-five thousand in medical bills."

"Your wife didn't have life insurance?"

Lester let out a grunt. "No. Stupid huh? For whatever reason, we just never took out life insurance on either of us. It's something we never even discussed." Lester paused. "Anyway, the creditors came after me for my wife's bills and they were relentless. They didn't even give me time to mourn. I only owed four years on my mortgage, so I tried to take out a second one, to pay everybody off. But the bank wouldn't give me one. I mean I was already behind on my current mortgage. Then someone told me to file for bankruptcy, which I did. That actually got most of the creditors off my back. But it didn't stop the bank from foreclosing on my house."

"Don't tell me they took your house when you only had four years left on your mortgage."

"Yep, they sure did. I had already burned through all my savings. The only thing of value I had to sell was my car, which I sold for six thousand dollars. I used that to get a small apartment and tried to find a job. But no one's hiring young college graduates or someone with experience, let alone a fifty-five-year-old black man who used to sell flowers. Anyway, after the six thousand was gone, I was broke again and out on the streets. And that's how I wound up homeless."

"Didn't you have any family that could help you out?"

"My two brothers died some time ago. Edith didn't really have any family. Our daughter, Tina, died in a car accident when she was just eighteen."

Julie-Ann put her hand over her mouth. "Oh, my God. That's terrible."

Lester nodded. "I do have a son, Tony. But he's…well, he's in prison," Lester said with shame in his eyes. "He was always a good kid, with good grades, but then when he was about seventeen, he started hanging out with the wrong crowd. He wound up joining some stupid gang in Indianapolis. Anyway, he was arrested for armed robbery." Lester shook his head in disgust. "I thought I taught him better than that. But then again, I never stole anything in my life, never touched a drug, busted my ass and made an honest living, and look where I am."

Julie-Ann could feel her heart breaking. It was such a tragic story. Lester had done everything right, everything society told him he was supposed to do, and yet there he was broken, homeless, without a penny to his name. He had lost his daughter, his wife, and for all intents and purposes, his son. It just wasn't fair. It was downright cruel.

Julie-Ann apologized to Lester for asking about his story and having him relive it.

"Don't be sorry. You didn't do it to me. In fact, if it wasn't for people like you, volunteering, and if it wasn't for places like the Christian Center, I'd have it a lot worse off. I mean, here I am eating a hamburger and corn. I have a room with a roof over my head. There's plenty of people around the country that don't even have that."

Lester was trying to be optimistic, but Julie-Ann just kept thinking about his heartbreaking tale. Then, as she looked around the courtyard, she was reminded that this was no ordinary joyful party. It was filled with sorrowful stories, many just as tragic as Lester's. And though some of the people had only themselves to blame, from either drugs or other bad decisions, some were just victims of circumstance, just victims of the times that the country was in.

By 4:00 p.m., the barbeque had wind down at the shelter. A few of the volunteers went back to Rory's house, and a couple of his neighbors also came by. It was still daylight out, and everyone congregated in the backyard. Unlike at the center, there were two coolers of beer, and everyone seemed to have one in their hand. Music was playing on a portable stereo. The atmosphere was festive, and there was a sense that the party would last well into the night.

At one point, Rory found Julie-Ann sitting on a patio bench, drinking a beer. "What are you doing here by yourself?" He asked with a bottle of Budweiser in his hand.

Julie-Ann smiled. "Just thinking."

"Mind if I sit down?"

Julie-Ann patted the spot on the bench next to her. "Please."

Rory sat down. "Is everything okay?"

"I was talking to Lester today at the center. He told me about his story, about his wife dying, and how he lost his business and house."

Rory let out a sigh, like air being let out of a party balloon. "Yeah. It's a sad story. And Lester's a real good guy."

"And it's not just him. There are so many people like him. It's just not fair."

Rory nodded in agreement. "Yeah. If only life was fair, huh. But if you let it get to you, if you let it take over, it'll drive you mad. It'll make you want to crawl in a ball and hide. But you can't let it beat you down Jules. All you can do is try and help, try and play some small part in feeding someone who's hungry, finding shelter for someone who has none, helping someone get back on their feet. And that's exactly what you're doing. Not just with the money you've so graciously given, but with your time and your caring. Especially now, with times so tough. We can't look to the government for all the answers. Hell," Rory laughed, "all they seem to do is make things worse."

"Well, I'm certainly going to continue to do my part."

"It's a noble cause. But you know Jules," he said as he raised his bottle, "life ain't worth living if you can't enjoy it every now and then."

Julie-Ann smiled. "I guess you're right." With that, she clanked her beer with Rory's and then took a swig.

"Now come on and join the party. There's someone I want you to meet."

Rory introduced Julie-Ann to an old partner of his at the sheriff's department. He said that she was a cousin visiting from New York. Rory never told anyone who Julie-Ann really was, that her father was a Wall Street CEO. If she wanted to divulge that, it was her prerogative.

Julie-Ann was able to put away her thoughts of Lester and the sorrows of the world, at least for the time being, and enjoy the party. She mingled and the beer was going down easily. In fact, everyone seemed to be getting a little drunk. Julie-Ann realized it was the perfect opportunity to take some pictures. She took some of Rory and Kathy, then her with each of them, and had someone take a few shots of the three of them together. Julie-Ann also had Rory take a picture of her with Mickey.

As the sun began to set, Rory grilled some more burgers and dogs. Then, one of his visibly intoxicated neighbors, broke out an acoustic guitar and began to play and sing cover songs. When he started playing Neil Young's Heart of Gold, those gathered around drunkenly sang along.

By 9:30 p.m. the crowd started to thin out. A half hour later everyone had gone home. Feeling a good buzz, Julie-Ann helped Kathy and Rory clean up.

"I'm really happy you got to stay for the barbeque," Kathy said as she threw some empty beer bottles into a recyclable container. "I hope you had a good time."

Julie-Ann picked up a bottle and can. "Oh yes. Thank you. I had a great time. I really appreciate you and Rory letting me stay here for so long."

"It hasn't been that long. And like we said, you're welcome to stay here for as long as you like. We love having you."

"Thank you. That's very kind. And you've both been so gracious. But I've already been here for a week. I don't want to overstay my welcome. I think Monday I'll be heading on my way."

Kathy stopped what she was doing and turned to face Julie-Ann. "Jules, please don't think you're overstaying your welcome. If want to continue your journey, that's one thing, but don't feel any pressure. Rory and I mean it when we say you can stay as long as you like."

Julie-Ann smiled. "I know you do."

Just then Rory walked over. Kathy explained that Julie-Ann was planning on leaving.

"Do you know where you're going?" He asked in a slightly slurred voice.

Julie-Ann let out a laugh that faded into the night air. "Not really. I figured that I would just continue my drive, stop in various towns, and see what happens. After all, that was my original plan—to get out there and meet people. I mean I just happened to meet you two."

"Well, we're certainly glad you did. But you also have to be careful, Jules. Some people don't have the best intentions—even if they seem like they do."

"There's a lot of sick people out there," Kathy added.

"And not every homeless shelter is like the Christian Center," Rory continued. "Some shelters are dangerous places. Some cities and towns are dangerous places." Rory paused. "I commend what you are doing. I really do. I'm just saying be careful. And also, don't feel like you have to leave. If you want to take your time, think about where you want to go. You can stay here as long as you like."

"That's what I told her."

Julie-Ann finished helping Rory and Kathy clean up. The conversation turned from her journey to the party. Kathy did a little gossiping, telling stories about different people who had attended.

By the time Julie-Ann went up to her room it was after 11:00 p.m. Tired and feeling the aftereffect of the beers, she languidly took off her wig and what little make-up she had on and got ready for bed. It had been a long day and as soon as Julie-Ann hit the pillow she was out.

Julie-Ann had originally thought about leaving on Monday, but changed it to Tuesday. She wanted to say goodbye to the friends she had made at the center and the VA hospital. There was something else she also wanted to do.

Monday morning, while at the center, Julie-Ann sought out Lester. She wanted some privacy with him, but no females were allowed in the dorm rooms, even staff and volunteers. So instead, they went out to the courtyard and sat at an empty table, where no one else was around.

"Lester, I want to help you. I want to give you some money."

Lester looked down towards the table. He could definitely use any money she was willing to give him, but he was ashamed that he had to rely on the charity of strangers. He had always been such a proud and hardworking man.

"But I don't want to just give you cash," Julie-Ann continued. "You shouldn't just have cash lying around. So I was thinking about opening a bank account in your name. But you'll probably have to come to the bank with me."

Lester looked back up. How much money was she talking about, he wondered?

Julie-Ann could see the puzzled look in Lester's eyes. She leaned across the table, closer to him. "I'm going to write you a check for ten thousand dollars. That should help you find your own apartment. You shouldn't be homeless."

Lester's jaw dropped. "Are you serious?"

Julie-Ann smiled. "Yes, I'm serious."

Lester's eyes started swelling up with tears. "I…I don't know what to say. I mean you don't even know me. I…you…are you some kind of guardian angel?"

Julie-Ann laughed. "No. I'm just someone who has some money and cares. There's no string attached. I've had a very fortunate life and I just want to give a little back."

Tears were now escaping from Lester's eyes. "Can I give you a hug?"

"Of course," she said with a smile.

As Lester hugged her and thanked her, Julie-Ann could feel her own eyes start to tear. It meant so much to her that it meant so much to him.

Julie-Ann took Lester to a local bank and opened a checking account for him. But before she did, she gave another $5,000 to the Christian Center.

After dropping Lester back off at the center, Julie-Ann went back to the house and met up with Rory. The two then drove to the VA hospital in Indianapolis so she could say goodbye to the people she had met there.

Julie-Ann ran into Rich, Frank, and a few of the other vets she had met. She said her goodbyes, but promised to keep in touch through email and/or Facebook. She was hoping to see Sergeant Francisco, but he was not there. However, she had already exchanged contact information with him.

Before leaving, with her credit card, Julie-Ann made a $7,000 donation to the hospital. She did not let the any of the vets know, but

Rory was right there with her and she could not hide it from him. Naturally, the hospital administrator and Rory both thanked her profusely. Rory did not know about the money she had already given Lester, or her second donation to the Christian Center. Julie-Ann was not looking for recognition or praise—she just wanted to help.

After the hospital, Rory took Julie-Ann out for lunch in Indianapolis, before the long drive back to Anderson.

"I still can't believe everything you've done," Rory said in a subdued voice, as they waited for their meal. "The money you gave to the center and the hospital. And also all the volunteering you did. You've been a real Godsend."

Julie-Ann scoffed at the idea. "I'm no Godsend. I'm just glad I could help out in some small way. Besides, meeting you and Kathy and Sergeant Francisco and everyone else, learning what I've learned here, it's worth more than anything money could ever buy."

Rory smiled. He was so touched he didn't know exactly how to respond. "So, you figured out where you're going?"

Just then, the waitress came with their food. Rory and Julie-Ann thanked her.

"Well, I've been watching the news," Julie-Ann said, finally answering Rory's question. "I was hoping to see something like the segment I saw on Anderson, that brought me here. But you're right, either they're talking about some celebrity—who's dating or breaking up with who—or they're arguing about politics."

"I remember when the news actually reported the news," Rory replied as he cut his steak.

"Anyway, then I just started Googling stuff, like homelessness, unemployment. I did find some good articles and information, but nothing that would point me in any direction." Julie-Ann took a sip of her ice-tea. "So I guess to answer your question, I don't have a particular destination. I've just decided to head west, see where it takes me, play it by ear."

"Well I think you should at least figure out where you want to spend the night tomorrow. This way you even book a room. You certainly don't want to be stranded in the middle of nowhere."

Julie-Ann nodded.

"I'll tell you what, when we get back to the house we'll go on Google maps and plot out a course for you—at least for tomorrow."

As they ate lunch, Rory talked about some of the self-defense techniques he had shown Julie-Ann, such as the body's pressure points. He also told her what to stay away from and various red flags. Julie-Ann could not help but be moved by Rory's concern. She couldn't believe that in a week's time this man, whom she had never known existed before had become like a father figure.

When they arrived back at the house Rory took out his laptop and he and Julie-Ann plotted out her course. On Google Maps, he showed her what towns and cities lay to the west and southwest of Anderson, no more than a day's drive away. Julie-Ann saw Nashville on the map. Though it did not fit the bill of a small town she envisioned on her journey, she had always wondered what it was like. Rory put it in the driving directions; it was only five hours away.

"It's a fun town. I've actually been there twice."

"I don't know," Julie-Ann said with hesitation. "I mean I'm not out here to be having fun and partying. I want to meet people and help those in need."

Rory sat back in his seat. "It's up to you Jules. But don't feel guilty about having a good time and listening to some music. I mean you can just stay there for a day or two." Rory paused. "And Nashville isn't Beverly Hills. Just because it may be somewhat of a tourist destination doesn't mean there aren't people there on hard times. Besides, I thought part of your journey was seeing places you've never been to before."

Julie-Ann smiled. "You're right. I mean I've always wondered about Nashville and this is my golden opportunity to go there."

With her destination figured out, Rory went on Expedia and helped Julie-Ann find a hotel.

That night, while in her room, Julie-Ann thought about how much she was going to miss Rory and Kathy—and even Mickey.

She promised herself that she would not only keep in touch, but also see them again. Before going to sleep, she posted an update on her Facebook page.

So I'm leaving Anderson IN tomorrow. I've met some great people here. Though I've only been here a week, I've forged friendships that I will never forget until the day I die. I will particularly miss my unbeliev-ably gracious hosts, Rory and Kathy. If there were more people like them the world would be a much better place. But my journey must continue. I will post an update when I reach my next destination. Hopefully, I will meet some more amazing people and learn new amazing stories. Until next time, goodnight.

Chapter 18

Tuesday morning, June 19. Julie-Ann woke-up early to the smell of bacon, onion, and peppers. Kathy had made a ceremonious last breakfast for Julie-Ann before she hit the road. God, she was going to miss Kathy's home cooking.

Over breakfast Julie-Ann thanked Rory and Kathy once again for all their hospitality, as well as everything they had taught her.

"Kathy, there's something I want to give you," Julie-Ann said as she reached into her cargo shorts' pocket and pulled out a folded check. "I want to help you start your foundation."

"Jules, you've done so much already."

"Please," Julie-Ann said as she reached across the table and handed Kathy the check.

Kathy looked at the check and couldn't believe what she saw. "Jules, this is for fifteen thousand dollars! I can't take this from you. I'm sorry," she said, trying to hand the check back to Julie-Ann.

But Julie-Ann wouldn't take it. "Kathy, it's not like I'm giving you a diamond necklace. This money is so you can start your foundation and help female veterans—help them find housing. I know you're going to turn this money into good. It's going to do so much more for someone than it will ever do for me."

Kathy's eyes began to tear. "I don't know what to say."

"You don't have to say anything."

"God bless you Julie-Ann," Rory added in a long, drawn-out voice.

After breakfast, Julie-Ann went out back and played fetch with Mickey one last time. She was going to miss the happy-go-lucky chocolate lab.

While she was playing with Mickey, Rory came out back with something in his hand. It was a stun gun and a can of mace. He quickly showed Julie-Ann how to use it in case of an emergency. She appreciated the gesture.

Rory helped Julie-Ann load her suitcases into the car. It was then time to say goodbye. Outside, by the front lawn, Julie-Ann gave Rory a tight hug and thanked him once again. He thanked her. Then it was Kathy's turn. Kathy said that she would never be able to repay Julie-Ann for her donation. Julie-Ann explained that she already had. She knelt down and gave Mickey, who had also come out to bid her farewell, a kiss on the top of his snout.

The three promised to stay in close contact and with that, Julie-Ann climbed into the car. It was a warm, June morning and she decided to put the top down. After putting the hotel into the GPS, she gave a final smile and a wave to the McAlisters. As she slowly pulled away, Julie-Ann watched Rory and Kathy standing on the edge of the lawn waving, with Mickey by their side. She felt so grateful for having met them, for having them let her into their home and lives. She also felt a sadness for leaving. For she already missed them. However, it was not just her relationship with the McAlisters that Julie-Ann thought about. As she pulled away, she felt as though she was looking back at a living, breathing portrait of the true American spirit.

As Julie-Ann turned her attention to the road ahead, she could also not help but think of the other people she had met in Anderson, the friendships she had forged, the lessons she had learned.

Though there were stories of hard times and tribulation, she smiled.

It was 325 miles to Nashville and Julie-Ann settled in for the long haul. She turned on the satellite radio and glided along the highway. Still cognizant of her near miss with the truck on the way to Indiana, she remained vigilant.

After two hours, Julie-Ann decided to stop at a rest area for refueling, use the restroom, and to stretch her legs. As she was walking to the building, her phone rang. It was her father. The last time they had talked they argued, but Julie-Ann was ready to put that behind her.

"Hey Daddy."

"Julie-Ann"—he rarely called her by her full name—"have you been posting things on Facebook about the company?"

Julie-Ann was taken completely off guard. "What company? What are you talking about?"

"My company. How Wall Street ripped off veterans and how the government gave billions of dollars to Wall Street firms, but there was no bailout of the American people?"

Julie-Ann could hear the anger in her father's voice. "I…I never ever mentioned anything about Diamond & Russell or you. I was just talking in general terms. Besides, that's my private Facebook page. It's not like I did an interview with a reporter."

"Julie-Ann, you're the daughter of Diamond & Russell's CEO. Nothing you put on the Internet is private. You know that. If this gets out the media would have a field day with it. I can hear it now: James Crown's own daughter think's he's a thief and destroying the American dream."

"That's not what I said." Now Julie-Ann was getting mad.

Her father grunted. "What did these people do to you? I knew they were trying to brainwash you. And I told you to come home!"

"I'm twenty-five-years-old Dad! You can't order me to come home! And no one brainwashed me. And I meant what I said. There are a lot of people suffering out there. A lot of hardworking people, honest people, lost their jobs and their houses. And no one is helping them out."

James let out a frustrated sigh. "First off, there are plenty of government programs to help people in need. Secondly, every-thing you have, the car you're driving now, the good life you've had, to the top healthcare you received in the hospital—it's all be-cause of my job. And despite what anyone might tell you, I work damn hard at my job. And I'm certainly not going to apologize to anyone for it. Besides, the money that you've given these people—and yes, I know about that too—where do you think that came from? They're so fast to demonize people like me and my firm, but they have no problem taking the money that we make."

"Dad...I...it's not like that."

"What is it like? Hold on."

Julie-Ann could hear his assistant telling him something.

"Listen, I've got to go. But remember where you come from, who your family is and what side you're on. I want you to come home. And whatever you do please don't post anything else—anywhere—about the evils of Wall Street."

After hanging up, Julie-Ann's initial reaction was anger at There-sa. Her father was not on Facebook, but Theresa was a "friend" and she figured it had to be her that told him about the posts. Also, Theresa had to be the one to tell him about donating money. Julie-Ann was thankful at least, that Theresa only knew about one of the donations to the Christian Center and the VA hospital, and not about the money she had given to Lester, Kathy, or Connie.

Though her initial feeling was anger, it quickly turned to confu-sion. Her father was right about one thing: the money he made at Diamond & Russell had provided her with not only a good life, but also a lot of fond memories. It did also provide her with the best possible care for her tumor. In addition, though Julie-Ann had worked for a while, she would have never been able to give the money she had to the Christian Center, or the hospital, or Kathy, if her father was not the CEO of Diamond & Russell.

Also, Julie-Ann didn't want to fight with her father or cause him any hardships. They had always been so close. He had always been there for her. Julie-Ann wanted to cry.

Continuing her drive, Julie-Ann was still conflicted. She had no doubt that she had done the right thing in helping those that she had. But at the same time, she didn't want to drive a wedge between her and her father. Ideally, she just wanted him to see her point of view, but she would at least settle for peace. She told herself that going forward she would not post anything negative about his business—directly or indirectly. As far as going home, she was not yet ready.

After four hours, Julie-Ann was sick and tired of driving and just wanted to get to the hotel. Suddenly the landscape changed, from flatlands to rolling hills. And as much as she wanted to be out of the car, she could not help but be in awe of the sprawling, green, mountainous backdrop. It seemed so alive, so vivid.

Julie-Ann reached the Nashville city limits at 4:17 p.m. Fifteen minutes later she arrived at the Hilton. She happily gave the car keys to the valet attendant and her bags to the porter. She didn't want to get into the car again for the next two days.

Julie-Ann checked in and went up to her room. It was much nicer and larger than the Best Western, but nevertheless, she was once again alone. She turned on the television for background noise and took her time unpacking and setting up her things in the bathroom. Afterwards, she realized she was hungry, not having eaten since breakfast. It was a beautiful day out and the hotel was situated right in downtown Nashville, near plenty of restaurants and bars. The long drive had taken all the life out of her, so she just ordered some room service.

As Julie-Ann waited for her food, her cell phone rang. It was Amber, who had returned from Europe several days earlier. Excited to hear from her friend, Julie-Ann picked-up the phone.

"So, are you still in Indiana?" Amber asked.

"No, I'm actually in Nashville. I just got here a little while ago. I'm just staying for three days."

"Nashville," Amber said with enthusiasm. "I love Nashville." She had been to Nashville several times before with her father. "Oh man, I wish I was there with you." There was a slight pause. "Hey, I have a great idea—how about I come out and visit you! It'd be great! Besides, I feel like we haven't seen each other in forever."

Julie-Ann did miss her friend and Rory's words popped in her head about it being okay to let loose and have some fun. Still, she felt a little hesitant, almost guilty, for some reason. "I don't know. I mean that'd be great, but I was only planning on staying here until Friday."

"So, I'll come out tomorrow morning. I think my father is using the plane, but I'm sure I can get a flight. Besides, so what if you stay an extra day or two—it's not like you're on a schedule. Come on Jules, it'll be fun. What are you going to do in Nashville by yourself anyway?"

"Okay. Yeah sure. I mean if you're down for it. I know you just got back from Europe."

"So, who cares? Excellent! We're gonna have a great time—I promise you. My father has plenty of connections in Nashville."

"Listen Amber, don't get crazy with any planning. I mean I just want it to be me and you."

"Okay, okay. Don't worry. This is so exciting. I'm gonna look for flights right now."

Twenty minutes later, Amber called back with her flight information. She would arrive in Nashville at 12:30 the next afternoon. Amber said she would get a limo to the hotel, but Julie-Ann insisted on picking her up at the airport.

As soon as Julie-Ann hung up the phone, her room service arrived. She asked the server to set it up on the table in the living room in front of the TV. She tried to find something good to watch. However, as she ate, she mostly thought about Amber coming out. Now that it was written in stone, the more she thought about it, the more excited she became. It would be good to see her best friend, and it would only be for a couple of days. Then she could get on with the rest of her journey—wherever that was to lead and for however long it would take to complete.

After eating, Julie-Ann's cell phone rang again. This time it was Kathy. She wanted to make sure that Julie-Ann had made it to

Nashville without any trouble. Julie-Ann explained that everything went smoothly and told Kathy about Amber coming out.

"That's great Jules. It's very noble to volunteer and help people, but you can't be serious all the time. Especially, when you're young. Go out and have a good time. Enjoy yourself."

"I know. That's exactly what your husband told me."

The two talked for a little while longer. Kathy said that Mickey had been going all around the house looking for her. Before hanging up, Kathy told her again to have a good time and that they would talk again soon.

As soon as Julie-Ann hung up, she noticed on her phone that she had new unread emails, so she went to see what they were. One was from Michelle. She was just checking in and seeing where Julie-Ann was on her journey. Instead of typing her reply on the phone, Julie-Ann took out her laptop to compose an email. Having not communicated with Michelle in several days, she told her about the barbeque and Lester. She also wrote about what a learning experience Anderson was and how she will always remember the people she met there.

After checking her other emails, Julie-Ann went on her Facebook page. Despite what her father might have thought, Julie-Ann was getting a lot of positive feedback and encouragement about her posts, not only from her long time friends, but also new followers. Of course, it made her feel good and gave her even more reason to continue her quest of helping people and talking about issues such as homelessness and the problems many troops faced once they returned home. Julie-Ann replied to several comments. Then she posted that she was now in Nashville for a few days. She left out the part that her friend was coming to visit.

After Facebook, Julie-Ann went on Twitter. She was new to the Twitter world and certainly did not tweet as much as many of its members. Starting off in Anderson, she would just tweet things such as:

Met a war hero today. Amazing man.

Volunteering at the Christian Center. They need your dona-tions if you can help.

Beautiful day in Anderson today. Going into Indianapolis to visit the VA hospital.

Her profile read: Julie-Ann Crown. Twenty-five-years-old. On a journey across America to find the people and stories who are the real heart of this country.

Though she only had the account for six days and did not tweet that much, Julie-Ann had somehow already amassed over forty followers. She realized she had a direct message from a new fol-lower named Lisa Hendricks. Curious, she clicked to see what it was. *My name is Lisa and I am fifteen-years-old. My father, a Marine, was killed seven months ago in Afghanistan. I think it is great that you are trying to help our troops and veterans. God bless you!*

Julie-Ann sent back the following message: *Lisa, I am so sorry about your father. I can't begin to imagine how difficult it must be. I am just trying to play some small role in helping those brave men, like your father, and women, who protect our freedom.*

Twitter limits the length of a message, keeping it short. But as soon as Julie-Ann sent it she wished she had wrote more. And she could not help but wonder about this girl. Who was she? Where was she from? What was her full story? Then it dawned on Julie-Ann; she went to Lisa's profile page. It read: *I'm a teenager living with Leukemia. But making the most out of life and trying to help oth-er people less fortunate than me.*

Julie-Ann was beside herself. This poor girl—only fifteen, suffer-ing from Leukemia, and her father had just died. Yet she wanted to help people less fortunate than herself. And here Julie-Ann was patting herself on the back for donating some money and volun-teering for a few days. She felt embarrassed.

Now, Julie-Ann wanted to know even more about Lisa Hen-dricks. She read some of her tweets. They ranged from the mun-dane to the heartbreaking, to the benevolent.

Me and mom went shopping today, got new shoes.

On my way to chemotherapy. I hate feeling weak, but I have to suck it up. I hate feeling sorry for myself even more.

Was thinking of my dad today. I miss him so much.

Then there was another post with a link attached. Danny has a rare bone disorder and his father lost his health insurance. We must help him out!

Julie-Ann clicked on the link. It was a news article about a six-year-old boy who had recently been diagnosed with something called hypophosphatasia. It went on to say how his mother was a stay at home mom and his father had lost his job six months earlier, and with it, his health insurance. At the end of the article was a link to a website that his mother had created for donations to help them pay their medical bills. Julie-Ann went on the website and used her credit card to donate $5,000.

Chapter 19

The next day, Julie-Ann, thankful for her GPS, went to the airport to pick-up Amber. She arrived at the terminal twenty minutes before Amber's flight was supposed to arrive, but after looking at the monitor, found out that it was a half hour late. She slowly passed the time going on Facebook and Twitter. She was hoping that Lisa had some new tweets, but there were none.

The minutes passed slowly, but alas the monitor showed that the flight had landed and was at the gate. Julie-Ann knew that Amber would be flying first class and thus would be one of the first ones off the plane. She eagerly went to the spot where arriving passengers entered the baggage claim.

As soon as Julie-Ann saw Amber walking towards her, she could not help but smile. Amber waved vigorously in the air. The two then hugged and jumped like two teenage girls.

"Oh Jules, it so great to see you!"

Julie-Ann let go off her embrace. "It's great to see you, too! I can't believe you're really here!"

"I know! We're gonna have a blast!"

The best friends finally started walking towards the baggage carousels. "So, how was your flight?"

"I hate flying commercial, especially American Airlines. Their first class sucks. Then we were delayed for like forty-five minutes. On top of it, we hit turbulence most of the way here. I'll tell ya' I need a drink."

"Well, I'm glad you're here."

Amber smiled. "I know. Me too!"

The two walked over to Amber's flight's baggage claim. "How many bags did you check in?"

"Just two," Amber replied. A carry-on was already slung around her shoulder.

"Two? I thought you were only staying for two nights?"

"You know me. I like to be prepared." Amber pulled out her phone and started texting. "I told my father I would let him know when I got here." She finished her text and put the phone back in her purse. "Oh, I didn't know what kind of room you had, so I reserved the best suite they had available just in case."

"You didn't have to do that. You could've stayed with me. I thought we would room together."

"Of course we're gonna stay together. I just didn't know what kind of room you had. I got the suite so you can just move your stuff in there. Or whatever."

Amazingly, Amber's bags were one of the first ones off. As they walked to the car, Amber said she was starving. Julie-Ann said she was as well and asked if Amber wanted to eat first, before checking into the hotel. But after a quick discussion, they decided to go to the hotel first.

On the car ride to the Hilton, Amber told Julie-Ann all about France and Belgium. She talked about the exclusive clubs and restaurants that she and Tyler went to and all the shopping she did. The more she talked, the more excited she became. She told Julie-Ann that they should go to Belgium together. Julie-Ann reminded her that she had been there once with her father and Theresa.

"Oh yeah, that's right," Amber remembered, before going on about the luxuries of her trip.

After checking in at the front desk, Julie-Ann followed Amber up to her room. It was a two-bedroom suite with a full living room, kitchen, and two bathrooms, one of which had a whirlpool.

"Hey, I got an idea," Amber said as she threw her purse on the couch. "Why don't we just order some room service for now. That way I can unpack, you can bring up whatever you want to bring from your room, and we can have a few drinks and unwind."

"All right. Sounds good to me."

Amber retrieved the room service menu from atop a table and handed it to Julie-Ann. "Here, see what you want."

Julie-Ann scanned through the menu and told Amber she would have a grilled chicken wrap and a diet Coke.

Amber looked over the menu for a minute and then called room service. "Yes, I'd like to have a grilled chicken wrap, a diet coke, the Caesar's salad with chicken, two shrimp cocktails, and an ice-tea. And I'd also like to order up a six-pack of Heineken, a bottle of Grey Goose—I guess you can also bring some more diet coke—and a bottle of Dom Perignon. What? Yes. Okay, I'll hold." While holding, Amber gave Julie-Ann a look and shook her head. "Yes. That's fine," Amber said. She then held her hand over hand over the receiver and looked at Julie-Ann. "You believe this? Like I care how much it costs." She turned her attention back to the receptionist. "Okay. About how long? All right, thanks." Amber hung up the phone. "They said it'll be about a half hour."

While they waited for the food and booze, Amber started unpacking. Julie-Ann went down to her room and brought back some of her clothes and personal items, as she planned on staying with Amber.

When the room service arrived, before digging into their food, Amber popped the bottle of Dom. "Here's to the two of us being together again," she said as the cork went flying into the air and foam spewed out the top of the bottle. She then poured two glasses.

"Well I'm glad you came. It's good seeing you again."

"Same here," Amber said, before they touched glasses and took a drink.

Over Champagne, the friends ate their lunch. As they did, Amber asked Julie-Ann more about her trip thus far.

"I wish you could've met Rory and Kathy—they're the people I stayed with. They're so incredible. You would love them."

"They're the ones that lost their son in Iraq, right?"

Julie-Ann sighed. "Yeah. It's so tragic. And their daughter is still in the Navy overseas. And the oldest son also served in the Marines. And Rory was in Vietnam. It's amazing how much sacrifice one family can make for the country. And they do so much volunteer work."

"Well they sound like real good people from everything you've told me."

"Hey, you wanna see some pictures?" Julie-Ann asked with excitement as she went into her purse and retrieved her phone. She then kneeled by where Amber was sitting and started showing her the photos from Anderson. "That's Rory and Kathy," she said with enthusiasm. "And this is me with their dog, Mickey. Oh, I love that dog! This is Rory with his old partner from the sheriff's office."

"He used to be a cop?"

"Yeah," Julie-Ann replied before moving onto the next picture. "This is some of their neighbors. Oh, this is outside the homeless center that I told you about. This is Lester."

"Who's Lester?"

Julie-Ann pulled the phone away, sat down, and told Amber Lester's story.

"Oh my God Jules, that's so depressing." Amber took a sip of Champagne. "Oh, I want to show *you* something." She then sprung from her seat, scurried into the bedroom, and came back with a purse. "This is the Birkin I bought in Paris. It cost forty two thousand dollars," she added, almost with pride.

Julie-Ann was exasperated. First, Amber completely blows off the story she was telling about Lester, a story that meant a lot to her. Then she brags about spending $42,000 on a handbag. All the money Julie-Ann had donated—to Connie, the center, the hospital, Lester, Kathy, the boy with the bone disease—amounted to a total of $57,000. She thought she had given so much. Yet there was Amber, spending nearly that much on a purse.

Amber could tell that Julie-Ann was perturbed. "What's wrong? Don't you like it?"

"Amber, I was telling you a story about this poor man's life, about his wife dying, his kid getting locked up, and him having to live on the streets."

"I'm sorry Jules. But it's just so depressing. And we're trying to eat. I didn't mean anything by it."

"And who pays forty two thousand dollars for a handbag? You know how many people that money could've helped?"

Amber gave Julie-Ann a look as if she was crazy. "Are you serious? You have a Birkin. And I know for a fact that yours cost even more than forty thousand dollars. And that's not counting all the other expensive purses you have."

Amber was right—and that killed Julie-Ann. Here she was, so proud of the money she had given to charitable causes, thinking she did so much and Amber reminded her that just her collection of handbags was probably worth two times all the donations she had made.

"I'm sorry," she said to Amber. "You're right. I don't mean to preach. It's your money and you can spend it any way you want to. It's just that lately I've been seeing things in a different light. Listen, I don't want to argue. I'm glad you came."

Amber smiled. "So am I." Amber then walked over to where Julie-Ann was sitting and gave her a hug.

As they finished their lunch and the bottle of Champagne, Julie-Ann and Amber discussed what they should do with the rest of the day, until they went out that night. Julie-Ann said that she really didn't have any "going out clothes" with her. Amber explained that downtown Nashville was casual, but if Julie-Ann wanted to pick up something they could go to the mall.

"There's this great big mall right next to the Grand Ole Opry," Amber continued.

"Oh, I always wanted to go there. That sounds like fun. We can stop in the mall—I won't be long—then we can check out the Grand Ole Opry."

By the time Julie-Ann and Amber finished lunch it was 3:00 p.m. Since they had a few drinks, they decided to take a cab to the mall.

The Opry Mills Mall is massive and there was a time when Julie-Ann could have easily spent the whole day there shopping. But on this day, after an hour, and two stores, she picked out a single out-fit at Calvin Klein and was done. Of course, Amber could not leave a mall without also getting something for herself.

After shopping, as agreed, the two walked over to the Grand Ole Opry Hotel. Much more than a hotel, it is a national tourist at-traction, with its massive atrium of sprawling walkways, bars, res-taurants, and stores.

After walking around for a while, Amber suggested they stop at one of the bars. The Champagne was wearing off and Julie-Ann's feet were getting sore, so she happily agreed. They followed one of the many signs that were posted throughout the atrium and found a quaint bar/restaurant. Since it was a Wednesday afternoon, there were only a few people in the restaurant and two people sitting at the bar. Amber and Julie-Ann walked over and each pulled up a stool.

The bartender was a handsome fellow with thick blonde hair and a chiseled chin, and looked to be in his late thirties. "Hello la-dies, what are we having today?"

"I'll have a Grey Goose with cranberry please," said Julie-Ann.

"The same for me please," added Amber.

"So you ladies from New York?" He asked as he mixed their drinks.

Amber laughed. "It shows that much?"

The bartender smiled. "Well I guess it's just easy for me to tell. I from New York myself."

"What part?" Julie-Ann asked.

The bartender handed them their drinks. "Long island, Massa-pequa."

"How long have you been living out here?" Amber asked.

"About six months. I love it. The cost of living on Long Island was killing us—heating oil, insurance, taxes. We were paying almost as much in real estate taxes and homeowners insurance than our actual mortgage payment. It's crazy. Everything out there is so much more expensive. Then my wife—she's in the hotel business—got a job offer working at a hotel in downtown Nashville."

Julie-Ann took a sip of her drink. "You were able to sell your house right away in this market?"

The bartender let out a sarcastic laugh. "Believe me, it wasn't easy. And we took a big hit. I'm sure you know how much home prices fell on Long Island after the crash." He then leaned across the bar. "We bought our house in two thousand one for three-hundred-eighty thousand. We wound up selling it for three-hundred-ten thousand. And we put a lot of work into it after we bought it."

"A seventy thousand dollar hit?" Amber said.

"Yeah. And we really didn't have that much equity in it, so we basically got no cash back. But luckily we had some money saved up that we used to put down on our new house. It was three-hundred-fifteen thousand and twice the size of our house in New York. And our real estate taxes and insurance is a fraction of what it was on Long Island. And my wife is making the same money as she did in Manhattan. I was able to get this gig working here. It's not bad."

"So, the economy is doing well here?" Julie-Ann asked.

The bartender waved goodbye to someone leaving the bar and thanked him. He then turned his attention back to the girls. "It's slowly coming back. I mean there are still a lot of people out of work. But it's certainly not as bad as a lot of other places around the nation. Unfortunately, I think it's going to be a long time until the country fully recovers from the 'Great Recession.'" Just then, a couple walked in and sat at the bar. "Excuse me," the bartender said as he went over to help them.

Julie-Ann and Amber leisurely finished their drinks and chatted some more with the bartender. They decided to catch a cab back to the hotel.

By the time they arrived back at the suite it was 5:45 p.m., so they decided to start getting ready to go out for the night. While Amber was in the shower, Julie-Ann kicked back on the couch in front of the television and drank a Heineken.

At one point, she pulled her phone out of her purse to see if she had gotten any calls or messages. She had several new emails and also a Facebook friend request. It was from Lisa Hendricks. Julie-Ann excitedly accepted it and then went to Lisa's Facebook page. She browsed through some of her profile pictures. There was one picture of Lisa standing next to her father, a handsome, tall man wearing Marine dress. It broke Julie-Ann's heart. She could not imagine how it would have been losing her father at fifteen-years-old. Then she saw a picture of Lisa, probably around ten-years-old, lying in a hospital bed, with an IV and completely bald, but wide-awake and actually smiling. Under, read the caption: *You have to always keep your spirit up.*

Julie-Ann went on to read some of Lisa's posts. They were mostly about hope and encouragement, or about someone that needed help. None of them were 'woe is me' or laments of self-pity. The more Julie-Ann learned about Lisa the more she was amazed by her outlook on life. She had suffered with Leukemia most of her life and she had recently lost her father. Surely she had to be bitter, had to feel anguished. The only traces of it were some brief comments about missing her father. It made Julie-Ann think back to little Allie, who she had met while receiving her radiation treatment.

Julie-Ann decided to send Lisa a message.

Lisa, I am glad we are now Facebook friends. I have been going through your profile, reading about your story and looking at some of your pictures. As I said in my Twitter message, I am so sorry about your father. I also see that you have Leukemia. This year I learned that I had a brain tumor. But I was very lucky, as it was not cancerous. They found it at an early stage and they were able to remove it. Although they will have to periodically monitor me, I feel fine now and am actually journeying across the country. I pray that you have the best prognosis possible and beat this god-awful disease. But I must say, I am amazed at your attitude and positive outlook on life after all you have been through, and the fact that you seem more concerned about others than yourself. You are a true inspiration. I hope we can stay in close contact and maybe one day we can even meet.

As soon as Julie-Ann hit the send button Amber came out of the master bedroom, wearing a robe and her hair wrapped up in a towel. "Okay, I'm done. Are you going to take a shower?"

Julie-Ann nodded. "Yeah, I think I'll take a quick one."

"Is something wrong?" Amber asked, due to the tone of Julie-Ann's voice and serious look on her face.

Julie-Ann didn't want to get into the whole story about Lisa Hendricks with Amber. "No, nothing's wrong," she replied. "I'm gonna take a shower now."

"You can take it in the master bathroom if you want."

"No, that's okay. I'll take it in the other one. This way you can finish up getting ready."

Though Julie-Ann said she was just going to take a quick shower, once the hot water poured down on her she could not help but just stand there for a while, engrossed in serenity.

After her shower, Julie-Ann put on a robe and went into Amber's bathroom, to put on make-up with her. Amber finished taking a swig out of her beer bottle and turned to look at Julie-Ann. "Hey, your hair is growing back."

Julie-Ann ran her hand over the back of her head and smiled. "Yeah. It's almost getting to be like a short haircut. I can almost go out without my wig now."

"I've been meaning to tell you, that's a really nice wig you had on. It looks so natural."

"Thanks."

By the time Julie-Ann and Amber were finished getting ready it was 7:15 p.m. Before hitting the bars, the girls agreed they should probably get some dinner first. Rather than walking around downtown, they decided to eat at the hotel's restaurant.

Afterwards, the girls hit Main Street. It was already dark out and the neon signs that hung above nearly every establishment were lit in bright colors. The drag was lined with bars, many of them with live music, which easily carried outside and permeated through the air. People loudly walked down the block in groups and waited in line to enter certain establishments. The area was alive and pulsated with electricity.

The girls ventured into a bar that Amber recommended. She said it was a good place to start out—whatever that meant. It had a good amount of people in it but was not overcrowded. There were instruments on the stage, but the band must have been on break. The girls made their way to the bar and Amber ordered two beers. As they drank them, Amber told Julie-Ann more about downtown and some of her experiences.

Just as they were finishing their drinks, two guys came up to them. One of them asked if they could buy the girls a round. Amber knew right away she would not be interested in either of them, but that did not stop her from letting him buy them a round of beer.

As the four of them huddled around the bar, one guy started talking to Amber and the other one to Julie-Ann. The one that was talking to Julie-Ann was already visibly drunk and after only two minutes started talking about his ex-girlfriend. Julie-Ann just drank her beer and nodded every once in a while.

Julie-Ann felt a tug on her arm. It was Amber, who already had an empty glass in her hand. "Jules, we have to go. We have to meet Rob and the others."

"You guys leaving already?" Asked the guy who had been talking to Amber. "Let us buy you another round."

"Sorry," Amber replied. "We have to go. We have to meet our

friends." Amber looked at her watch. "We were already supposed to be there ten minutes ago."

The guy asked where they were going. Amber didn't say, but assured them they would be back and thanked them for the beers.

As soon as the girls hit the outside, Julie-Ann turned to Amber and thanked her for saving them. "That guy was already talking about his ex. And he was slurring."

"My guy was telling me how pretty I was. What a bunch of dweebs."

Julie-Ann and Amber wandered to a different bar. They ordered a drink and were able to get a small table not far from the stage. There was a band playing the slow blues. The lead singer and guitarist was an older, weathered looking black man with gray hair. Wearing a button down dark gray shirt, black slacks, and rattle-snake skin boots, he played the faded Les Paul slung around his neck without a pick and sang in a deep, bluesy voice. The music was loud and Julie-Ann and Amber had to practically yell to hear each other.

Julie-Ann had never really listened to the blues before. But she was getting into the band's set. There was something moving about it.

After the band finished their second song since the girls had entered, the bassist and drummer went into a slow, melodic blues beat. The front man stood there for about thirty seconds, his eyes towards the ground, his left foot tapping the rhythm, his guitar silent. Then he walked back up to the microphone and looked at the crowd.

"I want to take this opportunity to tell you a little about the blues," he said in a deep, growling voice. "You see, you don't just play the blues, or listen to the blues—you live the blues." He then plucked a bending note on his guitar. "And unfortunately, right now, all across this country, there's a lot of folks living the blues. It's hard times out there my friends. Lotta folks suffering—outta work, on the street, goin' hungry." He played another reverberating note, which he seemed to bend into infinity. "This song goes out to all those people out there, just tryin' to get by, just tryin' to make it through another day. This is a old song by Skip James called Hard Times Killin' Floor."

The band then went right into the song.

Amber leaned across the small table. "Let's go," she yelled at Julie-Ann over the music.

"Wait, I wanna stay and hear this song," she yelled back.

"You don't listen to this music. This is old people's music."

Julie-Ann was able to convince Amber to stay through the end of the song, but agreed to go up to the bar for another drink. At the bar, as Julie-Ann worked on her beer, she listened intently to the music as some guy tried to hit on Amber.

After the girls finished their drinks, and the band was well into another song, Julie-Ann and Amber left to go find another bar.

"I know a place that'll be real happening and have a bunch of hot guys," Amber said excitedly.

"Amber, I'm not looking to hook up with anyone."

"Jules, you have to get over Ken." Amber stopped walking and faced her friend. "Jules, when was the last time you got laid?"

Julie-Ann let out a sigh. "I've just had other things on my mind Amber."

"I'm not saying you have to be obsessed with it, but everyone needs to get laid. Especially with all you've been through. It'll help you…"

Julie-Ann cut her off. "Amber, just please promise me you won't hook us up with anyone and you won't take anyone back to the hotel. I just want this time to be for you and me."

Amber looked at her friend. "Okay," she reluctantly replied. "But that doesn't mean we can't talk to guys."

The girls started walking again. Amber led Julie-Ann down a side street in search of the bar she was looking for. About halfway down the block, a ragged looking vagrant came up to them and asked for some change. Julie-Ann was about to go in her purse.

"No, we don't have any money," Amber said sharply. She then grabbed hold off Julie-Ann's arm and whisked her away.

"I was going to give him some money."

Amber made a scrunched-up face. "Eww Jules, did you smell him? You'd probably get fleas or some disease by just standing close enough to him."

Julie-Ann shook her head. "Amber, the poor guy is homeless. It doesn't mean he's a bad person. You don't know how he got that way. Maybe he just lost his job and his house."

"Jules, not everyone that is one the streets begging is some poor victim. A lot of them are drug addicts or criminals or only have themselves to blame. God, what is your fascination with these people?" Amber paused. "Listen, I'm sorry. I don't want to argue. We're here to have a good time. Right?"

Julie-Ann let out a breath and nodded. "Yeah. I don't wanna argue either."

The girls continued walking and found the bar just down the street. It had a line to get in, but Amber went up to the bouncer, flashed her pearly whites and said that they had just been inside. The bouncer let them both in.

The bar was crowded and loud from the live music and the people trying to talk over it. There was also a floating layer of cigarette smoke, as Nashville had no laws prohibiting smoking in bars and some establishments allowed it. Julie-Ann would rather have gone back to either of the other bars they had been, but not wanting to cause a debate, didn't say anything to Amber.

The girls wound up staying at the bar for nearly two hours. Amber entangled them with a couple of guys who were trying to pick them up. The guys ordered two rounds of shots and everyone was getting wasted. Julie-Ann was having a good time, but saw that Amber was getting touchy-feely with her guy and was worried that she was going to invite them back to the hotel. But when they went to the ladies room together, she told Julie-Ann that she would abide by their deal to not take any guys to the suite.

At one point, the guy who was interested in Julie-Ann put his hand on her thigh. She instantly brushed it away and told him that she had a boyfriend. Truth be told, Julie-Ann had been longing for a man's touch, longing to have wild, passionate sex, but she wasn't ready to get together with some guy she just met at a bar. She wanted to spend her time in Nashville just hanging out with Amber.

He naturally looked disappointed, but kept talking to her, hoping that another drink or two would soften her up.

By the time Julie-Ann and Amber left the bar it was approaching midnight. But downtown was still happening. The guys, to whom the girls had been talking, left the bar with them and out front they tried to cajole Julie-Ann and Amber into going to another bar. Julie-Ann was drunk and was happy just to go back to the hotel and call it a night, but Amber pleaded with her.

"Come on, it's not even midnight," she whined in a loud, slurred voice. "Last call isn't till two am."

Julie-Ann had been having a good time and didn't want to seem like the party killer. "Excuse me," she said to the guys before pulling Amber away so she could talk to her in private. "We'll go to another bar, but we are not taking these guys back to the hotel— or going back to their place. We don't even know them."

"Okay, okay."

"Promise me Amber."

Amber gave Julie-Ann the look of a child forced to make a deal with her parents. "I promise."

The group walked back to Main Street and went to a large, three-story bar with live music. It was jam-packed but they were able to get in right away and hung out on the first floor, by the wide horseshoe-shaped bar.

As they were drinking their beers, Julie-Ann's guy started getting frisky again, putting his hand on her arm and getting within inches of her face. Julie-Ann told him once more that she was taken. This time he seemed more perturbed.

Not long afterwards, the guy who Amber was talking to tried to kiss her right there by the bar. She gently pushed him away. That did not deter him as he went in for another try. This time she pushed him back with force. "That's not going to happen," she sternly said. Amber then turned to Julie-Ann. "I think it's time we go."

Julie-Ann was surprised by her friend's reaction. Amber was drunk and could be promiscuous. Julie-Ann didn't know if Amber had finally become monogamous with Tyler or if she was doing it because she had promised not to bring the guys back to the hotel and didn't want to start what she couldn't finish. But Julie-Ann didn't care what Amber's reason was; she was just happy to be leaving what was becoming an uncomfortable situation.

"Thanks for the drinks," Amber said to the guys. "We had a good time."

"Thanks for the drinks," the guy Amber had been talking to spewed back. "That's it? We wasted the whole night with you two."

Amber got right into his face. "Wasted the whole night? You know what—fuck you!"

"Fuck you, you fuckin' bitch!"

Amber grabbed a cup off the bar that still had some beer in it and threw it at him. After that all hell broke lose. He went to push her, but was grabbed by some other guy. He pushed the guy back but the man then decked him and knocked him on the floor. Then the guy who had been trying to pick up Julie-Ann got into it with Amber's protector. They inadvertently bumped into a third party and he and his friends entered the melee. Everything happened so fast. In a matter of seconds the bouncers were circling around, grabbing people, trying get a hold on the situation. Meanwhile, Julie-Ann grabbed Amber by the arm and whisked her out of the bar.

Once they were safe outside and a bar away, Amber stopped. "Oh my God!" She said with bated breath. "Can you believe we just started a bar fight?"

Perhaps fueled by alcohol, Julie-Ann couldn't help but laugh. "I know! That was crazy!"

But the girls had had enough for the night. They walked back to the hotel and called it an evening.

Chapter 20

Julie-Ann woke-up with a splitting headache. She looked to the digital clock on the nightstand. It was 11:27 a.m. Still wrapped in covers, she grabbed for the open water bottle next to the clock, gingerly propped herself up, and took a drink. After a few minutes of just absorbing her hangover, Julie-Ann went looking for Amber. She found her in the master bedroom, still in bed. She had been asleep, but heard Julie-Ann come into the room and lifted her head.

"Jules, I have a bad hangover," she whined in a coarse voice.

"So do I."

After getting their wits about them, the girls ordered room service. They sat around the television in the main room, talked about the night before, and slowly ate their food.

By the time they finished eating it was nearly 1:00 p.m. and neither of them had yet taken a shower. Feeling a little better than when they woke up, but now both full, they seemed intent with pissing the day away. Amber laid on the couch and Julie-Ann the love seat, watching TV, fading in and out.

"Can you believe it's three o'clock already?" Amber moaned.

"Yeah, I know. Maybe we should take showers and do something. If we just stay in this room the whole day we'll never be able to sleep tonight."

Amber let out a deep sigh. "Yeah, I guess you're right."

The girls were in slow motion and by the time they were finished with their showers and getting ready it was 4:45 p.m. They talked about what they could do. Amber suggested walking around downtown in the daylight, but Julie-Ann didn't feel much like trekking around. As they threw out ideas in front of the television another half hour ticked by.

"How about we just go out for a nice dinner?" Amber suggested.

"That sounds good. But I'm really not too hungry yet."

"Well, how about we make reservations somewhere for seven o'clock? Then we can just kick back or something until then."

Julie-Ann nodded. "Yeah, that sounds like a plan."

"Hey, are you in the mood for Sushi?" Amber asked. "I know this real good place in Nashville—Vigaro. I mean it's not Nobu, but then again, what is?"

"Yeah, that actually sounds good. I can go for some sushi."

Amber looked up the number of the restaurant on her iPhone, called, and made the reservations.

"Well we have an hour before we need to leave," Amber said in a drained voice. "I feel like we've been sitting in this hotel room forever. I'm starting to get cabin fever."

"Me too."

"Maybe we should venture down to the hotel bar until we need to leave."

Julie-Ann grunted. "Amber I don't know. I had enough to drink last night. In fact, I'm starting to feel shitty again."

"You know what that means—you need some hair of the dog. I'm not saying get drunk, but just enough to get rid of your hangover. Otherwise you're going to feel like crap at the restaurant."

Julie-Ann knew Amber was right. So she begrudgingly agreed to go down to the bar.

Julie-Ann ordered a Grey Goose and cranberry and it was going down hard. But she did feel better just getting out of the suite. As the girls chitchatted, Julie-Ann zoned in on the conversation the man sitting close to them was having on his cellphone. Wearing a fitted tan suit, matching expensive-looking tie, and an Omega wristwatch, the man had slicked back black hair and looked to be in his late forties or early fifties.

"That's right, eighty-five employees," he said in a matter-of-fact voice as Julie-Ann eavesdropped. "You can work with Miriam and Ralph C to come up with the names, but we need them by the end of next week because I want to give them their notices by the following week." The man paused as he casually took a drink from his glass of what looked to be scotch on the rocks. "You can get the names from across all the departments. Try and find people that have been with the company the longest and have been getting pay increases through the years, but have younger, less expensive counterparts. It's time we trim the dead fat anyway." There was a pause. "Well, then other people will just have to pick up the slack. They'll be so afraid of losing their jobs they'll come in on the weekends if we tell them."

Julie-Ann couldn't believe the callousness in which the man was talking about laying off his employees.

"I'll be back in town on Monday," the man continued. "Yeah, that's right. So, I was thinking we would have the golf outing in Bermuda this September." There was a pause as he listened to the person on the other end. "Yeah, why not, we deserve it. We've weathered some rough storms. I mean Boca is nice, but it's not Bermuda."

"Are you even listening to me?" Amber said in a loud voice.

Julie-Ann realized that she had completely been ignoring her friend. "I'm sorry." She then leaned forward towards Amber. "I was listening to that guy's phone conversation," she said in a whisper.

"What was he saying?" Amber blurted out.

"Shhh!" Julie-Ann watched through the corner of her eye as the man, apparently finished with his phone call and drink, walked away from the bar. Once he was out of earshot, she told Amber about his conversation.

"Jules, no one wants to lose their jobs," Amber replied. "But it's just an unfortunate fact of life, especially these days. You gotta understand, a lot of times, if they don't cut the workforce than they might have to close the entire company and everyone would lose their jobs."

Julie-Ann understood that there were certain situations where businesses were forced with hard choices and had to let some people go in order to save the entire company. It was the heartlessness in which the man gave the orders and how he then boasted about some golf outing in Bermuda. That part apparently went right over Amber's head, but Julie-Ann didn't feel like getting into a debate with her, so she just let it go.

The girls had one more drink at the bar and then caught a cab to the restaurant. The hair of the dog had helped. Julie-Ann was no longer hung-over. She was also getting hungry.

The maître d sat them in a corner booth, giving them some privacy.

"We have to get some Thai lobster shooters," Amber said as soon as they sat down. "They're great."

Within a minute, a waitress came over to take their drink order. Amber ordered Kirin beer for the both of them and opened up the sake menu.

"Oh, I don't know if I want any sake," Julie-Ann said.

Amber waved her off. "Oh, come on Jules. We're in Nashville together, out for dinner. Have a good time."

Julie-Ann smiled and nodded in agreement. Then, with the help of the waitress, Amber picked out a bottle of good sake.

As the waitress went to go get their beer and sake, the girls looked over their respective menus. Julie-Ann was well versed in sushi, but listened to Amber's suggestions since she had been at the restaurant before.

It did not take long for the waitress to come back with their drinks. She opened the bottle of sake and filled their small, white, ceramic cups. She then took their dinner order, which consisted of various sushi rolls, sashimi, and the Thai lobster shooters.

Once the waitress left, Amber raised her sake cup in the air. "To best friends."

Julie-Ann smiled and raised her sake. "Forever."

They then touched cups and took a drink.

"Mmmm," Julie-Ann said. "I usually don't like sake, but this is pretty smooth."

"It is, right?"

Over drinks and sushi, the girls talked and laughed. The mood was light and festive. Julie-Ann commended Amber for her suggestion of the restaurant and said how good the food was.

Amber poured them each another cup of sake. She then raised her cup in the air. This time, without any words, they touched cups and took a drink. Then, Amber went into her purse and pulled out a folded piece of letter-size paper and handed it to Julie-Ann.

"What's this?" Julie-Ann asked with a puzzled look as she unfolded it.

"It's your itinerary. I bought you a ticket with me tomorrow. I want you to come back to New York with me."

Julie-Ann let out an uncomfortable laugh. "Amber, why would you do that? I can't go back with you. I'm not finished with my journey yet. Besides, I have my car."

"You can leave your car here and we can get someone to transport it back to New York."

Julie-Ann put down her chopsticks. "Forget the car. I don't think you understand—I'm not ready to go back yet."

"Jules, you've been gone for three weeks now. Isn't that long enough? Your father's starting to worry about you."

The festive mood that hung in the air was now gone. "My father? What does my father have...Have you been talking with my father about me?"

"Jules, don't get all defensive. It's not like that. He's just worried about you and doesn't understand what you're doing out here. I don't understand. I mean, if you're having some kind of crisis..."

That was is it. Julie-Ann's blood began to boil. Had everything she told her father and Amber about what she was doing gone in one ear and out the other? "I'm not having some kind of crisis," she said in a low, but stern voice. "I'm living my life! And I've never felt so alive. I've never experienced so much. The people I've met already on the road—I'll have a bond with them for the rest of my life."

Amber shook her head. "Do you hear yourself? You don't even know these people. You were around them for a couple of days. They could be con artists."

Julie-Ann was fuming. "You're just like my father—so close minded, living in a rose-colored, Champagne bubble. These people let me into their homes, into their lives."

"And what did you give to them in return?" Amber asked in a sarcastic tone. "You act like they did it all out of the kindness of their hearts."

"Why am I even arguing with you? You'll never get it. You just don't understand." Julie-Ann reached into her purse and pulled out her wallet.

"What are you doing?"

"Here's a hundred dollars for dinner," she said, throwing a hundred-dollar bill onto the table. "I'm going to get my own ride back to the hotel," she continued as she stood up. "I'll get my stuff from your room. I'm going to stay in my own room tonight."

Amber let out an exasperated sigh. "Jules, come on. Don't overreact. Don't be like this. I'm you're best friend."

"I thought you were." With that, Julie-Ann walked away.

Julie-Ann went back to the hotel, and using a key Amber had given her, moved all of her stuff back to her own room. She then called the front desk and extended her stay until Saturday, as she was scheduled to checkout in the morning. She was ready to get on with her journey, but still had no idea of her next stop.

Alone in her hotel room, Julie-Ann took out her laptop. She saw from her phone that she had unread emails and Facebook notifications and figured it would be easier to look through them on a larger screen. Not unusual, most of the emails were spam and other notifications. There was one email from someone named Jane. It turned out to be the mother of the boy with hypophosphatasia, to whom she had donated $5,000. Jane thanked Julie-Ann profusely, explaining that her son needed constant medical care and how they had lost their health care insurance when her husband lost his job. Julie-Ann felt terrible for the boy and the family, but felt some solace in playing a small part in helping them.

After going through her emails, Julie-Ann went on Facebook and was happy to see that she had a message from Lisa Hendricks.

> *Dear, Ms. Crown, I was so glad to hear from you again. And I am so happy that you have beaten your tumor. I went through your profile and some of your posts. Like I had mentioned on Twitter, I thank you so much for your support of our military men and women. You are right, there are so many who returned from Iraq and Afghanistan and can't find work, or are wounded and are having trouble getting their benefits. But until I started following you, I was really unaware that there were so many homeless veterans, especially women veterans. It is a real eye opener and very, very sad. The brave men and women who served so we can be free should always come first. I know my father would have been proud of the work you are doing. I know I am. Because of you I have reached out to Ms. McAlister to find out more about the foundation she is trying to start. Like you, I hope that we can meet someday. I told my mother about you and she would also like to meet you and thank you. Hope to hear from you soon.*

Julie-Ann was so touched by Lisa's message that her eyes started to fill with tears. She still could not believe that she was only fifteen-years-old. She exuded such courage and altruism.

Hearing from Jane and Lisa, Julie-Ann was eager to continue her journey through the country and meet more people, learn their stories, and hopefully help those she could. So she started thinking about her next destination. She brainstormed and read some articles on the Internet, hoping that something would give her a sign. She could not help but coming back to Lisa Hendricks. Not only was she fascinated with Lisa's story, but she knew from her Facebook page that Lisa and her mother lived in Hastings, Nebraska and that intrigued her as well. Where was Hastings anyway, she wondered? And what was in Nebraska? It seemed just the place where her journey was supposed to take her. It was the heartland of America, yet a place she probably would never have visited in her life.

The more Julie-Ann thought about it, the more Hastings seemed like her next destination. But then came the reservations. *Wait, I just exchanged a few messages with this girl on Twitter and Facebook. I know she said that she would like to meet me someday, but I can't just show up on her doorstep. That's just crazy. And she's only fifteen. I've never even corresponded with her mother. I'm moving way too fast.* But Julie-Ann also couldn't just let it go. *But what if I tell her that I just happened to be in the area and ask if I could meet her and her mother? Wait, that sounds even crazier! Who just happens to go to Nebraska? And she'll see right through it—happening to be there a week after I first made contact with her. What if I just tell her the truth? I already told her that I'm traveling through the country. Maybe I'll say that I'm heading out west and I'll be driving by Nebraska? But Nebraska is a big state. But it makes sense. She already knows about my journey. Anyway, if she or her mother doesn't want to meet me then the worst that can happen is she says no or tells me some excuse. I want to see Nebraska anyway. I want to know what it's like there, what the people are like.*

In the end, Julie-Ann decided that she would head for Nebraska. However, instead of driving straight there, she would take the opportunity to make some stops along the way and see as much of the heartland as she could. Remembering Rory's advice, Julie-Ann went on MapQuest and plotted her course, and to decide where she would spend the next night.

Hastings was 856 miles from Nashville and the most direct route would take thirteen and a half hours. But Julie-Ann was not interested in the fastest way to get there. She told herself that she could not take a journey through the heartland of America without visiting Kansas. Kansas was still over an eight-hour drive and that was driving straight through.

After looking over an interactive map, Julie-Ann eventually decided that her first stop would be Jefferson City, Missouri, a six-hour drive. Next, she went on Travelocity and booked a room at the Doubletree hotel for two nights. She thought about researching what Jefferson City was like, what was there, but then decided that she wanted to be surprised. She wanted to go there without any preconceived notions.

Julie-Ann woke up early the next morning. She knew Amber's flight was scheduled to leave at 11:30 a.m. Feeling bad about their fight the previous night, she called Amber's room to apologize for storming out and to offer her a ride to the airport.

"That's okay, I'm just going to take a cab," Amber replied in a somber voice.

"Amber, don't be silly. Please. I'm sorry about last night. I know you're just worried about me." That's not exactly how Julie-Ann really felt, but she did want to make amends with her friend.

"Listen Jules, it's okay. I'm not mad, really. I think it's best if I just take a cab to the airport. It's no big deal, really." Amber paused. "I wish you the best on your journey Jules, I really do. I hope that you find what you're searching for. Just please be careful out there. And remember that you have friends and family back in New York and whenever you decide to come back, we'll be there waiting for you."

Julie-Ann was starting to choke-up. "Amber, please realize that I miss you guys so much and I really appreciate you coming out here. I had a great time Wednesday night. But this is something that I just have to do."

"I know it is, Jules. I know it is."

"Are you sure I can't give you a ride to the airport?"

"Yes. I'm just going to take a cab. But like I said, I'm not mad and

I don't want you to be upset. You take care of yourself Jules—and stay in touch."

"I will."

As soon as Julie-Ann hung up the phone she began to cry. She felt terrible about the wedge that had been driven between her and Amber, as well as her father. She so much wanted them to truly understand what she was doing and why. She wanted them to be a part of her awakening, to let them in, to be able to talk to them about her experiences. She thought it should have brought them even closer together. Julie-Ann had stepped outside the crystal palace she had lived in her whole life and saw the world in a new light. However, it appeared to Julie-Ann that Amber and her father—and probably most of the other people she had known—were still stuck inside that palace. She still loved Amber, and of course, her father, but it seemed that they had less and less in common with each passing day. In fact, their views on the world now seemed diametrically opposed to hers and that filled her with great sadness.

Julie-Ann was feeling a little hung-over, but she didn't want to just sit in the hotel room by herself all day. So after getting ready, she went down to the lobby and grabbed some tourist pamphlets. She went to the hotel's restaurant for a late breakfast while eating an egg white omelet and some toast she browsed through the pamphlets. Finally, she decided to take a tour of The Hermitage, the plantation, and historical national landmark, which once belonged to Andrew Jackson and his family.

Being out of the room and after having a healthy breakfast, Julie-Ann was feeling better. She picked up her car from the valet and decided to make the twenty-minute drive with the top down. Trying to forget about how things went down with Amber, or at least push it aside for a while, Julie-Ann basked in the sun and the fresh Tennessee air as she followed the directions of the GPS.

Julie-Ann wound up staying at The Hermitage for over two

hours, taking a tour of the main house, walking around the sprawling grounds, and then browsing through the small museum.

While walking through the grounds, Julie-Ann heard her phone ring from inside her purse so she retrieved it. It was Dr. Libowitz. He was checking in, to see how Julie-Ann was feeling. She told him the truth—that she was feeling fine and had not had any more headaches (of, course she wasn't counting hangovers) or any other symptoms. He reminded her that she should schedule a follow-up MRI and blood work in three more weeks. Julie-Ann obligatorily agreed. She had every intention on getting the MRI and blood work, but not knowing if she would still be on the road, she was not prepared to schedule anything just yet. She figured it wouldn't matter to push it back a week or two. Of course, she also didn't need to get an MRI or have blood work done in New York. If it came to it, that could be done nearly anywhere.

After the Hermitage, Julie-Ann parked the car back at the hotel and sauntered around downtown Nashville. It was Friday afternoon and the sidewalks were filled with people. There was electricity in the air that was only growing as the evening approached. Many of the bars were already happening. A part of Julie-Ann wanted to get caught up in the excitement. But she promised herself to stay away from the bars, instead, looking around the various little shops that lined Main Street. She was afraid that if she stopped in one of the bars and had a few drinks one thing might lead to another and she would become a prisoner of the Friday night festivities. Not only had she already drank two days in a row, but she did not want to have a hangover for her six-hour drive to Jefferson City. So, by 5:30 p.m., summoning up her willpower, she went back to the hotel.

That evening Julie-Ann stayed in her room, watching TV and ordered room service for dinner. But by 8:00 p.m., she was feeling restless and like she was missing out on the Friday night Nashville scene. Thinking about her long drive the next day, she stuck to her guns and was a good girl.

In bed, Julie-Ann flipped through the channels, trying to find something to watch. She finally settled on a show called Million Dollar Rooms. It showed various exorbitant rooms that people had built in their houses, all in the United States. One man built a massive party room in his Colorado mansion, which housed a thirty foot long indoor pool, a giant hot tub, two professional bowling lanes, a full bar, two tournament billiards tables, and an indoor shooting range. The main area was floored with imported marble tiles, and overlooked the mountains.

Another mansion had two rooms worth over a million dollars each. One was a massive bathroom adorned in marble and granite. The host explained that the colossal bathtub, which had elaborate scenes of antiquity carved on the outside and marble steps, used to actually belong in the Vatican. The room also had a seven-person steam room designed to replicate an ancient Roman bath-house. The other room was an auditorium, which the owner of the house had built specifically for his wife, who was a pianist. The walls and ceiling were hand painted in the fashion of the Sistine Chapel. The host said that it took the artist eight months to complete. At one end of the room, sat a grand piano. Facing it was the viewing section, rows of elegant seats on four stepped levels. The floors of the auditorium were cherry wood and the entrance to the room was two, seven-foot tall doors, also cherry wood, but with a swirling gold-inlayed design and solid gold handles.

Yet another mansion, in San Diego, showcased its garage. The owner, a record producer, had such a large collection of expensive and exotic cars that they wouldn't all fit in his garage. So he had built another, underground garage and a hydraulic lift to raise cars from the lower level to the ground level so he could display and drive them.

Julie-Ann was intrigued by the show. She was not surprised by people's wealth or lavishness. She had lived in an exclusive club and as rich as her father was, she had been around those who had even more money.

After the show was over, Julie-Ann scrolled through the channels again, until she came to an episode of 20/20. It was on the

housing crisis, in particular, how many houses were still being foreclosed on. She watched intently as they talked about Nevada, and
how it was one of the worst hit states from the financial collapse.
Julie-Ann had known that the Nevada economy and housing market was devastated by the meltdown. She did not realize that one
in fifteen homes were still being foreclosed on. The show explained that many of the families that lost their homes were considered middle class, and interviewed several people who had
their homes foreclosed.

The show moved on to Detroit, without a doubt the city most
decimated by The Great Recession. It showed entire rows of empty
houses. The host interviewed a man who had recently lost his
house there to foreclosure.

"It's like a modern ghost town," he said with pain in his eyes.
"Thousands of people were laid off from the auto companies as
they downsized," he continued. "Other businesses in the area followed suit, like a domino effect. It's like a third world nation out
here. Crime is rampant. There's no future here for the younger generation."

Julie-Ann watched as they showed one block of houses that
were burned out and were actually still smoldering, as if they were
showing footage from some warzone in a foreign country.

Next, the show interviewed a homeowner that was fighting
foreclosure proceedings in Tempe, Arizona. "So what do you say to
the experts that say the economy is recovering?" The interviewer
asked. "That the stock market has seen some of its biggest gains
and the housing market is showing signs of a rebound?"

The fit young man, who looked to be in his late thirties, let out a
laugh of cynicism. "Well I'm sure if you're on Wall Street, or are rich,
the economy looks good. The stock market has nothing to do with
what's really going on across America. Maybe once it did—but it
doesn't anymore. Of course, the experts are saying things are getting better, because they're usually well off. But these are the same
experts that said everything was fine, right before the collapse,
that said invest in the stock market right before it crashed."

"Well, you owned a restaurant here in Tempe," said the interviewer. "How would you say things are today here?"

The man paused and then let out a sigh. "Not good. Not good at all. I mean I lost my restaurant. People just don't have the money they did before to go out and eat. And the people that do have jobs are scared of losing them so they're not spending. And Arizona is just a microcosm of what's going on throughout the entire country. People are suffering and the government keeps printing more money, talking about all these programs that are going to bring new jobs. But here we are at two thousand eleven, over three years after the crash, and the unemployment rate is still over eight percent. And that doesn't include all the people whose benefits have run out or who have just stopped looking for work."

"It also doesn't take into account people who have had to find new jobs making much less than they were before," the interviewer added.

"You hear officials saying that we've been living above our means," the interviewee continued, "that we, as a country we are just going to have to learn to get by with less. But that's hogwash. That's just their politically correct way of saying that the middle class is disappearing. The day's coming—in the not too distant future—that there will be no middle class; there will just be rich and poor."

Julie-Ann watched the rest of the show. She watched a little more TV before turning off the set so she could go to sleep. She found herself awake in bed, thinking about the 20/20 episode, as well as the episode of Million Dollar Rooms. It was seeming more evident than ever to her that there were two Americas: one that the wealthy, elite lived in and enjoyed; and what was becoming everyone else. Perhaps the man in the 20/20 episode was right— one day soon there would just be the rich and the poor. Maybe America was heading towards a Saudi Arabian society, where ninety percent of the wealth of the entire country was enjoyed by ten percent of its populous.

Chapter 21

Julie-Ann woke up early the next morning and finished packing. After taking a shower, she stood in front of the mirror, a towel wrapped around her still damp body. As she looked at herself, she decided, for the first time, to go out without her wig.

With a long drive ahead of her, Julie-Ann went to the hotel's restaurant and ate a hearty breakfast. After she was finished, she went back up to the room and checked out on the television set. She lugged her bags downstairs and went to the valet for her car.

By 9:45 a.m., Julie-Ann was on the road, headed for Jefferson City, Missouri. When she put it into the GPS, she could not help but laugh, thinking that several months earlier she couldn't imagine ever going to Jefferson City, let alone driving there.

The sky was dark with ominous clouds, and though there was only a light rain, the forecast—which Julie-Ann watched on TV that morning—called for the rain to become heavy, with possible thunderstorms. It was also a large system coming in from the west, which meant she probably wasn't going to be able to miss it by merely driving a half hour or so out of Nashville.

Once Julie-Ann hit the highway, she turned on the satellite radio. Instead of stopping at the channel she would usually listen to, she kept going, trying to find something different. Then she came to a channel with blues music and left it alone, thinking about the band she had heard in Nashville with Amber. The display said the artist was Freddy King, and the song, *Same Old Blues*. Julie-Ann immediately was moved by King's powerfully, soulful voice, as well as the strategically wailing guitar. With its lyrics of rain and gloom, it was also a fitting song for the weather outside. Still, she kept it at a low enough volume, so she could concentrate on the road

After the song was over, Julie-Ann kept it on the station. But she was beginning to worry about the road conditions as the sky opened up and it began to pour. Thick sheets of rain greatly diminished the visibility. Cars and trucks began to back-up. With her windshield wipers on full power, Julie-Ann gripped the steering wheel harder she lowered the music until it was barely audible against the pounding rain.

Julie-Ann hoped that the rain would at least let up, but the deluge continued. Staying in the middle lane, she tried to maintain a reasonable speed. She didn't want to go too fast, but she was also worried about going too slow and having a car rear-end her. Once in a while, a car or truck would zoom by in the passing lane, splashing buckets of water onto her windshield and rattling her already fraying nerves. *It's okay, Jules, it's just rain,* she told herself. Then, for the first time, lightning illuminated the dark sky. A second later, the roar or thunder. As soon as it faded, a spider web of fantastic blue and white lightning flashed just to the east.

"It's okay, just focus," Julie-Ann said aloud as another, even louder round of thunder crashed.

Just then, the car's navigation system came to life. "In one mile, take exit ninety-six on the left, towards I-64 West."

Julie-Ann looked through her rearview mirror and, through the sheets of rain, saw a pick-up truck pulling up to her in the left lane. There were also several cars ahead of her in the left lane. She began to panic. Julie-Ann put on her left turn signal and slowed down to let the pick-up truck pass her. But it felt like it was taking forever.

"In a half a mile, take exit ninety-six on the left, towards I-64 West."

"Come on," Julie-Ann yelled, trying to will the truck to pass.

As soon as the truck was far enough ahead of her, she went to make her move, but there was a car, not too far behind in the left lane. Julie-Ann had no idea how far out of the way she would have to go if she missed the turn. Stepping on the gas, she cut hard into the left lane. As she did, the car began to fishtail. Luckily, she was able to quickly regain control, but it was enough to make her heart pound out of her chest. The car behind her blew its horn.

Her senses on high alert, and her heart palpitating, Julie-Ann made the exit.

"Drive fifty-two miles on I-64 West."

Fortunately, Julie-Ann did not have to take any more turns or exit for a while. But her nerves were shattered. With a death grip on the steering wheel, and still fighting to see clearly out the windshield from the driving rain, she tried to slow down her breathing. After another five miles, Julie-Ann saw a sign for a rest area up ahead. She decided to stop there to settle her nerves, and wait until the rain let up.

It was a full service rest area, with a gas station, fast food court, and convenience store. Julie-Ann parked the car, and not having an umbrella, ran inside. It only took her probably twelve seconds, but by the time she entered, she was drenched. However, she was just glad to be off the highway.

With time to kill, Julie-Ann went into the convenience store and looked at the magazine rack. The cover of Time magazine immediately caught her attention. The headline was: *What Recovery?* It featured an image of a cut-up U.S. dollar bill. Julie-Ann bought it—and an umbrella.

After the convenience store, she bought a cup of coffee from the Starbucks that was nearby, and found a vacant table to sit and read her magazine.

After about forty-five minutes, Julie-Ann took a look outside. The sky did not look as dark and the rain, not as heavy. So she ventured out, to get a better feel. Though still raining, it had turned to a drizzle. She decided it was safe enough—and her nerves had settled enough—to continue the drive. Before leaving the service area, she filled up her tank.

The driving conditions were better. Though the highway was still slick, Julie-Ann could clearly see out her windshield. After about fifteen minutes, she felt calm enough to turn back on the XM Radio. Though she had enjoyed the blues, for a change of pace, Julie-Ann decided to see if there was anything on any of the news channels. She scanned a few stations, listening to them for a minute or two, until she came to a news talk show.

"They're destroying America," the host hollered.

It immediately caught Julie-Ann's attention.

"So now the town is taking this guy—this veteran who fought for our country—to court to make him take down his American flag, saying it's against the zoning."

Intrigued, Julie-Ann stayed on the station, and even turned it up.

"Is this what this country's come to?" The host went on in a raised, angry voice. "Now they're going to make us take down our flags? We already had the war on Christmas. Employees at department stores can't say 'Merry Christmas' anymore; now they have to say 'happy holidays'. Schools throughout the country were made to take down their nativity scenes. Last year, in California, we had a sixth grader bring cupcakes to school for a bake sale and was told that she couldn't sell them because they said Merry Christmas and that might offend some people! Offend some people? Look it up— it's called Christmas—and it's a federal holiday!"

Julie-Ann was aware of the recent, and growing, ongoing agenda to change the meaning and celebration of Christmas into some generic holiday. She had heard at least some of the stories about stores and public places taking down anything that promoted Christmas and replace them with "Happy Holidays". And she thought it was ridiculous. Growing-up, she remembered walking through Macys or other department stores and there being signs that said Merry Christmas, and smiling employees greeting people by wishing them a Merry Christmas. She never remembered anyone being offended. She also never remembered anyone making a big deal about a nativity scene. She truly just didn't understand—after all these years, why now was there some kind of problem with Christmas?

"Then we have the general war on God and Christianity," the host continued his tirade. "First you had them take any prayers out of schools, even before high school football games. Then you had them take the Pledge of Allegiance out of school—that's right, the Pledge of Allegiance—because it has the word 'God' in it. They made those courthouses take down the Ten Commandments. They want no mention of God or Christianity—the religion this country was based on—to be displayed in any public building or area. And they're getting their wish!" The host paused to catch his breath. "Now they're going after the American flag! It's okay to burn an American flag, but you can't hang it on your house. What is this country coming to? You better wake up people! The country that the Greatest Generation fought for is gone."

Julie-Ann could not help but agree with everything the host was saying. She listened as he opened up the phone lines to callers, most of them who went on their own diatribe on the direction of the country and the dismantling of what it was founded on. Julie-Ann could feel herself getting fired up. A few times, she even yelled aloud. "Yeah, that's right! How can they do that? That's bullshit!"

Julie-Ann felt like she was listening to the show for hours, but when it went off the air, it was only 1:00 p.m. With her nearly one-hour pit stop at the service area, and the slow start, due to the rain, she still had over four hours to drive. She had enjoyed the radio show, but was getting a slight headache and decided to take a break and drive with the radio off for a while.

It was 5:07 p.m. when Julie-Ann reached Jefferson City. Exhausted and wanting to get out of the car, she followed the GPS to the Doubletree. The area around the hotel was somewhat commercial, but appeared safe and clean. Though there were trees around, the landscape was flat and more urban than Julie-Ann had envisioned. She had an image in her mind of some small, country town.

Julie-Ann parked her car and went inside, wheeling a large suitcase and carrying an overnight bag on her shoulder. The hotel itself seemed nice and made her feel comfortable. Feeling good just to be out of the car, Julie-Ann went up to the front desk.

"Good evening," a young woman said with a smile. "How can I help you?"

"Yes, I have reservations," Julie-Ann replied as she went into her purse for her wallet. "The last name is Crown."

The woman looked her up on the computer and checked her in, all the while with a pleasant, welcoming demeanor. She asked Julie-Ann how her trip was and told her about the hotel and the surrounding area. She called over a bellhop to help Julie-Ann with her bags, but Julie-Ann said it was not necessary.

The room was clean, but nothing fancy or too spacious. There was a queen-size bed, a small desk, dresser with a TV, closet, and bathroom. Julie-Ann threw her purse and overnight bag on the chair, and then she plopped down on the bed. She was only there for a minute before she heard her cellphone ring. She reluctantly sprang up from the comfort of the bed and hurried to get it. However, she was pleasantly surprised to see that it was Kathy.

Kathy asked how she was doing and where she was. Julie-Ann filled her in. Then Kathy excitedly explained that she was in the process of incorporating the foundation. Julie-Ann said that if there was anything else she could do to help, to please let her know. But of course, Kathy replied that she had already done more than enough.

As soon as Julie-Ann hung up with Kathy her phone rang again. It was Theresa. She didn't want to hear a speech similar to Amber's, about abandoning her journey and coming back to New York, but it had been a while since she talked to Theresa and she did miss her. So, with some trepidation, Julie-Ann answered the call.

"Hello."

"Jules," Theresa said with a vibrant voice. "I'm glad you picked up. It's been a little while. How are you doing?"

"I'm good. Everything is fine."

"Where are you?"

"I'm in Jefferson City, Missouri. I just got here."

"Jefferson City? What's in Jefferson City?" Theresa asked with puzzlement.

Julie-Ann didn't want to explain her whole journey and its purpose for the umpteenth time—and there was no real great specific reason to be in Jefferson City. "I'm just passing through. I'm just going to be here for two days."

Theresa could tell Julie-Ann was being hesitant. "Listen Jules, I wasn't asking to get in your business," she said in a calm tone. "I didn't call to try and convince you to come back to New York or patch things up with your father. I mean, he genuinely worries about you and loves you very much, and I'm sure you guys will patch things up in your own time. I just miss you and wanted to see how you were doing."

Julie-Ann relaxed. "I'm sorry. It's just that I've met some amazing people out here and learned so much. It's really opened my eyes. I just wish everyone back home could understand it, could be a part of it. I want to be able to talk to you guys about it."

"Jules, I do understand what you're doing. I never said that I didn't. All I said was just to be careful." Theresa paused. "I would love to hear your stories."

Theresa's words were comforting and such a relief—and Julie-Ann believed her. With eagerness, she told Theresa about Lisa Hendricks, all that she had been through, and her seemingly indelible positive outlook and benevolence. She went on to explain that her goal was to meet Lisa and her mother. Theresa listened attentively and asked questions here and there. Julie-Ann could tell that she was genuinely interested and moved by Lisa's story. They talked for about half an hour. Julie-Ann asked how things were back home and what Theresa was up to. She promised that she would start calling Theresa everyday again—or at least text her—to keep her updated on her whereabouts and wellbeing.

When she hung up the phone, Julie-Ann felt much better about things. She still wished her father would fully understand what she was doing, but she was glad that she could talk to Theresa again about her journey, without getting pressure to come back to New York. She also hoped that maybe Theresa could work on her father to get him to see her point of view—though she knew that would be a tough nut to crack.

By the time Julie-Ann got off the phone with Theresa it was 6:40 p.m. She had not eaten anything since breakfast and was starving. Not wanting to go back in the car again or walk around looking for a place to eat, she just ordered some room service.

As Julie-Ann waited for her food, she took out her laptop and sent Lisa a message on Facebook.

> *Lisa, first off, please call me Jules. I am currently in Jefferson City, Missouri. I am going to be here until Monday. Then I am heading to Topeka for a few days, continuing my journey out west, through Nebraska and Wyoming. I would love to be able to stop and meet you and your mother. Please talk it over with your mother and let me know if it is something the both of you would be interested in. If you can't do it for any reason, it's ok. I won't be offended in anyway and we will still keep in touch. I just thought that since I'm going to be in the area we could meet.*

Right after Julie-Ann sent it, she read it again and realized that she had not included her cellphone number, so she sent another message. She told Lisa that her mother could call her. She didn't want her mother thinking that she was a stalker that her daughter had met on the Internet, pretending to be some other person.

By the time her room service arrived, Julie-Ann was famished. Still, she ate her cheeseburger and fries at a leisurely pace, while watching a rerun of Seinfeld. After she finished she felt full, but also super relaxed. Though it was only 8:00 p.m., she changed into her nightclothes—gym shorts and a t-shirt.

Sitting Indian-style on the bed, with her laptop in front of her, and the TV still on, Julie-Ann went online to see what there was to do in Jefferson City. It turned out that there were not too many tourist attractions. Then it dawned on her and she searched for homeless shelters in the area. The first one to come up was The Salvation Army. Julie-Ann decided to visit it in the morning.

Before putting the computer away, Julie-Ann checked her emails and went on Facebook to post that she was now in Jefferson City. Lisa had already responded to her message.

> Yes, I would love to meet you in person. That would be great. I would really like to know more about your story. I had already told my mom about you (we're very close and tell each other everything). After reading your last message I told her that you were passing through and would like to meet both of us. I had her go on Facebook and read your profile and some of your posts. She said she would also like to meet you. She said she will call you tomorrow. I'm excited!

Julie-Ann was obviously happy that it sounded like she was going to be able to meet Lisa. In fact, while she was under the covers for the night, watching TV, her mind kept on thinking about meeting the teenager that a week ago she never even knew existed.

The next morning, after getting ready, Julie-Ann went downstairs for a complimentary continental breakfast.

After breakfast, Julie-Ann drove to the Salvation Army shelter. In a more rural part of town, it was a one-story stand-alone building that looked more like a ranch house than a homeless shelter. Julie-Ann parked in the parking lot. As she climbed out of the car, a sense of nervousness befell her. However, it was not enough to deter her. She just sucked it up and went inside.

There were two women talking to each other in the lobby. As Julie-Ann stood and looked around, one of the women, a plump, middle-aged woman with thin, metal framed glasses and short, but thick, curly red hair, turned to her.

"Can I help you?" The woman politely asked.

Julie-Ann could now see the red, short sleeve Salvation Army shirt she was wearing. "Oh, please, I'm sorry, I didn't mean to interrupt."

"Well thank you Nancy," said the other, younger woman, who looked frail and had eyes of shame that looked towards the floor. "I'll see you later." With that, she scurried away down one of the hallways.

"Oh, that's okay," the older woman said with a smile. "She just had a question for me. Now what can I help you with?"

"Well, I was wondering if…well, if I could maybe learn more about the shelter, maybe take a look around."

The woman looked over Julie-Ann. "I can certainly tell you about the facility and show you around, but I'm sorry, right now all of our beds are full. In fact, unfortunately, we have a waiting list. But if you need help…"

"Oh no, no," Julie-Ann politely interrupted. "I…I don't need a place to stay," she said. "I would just like to help. Make a donation, maybe even volunteer—though I'm only going to be here until tomorrow."

The woman let out a sigh of relief. "Oh yes, of course. Not a problem. You didn't look like you were homeless, but these days you never can tell. I just hate having to turn people away. Oh, I'm Nancy by the way," she said, extending her hand.

"Jules," she replied with a smile, as she shook Nancy's hand.

Nancy told Julie-Ann about the shelter, which was called the Center of Hope. Unlike the shelter in Anderson, the Center of Hope actually housed women and children, as well as men. In fact, many of the shelter's forty beds were currently filled with families. Julie-Ann was glad that women and children were able to be accommodated, but on the other hand, was heartbroken to know that so many families were homeless.

Nancy took Julie-Ann for a tour around the shelter. They ran in-to some of the residents, but Julie-Ann didn't really have an oppor-tunity to talk to any of them. However, Nancy briefly whispered here and there about some of their stories. The woman, she had been talking to when Julie-Ann walked in, Nancy explained, was a thirty-three-year-old single mother of two, named Helen. Her hus-band, who had been the sole provider for the family, committed suicide a year earlier. He actually had a $100,000 life insurance pol-icy, but it excluded suicide, and his wife didn't wind up getting a dime. Now homeless, she was living at the shelter with her seven-year-old daughter and ten-year-old-son.

Nancy wrapped up the tour of the facilities back by the front entranceway.

"I really want to thank you for showing me around, and telling me about the shelter," Julie-Ann said in a subdued voice. "You're really doing great work here and I would like to make a donation."

Kathy smiled. "Thank you. That would be very generous of you. We accept checks or credit cards."

Julie-Ann said she would write a check and Nancy led her to a nearby office where they sat down at a small, round table. As Julie-Ann retrieved the checkbook from her purse, she asked to whom she should make it out.

"The Salvation Army, Center of Hope," Nancy replied. "And again, we thank you very much for your contribution. We wouldn't be able to survive without donations."

Julie-Ann wrote the check and handed it to Nancy.

Nancy instinctively glanced at the amount. "Thi…this…this is for seven thousand dollars," she said in a shocked voice.

"That's right. I've been very fortunate in my life."

Nancy sat there for a second just staring at the check, her mouth open. "I…I don't know what to say."

"It's okay," Julie-Ann replied with a smile. "I'm just glad I can help in some small way." Julie-Ann paused. "But I was wondering if I could ask you a favor?"

"What is it?"

"I'd like to write one more check—for Helen, who you were telling me about. It's just heartbreaking to hear what happened to her and her children. They shouldn't be homeless—they did nothing wrong. I'd like to give her just a little bit of money, just to help her out, but I don't know how to go about it. I mean I would just write her a check, but she probably doesn't have a bank account. Can I write a check to the Salvation Army in her name? I don't want her just to be carrying around a bunch of cash."

"Well if you don't mind me asking, how much money are you talking about?"

Julie-Ann thought about it for a second. "I don't know, maybe ten thousand. I know that's not going to get her a house, but at least..."

"You want to give this woman, who you don't even know, ten thousand dollars?"

"Well I mean it's kind of the same as donating to the Salvation Army—it's going to help people I've never met before. But instead, it's going to help a specific family. I mean I know there's so many families out there that need help, especially now, but her story is just so tragic."

Nancy wiped away a tear from under her glasses. "God bless you Jules. God bless you." Nancy then thought about Julie-Ann's question for a few seconds. "I'll tell you what, I can go get Helen. You can meet her and give her the check yourself. Then when she goes to cash it, she can open up a checking account, so she won't have a bunch of cash lying around."

"You know what—I would love to meet her, but I don't want her to feel embarrassed or uncomfortable."

"I don't think she'll feel uncomfortable. I'm sure she'll be overjoyed."

"Well I'm sure she can use the money, but...I don't know...I don't want her to feel like such a charity case. I'll tell you what—if you can give me her full name, I'll make the check out to her, and then later you can give it to her. I'll leave my contact info and if she has any problem opening a checking account with it she can call me."

Nancy said that would be fine and provided her with Helen's last name, saying she knew she had a driver's license. Julie-Ann wrote out a $10,000 check.

After she handed it to Nancy, Nancy stood up. "Do you mind if I give you a hug?"

Julie-Ann smiled. "Of course not."

Nancy came over and wrapped her portly arms around Julie-Ann's slender frame. "Thank you so much."

"You're welcome," Julie-Ann simply replied as she hugged Nancy back.

After they let go of each other, Nancy looked at Julie-Ann. "Do you mind if I ask you a question?"

"Not at all."

"How did you become so involved with the homeless? I mean was it anything specific that made you focus on the homeless?

Julie-Ann felt comfortable telling Nancy her story—how she found out she had a tumor, how she decided to drive across America, and how she wanted to help those less fortunate than herself. She explained that she was from a "well-to-do" family, but didn't mention that her father was the CEO of Diamond & Russell.

As Julie-Ann left the center and walked to her car, she felt good about herself, good that she was able to play some part in the solution, not the problem. Before driving off, she sat in the driver's seat, pulled out her phone, and posted on Facebook that she had just visited the Center for Hope in Jefferson City, and that it was a humbling experience and praised them for the work they did. She once again urged people to help the less fortunate in anyway they could. Then she went on Twitter and tweeted about it. *Just visited homeless shelter in Jefferson City. Glad I could help. Great to see they allow families.*

Julie-Ann was glad she had visited the Salvation Army, but she had only spent less than an hour there. With no other particular place to go, she decided to drive back to the hotel, park the car, and walk around the area.

After parking the car, Julie-Ann went back to her room to use the restroom. On her way up, in the elevator, she checked her phone and realized that she already had several replies to both her Facebook post and tweet. She quickly browsed through them. They were mainly comments commending her and also saying what a shame it was that there were so many homeless people in the country. But as she exited the elevator and walked towards her room, one tweet in particular caught her attention. *I live in Henderson, NV. Big homeless problem here. People have set up camps, living in cars & tents.* Julie-Ann immediately envisioned some flat piece of land where families were living out of their automobiles and tents, refugees of the recession.

As Julie-Ann opened the door to her room, her phone, which was still out, rang. She looked down and didn't recognize the number, but the caller ID said it was from Nebraska. Then it dawned on her—it must be Lisa Hendricks' mother. Somewhat nervous, she picked up the call.

It *was* Lisa's mother, Adele. She was very polite and her voice welcoming. She thanked Julie-Ann for her support of America's troops. Julie-Ann said how sorry she was about the loss of her husband. Adele thanked her. She then said how she had looked at Julie-Ann's Facebook page and asked more about her story. Julie-Ann filled in the blanks, but once again, didn't let on who her father was. Adele seemed fascinated by her story. After talking for about fifteen minutes, Adele said how Julie-Ann had mentioned she would be driving through southern Nebraska and would like to meet her and Lisa.

"I would love to," Julie-Ann replied with excitement. "If it's at all possible. I mean we can meet at a restaurant or my hotel."

"Yes, I would love to meet you, too—and I know Lisa want's to meet you. I know you guys have only just exchanged a few messages, but it seems you really struck a chord with her."

Julie-Ann said that she would be in Hastings on Thursday, but if that was a bad time, she could push it back a few days. "I really don't have a set schedule," she explained.

Adele did not want Julie-Ann making a schedule around her.

She said Thursday or Friday would be fine, but that she worked during the day at a local supermarket. The two women agreed that Julie-Ann would call when she was in the area and they would hammer out the details of when and where to meet.

As soon as Julie-Ann hung up the phone, there was another incoming call. The caller ID read: Salvation Army, Jefferson City, Missouri. Figuring it was Nancy calling back for some reason, she picked it up.

"Nancy?"

"No," said a sheepish voice. "This is…my name is Helen Vigman. Is this Julie-Ann Crown?"

"Yes it is."

"You wrote me a check? Nancy gave it to me."

"Yes. Yes, that was me. Please don't be mad at Nancy, but she told me about you. I'm so sorry about your husband." Julie-Ann tried to find the right words to say. "I just wanted to help."

Julie-Ann could hear Helen sniffling, as if she was crying. "This check is for ten thousand dollars."

"Yes, that's right. Hopefully it can help get you back on your feet."

Now it was clear that Helen was crying. "Why would you give me ten thousand dollars? I don't even know you."

"Like I said, Nancy told me about you, that you're living at the shelter with your two kids. Please understand it's not pity. I don't want you to feel…I mean I know anyone can become homeless. I…I've been very fortunate and have some money and I just want to be able to help where I can. I just want to be able to give something back."

"God bless you Julie-Ann. It's people like you that proves there's still hope for humanity. Never in my wildest dreams…I can never repay you."

Now Julie-Ann was fighting back tears. "Oh, don't ever worry about repaying me. If you want to repay me then one day just do something to help someone else."

"I will. And I want you to know that I'm going to use this money to find an apartment and be able to get someone to watch my kids so I can find a job. I don't want you thinking that I'm going to blow it, or use it to party. I don't do drugs..."

"Please," Julie-Ann politely cut her off. "The thought never crossed my mind. I'm sure you will use it wisely. And I hope you and your children see better days."

Helen thanked her again and promised to give her an update at some point of how she and the kids were doing.

After finally getting a chance to use the restroom, Julie-Ann went back outside and ventured around the area. It was a hot and sticky day, and even in shorts and a t-shirt, she was sweating. She stopped in a few stores. Afterwards, while walking around some more, she stumbled upon a Mexican restaurant. By this time it was 1:40 p.m. and she hungry. So she sat down and ordered chicken fajitas—figuring they would be safe—and a margarita.

That evening, Julie-Ann stayed in the hotel. After watching some TV, she went on the Internet to find a hotel in Topeka, her next stop. There was a Hyatt and she was shocked to see that a regular room was $75 a night. She laughed, thinking how much the Hyatt in New York City cost. She booked a room for three nights.

Then, feeling bored, Julie-Ann searched for a hotel in Hastings. There were not many choices. She picked the Holiday Inn, as it looked to be the nicest hotel. She did not know how long she would be in Hastings, but reserved the room for four nights just in case. Not worried about the money, she figured she could always leave earlier—or extend her stay.

Chapter 22

It was only a three and a half hour drive from Jefferson City to Topeka, so Julie-Ann took her time getting ready in the morning and went downstairs for breakfast. Still, she was on the road by 10:15 a.m.

Julie-Ann tried to find the talk radio show she had listened to the other day, but she could not. So she scanned through some other talk shows. She found one that was talking about the high cost of healthcare in America and kept it on.

"Listen, I have no problems with immigrants," the host said in a calm tone. "My father was from Ireland. But we can't have people coming into this country illegally and getting free healthcare and then having everyone else that is here legally and paying taxes, pay for it."

Julie-Ann listened as the host went on not just about undocumented immigrants, but also other reasons healthcare was so expensive and how the cost was only rising and becoming more and more unaffordable. Then he opened up the phone line to callers.

"If I have to go to the emergency room you better damn well

believe I'm getting a bill for it," one angry caller lamented. "And if I don't pay that bill they'll go after me, ruin my credit, put a lien on my property. But if someone that's here illegally doesn't pay their hospital bill what happens? The taxpayers—you and me—are stuck paying for it. Not to mention that we then all have to pay more for insurance."

Another caller phoned in. "I'll tell you the real problem with high cost of healthcare, and neither the Democrats nor the Republicans ever mention it—tort reform. These doctors have to pay an astronomical amount for malpractice insurance. These lawsuits are out of control in America."

Yet another irate caller pointed out the pharmaceutical companies being in bed with doctors. "Everyone's going to the doctors, because they keep everyone medicated. Everyone's on medication now—many people more than one medication—because the pharmaceutical companies give these physicians incentives. And then you have the pharmaceutical lobbyists. You want to know the people with the real power in Washington? The lobbyists! They don't get voted in, we can't impeach them, and you've probably never even seen one, but every politician is beholden to them, because they contribute massive amounts of money to their campaigns."

Then, one caller seemed to have a solution. "I'll tell you the answer to all this—give every taxpayer in the country the same health insurance as Congress has!"

Julie-Ann listened to the show for nearly an hour, until she stopped at a rest area to use the bathroom and fill up her tank. When she continued on her way, she decided to leave the radio off. Julie-Ann just wanted to relax, look at the scenery, and enjoy the rest of her drive. In fact, though it was already hot and humid out, she put the top down on the Camaro.

It was a bright blue sky, speckled only with a few, sporadic, small, transparent white clouds. On both sides of the highway were sprawling flatlands as far as the eye could see. There was not a mountain nor hill to be found. Eventually, the land turned to seemingly infinite wheat fields. With the wind blowing in from the open top, Julie-Ann gazed out at the fields and could not help but think about the Native Americans, and later pioneers that crossed the vast land. In her mind's eye she could see thousands of buffalo roaming the prairie. If only she could go back in time and witness what it was like, she wondered.

Julie-Ann entered Topeka at 2:05 p.m. Like the land that led to it, the city was flat. She went straight to the hotel, which seemed to be on the outskirts of town, but in what looked like a safe area.

Compared to her other drives, this one was short and instead of being worn out, Julie-Ann actually felt energized as she walked into the hotel's lobby. Though not as luxurious as some of the other Hyatt's she had stayed in throughout the world, it was very clean and modern. After looking around, Julie-Ann went up to the front desk, where a friendly young gentleman checked her in.

The room was even more spacious than it seemed on the Internet. Like the rest of the hotel, it also looked new. There was a couch in a separate seating area, though it flowed into where the bed was via an open wall. The flat screen TV, which was in front of the bed on a dresser, was also larger than in most normal hotel rooms. There was even a stocked mini-bar (of course, nothing was complimentary). Everything was adorned in light, beige colors and exuded a welcoming brightness to the room. After putting down her bags, Julie-Ann went to check out the bathroom, which was also clean and quite spacious. The shower had a large head on it and she turned it on to inspect the water pressure and to her delight it was powerful.

As Julie-Ann put some of her clothes away and set up her toiletries on the bathroom counter, she contemplated what to do with the rest of the day. The man that checked her in said that the hotel had a pool. It was hot and humid out and jumping into a pool sounded refreshing. But then Julie-Ann realized that for whatever reason, she had not packed a bathing suit. *I'll just find a mall and get one,* she thought. *I'm going to need one at some point anyway. The pool sounds so good right now. But wait, you're not going to spend four hours in the mall looking for the perfect bathing suit. You're just going to go in, find something and leave. Yes, I promise.*

Julie-Ann went down to the lobby and asked the concierge where the nearest mall was. He explained that it was about ten minutes away and gave her quick directions. However, when Julie-Ann got into the car, she still used the GPS. It was just habit—and she was not too good with directions.

Julie-Ann found a Dillard's and went straight to the swimsuit section. Sometimes, finding the right bathing suit for a woman could literally take days and a plethora of stores, but she was determined to keep her promise to herself to not go crazy. Besides, she was in Topeka, not Midtown Manhattan. There were not an unlimited number of clothing stores. As she browsed through the choices, she tried to narrow them down. She did not want something too revealing or sexy, but neither did she want a one piece. Finally, after about a half hour of going into the changing room and trying different ones on, she settled on two bikinis. She figured if she went back to the hotel and for some reason didn't like the way one looked in front of a different mirror, then she could have an alternative.

Julie-Ann was proud of herself—and amazed—that it only took her a half hour and one store. Having eaten only a light breakfast, and not wanting to drive around or wait in a restaurant, she decided to go to the food court. She ordered a quarter-pounder and fries and found a small table, where she sat and ate. It dawned on her that she had just bought a bikini and there she was gobbling down fast food. Though not sickly thin, Julie-Ann didn't have an ounce of fat on her. Still, a woman always has her waist on her mind.

Once back at the hotel, Julie-Ann changed into her swimsuit, a black bikini with subtle gold trim. She stood in front of the mirror, making sure she liked the way it fit; Julie-Ann looked at the long, blonde wig she was wearing. *Wait, I can't go into the pool with my wig. I can't get it wet. Can I? I think she said I can. But what if it comes off? I can't have that happen. What if I just don't put my head in the water? But I wanted to maybe swim. I'll just take it off. It's not like I'm bald. But the people at the desk already saw me with it on. If I go down without it they'll know it was a wig. So, who cares what they think. Stop being so vain.*

Julie-Ann took off the wig revealing her short, blonde hair, and looked into the mirror. "You look fine," she said aloud.

Julie-Ann took some money out of her wallet and then put her purse, car keys, and laptop in the room's safe. She grabbed a bottle of water from the minibar, her sunglasses and headphones, and headed downstairs. Before going to the pool, she stopped in the hotel's gift shop and bought a bottle of sunscreen. Wanting to get tan, but not burn, she went with a fifteen SPF.

The pool area was nicer than she had expected. Though the pool itself was not a sprawling body of water that one might find in a resort, it was big enough to go swimming. The area, like the rest of the hotel, was clean. There were lounge chairs, tables, and adjacent to the pool was a small, outside bar.

Julie-Ann grabbed two towels—one to lie on and one to dry herself with—and went to find a lounge chair. Though she had tried to find to find a bikini that was not too provocative, it was still a bikini and showed off her alluring figure. The few men that were by the pool—two of whom were with women—turned their heads and watched as she walked by. Even a boy, who appeared to be around twelve-years-old, could not help but sneak a peek.

Julie-Ann set up camp at one of the lounge chairs, facing the sun, and not next to anyone else. Though she had wanted to go in the pool, she decided to lay out for a while first. As she rubbed on her sunscreen, she noticed a middle-aged guy looking at her, though he was trying to be inconspicuous. Then she saw another, younger man, walking from the bar with two drinks in his hands, to bring to either his wife or girlfriend. He had sunglasses on, but Julie-Ann could feel him watching as she put on her lotion. None of it made her feel uncomfortable. To the contrary, she enjoyed the attention—as long as it was from afar. Every girl wants to be able to turn heads. Besides, though she was alone, it seemed like a safe, family-oriented place.

After putting on her sunscreen, Julie-Ann was ready to lay out, but then realized that something was missing. She walked over to the outside bar and ordered a pina colada to bring back to the lounge chair. She then laid back, put on her headphones, and turned on Pandora on her iPhone. Though she had enjoyed the blues, she was in the mood for something more upbeat and more apropos, so she turned to her Jimmy Buffet station.

With Margaritaville playing in her ears, and the sun caressing her body, Julie-Ann leisurely sipped her drink from a straw. For the first time since her journey began, she felt as if she was on vacation and it was a relaxing, liberating feeling. Julie-Ann took another sip of her pina colada and then exhaled. *Yeah, this is good,* she thought.

While still listening to music on her iPhone she text Theresa. *Got to Topeka safely. Laying out by the pool having a pina colada. I'm so glad we talked yesterday. Thank you for understanding me. I'll call you soon.*

After about fifteen minutes, and with her drink empty, Julie-Ann went into the pool. Her body hot and sweaty from the still powerful sun, the water felt exhilarating. She was so glad that she had decided to forgo the wig, as she dunked her head into the clear water.

After chilling in the pool for ten or so minutes, Julie-Ann got out and loosely dried herself off. She walked back to the bar for another drink.

A young couple, maybe in their twenties, was sitting at the bar. Julie-Ann stood next to the woman, who was attractive and wearing a bikini, to order a drink.

The bartender, a young, slender Latin-looking male, turned his attention to Julie-Ann. "Another pina colada?" He asked with a smile.

Julie-Ann smiled back. "Yes please. It was very good."

The woman turned to Julie-Ann. "How is the water?"

Julie-Ann noticed the wedding ring on the woman's hand. She then glanced over and saw that the man also had a ring. "Perfect. Not cold, not too warm. It's just the right coolness."

"I can't wait to go in, but he wanted to have a drink first," she said, tilting her head towards her husband.

The young man, physically fit with washboard abs, and a handsome face, turned his head. "And what's that in your hand," he said lightheartedly, pointing at her bottle of Corona.

"Well hey, there is nothing like drinking a beer by the pool. Besides, I'm on vacation. I'm Lexi by the way," she said, extending her hand.

"Jules," she replied, shaking her hand.

"This here is Evan."

Julie-Ann and Evan acknowledged each other with a smile and nod of the head.

Just then, the bartender gave Julie-Ann her pina colada, which she paid for with the money in her hand.

"So, what brings you to beautiful Topeka?" Lexi asked.

Julie-Ann could not tell if she was being sarcastic or not about Topeka. She didn't want to get into her whole story. "I'm on my way to visit a friend in Nebraska and am just passing through."

"Oh, you're driving? Where from?"

Julie-Ann thought about it for a second. "From New York," she said with a chuckle. "I've just always wanted to drive across the country and I figured it was the perfect opportunity."

"That is so cool. All by yourself?"

"Yep."

"That is great. Good for you."

"I would love to do that," added Evan.

Lexi asked about her trip so far and some of the places she had stopped at. Without getting into the people she had met, and the real purpose of her journey, Julie-Ann told them about being in Blacksburg and Anderson.

"So what about you guys?" Julie-Ann then asked. "You're on vacation?"

Lexi took a swig of her beer. "Well kind of. We're visiting Evan's parents. I love his parents, but I just rather stay at a hotel, you know what I mean? You just have more freedom. You can do whatever it is you want to do."

Evan swiveled in his barstool and put his arm around his wife's shoulder. "Don't listen to her—she can't stand my mother."

"Evan!"

"Oh come on, I don't blame you. She's completely overbearing. I don't even want to stay there."

Evan and Lexi laughed together.

"Well it was a pleasure meeting both of you," Julie-Ann said with a smile, pina colada in hand.

"Well we're here for a couple of days. Hopefully we can have some drinks together," Lexi said.

"Lexi loves her shots," Evan added jokingly.

Julie-Ann nodded. "Yes, definitely. I'll be here till Thursday."

With that, Julie-Ann went back to her lounge chair by the pool. She was happy to see that her stuff was still there, including her iPhone, which she had left under the towel. As she went to lay back down, she looked across the pool area and could see Lexi and Evan sitting at the bar. Evan was saying something to his wife, a few inches away from her face. Then they kissed. Seeing this, suddenly Julie-Ann felt lonely. She wanted someone to laugh with, to hangout with, to kiss—to sleep with.

Having already laid on her back, Julie-Ann wanted to turn over and lay on her stomach. She had no one to rub sunscreen on her back that made her feel even more alone. Not about to ask a stranger to put lotion on her back, she told herself that she would just lay on her stomach for ten minutes or so.

After about ten minutes, Julie-Ann was feeling hot again and decided to go back into the pool. She had only drunk half of her pina colada, but the rest of it had melted from a frozen, frothy concoction into liquid. So she left it by the chair and instead took her bottle of water.

Julie-Ann was not in the water more than a few minutes when Lexi came in and waded over to her. "Oh, the water feels so good," she proclaimed.

"I know."

"That's one of the things I love about summer the most—that it stays light out for so long. We live in Chicago and in the winter, which lasts forever, it's completely dark by five o'clock. But what am I telling you for, you live in New York."

Julie-Ann and Lexi stood in the water for a little while chatting. Lexi explained that Evan was a graphic designer and she was a paralegal. They had been married for two years and this was their first trip out of state since their honeymoon, in Aruba. Lexi went onto say that her first choice was not Topeka, but Evan had not seen his parents in a while. Lexi asked what Julie-Ann did for a living. Not wanting to get into who she was and what had happened, she reverted to the white lie of saying she worked for a publishing company.

When Evan jumped into the pool, Julie-Ann saw her opportunity to exit. It was not that she had anything against Lexi or Evan. They appeared to be good, fun people. In fact, she wouldn't mind hanging out with them again at some point during her stay. But for right then, she just wanted to go back to the room. She said good-bye and that they would probably run into each other again over the next few days.

That evening, Julie-Ann stayed in her hotel room and ate a Cobb salad from room service. She could not shake the feeling of loneliness. Looking at the empty side of the bed next to her, she longed to be held, to be caressed, to have sex. Flipping through the channels, she found a cheesy soft-core porn movie on Cinemax. As she watched a sex scene, she slid off her shorts and panties and began to pleasure herself. Getting more excited, her heartbeat accelerated and a warm tingling sensation flowed through her body. Breathing heavy, her legs spread wider as she slid her finger inside of her. Knowing just the right spots, the exhilaration continued to build as she squirmed under the covers, until finally, she climaxed. Once the euphoria was over and her breathing slowed, the loneliness quickly returned.

Julie-Ann woke up the next morning at 7:30 a.m. and felt well rested. Still, she laid in bed for a while, watching TV, before slowly getting ready. But for what, she had no idea. She just knew she did not want to spend the day in the hotel room.

While getting ready, Julie-Ann ordered room service; an egg white omelet, wheat toast, and a bowl of mixed fruit. While eating she went on her laptop and searched for things to do in Topeka. She whittled it down to two choices: the Kansas Museum of History, and the zoo. After giving it some more thought, she decided to go to the museum. She could always go to the zoo afterwards, or even the next day.

Julie-Ann decided to once again, forgo her wig. This time she did not even fret over the decision. In fact, she would never again wear a wig.

By 10:00 a.m., Julie-Ann was in her car, on her way to the museum. It was smaller than she thought it would be, but still had plenty of artifacts, such as stagecoaches, an old steam locomotive, and the inside of a pioneer log house. It also has a section dedicated to the Civil War, which Julie-Ann found fascinating. She wound up spending over two hours in the museum, slowly snaking her way through, looking over every exhibit and reading every story.

Though it was hot out, Julie-Ann decided to drive back to the hotel, park the car, and walk around. The Hyatt was not in a centrally located area, but she didn't mind getting some exercise.

There were not many stores or businesses by the hotel, but after about ten minutes Julie-Ann came upon a convenience store and went in to buy a bottle of water. It was a hot, humid, late June day outside and she was already overheating. After chugging down some water, she continued her trek. She walked for about another twenty minutes before coming to what appeared to be a centralized area. Sweating and panting, she bought another bottle of water. She then saw a bank and used the ATM, needing some more cash. Julie-Ann strolled around the area, stopping in several stores, mostly just to take advantage of their air conditioning.

Periodically cooling off with a dose of cool air was nice, but Julie-Ann was getting tired of walking around and wanted a place to sit and rest. Though she wasn't too hungry, she started looking for a restaurant where she could sit down for a while. She happened to walk right past a bar. *A cold beer does sound good right now,* she thought. Trying to be inconspicuous, she peeked in through the glass facade. She saw a woman bartender, another woman at the bar, as well as one male customer. She decided to go in. Julie-Ann walked up to the bar and took a seat.

"How are you doing today?" The barmaid, who looked to be in her thirties, asked in a welcoming voice.

"Hot," Julie-Ann replied as she fanned herself off with her hand.

"Yeah, it's supposed to be ninety today."

Julie-Ann nodded in agreement.

"Well what can I get for you?"

Julie-Ann thought about it for a second. "You know what, do you have Corona?"

"Yes we do."

It tasted so good and cold, that Julie-Ann gulped down a quarter of the bottle.

As the barmaid went back to the other woman customer she had been talking to, Julie-Ann enjoyed her beer and turned her attention to the television above the bar, which had the news on. They had just started talking about the Occupy Wall Street movement, showing dozens of people camped out in lower Manhattan, many of whom held placards protesting Wall Street and the rich.

"Will you look at these assholes," the man at the bar ranted, as he pointed towards the television. Wearing faded jeans, a t-shirt, and work boots, he was tall with broad shoulders, and looked to be middle age.

"I thought you hated Wall Street, Bill," the barmaid said as she walked over.

He shook his head. "I do. Believe me. But these idiots don't even know what they're protesting, Heather. They don't know the first thing about Wall Street. They just think they're entitled for some reason, like the government should give them money and houses just for taking up space."

Everyone in the bar turned their attention to the TV, as a reporter asked one of the protesters, a young woman, maybe in her early twenties, exactly what she was protesting against.

"I'm protesting against the machine," she said defiantly. "Down with capitalism!"

The reporter than asked a young man the same question.

"I'm not sure really. I guess everything. I just heard there's a party going on here."

Bill, the man at the bar, let out a loud, hardy laugh. "See! What did I tell you?"

"You hear that a lot now, about how capitalism has failed," the other woman at the bar said.

Bill took a swig of his beer. "That's a bunch of bullshit. You see, if you're against Wall Street, the media tries to paint you as being against capitalism and free market. That couldn't be further from the truth. I believe in free markets. It's Wall Street that is anti-capitalism and free markets. You name me one single financial firm that hasn't been embroiled in scandal. Manipulating the markets, fixing interest rates, using insider information, creating bogus investment vehicles. That's the opposite of free market."

"But you're right," Heather replied. "These occupy people aren't just protesting Wall Street, they're against anyone who's rich."

"Look, if you invent something, or work hard and have a great idea and start a company, than as long as you're not ripping anyone off, you deserve all the money you can make. I have no problem with that." He took another drink from his bottle and then motioned Heather to get him another. "But it's the people who built this country and make this country run—the working class, the middle class—that are always getting squeezed the hardest. No one's ever looking out for us."

"Do you think we're really seeing an end to the middle class?" Julie-Ann asked, finally joining the conversation.

Bill took a drink of his new beer and then let out a deflating sigh. "Unfortunately, young lady, I think we are. People like me; I'm part of a dying breed. I'm not looking for any handout from the government or to take from anyone else. I believe in working hard for a living, being able to provide for my family, and hopefully leave my kids better off than I had it. When I was growing up that was the American Dream. But now, thanks to these billionaire crooks on Wall Street everything I have is worth less. And what money I do have left, Obama is trying to take and give to these freeloaders. As if I owe anyone anything. I've worked hard my whole life for everything I have, and pay my taxes every year."

"But what about all those people like you that worked hard and were making an honest living, but through no fault of their own, when the collapse happened, lost their jobs—and many, their homes?"

Bill took another swig of his beer and nodded. "You're right about that. A lot of good, hardworking Americans did lose their jobs and I have no problem with them collecting unemployment so they don't have to be forced out onto the street. But it can't go on forever. There's a lot of people just living off the system. People who've contributed nothing, but always have their hands out."

"Well, I guess that's true," Julie-Ann agreed.

"If you can't make your mortgage payment," he continued, "there's programs now to help you out. But what about someone like me, who's never missed a mortgage payment? Don't I get credit for that? You see, if you're rich, you get all the breaks. If you can't work or need assistance, then the government helps you out. But if you're a working stiff, if you're the middle class, then the only thing you get is screwed." Bill paused as he took another drink. "There's no incentive anymore for busting your ass and making an honest living. It's like everything's backwards."

"You're right about that," the barmaid chimed in. "I work six days a week—here and at another bar. And nobody's helping me out. I don't qualify for any special programs."

"Well I've got to get going Heather," the other girl at the bar announced as she stood up. "I'll see you later on tonight." She then said goodbye to Bill, and even Julie-Ann.

As the woman and Heather exchanged a few last words at the end of the bar, Bill turned to Julie-Ann. "I'm sorry, I didn't mean to be rude. It's just that it really pisses me off. I love my country and I see it going down the tube." He paused and took a breath. "But you didn't come in here to hear me lecture."

"Oh no, please, don't apologize. I was the one asking you questions."

Julie-Ann talked to Bill and Heather for a while and they seemed like good people. Bill told her that he currently worked as a manager of a lumberyard. He also said that he had three children, and that his oldest daughter, who just turned twenty-four, reminded him of Julie-Ann. Bill asked where Julie-Ann was from and what she was doing in Topeka. She told him the same story that she had told Lexi and Evan—that she was from New York, worked for a publishing company, and that she was driving to see a friend in Nebraska.

"You're driving from New York to Nebraska by yourself?" Asked Heather.

Julie-Ann finished drinking her beer. "Well I was able to take some time off work," she lied. "And I always wanted to drive across the country, stop at different places."

"Well good for you. It's good to see a young, independent woman," Bill replied.

Just then another man walked into the bar. He said hello to Heather and Bill and before he could even sit down, Heather had a bottle of Bud waiting for him. Bill introduced the man to Julie-Ann and he joined in on the conversation. Heather asked Julie-Ann where she had stopped thus far on her journey and she told them.

Julie-Ann was feeling comfortable and enjoying talking to the locals. She asked about Topeka. Heather poured everyone a free shot—including herself. Julie-Ann chose tequila. The time seemed to fly by. As two more customers came into the bar, Julie-Ann looked at her watch and realized that she had been at the bar for nearly two hours. After four beers and a shot, she was also starting to feel drunk. So she decided it was time to go back to the hotel.

Julie-Ann was ready to say her goodbyes and to walk back to the hotel, but then she remembered that she had walked for probably two miles to get to the bar and didn't feel like trekking all the way back. So she asked Heather if she had the number for a local taxi. Heather asked where she was going and called the cab company for her. Heather said it would be about ten minutes.

As Julie-Ann waited, she said her goodbyes and what a pleasure it was meeting Heather and Bill (the other man whom she had been talking with was now locked in a conversation with someone else). Heather and Bill reciprocated and Bill said she had to do another shot before she left. Julie-Ann thought what the hell and did a shot with him.

By the time Julie-Ann arrived back at the Hyatt it was 3:40 p.m. She was feeling happy, but realized she had not eaten any lunch. Not wanting to just go sit in her room and order room service, she went to the hotel restaurant. There, she sat by herself and ate a turkey club. As she did, she checked her messages and emails. There was an email from Michelle, who was just checking in. Always glad to hear from her, Julie-Ann emailed her back telling her she was in Topeka and about the people she had just met at the bar.

Julie-Ann also had a text message from Amber, apologizing again for their fight. Julie-Ann text her back. *Don't apologize. I told you I'm not mad. It really was great seeing you. I wish you were here with me now in Kansas. There are some really cool people here. You'll always be my BFF Amber! We'll talk soon.*

After eating Julie-Ann felt energized. She did not overeat and stuff herself and she still had a buzz from the alcohol. As soon as she walked out of the restaurant, she ran into Lexi and Evan.

"Hey!" Lexi said with a grand smile.

"Hey. How are you guys doing?"

"We just got back from spending the day at his parents. Now I'm ready to go to hang out by the pool and get drunk. You should join us."

Julie-Ann thought about it for a second. It was only 4:30 p.m. She was feeling energized and she certainly didn't want to just sit in her room for the rest of the day. "Are you sure?"

"Of course," Evan said. "We're just going up to the room to change."

"Go put on your bathing suit," Lexi added. "We'll meet you down by the bar in like twenty minutes."

"Okay," Julie-Ann replied with excitement.

Happy to have someone to hangout with—and something to do—Julie-Ann went back to her room and changed into her bikini.

As planned, Julie-Ann met Lexi and Evan down at the bar, where they stayed and had a drink before going to the pool. Though beginning its descent, the sun was still blasting through a clear sky. Lexi and Julie-Ann went in the pool with their beers in plastic cups, as Evan lay on a lounge chair. Eventually, they all made their way into the water. Lexi sucked down her beers and encouraged Julie-Ann to do the same. Evan kept going back to the bar to get more. At first he would not take Julie-Ann's money, but after the third round she insisted on buying the next one. As the summer evening pushed on, time ticked away unnoticed. The drinks kept flowing, voices grew louder, and laughs were a plenty. The atmosphere was light and energetic.

At one point, as they were sitting around a patio table, Lexi asked Julie-Ann more about her drive from New York.

Julie-Ann paused before answering. "You know, I want to tell you guys something."

"What is it?" Lexi asked.

Julie-Ann decided to tell them the real reason she was on her journey and what she hoped to accomplish. Both Lexi and Evan seemed fascinated and commended her.

Then, as they asked more about the people she had met on her journey, Julie-Ann told them about the McAlisters and the veterans at the hospital. She went on to tell them about the epidemic of out of work and homeless veterans. Evan said that he had a cousin that did three tours in Iraq and luckily came home safe. Lexi had a good friend that was still in Afghanistan. They all agreed that more should be done for the troops that return home, especially helping them find jobs.

"They should get first priority," Evan said.

"You would think companies would want to hire vets," added Lexi.

Julie-Ann then told them about the specific problem of homeless female veterans and how Kathy was starting a foundation to help them.

They talked for a while about returning troops and the wars overseas. But eventually the conversation turned more lighthearted again and the three of them found themselves sitting at the outside bar as the sun began to set.

Lexi mentioned that she was hungry. The bartender overheard and said that they could order food to be brought out to the bar until 8:00 p.m.

Evan looked at his watch. "Well it's seven-forty now. We better hurry up. Let's order some appetizers."

"Yeah, that sounds good," Lexi replied. "I'm too relaxed and drunk to go up and change and go out for dinner. How does some appetizers sound Jules?"

Julie-Ann had just eaten less than four hours earlier, but she decided to go with the flow. She also figured that some more food might be needed to soak up all the alcohol. "Yeah sure, that sounds good. I mean as long as you guys don't mind."

"Don't be crazy," Lexi said as she waved her hand. "We're having a good time."

Evan asked the bartender for menus—and another round of drinks.

They stayed outside by the pool until 9:30 p.m., when the patio bar closed. All three of them were blasted, especially Julie-Ann, who had already had several beers and two shots earlier in the afternoon. Lexi suggested they go back to their room and continue the party, but Julie-Ann knew she had to call it a night. Before parting ways, in case they did not see each other the next day, Lexi and Julie-Ann exchanged numbers, email addresses, and befriended each other on Facebook. They also took several pictures; a few of Lexi and Julie-Ann, one of Julie-Ann and Evan, and the bartender took a few of the three of them together.

Chapter 23

Julie-Ann woke up late the next morning with a crushing hangover. She forced down some water and took two Advil, but it seemed of little help. Feeling sick to her stomach, she went into the bathroom and threw-up. She then went back to the bed and crawled under the covers. Her head hurt, her stomach hurt, her muscles hurt. She wanted someone to take care of her, to coddle her. But she was all alone.

Finally, around 1:00 p.m., Julie-Ann ordered some room service. She still wasn't exactly hungry, but hoped food would make her feel better. But when it came, she could only eat half of her burger and some fries.

Julie-Ann spent the whole day in the hotel room. At one point she thought about going down to the pool, thinking that the fresh air and water might help her, but she was feeling too sick.

Later on in the afternoon she received a text from Lexi. *How are you feeling? I'm so hung-over, but we had to go to Evan's parents. I'm there now. Kill me! I just want to go back to the hotel and go to bed!*

Julie-Ann responded. *I can't even imagine that. I've taken aspirin, ate something, and I still feel like I'm going to die! I haven't left the room all day. How much did we drink last night? And remember I stopped at a bar before I even got back to the hotel. Oh God, I'm never drinking again. I'm going to try and take a shower now. Talk later.*

That evening Julie-Ann ordered an in-room movie and watched it on the couch. As she was watching it, her phone rang. It was her father. She debated whether to answer. Still feeling like shit, the last thing she wanted to do was hear a lecture or argue. However, on the third ring, she reluctantly answered.

"Hey Dad," she said, trying to force an upbeat voice. She didn't want her father thinking that something was wrong.

"Hey sweetie. How are you doing?"

"I'm doing fine."

"Good. So I hear you're in Topeka."

Julie-Ann didn't know where her father was going, but wanted to nip it in the bud if he was calling to pressure her to come home. "Dad, I really don't…"

"Listen Jules," he cut her off. "I didn't call to ask you twenty questions about what you're doing or tell you to come home. In fact, I want to apologize about the way I've acted. You know I love you."

Julie-Ann felt like crying. "I love you to, Daddy. I always will."

"I know sweetie. And I've thought about it and I'm behind what you're doing. I just worry about you out there by yourself. I don't want anyone taking advantage of you or trying to turn you against me because of what I do."

"Dad, no one is ever going to turn me against you. And I'm not going to let anyone take advantage of me. I know you worry about me, but you have to trust me. I'm not a little girl anymore."

Her father let out a breath. "I do trust you sweetie. I really do. And though I'm always here if you need me, you take as long as you want on your journey. And whatever you want to do with your life I'll be behind."

Tears began to swell in Julie-Ann's eyes. "Thank you, Daddy. That means the world to me. It really does."

"I don't want us to argue anymore. I miss you and I want us to be able to tell each other things—like we always have."

"Me too."

Julie-Ann talked to her father for a while longer. She told him that she was going to Nebraska in the morning. She didn't tell him why and he didn't ask. But he did ask about Topeka. She told him that she had met a nice couple at the hotel and had some drinks and dinner with them. She also told him about the museum.

When Julie-Ann hung up, she felt much better about everything. She was actually smiling, thinking about her father and home when her phone buzzed. It was an incoming text from Lexi asking if she wanted to meet for breakfast before leaving in the morning. Julie-Ann replied that she would love to, but wanted to leave by 9:00 a.m., because it was a five-hour ride and she wanted to check into the hotel and have a breather before she had to meet Lisa and her mother. Lexi replied that she could meet Julie-Ann at 8:00 a.m., but she did not want to pressure her. Julie-Ann agreed to meet Lexi at the hotel breakfast buffet at 8:00 a.m.

Julie-Ann woke up the next morning to the piercing, annoying chirping sound of the alarm clock. Although she had rested the whole previous day and went to bed early, she still felt exhausted. Nevertheless, she got herself ready and packed.

As planned, Julie-Ann met Lexi down at the buffet at 8:00 a.m. She was alone, saying Evan was not feeling well and still asleep, but sends his regards and wished Julie-Ann well on the rest of her journey.

Over breakfast Lexi asked Julie-Ann more about her travels and plans. Julie-Ann talked more about Lisa's story and how much she was looking forward to meeting her. Beyond Hastings, Julie-Ann explained, she would play it by ear.

"I guess I'll probably wind up driving all the way to the west coast at this point."

"Well I think it's great what you're doing," Lexi replied. "Not just for yourself, but how you're trying to help others. You're a real inspiration."

Julie-Ann laughed. "Please, I think you're giving me too much credit. I've been blessed my whole life. Everything's been handed to me. I'm just trying to give a little back, that's all. It's the least I can do."

"You may have had an easy life growing up, but I'm sure you always had a good heart. And you're just twenty-five, Jules. Most twenty-five-year-olds are still worried about partying and having a good time. And you're not just giving something back. You really care." Lexi paused. "I don't care what you say, you're an inspiration to me."

Julie-Ann blushed and smiled. "Thank you."

After breakfast Lexi made Julie-Ann promised to keep her updated on her journey. Julie-Ann said she would, but also wanted Lexi to let her know how she was doing.

In front of the restaurant, the two new friends embraced in a hug. "Take care of yourself Jules."

"I will. And you take care of yourself. And tell Evan I said goodbye. It was a pleasure meeting him. You two are great together."

They let go of each other and stood face to face. "Hopefully some day we can meet again," Lexi said. "Maybe in Chicago or New York."

"I would like that very much," Julie-Ann replied with a smile.

After leaving Lexi, Julie-Ann brought her bags down to the car and checked out of the hotel. She was on the road by 8:50 a.m.

Julie-Ann was glad she had met Lexi for breakfast, and although feeling much better than the previous day, she still felt some lingering effects from her hangover. Though she was excited to meet Lisa and her mother, and continue her journey, she was not looking forward to spending the next five hours in the car. But there was nothing she could do but suck it up.

With music on low and the air conditioner on, Julie-Ann headed out to the highway. Thick clouds were rolling in and she prayed that it would not rain like it had when she was driving to Jefferson City.

About a half hour out of Topeka, the open highway started to congest. Suddenly there was a stream of brake lights and a traffic jam in the middle of nowhere. As she slowed down to a standstill, Julie-Ann noticed flashing red and blue lights about a half-mile down the road to the left. There had to have been an accident she surmised. She figured that it would just be a slight delay, but after twenty-five minutes, she had only moved up several car lengths.

As she was impatiently waiting for the accident to be cleared and gridlock to dissipate, her phone, which was lying on the center console, rang. It was Adele. Julie-Ann quickly put in her Bluetooth and answered the call. Adele asked how things were going and when she wanted to meet. Julie-Ann explained that she was planning to get to her hotel in Hasting by 3:00 p.m., but was currently stuck in standstill traffic because of an accident.

Adele could hear the frustration in Julie-Ann's voice. "Well don't worry about it. I don't get off until five. But listen, I don't want you to drive all day, check into your hotel, and then rush to meet us. I know how I feel after a long drive. If you just want to meet tomorrow we can do that. In fact, though I usually work Fridays, I offered to change my schedule with someone and I actually have tomorrow off. But it's up to you. We can still meet tonight if you want to. I mean I don't know if you were just staying in Hasting overnight."

Julie-Ann thought about it for a second. "Are you sure it wouldn't be an inconvenience if we met tomorrow?"

"Oh, not at all. I'll make lunch. I just don't want it to be an inconvenience for you."

They agreed to meet the next afternoon at 1:00 p.m. Later, Adele would text Julie-Ann her address. Once she hung up, Julie-Ann felt relieved, since she was not sure exactly how she would feel after the long drive. This way, she could just relax and not have to worry about anything.

After being stuck in traffic for a while and making two pit stops at service areas, Julie-Ann arrived in Hastings at 4:10 p.m. Exhausted, she just wanted to check into the hotel and lay around. Though the website she used to book the room said that the Holiday Inn was close to downtown Hastings, it was right off the side of the highway and there was a Wal-Mart Supercenter adjacent to it.

The hotel itself, a three-story rectangular building, was very clean. While checking in, the receptionist explained that they had an indoor pool and whirlpool, fitness center, and a complimentary hot breakfast. Unfortunately, the hotel did not have a restaurant or room service.

The room was modest but was spotless and draped in bright colors. Julie-Ann threw her purse and shoulder bag on the chair and then collapsed onto the bed. It felt so good to be out of the car and lying down. The mattress was just the right firmness for her and there were a plethora of pillows.

Eventually, Julie-Ann did some unpacking. She then updated her Facebook page saying that she was now in Hastings, and replied to some messages. Afterwards, she lounged around and watched some TV.

By 6:00 p.m. Julie-Ann was hungry. She really didn't want to drive anywhere, but without room service or a hotel restaurant, she had no choice. So she went downstairs and asked the woman at the front desk if there were any places nearby that she could get some food and bring it back to the room, as she didn't want to sit down anywhere. The woman replied that there was a Burger King about a five-minute drive away. So she drove there, went through the drive-thru, and brought it back to the room.

After eating, Julie-Ann figured that she should call and let Theresa and her father know that she had reached Hastings okay. Thinking that they would both be home by this time, she called the house phone so she could talk to both of them. She was pleasantly surprised when Rita answered the phone; she had not spoken with her since leaving New York. They talked for a while. Rita asked about her journey thus far. Julie-Ann felt that Rita would really understand what she was doing out on the road and why. Rita said she was proud of her and blessed her on the rest of her journey.

After talking with Rita, Julie-Ann talked with both her father and Theresa. Having talked with both of them recently, she did not have a long conversation with either. She just said that she was checking in and that everything was okay.

Julie-Ann woke up early the next morning. She felt well rested and energized. All signs of her lingering two-day hangover were completely gone. Before even taking a shower, Julie-Ann threw on shorts and a t-shirt and went downstairs to take advantage of the hotel's complimentary breakfast bar.

Julie-Ann was ready by 11:00 a.m. Not wanting to go to the Hendricks' home empty handed, she decided to go into town and pick up a cake or some pastries.

About three miles from the hotel, Julie-Ann drove to downtown Hastings. It was a small, rustic town, with one and two-story brick buildings adjoined to each other. Though clean, everything looked like it had been there for a while. Most of the vehicles that rolled down the uncongested streets were pickup trucks.

Julie-Ann had put "bakery" into the GPS, hoping that something would show up, but nothing did. So she parked the car and wandered around. After two blocks she asked a woman walking down the sidewalk if she knew of a bakery. She gave Julie-Ann directions to one a couple blocks away, saying that it was excellent. Julie-Ann walked there and bought a chocolate pudding pie and a carrot cake, which the woman behind the counter recommended.

After getting back to the car, Julie-Ann put the address Adele gave her into the GPS and headed over to meet her and Lisa. She was excited, but somewhat nervous. What was she going to say? Did Adele really want to meet her, or was she just trying not to be rude? Luckily, they were fleeting thoughts. Her attention quickly turned to the rural landscape. Adele had said they lived a few miles out of town, but Julie-Ann could see nothing but sprawling farmland. She wondered if the GPS was taking her off course. But then the GPS' voice told her to turn left at a narrow, long, straight road. Julie-Ann knew it was the road that Adele and Lisa lived on. Up the road, there were several houses on both sides, each with an abundance of land.

Julie-Ann pulled up to the front of the Hendricks' property, an expansive, flat grassy lawn with a recessed two-story house. As Julie-Ann was grabbing the cakes and getting out of the car, she saw a woman and a girl coming out of the house towards her. The woman was casually walking, but the girl was at a faster pace.

"Jules," Lisa said with excitement. "I'm so glad you were able to come."

Julie-Ann looked at Lisa. Standing about 5'6", her skin was pale, but she appeared vibrant. A white bandana covered her bald head, but did not detract from her pretty face and beautiful, light blue eyes. "Me too," Julie-Ann replied with a smile as she extended her hand. "It's so nice to be able to actually meet you."

Lisa shook her hand. "It's a pleasure to meet you, too."

Just then a woman came out. Slender and slightly taller than Lisa, she had long, straight dirty blonde hair, blue eyes, and a sunny disposition. Julie-Ann could immediately see a comparison to Lisa.

She put out her hand for Julie-Ann to shake. "I'm Adele."

"It's a pleasure to meet you," Julie-Ann said as she shook her hand.

"Were you able to find the house okay?"

"Yes."

"Oh, good," Adele replied in a welcoming voice. "Like I said over the phone, some GPS's don't work so good out here."

"No, I didn't have any problem. Oh, I didn't know what kind of dessert you like," Julie-Ann said, giving Adele the two boxes, "so I got a chocolate pudding pie and a carrot cake."

Adele took the boxes from Julie-Ann. "Oh, you didn't have to bring anything. That's so nice of you."

"Mom loves chocolate pudding pie," Lisa said with a grin.

"Oh, good," Julie-Ann replied.

"Well, come on in," Adele said as she led the way. "Let's go inside."

As soon as they walked into the house, they were greeted by a full-grown golden retriever. Feverishly wagging its tail, it went right up to Julie-Ann and started sniffing her.

"This is Sadie," Lisa said. "She's friendly. She just wants to sniff you."

Julie-Ann knelt down and pets her on the head. "Oh, she's beautiful. Hi Sadie," she then said in a baby voice.

After putting the bakery boxes in the kitchen, Adele, with Lisa, gave Julie-Ann a tour of the house. It was bigger than she had expected and it was well kept. There was no clutter and everything was clean. It had a very homey feel to it, with plenty of strategically placed framed, family photographs.

"You have a beautiful home."

"Oh, thank you," Adele said in a prideful voice.

"Mom's a neat freak."

Julie-Ann laughed. "It's good to be neat. I can't stand clutter."

"Neither can I," agreed Adele. "So listen, I'm sorry, I should have asked you what you like to eat. I made a cheese platter and some sandwiches. But I can easily make something else."

"Oh, no, no, that sounds great."

Lisa and Julie-Ann sat at the dining room table as Adele brought out the food and her homemade ice-tea. Lisa asked about Topeka. Julie-Ann gave an abridged version, leaving out the part about getting wasted. Once Adele sat down, she asked about Julie-Ann's journey in general. More than the places she had been to, Julie-Ann talked about the people: Michelle, Connie, Frank and Kathy, Lester.

"What about the people you befriended at the veterans hospital in Indiana?" Lisa asked. "I read about them on your Facebook."

"Yes, they are great people," Julie-Ann said with hesitation in her voice. "I...I don't mean to bring up such a sensitive subject, but...I'm really sorry about your husband—and your father."

"Thank you," Adele replied with a half smile. "Lisa was only four-years-old when September eleventh happened. Jim came to me and said he had to enlist, to help protect the country. Of course, I didn't want him to go, especially with a four-year-old at home. But at the same time, I couldn't tell him no. I mean how many young men left their families after Pearl Harbor to fight in the war. I felt it was our duty, my duty. Besides, at first, everyone thought that we would go into Afghanistan, take care of business, and have all of our troops home within six, seven months." Adele paused. "Jim was on his fifth tour of duty when he was killed."

"I can't even imagine."

Adele could tell how sincere Julie-Ann was. "I want you to know that we really appreciate and admire the awareness you're trying to bring to those brave men and women who are struggling once they return home. There are way too many of them that aren't able to find jobs and who have actually become homeless. And I have to tell you, until Lisa showed me your posts on Facebook, I really wasn't aware that there was such a specific problem of homeless women veterans."

Julie-Ann let out a deflating breath and nodded. "Yes. It's such a shame. There really needs to be more done."

"Well I know the VA and other agencies have some programs in place, but it doesn't seem to be enough. It's really up to private businesses." Adele paused. "And it doesn't help when you have people and big companies actually taking advantage of them— like that scandal where JP Morgan, Diamond & Russell, and others were screwing military families with their mortgages. And then you had the Walter Reed debacle and even phony charities. There're some disgusting people out there."

"They should all rot," Lisa added.

"But don't get me wrong," Adele said in a more upbeat tone, "the vast majority of Americans support are troops, appreciate the sacrifices that they've made, and really want to help them. People like you."

Julie-Ann felt uneasy, thinking about her father being the CEO of Diamond & Russell. But she did not let her uneasiness show. "Well I'm just trying to do my very, very small part."

They sat around the table for about forty minutes, talking and eating.

"Would you like to see our horse," Lisa said after everyone's plate was finished.

"You have a horse?"

"Yes. His name is Champ," Lisa replied with excitement.

"That's a great idea," Adele said as she slowly stood up. "Lisa, why don't you show Jules out back while I clean up."

Julie-Ann stood up. "Oh, no. I mean please let me help you clean up first."

"That's very kind, but really, it's no big deal. It's just a few plates and glasses. Plus you're our guest. Besides, I know Lisa's eager to show you Champ."

Lisa happily led Julie-Ann outside. Sadie, wagging her tail in excitement, came along. The back property was at least two acres. Right behind the house was a brick patio with a table, chairs, and gas grill. Attached to the patio was a gated pool. Beyond that, about thirty yards away was a huge dirt area that was cordoned off by a wire fence with wooden posts. Inside the area was a rustic looking stable. Julie-Ann scanned the area with wide-eyed wonder. It was so picturesque. Driving through the heartland she had seen plenty of countryside and open space. But this was someone's home—and from what she gathered, not the property of a wealthy person.

"Champ is in the stable," Lisa said as she led Julie-Ann there.

"You have a beautiful back yard," Julie-Ann said as she continued to look around.

"Oh, thank you."

"I was brought up in New York, where everything is so cramped and space at such a premium. Even on Long Island, a place like this, with so much property, would be at least one, two million dollars."

Lisa laughed. "I don't know how people can afford to live there. I need space. I couldn't live in an apartment or some small house with no backyard. Out here you can probably get a four-bedroom house with a nice yard for two-hundred-fifty thousand. Or even less. But our house is paid for. It's been in the family for years. My grandparents—on my father's side—used to own it and when my grandfather passed away about ten years ago, he left it to my father."

They had arrived at the stable. Lisa led Julie-Ann inside and then practically ran over to a lone grey and black peppered horse standing in a gated stall. "This is Champ," she said with great enthusiasm as she pets his snout.

Julie-Ann, with Sadie by her side, walked over. "He's beautiful."

Lisa turned to Julie-Ann, her face lit up. "You can pet him. If fact, here," she said going over to a metal canister hanging on the wall, "you can feed him a carrot."

Julie-Ann had been near horses before and even ridden them in the Hamptons, and once in the countryside of France. But it had been a while. She took the carrot from Lisa and gave it to Champ, who gently plucked it from her hand.

"I think he likes you."

"I like him."

"Let's take him out," Lisa said. "He's been cooped up in here all day."

Lisa reached to grab the headstall and reins that were hanging on the wall. While retrieving them, she dropped them and they fell to the ground. As she bent down to pick them up, a silver necklace came out from under her V-neck t-shirt and dangled in the air. It was a dog tag. Holding the headstall and reins in one hand, Lisa stood up and stroked the tag with her other hand. "It was my father's. I talked my mother into letting me keep it and wear it. This way he's always close to my heart. I mean he would always be close to my heart and on my mind anyway, but…" Her sentence trailed off. "I never take it off—except when I have to go for treatments."

Julie-Ann wanted to cry. Suddenly, she no longer saw a happy-go-lucky, seemingly normal teenage girl. She saw a fifteen-year-old that had endured more hardship and suffering than anyone her age should ever have to live through. "Again, I'm so sorry about your father. I can't even imagine."

"Thank you. I miss him a lot." Lisa could see Julie-Ann was trying not to cry. "But please don't feel bad. There are people that have it a lot worse than I do. I have the world's greatest mother. I have a wonderful family and friends. I have Sadie." She leaned over and patted Sadie on the head. "And I have Champ," she added as she opened the stall. "Isn't that right Champ," she said while putting on his headstall and reins.

Julie-Ann was amazed. Where did this fifteen-year-old find such appreciation and optimism?

Lisa led Champ out of the stable. "I would let you ride him, but sometimes he gets a little skittish. In fact, the only person that rides him is my mom, and that's just once in a while." Lisa paused. "I wish I could ride him, but I can't because of the Leukemia. It's very easy for me to bruise and if I fell off…well, it would be bad."

As they watched Champ trot about, Adele came out. Julie-Ann told her what a lovely backyard and property she had. Adele thanked her and told her about Hastings and the people.

"The media likes to portray people around this part of America as country bumpkins or evangelical right wing fanatics," Adele said matter-of-fact. "But really we're just hard working people who care about each other and the country. I know here in Hastings, we're a very tight-knit community."

They stayed by the stable area, talking. Adele asked Julie-Ann about New York and her parents. Without saying exactly who her father was, she explained that he was a successful businessman and that she was spoiled growing up. She also told about her mother dying in a car accident when she was six, but that she was very close with her stepmother.

Julie-Ann had been at the Hendricks' for nearly three hours. Though Adele and Lisa had been extremely gracious hosts, she did not want to overstay her welcome, and feeling that they were never going to ask her to leave, she eventually thanked them and said that she was going to be on her way.

"How long are you staying in Hastings?" Adele asked, as they walked back inside the house.

"Well I was planning on staying until Monday, but as you can imagine, I really don't have a set schedule."

"Well I don't know what your plans are for tomorrow, but there's a flea market in town every Saturday. We were going to go tomorrow afternoon. It's got some interesting things there. If you're interested we can pick you up or meet you in town. But I don't want you to feel obligated."

Julie-Ann looked at Lisa and could tell that she wanted her to go. Besides, what else was she going to do all day? "Sure. I would like that. It sounds like fun."

"Great," Lisa said.

Adele and Lisa walked Julie-Ann to her car. Adele said she would pick her up the following day at the Holiday Inn at noon.

As Julie-Ann drove-off, she looked back at Adele and Lisa, standing on the front lawn, waving as she left. Adele had her arm around her daughter's shoulder. Julie-Ann started thinking about Theresa and all the times they had together, and how lucky she was that they had such a loving a close relationship. However, for the first time in a while, she also thought about her real mother and the few memories of her she had. Though she loved Theresa with all her heart, Julie-Ann wondered what could have been.

Chapter 24

As Julie-Ann was getting ready the next morning, Adele called on her cell phone.

"We're still going to pick you up at noon," she said, "but Lisa and I were talking last night. I don't want you to lose any money on your hotel room, but why don't you stay with us? There's no reason you should be holed-up in that hotel room all by yourself. We have a guest room. You can eat home cooked meals."

"Oh, that is so generous of you—really. But I don't want to impose." However, by the end of the call, Adele had talked Julie-Ann into spending the rest of her time in Hasting with them.

Adele and Lisa picked Julie-Ann up at the hotel at noon. The plan was that after the flea market, she would go back and get her bags and car.

It was a short ride to town. Adele parked on a side street and the trio walked to the market. It was sunny and hot, but Julie-Ann was thankful that Hastings was not as humid as Nashville, Jefferson City, or even Topeka.

They strolled around the rows of tables and booths. At one

point, Lisa saw one of her friends and went over to him, leaving her mother and Julie-Ann alone.

"Do you mind if I ask you a personal question?" Julie-Ann asked in a hesitant voice.

"It's okay. What is it?"

Julie-Ann let out a breath. "What is Lisa's prognosis?"

"We found out that she had Leukemia when she was ten," she responded in a somber tone as they continued to walk. "They seemed to have caught it early enough, but she had to go through chemotherapy and radiation. After a while the cancer went into remission. Everything seemed normal for several years. But then, when she went in for a routine check-up, her blood work showed that her white blood cell count was extremely high. The cancer had returned. That's the way cancer is—sometimes you think it's gone for good, but it's just hiding, laying in wait."

Julie-Ann shook her head. "It's such a terrible disease."

"That it is," Adele replied. "But luckily, the cancer seems to be going into remission again," she went on. "But you never know. When she was first diagnosed with it one doctor told us that she had maybe five more years to live at the most. We got another doctor." Adele paused. "It really varies from case to case. It depends on the person, their immune system, what parts of the body have been affected. There're a lot of variables. Believe me, I've learned so much about Leukemia over the years that I feel like I can write a book about it. But like I said, thank God, at the moment it seems to be in remission and she is doing well."

Julie-Ann stopped walking. "Thank God. I can't even fathom how hard it must be on you. And then losing your husband. I'm sorry. I didn't mean to..."

"It's okay. Yes, it's been hard for sure. I was angry with God. I felt sorry for myself, wondering why me? What did I do to deserve all this? But at some point I realized that all that did was make it even worse. It didn't help anything." Adele paused. "All you can do is cherish the times that you do have. Jim was taken from us way too early. But I feel blessed with the memories I have of him, for having had him in my life, for him giving me Lisa. The same with her. I hope to God that Lisa lives a long, healthy life and that I die long before her. For now, I cherish every day, every moment I have with her."

Julie-Ann felt like crying. "I'm sure she will live a long, long life."

Adele let out a sigh. "I know she will," she said, almost trying to convince herself. "She's just had to endure so much for a fifteen-year-old. Losing her father, the cancer. She's been to the hospital so many times, had so many radiation sessions. But I'll tell you—through it all, she's been a trooper."

"You have insurance, right?"

Adele nodded. "We have health insurance for Lisa, but it's still a lot of money out of pocket. I couldn't afford it on my salary, working at the grocery store. But luckily my parents help me out. But Lisa doesn't know that. The last thing I would ever want to do is have her feel like a burden. She's always so concerned about everyone else."

Julie-Ann let out a heartfelt laugh. "Yes. Your daughter is quite amazing. She's always tweeting or posting on Facebook about someone that needs help."

"That's Lisa. She's always taking up some cause, trying to raise money and awareness for someone that needs it." Adele turned and faced Julie-Ann. "That's what drew her to you. She read about you trying to get people to help our returning troops, and those less fortunate. She really likes you."

Julie-Ann smiled.

Just then, Lisa came walking over and excitedly started telling her mother and Julie-Ann about the new dog her friend had just gotten. "We have to go over and see it," she said.

As they were standing there, a middle-aged looking couple with a teenage boy approached. They obviously knew Adele and Lisa, as they said hello and started talking.

"Jules, this is my brother, Mike," Adele said. "And his wife Cynthia and their son Jacob." She then turned towards her family. "Jules is a friend. She's staying with us for a few days."

They said hello to Jules and appeared very friendly. Mike was curious; his sister had never mentioned a Jules before. But not wanting to be rude, he didn't ask any questions in front of her. Later on that day, Adele would call her brother and explain exactly who Julie-Ann was.

They chatted for a few minutes. Adele asked Mike and Cynthia if they needed any help getting ready for the barbeque.

"Every Fourth of July we have this big barbeque," Mike explained to Julie-Ann. "Hopefully you'll still be around. It's a real good time. We have a big fireworks display. And plenty of beer for the adults."

"Oh yeah Jules, you have to go," Lisa added. "It's great."

They talked for a little while longer before Mike, Cynthia, and Jacob went on their way. They told Julie-Ann it was a pleasure meeting her and Cynthia said she hoped to see her at the barbeque.

As soon as they walked away, Adele turned to Julie-Ann. "I'm so sorry, I didn't even think of the barbeque before. I should have told you."

Julie-Ann waved off Adele. "Oh, please, don't worry about it."

"But really, we would love if you went. Everyone that's going to be there is real laid back and nice. You'll fit right in. I mean I know you were planning on leaving Monday, but the Fourth is Wednesday."

The Fourth of July had completely escaped Julie-Ann's mind. Usually, she would have spent it with friends or family. The thought of being all alone in some hotel room when everyone else was out celebrating did seem somber. But she also didn't want to impose. Everyone had invited her, but maybe it was just because she was there and they were talking about it. "Thank you. We'll see."

Julie-Ann, Adele, and Lisa walked around the market for about an hour, stopping at different booths, even going into stores. Adele and Lisa ran into more people they knew. Julie-Ann was always introduced. Everyone seemed extremely friendly. Julie-Ann took note that no one was rude. No one was arguing or showing impatience. If some one accidently bumped into someone else they said "excuse me." Beyond the blocked off streets, there was no sounds of honking horns or commotion.

At one point Lisa stopped at a funnel cake stand and made Julie-Ann try one. It tasted good, but with its powdered sugar, was messy and Julie-Ann couldn't imagine eating it every day.

As they strolled around, Adele asked Julie-Ann what she would like for supper. Julie-Ann insisted that she take her and Lisa out for dinner. Adele accepted the offer and mentioned that there was a good steakhouse on the edge of town. A nice steak sounded great to Julie-Ann.

After the flea market, Adele drove Julie-Ann back to the hotel to pick up her car. She told Adele she still had to get her bags and would meet them back at the house. She then checked out, grabbed her luggage, and checked the room over, making sure she didn't leave anything behind.

Back at the house, Adele showed Julie-Ann to her room and told her to make herself feel at home. She then showed Julie-Ann where the towels were (she already knew where the bathroom was from her previous tour). Adele then left Julie-Ann so she could unpack and get herself comfortable. Like the McAlisters had done, Julie-Ann was amazed that people she hardly knew let her into their homes and showered her with such hospitality.

As Julie-Ann was in the guest room doing some unpacking and texting Theresa and her father to let them know where she was, Lisa came by with Sadie.

"Is everything okay?" Lisa asked. "I'm sorry; I know there's no TV in the room."

"Oh please, that's no big deal. There is usually nothing on TV anyway. It's just so generous of your mother to let me stay here."

Sadie came over, wagging her tail, and put her snout on Julie-Ann's leg.

Julie-Ann bent over and pets the dog on its head. "Hello Sadie. You're such a good girl,"

"She likes you."

"I like her too," Julie-Ann replied in a childish voice as she continued to pet her.

"Well I'll let you get settled in. But once you're done, why don't you come by my room. I want to show you something."

"Sure. Just give me a few minutes."

With that Lisa left and took Sadie with her. Julie-Ann finished checking her emails and texts and replied to a few of them. She then walked down the hall to Lisa's room.

Lisa was sitting at her desk, in front of a laptop. When she saw Julie-Ann approach from the open door, she asked her to come over. Julie-Ann sat down in a spare chair, next to Lisa.

"I've been following this story and trying to find out more about it. It's so heartbreaking." It was a story about two twelve-year-old girls in Jacksonville, Florida that had walked to a store by their house in the early afternoon and never returned home. They had been missing for three days. "I hope they find them."

"Me too." But deep inside Julie-Ann feared the worse.

Later that evening they went to the steakhouse. Adele drove. The restaurant was big and noisy, but they were able to get a booth and hear each other talk. The décor and atmosphere was casual and fun, the opposite of many of the stuffy New York steakhouses Julie-Ann had been to.

Adele, Lisa, and Julie-Ann kept the conversation light. There was no talk of cancer or people's tragic stories. Lisa didn't bring up any causes she was trumpeting. Adele talked about her family and some of the people in Hastings. She told some funny stories that they all laughed at.

When the food came—they all ordered steaks—Julie-Ann could not believe how good it was. Her filet mignon rivaled some of the world's most expensive and famous steakhouses she had eaten at.

At the end of dinner Adele tried to pick up the bill, but Julie-Ann grabbed it from her. She was shocked when she saw that the entire tab came to only $73. Julie-Ann laughed inside, knowing that the same meal in a New York Steakhouse would be at least $350.

By the end of the night, Adele and Lisa had convinced Julie-Ann to stay for the Fourth of July barbeque. But they didn't have to twist her arm too much. She was glad not to have to spend it alone.

The next morning Adele went to work at the grocery store in town. She usually didn't work Sundays, but a co-worked had asked her to switch a day with her.

Julie-Ann spent the afternoon with Lisa. She took her out for an early lunch and then they went into a couple of stores together.

When they came back, Julie-Ann helped her wash down Champ. As they did, Lisa talked about a thirteen-year-old boy she had read about and subsequently corresponded with through Facebook and emails. He was suffering from non-Hodgkin lymphoma and his outlook was grim. In fact, doctors had told him there was only a twenty percent chance that he would live past two more years. He was using his time to try and find dogs homes that had been displaced by natural disasters, such as hurricanes and floods. He had even reunited several dogs with their original owners. He did most of it through a website that he designed himself, Lisa explained. It had pictures of the dogs—some in shelters and a few his parents let him keep at the house. Julie-Ann was naturally moved by the story and would later donate $2,000 through the website, without telling Lisa.

But Lisa did not stop there. Next, she told her about a fourteen-year-old boy she had been corresponding with who recently lost his father in Afghanistan. "Naturally, I can relate to him," Lisa said. "I just wanted to be supportive, tell him that he's not alone."

"You're an amazing girl Lisa—the way you care so much and try to help other people."

"Well you're the same way," Lisa replied as she scrubbed Champ's neck with a soaking wet brush.

Julie-Ann felt embarrassed to be even put in the same category as Lisa. "I certainly wasn't like that when I was fifteen. I was a spoiled brat. And I never had to go through the things you have had to endure. Despite everything you've been through, you have such a benevolent perspective of life."

Lisa stopped what she was doing and looked at Julie-Ann. "It does get me so mad sometimes. So many people are obsessed with money and materialistic things. I mean I realize that you have to pay the bills and provide for your family. And I also understand that money can be used to help so many people. But I guarantee you that no one says on their deathbed 'I wish I would've made more money, or drove a better car, or lived in a bigger house.' Sadly, sometimes it's not until people face the end that they realize what's really important: Times you spend with loved ones; the comfort you were able to bring someone that needed your help; a positive effect you were able to leave on the world—no matter how small."

Julie-Ann looked back at Lisa in awe. "Can I give you a hug?"

Lisa smiled. "Of course."

Julie-Ann gave the fifteen-year-old a tight hug. "You may not realize it," she said, still holding onto her, "but you *are* special Lisa. You are very special. I wished everyone thought like you, lived like you. The world would be a much better place."

Julie-Ann spent Monday and Tuesday hanging out with Lisa during the day while Adele worked. Upon Lisa's suggestion they went to the Hastings Museum. Lisa also showed her around the outskirts of town, pointing out some large ranches. On Tuesday they went to a hamburger joint and Lisa insisted on paying. Julie-Ann knew she must not have had a lot of money, probably just what her mother had given her, but saw how much Lisa wanted to pay, so let her. Besides, the total was only eight dollars.

Back at the house, they went in the pool. Sadie would go in with them. Julie-Ann enjoyed throwing a tennis ball in the water and having Sadie jump in and dog paddle to go get it. They also spent time with Champ. Lisa taught Julie-Ann all she never knew about horses.

Of course, Lisa also spent time showing and talking to Julie-Ann about other new causes and stories she had become aware of. Julie-Ann would post them on her Facebook page as well, and also tweet about them. A few, she even donated to.

Not wanting Adele to come home from work and worry about dinner, Julie-Ann went into town both Monday and Tuesday and brought something back so it was ready when Adele came home. She also tried to help her around the house and asked if she needed anything done or picked up during the day. Adele would thank her, but never asked her to do anything.

During the evening the three of them would watch television together, something that Lisa and her mother did often. Tuesday they even rented a movie.

Julie-Ann also found time over the two days to talk with Adele alone. She would tell stories of Lisa growing up, and talked about how well she did in school, even though she had to have private tutors for a while when she was very sick. She told Julie-Ann more about Lisa's past treatments and how Lisa's hospital was two and a half hours away in Omaha. Sometimes she could not help to talk about her late husband. But she never broke down in front of Julie-Ann.

Over the four days she had spent at the Hendricks', Julie-Ann's admiration and respect for Lisa only grew. But she also came to have great reverence for Adele. She had such amazing fortitude. She had lost her husband—way too early—and had to take care of a child with cancer over the years. Still, she worked, kept a spotless house, and never let her daughter hear her complain.

There had been a slight chance of rain for the Fourth of July, but luckily it held off. It was a hot, dry day. In the morning and early afternoon there was light cloud cover, but it burned off by the early evening, leaving a clear sky, perfect for watching fireworks.

Adele, Lisa, and Julie-Ann left for her brother's house, which was fifteen minutes away, by 1:30 p.m. Though Julie-Ann knew Adele and Lisa, and had certainly learned to talk with strangers during her journey, there was still a part of her that was a little apprehensive. Though she was introduced to Mike and Cynthia, and was sure she would be introduced to other people, she still really wouldn't know anyone at the party. She didn't want to wind up standing by herself.

Mike and Cynthia lived just outside of town. They had a spacious one-story house on a one and a half acre lot. Their backyard was expansive. Completely flat, it had a pool with a large, rectangular brick patio. In the other part of the yard was an elaborate backyard playground, with a slide, swings, monkey bars, and elevated wooden playhouse. There was also a huge wooden shed. *Does everyone have this much space in Nebraska,* Julie-Ann wondered?

Cynthia greeted Adele, Lisa, and Julie-Ann. Adele gave her sister-in-law the macaroni salad she had made for the barbeque. Cynthia thanked her. She then introduced Julie-Ann to a few of her friends. As they were talking, Mike came by. After saying hello, he walked Adele and Julie-Ann over to an oversized cooler, packed with various beers.

"Here's a Blue Moon for you," he said as he handed the bottle to his sister. "And what kind of beer can I get for you Jules? I have Blue Moon, Budweiser, Miler Lite, Sam Adams…"

"I'll have a Blue Moon."

Mike reached into the cooler and grabbed another bottle for Julie-Ann. He then retrieved a bottle opener from his shorts pocket and opened each of their beers. "Wait, let me get mine," he said as he fished out a bottle of bud and opened it. He then raised his beer in the air. "To having a good time with family and friends. Jules, I'm glad you were able to make it."

"Yes," Adele added.

"Thank you," Julie-Ann replied with a smile. "And thank you for inviting me."

With that, the three of them touched bottles and took a drink.

"Well I have to get back to the grill before Jake burns everything. The first round of food will be coming up shortly."

As Mike scurried away, Adele discretely told Julie-Ann some gossip about several of the people at the party. Julie-Ann listened as she sipped on her beer. It was the first beer that she had shared with Adele. But it felt natural. Though only knowing her for less than a week, Adele felt like an older sister.

There were already about fifteen people at the party, including several children running around the backyard. Two dogs—a mutt and a border collie—were playfully chasing after them. Soon more people would show up, adults, teens, and younger kids.

Julie-Ann quickly forgot her slight apprehension about not knowing anyone at the party. Between Adele and Cynthia she was introduced to nearly everyone at the party, including most of the kids. Moreover, everyone was very affable. In fact, Julie-Ann found herself without Adele or Lisa, having flowing conversations with people she had just met.

Naturally, there were some innocent questions: How did Julie-Ann know Adele; where did she live; what did she do for a living; what brought her out to Hastings. Not wanting to completely lie, Julie-Ann explained that she lived in New York, but met Adele through the Internet through volunteer work she had done with veterans. Julie-Ann was on a cross-country drive and they decided it would be the perfect opportunity to meet in person. Julie-Ann should have realized, but this spurred on even more questions, like how she became involved with veterans. Again, not wanting to lie, she told one couple about her story. She told them about the McAlisters, the vets she had met in the VA hospital, as well as the homeless shelters she had visited.

Not knowing what Adele was telling people about her, and not wanting their stories to conflict, Julie-Ann pulled Adele aside and told her what she had been saying.

Julie-Ann had not intended to get into heavy dialogue at the party. But in answering some of the questions it was unavoidable. Different people commended her for what she was doing. She found herself in several conversations about the need to make sure servicemen and women were taken care of once they returned from overseas. A few conversations were quite passionate.

Though there was some serious dialogue, it was still mostly a festive atmosphere. Much of the time Julie-Ann was laughing and joking with various people. At one point she even played horseshoe with some of the kids.

There was a wide age range of people at the party: the late twenties to forties group; several twenty-one to twenty-four-year-olds; teenagers; young kids; and some old timers. Everyone seemed to be having a good time. People of all ages were in the pool. The beers were flowing. Mike kept turning out seemingly endless hot dogs, hamburgers, chicken, sausage, and skirt steak. As with any party, the later it got, the more ruckus the crowd. Some of the guys were challenging each other to a beer chugging contest. Not to be left out, a few of the women stepped up to the challenge.

At 8:00 p.m., as the sun made its final descent behind the western horizon, Mike announced that it was time to light off the fireworks. With the help of several of his friends, he grabbed boxes of fireworks from the shed and began setting some of them up near the far end of the backyard. Meanwhile, everyone else gathered on the patio and awaited the display.

With a fresh beer in his hand, Mike turned and faced his guests. "Can I have everyone's attention please," he yelled.

The ruckus chatter of the crowd quieted down, as everyone gave Mike their attention.

"Before we light off any fireworks, I would like to take a moment to make a toast and remember what the Fourth of July is really about—our freedom and independence. May we always remember all those that made the ultimate sacrifice so that we may be afforded that freedom. From the Revolutionary War, to Iraq and Afghanistan. And may our prayers go out to those still overseas." Mike raised his beer high into the air. "To all those that have put on the uniform—past and present—thank you! And God bless America!"

The crowd raised their beers and roared. "Thank you!" "To the troops!" "God bless America!" Different people yelled in unison.

Julie-Ann stood on the patio by Adele and Lisa as she watched the fireworks. It was a much more elaborate display than she had been expecting. Three people at one time lit off a various assortment of rockets, mortars, and cakes of varying sizes. The partygoers oohed and ahhed as multiple streams of projectiles whooshed high into the air and erupted into crackling showers of glittering sparks, booming bright colorful chrysanthemums, and blasts of gracefully falling stars. There was never a pause, just a steady stream of aerial assault. Then, without interruption, came the grand finale, as the entire surrounding sky lit up with a brilliant kaleidoscope of thundering display of various shapes and colors.

After the fireworks were over, Julie-Ann sought out Mike. "That was a great display."

"Oh, thank you. I'm glad you enjoyed it."

"I did. But I also really enjoyed your toast. It's great to bring remembrance back to what this holiday is really about."

"I'm glad you feel that way. It's just like Memorial Day. We get so caught up in what we're going to do, having our barbeques, or going to the beach, having a good time with family and friends. And there's nothing wrong with that, as long as we take time out of the day to pause and remember those that made it possible to enjoy those liberties." Mike paused. "Especially now it's important to remember, with all the discord and hardship that's going on in the country."

Julie-Ann nodded. "I couldn't agree more."

The next day it rained all morning and afternoon. Julie-Ann, along with everyone else, was glad it had waited until after the Fourth of July. After waking up and having breakfast, which Adele had made, Julie-Ann went back to her room and went on her laptop. She was trying to figure out her next destination, as she was leaving the next day and really had not given it much thought.

A part of her actually considered going back to New York. She had been on the road for over a month. She had learned so much, met so many wonderful people, and was able to assist in some important causes. She had found her purpose. Perhaps it was time to go home and be with her father and Theresa. After all, she could always help people from New York. And just because she went home now, did not mean that she couldn't go on other long drives down the road. However, a larger part of Julie-Ann said that her journey was not yet over. She didn't know what, but something told her there was still unfinished business out there. There was something left to discover. She also figured that she had made it so far across the country that she might as well finish the trek and make it all the way to the west coast. If she wanted to go back to New York then, she could always fly back and have the car shipped.

Julie-Ann had talked herself into continuing her journey, on through to the west coast. But then the questions became which route to take to the coast, and where would be her next destination?

As Julie-Ann was sitting in front of her laptop, Lisa came by the room. The door was open. Julie-Ann saw her and told her to come in. She then explained what she was doing.

"Have you ever been to Wyoming?" Lisa asked.

"No. Can't say I have."

"We drove through it when I was eight. My father took us to see Yellowstone National Park. It's a beautiful state. And Yellowstone is amazing. It's really something everyone should see, especially that you're this close."

The idea of Yellowstone appealed to Julie-Ann. And when would she get another opportunity to drive through the state and the national park? "I think I'm going to do it. I would love to see Yellowstone."

Lisa explained that though Nebraska was next door to Wyoming, it was a long drive to Yellowstone. So the decision was made for Julie-Ann to stop at Cheyenne, which was five hours away. They were able to find a hotel and Julie-Ann booked it for one night.

From Cheyenne it was still over a nine hour drive to Yellowstone. It was longer than Julie-Ann wanted to drive in one day, but she did not want to make another stop in Wyoming. Figuring if she left at 7:00 a.m., even giving an hour of stopping along the way, she would get to Yellowstone by 5:00 p.m. So she decided to go for it.

After doing some research, with Lisa by her side, Julie-Ann realized that there were not really any hotels right by the South Entrance to Yellowstone, which was in Wyoming. However, she did find one, the Snake River Lodge and Spa, which looked amazing, that was about forty-five minutes away. It was right next to the Teton National Park, the gateway to the South Entrance, and a half hour—in the other direction—from Jackson Hole. When she tried to reserve a room, there were none available. She then tried some other hotels, a little further away and not as nice looking. However, they were also booked. After thinking about it for a few seconds, Julie-Ann put in different dates; instead of arriving on Friday, she tried Monday as the check-in date. It showed available rooms. Figuring she would not get there until the evening, and probably wouldn't explore the park until the following day, Julie-Ann reserved three nights at the Snake River Lodge, in a one bedroom suite. She then went back and reserved two extra nights at the hotel in Cheyenne, as now she wouldn't be driving to Yellowstone until Monday morning.

"So where do you want to go after Yellowstone?" Lisa asked. "If you want to make it to the west coast, you'll have to go through Idaho. Unless you want to go all the way south through Utah."

Julie-Ann thought about it. "You know what—I think I'm going to play it by ear the rest of the way. Maybe something will come to me. Besides, I know I said I wanted to make it all the way to the coast, but who knows, after Yellowstone I may decide to head back to New York."

That night Julie-Ann, Adele, and Lisa were sitting on the living room couch watching the evening news. They were talking about the national deficit and the government's deadlock in trying to reduce it.

"It's amazing," Adele said, "they way they talk about trillions of dollars like it's nothing."

"It's crazy, huh," Julie-Ann agreed.

"I mean listen to them. We can save fifty billion here, raise ten billion there. They give tens of billions of dollars to Pakistan and other countries that hate us. Meanwhile Americans are living paycheck to paycheck—if they're lucky enough to have a job."

"What happens if the national debt keeps on going up?" Lisa asked.

"The treasury will just print more money," her mother replied in a sarcastic tone. "Or we'll borrow more money from China. While we have to deal with real money, worry about paying our bills or feeding ourselves, it's just Monopoly money to the government. I mean really, what's the difference between thirteen trillion and fourteen trillion?" Adele paused. "Though at some point it devalues the dollar. That's one of the reasons prices keep going up. What used to cost five dollars two years ago now costs eight or nine. In the end, it's always the citizens who suffer, Lisa. Meanwhile the politicians sit on their thrones trying to one up each other, arguing about trillions of dollars, completely detached from the real world that the rest of us have to live in."

Lisa shook her head in disgust. "It's not fair. They should all be fired."

Adele laughed. "I wish they could be, honey."

Chapter 25

Julie-Ann woke-up early Friday morning so she could get ready and to talk with Adele before she left for work. She was surprised when she came downstairs at 7:30 a.m. and saw Adele cooking breakfast, as she usually only made it when she had a day off, because she had to be at work so early.

"Oh, I'm glad you came down," Adele said with a smile. "I was just going to come get you. I didn't want to wake you up, but I wanted to make you breakfast before you left."

"Adele, please, you didn't have to do that. I could've just gotten something on the road."

"Nonsense," Adele replied as she plated some bacon. "But can you do me a favor? Can you just knock on Lisa's room and wake her and tell her to come down?"

It was a pleasant surprise, as Julie-Ann sat down for breakfast with Adele and Lisa, enjoying one last meal with them before she left. Once again, she thanked both of them for their overwhelming hospitality and said what a wonderful time she had. They all agreed to keep in touch and Julie-Ann promised to update them on her journey.

After breakfast, Julie-Ann helped Adele cleanup. Afterwards, they said their goodbyes as Adele had to leave for work. Once she was gone, without letting Lisa know, Julie-Ann snuck into Adele's bedroom and left a white envelope on her bed. In it was a check for $40,000 and a letter. It read:

> *Dear Adele,*
>
> *I know you are a very proud and independent woman and that if I would have tried to hand you a check you probably would have turned it down. But I also know that even with Lisa's health insurance, the medical bills are difficult to keep up with. Please take this money to help pay for the bills, maybe put some into a college fund for Lisa, and also do something for yourself. You deserve it. Perhaps you and Lisa could take a nice vacation somewhere. And again, I want to thank you with all of my heart, not just for letting me stay at your house, but also for letting me into your lives. I truly feel blessed for being able to call you and Lisa friends and I hope we will always stay in close touch.*
>
> *Love, Julie-Ann*

Adele would find the letter when she arrived home that day from work. She was not surprised that Julie-Ann would try to leave them money, but was taken aback by the amount. Adele had to borrow money from family over the years and could certainly use the help. However, she did not want to take Julie-Ann's money, even if she had plenty to spare. At first, she told herself there was no way she would cash the check. However, as she stood there staring at it and the letter, she thought about Lisa. How could she deprive her daughter? Eventually Adele would cash the check, but put $30,000 of it in a custody account in Lisa's name. The rest of the money she used to pay some back medical bills and later on, took Lisa to Disneyland. But Adele never bought anything for herself with the money.

Lisa helped Julie-Ann bring her things down to the car.

"Well, I guess this is it," Lisa said after putting Julie-Ann's last bag in the trunk.

Julie-Ann looked at the fifteen-year-old. Though she had only known her for such a short time, Lisa felt engrained in Julie-Ann's soul. She wished she could spend years with her. Holding back tears, Julie-Ann was ready to say goodbye when Sadie, who had also come out to the sidewalk, jumped up on her.

Julie-Ann pets her and gave her a kiss on the snout. "Oh, yes Sadie, I'm going to miss you, too."

"She's going to be looking for you," Lisa said.

After Julie-Ann was finished with Sadie, she gave Lisa a big hug. "You take care of yourself, you hear. I'm so glad I came here."

"Don't sound like we're never going to see each other again," Lisa said as she clung onto Julie-Ann, "like this is goodbye forever."

Julie-Ann let go of Lisa and looked her straight in the eyes. "Of course not. I promise you. Maybe you can come out to New York. And we'll stay in touch online."

Lisa smiled. "I'm so glad you came too. And I know my mother was. She really likes you."

Julie-Ann climbed in the Camaro and programmed the GPS. But before driving away, she rolled down the window. "I'll let you guys know when I get to Cheyenne."

"Okay. Be careful."

With that, Julie-Ann pulled away. Through the rearview mirror she watched Lisa on the sidewalk waving, Sadie sitting by her side. After a few blocks, Julie-Ann started crying. She intended to keep her promise and see Lisa and Adele again, and to stay in touch. But she already missed them. Like the McAlisters, they had become family.

Julie-Ann passed the welcome sign for Cheyenne at 3:20 p.m. From there, it only took another fifteen minutes to reach the hotel.

Julie-Ann had chosen The Historic Plains Hotel mainly because of its location, which was in the middle of downtown. The website had also said that it was a national landmark—hence the name—built in 1911. Julie-Ann was impressed right away when she walked into the large, open lobby. Floored in white-patterned tile, with a posh seating area and gift shop, the ceiling went all the way up to the second level of the hotel, which wrapped around and overlooked the main floor. After taking in the area, Julie-Ann walked up to the marble check-in counter. There, a very friendly middle-aged man assisted her.

However, when Julie-Ann went up to the room, it was small and dated. Though clean at first glance, it looked like it had not been updated in a long, long time. The carpeted floor, walls, bed, and curtains looked like they were from the seventies. And as cramped as the main room felt, the bathroom was even smaller, with an old-time ceramic tub with a showerhead, diminutive stand alone sink with no counter, small mirror, and toilet that was compressed up against the tub.

More than five hours of driving, Julie-Ann just wanted to un-wind. She turned on the small, outdated tube television and slowly unpacked some of her clothes and belongings. But there were not many places to put them. Afterwards, she sat on the soft mattress and tried to find something to watch.

By 5:00 p.m. Julie-Ann was getting restless and hungry. Since the hotel was right in town, she decided to walk around and explore, hopefully find a good place to eat.

Julie-Ann's hotel was located in the historic district. Cheyenne was spread out, with wide roads, it was bigger than Julie-Ann had expected, much larger than Hastings. The area was clean, yet rustic, with old brick buildings. But like anywhere USA, it had the usual, modern staples, such as the Sports Authority, Kmart, Lowes, Wal-Mart, and Olive Garden. Yet even with its speckling of major chains, the historic district managed to keep its Old West charm.

After only walking for about three blocks, it started to rain. It began as a light rain, but the sky was darkening quickly and at any moment it seemed like it could start pouring. Julie-Ann didn't feel like hunting down a store with an umbrella, or waiting out the rain, so she decided to go back to the hotel.

Wet, she went up to the room and dried herself off. She thought about going downstairs to the hotel's restaurant, but decided to just order room service instead. As she waited for her food, Julie-Ann text Adele, Lisa, Theresa, her father, and Kathy to let them all know she had arrived in Cheyenne and was fine. She also updated her Facebook status, as well as tweeted that she was now in Cheyenne.

That evening, Julie-Ann stayed in her hotel room. As she laid on the bed, with the television playing in the background, she began to ponder for the first time what she was going to do once her journey came to an end. She knew that she wanted to help people, but exactly how was she going to make a living out of it? With millions to her name, she thought about starting a foundation, which would cater to various causes. But was that going to amount to a full time job? And exactly how would she go about putting it together? Julie-Ann figured Kathy would be a great person to talk to about it, since she was starting up her foundation to help women veterans. Her father no doubt also knew big time philanthropists and fundraisers who might be able to help her out.

After pondering her plans for the future, Julie-Ann started thinking about her current situation. She went on her laptop and Googled: *Homeless shelters Cheyenne WY*. The first result that came up was the Comea House. After exploring their website, Julie-Ann decided that she would visit the shelter the next day.

Julie-Ann then put away her computer and readied herself for bed. As she climbed under the covers and turned off the light, loneliness and longing for male companionship once again crept its way into her thoughts. Trying to brush it away, she looked for something funny to watch on TV.

Julie-Ann woke-up early the next morning, already wanting to get out of her small hotel room. After showering—the water pressure was weak, which didn't make her happy—she put on shorts and a t-shirt, and minimal make-up. She then went downstairs to the hotel's restaurant and sat down for breakfast.

After breakfast, Julie-Ann went upstairs to the room to use the restroom. While she was there, Lisa called. They talked for about fifteen minutes. As soon as she hung up, Amber called. Though they had corresponded through texts and Facebook since Nashville, it had been over a week since they had actually talked. They were on the phone for about a half hour, catching up.

After finally getting off the phone. Julie-Ann went downstairs and retrieved her car from the valet. Then, under a cloudy, drizzling sky, she drove to the Comea House. It was several miles outside of town, by the railroad tracks. The shelter itself, both inside and out, looked well kept. When approached by a young, male staff member in the lobby, Julie-Ann explained that she would like to make a donation and possibly learn more about the facility.

Larry, who volunteered at the shelter, showed her around and gave her an overview of the Comea House. He explained that it could accommodate fifty men, twelve women, and two families.

"Right now, we're filled to capacity," he said with a deflated voice. "In fact, there is currently a waiting list. We hate to turn anyone away, of course, but sometimes, unfortunately, we have to. From what I understand, it's like that all over the country now. There seems to be more homeless than ever before."

Larry took Julie-Ann into the large food pantry. However, its shelves were only a quarter full. He explained that people in Cheyenne were very generous, but many of them were going through their own tough times and with more people than usual using the pantry, it was hard to keep stocked.

Julie-Ann did not meet any of the shelter's current residence. Though she saw some of them walking by and hanging around, she did not ask about their stories and Larry did not volunteer. But before leaving, she went into the administration office and made a donation.

Julie-Ann handed Larry one of her credit cards as he sat behind a desk.

"And what amount did you want to donate?" He asked.

"Fifteen thousand," she said matter-of-fact.

Larry, who had been looking at his computer screen, stared at Julie-Ann in disbelief. "Wha…I'm sorry…what did you say?"

"Fifteen thousand."

"Seriously?"

"Yes. It's okay. I can give you a check instead if it's easier."

"No, that's not what I mean. I mean…it's just so…I…it's very generous of you." He let out an awkward laugh. "God bless you. This is going to do a lot of good."

Larry went to process the donation, but a message came up that said to call American Express. Julie-Ann had made most of her donations by checks. Since Amex did not recognize the Comea House, and it was a large, out of state amount, they wanted to make sure that in fact it was Julie-Ann using the card. But after a brief conversation with the American Express representative over the phone, the donation was processed.

Before leaving, Larry thanked Julie-Ann once again. As soon as she walked out the door, another staff member came over to him and asked whom the good-looking blonde was that he had been talking with. When Larry explained that she had just donated $15,000 to the shelter, he too was in disbelief.

After the shelter, Julie-Ann drove back to the hotel. It was only 1:30 p.m. and the rainy sky had cleared. Not wanting to sit around in the room, she had the valet park the car and wandered around town. It was Saturday afternoon and everyone was out and about. Not far from the hotel she passed a place called the Snake River Pub & Grill. It seemed like a casual restaurant with an outdoor seating area. Hungry, she decided to go in and give it a try.

It was a crowded, lively atmosphere. However, Julie-Ann didn't have to wait to sit down. As she looked over the menu, she ordered a Stone Indian Pale Ale, recommended by the waiter. Then she had another one with her turkey club. It was mediocre food, but did the job. Julie-Ann satisfied her appetite, but didn't overeat.

From the grill, Julie-Ann continued her trek around town. She had no destination. After about twenty-five minutes she found herself in a less dense area, with not as many people. But it still seemed safe. Hot and sweating, Julie-Ann thought how good another cold beer sounded, and a place to rest for a while with air condition. After another couple of blocks she came upon a nondescript bar. It looked like a local haunt.

Without sneaking a peek, she walked in. There were several gruff looking guys at the bar and one woman. Not thinking anything of it, she grabbed a stool at the front bar, near the entrance, and ordered a beer from the young, male bartender. Julie-Ann could feel a few of the guys checking her out, but that was something she was used to.

As Julie-Ann was drinking her beer, half-listening to the jukebox, which was playing southern rock, a man walked in and after scanning the bar for a place to sit, came over to Julie-Ann.

"Excuse me, is this seat taken?" He asked about the stool next to her.

Julie-Ann looked up at the man, who appeared to be in his late twenties or early thirties. Completely bald with a shaven face, he stood about six foot, and was wearing khaki cargo shorts and a maroon, V-neck t-shirt. He looked like he lifted some weights, but had a slight stomach.

Julie-Ann knew there were a few stools open at the end of the bar, but didn't want to be rude. "Oh, no," she said, motioning him to sit down.

Julie-Ann was waiting for him to hit on her right away, give her some stupid line, but he ordered a beer and left her alone.

After Julie-Ann finished her beer she was going to leave, but then thought what the hell, what else was she going to do with the rest of the day? So she ordered another one. But by this time she was starving for some conversation. She turned to the guy who had asked her about the seat. "So, what's it like living here?" She didn't know what else to say.

The man finished taking a drink of his beer and turned his head to face Julie-Ann. "It's nice. Real beautiful country. Everyone isn't running around like rats in a maze. It's not like LA. That's where I'm from. I've only been out here for about eight months."

"Oh? What made you move out here?"

He let out a fading sigh. "I lost my wife two years ago in a car accident. Then there was this lawsuit and I lost my house and most of my money. I just wanted to get away, clear my head, and try to start over."

"Oh my God. I'm so sorry. I didn't mean to…"

He smiled. "It's okay. Really. I didn't mean to bring you down. So what about you? You just move here or just visiting?"

Julie-Ann took a drink of her beer and thought about how she was going to answer. "I had a brain tumor—I'm all right now. I mean I feel perfectly healthy and am able to do everything a normal person can do. It made me really think—what am I doing with my life? There has to be more out there, some purpose. So I decided to drive across the country, take my time, and stop in different cities and towns. Now here I am in Cheyenne."

The man raised his bottle of beer. "Well here's to your health. I'm glad you're doing okay."

"Thank you," Julie-Ann replied with a smile as they touched beers.

After they each took a drink, he extended his open hand. "I'm Chris by the way."

"Julie-Ann. Well, everybody calls me Jules."

"Do you mind if I call you Julie-Ann?"

"Well no, I mean that is my name."

"It's just that I really like that name—Julie-Ann."

Julie-Ann and Chris talked some more. He told her about Cheyenne. He lived in an apartment complex not far away. He explained that he worked for himself, designing websites for people and companies. When their beers were done, he bought another round and asked Julie-Ann about her journey. She told him about the McAlisters and Adele and Lisa.

"She sounds like an amazing girl," Chris said about Lisa. "Makes you really put things in perspective, doesn't it."

"It sure does."

As Julie-Ann and Chris continued to converse, some more people came into the bar and it was starting to get livelier. Three guys, dressed like construction workers, and standing at the bar to the left of Julie-Ann, were getting particularly rowdy. They were ordering shots, talking loud, and generally acting obnoxious. Julie-Ann wished they were further away, but she didn't pay it too much mind. After all, it was a bar.

At one point, Chris excused himself to use the restroom. As soon as he left, Julie-Ann faced forward, took a sip of her beer, and thought about what she was doing. *He seems real nice. And he's good looking. Maybe something will happen. What am I talking about; he's a complete stranger. What if he's an axe murderer? Don't be stupid—he's not an axe murderer. But what am I going to do—just take him back to my hotel room? What am I a slut? But it's been so long.*

As Julie-Ann was lost in her own head, she heard one of the guys standing next to her yell at the bartender for shots. He then turned to Julie-Ann. "Hey honey, do a shot with us."

"Oh, no thank you."

"Come on, let me buy you a shot. Get drunk with us."

"We're fun guys," added one of his buddies, as they all got a good laugh out of it.

Now Julie-Ann was feeling uncomfortable. In fact, she started thinking about the can of mace in her purse that Rory had given her. "No, really. Thank you, but I'm okay. Besides, I'm with someone."

"That guy you were talking to? That guy's not gonna satisfy you."

Just then, Chris came back on the scene.

"Hey buddy, mind if we borrow your woman for a while," one of the other guys said. Again, they all laughed.

Chris looked at Julie-Ann. "What's going on?"

"Nothing. These guys just offered to buy me a shot and I said no thank you."

Chris could clearly see that it was more than just a polite offer being declined. He stood toe-to-toe with the ringleader. "Listen, we're all here to have a good time," he said in a calm, but strong voice. "There's no need for any trouble."

"Who said anything about trouble? You're right, we're just here to have a good time." There was a pause and for a second everything looked like it might cool down. "And she looks like a real good time."

"That's it," Chris barked. "Don't talk to her like that."

One of the other hooligans stepped up to Chris. "And what are you gonna do about it asshole?"

Still sitting, Julie-Ann grabbed Chris' arm. "Just leave it. Let's go somewhere else for a drink. It's not worth it."

By now, everyone had heard the scuffle over the jukebox and was looking over.

Chris took a deep breath. "If that's what you want," he said to Julie-Ann.

"That's right, run away," said the main culprit. "But leave your slut behind."

Without saying another word, Chris reared back and decked him with a right hook to the jaw. The hoodlum was knocked to the floor. In less than the blink of an eye, one of his buddies sucker punched Chris on the side of his head, knocking him down. Before he could get back up, the guy started kicking him in the stomach. Then the third friend went to kick him in the head, but Chris was able to cover himself with his hands. Julie-Ann leapt from her seat and grabbed one of the guys, but he pushed her away, back into the bar. However, the cavalry was on the way, in the form of several bikers, who had watched the whole thing from further on down the bar. One of them smashed a beer bottle over one of the attackers head, instantly laying him out. Another one grabbed one of the other guys in a headlock. The two remaining bikers started to pummel the original instigator.

Chris was able to get back on his feet and went to take a swing at one of the guys who had kicked him, who was now in a headlock. But before he could, Julie-Ann forcibly grabbed his arm.

"Lets get out of here," she pleaded.

Chris looked at her. Then his eyes caught the eyes of one of the bikers, who he had actually seen at the bar and talked to once before. "Just get her outta here. We got this covered," he said with a devilish grin.

Chris felt guilty to leave, since he had thrown the first punch. But Julie-Ann had already left money on the bar and was now pulling him towards the front door. He quickly thanked the biker, and with the melee in full force, he left with Julie-Ann.

"Are you okay?" Julie-Ann asked with bated breath as soon as they were outside.

"Yeah," Chris replied, though he was holding his stomach.

"I walked here," Julie-Ann said.

"So did I. But my apartment's only a few blocks away."

"Lets just get out of here before the fight spills out to the sidewalk."

Chris nodded. "That's a good idea. Come on, this way."

As they walked down the sidewalk, in the middle of the day, Julie-Ann looked Chris over. The left side of his face was already red and starting to swell, and he was still holding his stomach. "Are you sure you're okay?"

"Yeah. Listen, I'm sorry. I'm not a violent guy or anything. I can't remember the last time I was in a fight. It's just that guy called you...I mean..."

"Don't apologize. You were just sticking up for me. That was very honorable of you."

Chris let out a painful laugh. "Honorable? I got my ass kicked. That's not how it's supposed to work."

"I don't know, you got that guy pretty good. And there were three of them. But it was nice of those bikers to intervene."

"Yeah, they get a bad rap. I mean don't get me wrong, some of those guys are bad dudes that you don't want to deal with. But a lot of bikers are good people and actually do a lot for charity—toys for tots and everything." Chris stopped walking and started coughing.

Julie-Ann could tell that he was in pain. "Maybe we should take you to the hospital."

"No, no. I'm fine, really."

"Well at least let me walk you up to your apartment."

"Listen, I'd love for you to come up. I have some beer in the frig. We can talk some more, finish the conversation we were having before I got my ass kicked. But I don't want you to feel obligated. I mean…"

Julie-Ann could tell Chris was trying to find the right words. "It's okay," she said with a smile. "I want to."

After only five short blocks, they came to Chris' apartment complex. In a gated community, it looked new and extremely well kept. There were several, long buildings, each three stories high. Many of the apartments had balconies. The grounds were mostly grass, with strategically placed hedges, all perfectly manicured. Everything seemed spread out and inviting. Chris explained that the complex had two pools with two Jacuzzis, a playground for the kids, and a large recreational room with televisions and a pool table.

Chris' apartment was on the third floor. They walked up the stairs and he unlocked the door. "Well this is my humble abode," he said, as he led Julie-Ann inside.

It was clean, and like the entire complex, looked new. Julie-Ann could tell right away that he was not a slob. Chris walked into the kitchen, which had a sitting counter. He went into the refrigerator and grabbed two bottles of Heineken, opened them, and went to hand one to Julie-Ann.

"We should put some ice on your face, or it's going to swell up pretty bad. I mean it's already starting to swell."

Chris took a swig of his beer. "Well, I don't want to look like a wussy, holding a bag of frozen peas on my face. But I guess I don't want to look like the Elephant man, either."

Julie-Ann helped Chris put some ice in a Ziploc bag. She then made him sit down on the couch in the living room. As he sat there, holding the bag on the side of his face, Julie-Ann lifted up his shirt to see his stomach. It had a slightly discolored, black and purplish bruise.

"Are you sure you're okay?" She asked yet again.

"Yes, believe me."

While still holding up his shirt, Julie-Ann lifted her head and her and Chris' eyes met. There was a moment of silence as a connection was made—if it hadn't been already. Julie-Ann thought Chris was going to lean over and kiss her, but he didn't.

"I'm really glad that you came back with me," he said. "I know we just met, but if you had just left and I never saw you again I would have been wondering about you." Chris paused and looked away. "I'm sorry. I didn't mean to be all weird or anything."

Julie-Ann smiled. "It's okay. I think that's sweet. And thank you again for coming to my defense."

"Anything to be able to hold a bag of ice on my face."

They both laughed.

Julie-Ann and Chris sat on the couch together, drank their beers and joked about the incident at the bar. Chris then asked Julie-Ann more about her journey and the people she met.

When their beers were finished, Chris got up to go grab two more. Julie-Ann took the opportunity to excuse herself and use the restroom. Chris pointed the way. Like the rest of the apartment, the bathroom was cleaned, which impressed Julie-Ann. No woman likes a dirty bathroom. After she was washing her hands, Julie-Ann carefully opened the medicine cabinet. She felt guilty doing so, but could not help her curiosity. Inside were the usual items any man would have, shaving cream, extra soap, toothpaste, Neosporin, and aspirin. There were no prescription bottles.

On her way back to the living room Julie-Ann noticed a framed pencil etching hanging on the wall of the short hallway. It was a picture of a mountain range, with a large bald eagle soaring above it. "I like this etching," Julie-Ann said as she stared at it. "It's so beautiful and detailed. I mean you can see every feather on the eagle."

Chris walked over and handed her a beer. "Thank you. It's one of my favorites."

"Wait…you did this?"

"Yes. It's always been a love of mine. When I was a kid I used to draw aliens and other worlds. But then when I got older I started etching real people and places I'd go to. If I was stressed or going through a rough time, I would go somewhere by myself with my stencil and kit and etch the landscape. Not only did it help me forget what I was going through, but it made me immerse myself in what I was drawing—as if I was a part of it." Chris pointed at the framed drawing. "I like this one because the eagle reminds me of freedom and hope. It reminds me of the possibility of spreading your wings and flying away to start anew."

Julie-Ann turned so she was face-to-face with Chris. "That's beautiful," she said in a fading voice.

As their eyes locked, they once again found themselves in a silent pause. This time, Julie-Ann slightly moved closer to Chris. As she did, he met her the rest of the way and they kissed. At first, it was just a soft, moist meeting of the lips. But as they pulled away, just for a second, they gazed into each other's eyes once again and went back for another kiss. This time there was no restraint. With their lips and tongues still intertwined, Julie-Ann moved them over a few steps and put her beer down on an end table, near the couch. Chris did the same. Now, with their hands free, they caressed each other. Chris placed his left hand on Julie-Ann's neck and tilted her head up. He then slowly kissed her neck.

A part of Julie-Ann wondered what the hell she was doing. She had just met this guy at a bar. But it felt too good to stop. She put her hands underneath Chris' shirt and ran her fingernails down his back.

With his lips working their way around her chin and back to her open mouth, Chris put his hands under Julie-Ann's ass and lifted her up. In one motion, he brought her to the couch and laid her down. He then unbuttoned her shorts.

"Wait," Julie-Ann said through her heavy breathing, "do you have a condom?"

With one knee on the couch and his other leg on the floor, Chris lifted his head. "Yeah, I think I do—in the bedroom."

As Chris scurried to the bedroom, Julie-Ann followed. Watching Chris fumble through his sock drawer, hoping he would find a

condom, she laid down on the made bed. When she saw him retrieve that unmistakable square wrapper, she pulled off her t-shirt.
But before Julie-Ann could unlatch her bra, Chris was kneeling
over her on the bed. As she finished with her bra, exposing her
bare breasts, Chris began unbuckling his belt.

"Here," Julie-Ann said as she unbuttoned his shorts for him and
then slid them and his briefs down. Chris was almost completely
hard. She gently took a hold of his girth and began stroking it. Almost instantaneously, he was fully erect.

Chris grabbed hold off the sides of Julie-Ann's shorts and panties
and pulled them completely off. Next, he lifted his legs so he could
discard his own shorts and underwear. He then tore off his shirt. The
two of them were now completely naked. Still hovering over her, Chris
spread Julie-Ann's legs open and began to massage her wet insides.

"Let me see it," she said about the condom that was still in Chris'
hand.

Chris gave it to her. As she ripped open the wrapper, Chris in-
serted his finger inside her.

"Oh that feels so good," Julie-Ann said as she placed the flat
condom on the tip of Chris' erection and then rolled it down his
shaft. "But I want you inside me."

Chris spread Julie-Ann's legs even wider and then thrust himself
inside.

"Oh yes, harder," she moaned.

Julie-Ann's entire body was quivering. He felt amazing inside
her. She wanted it to never end.

Chris pulled out and Julie-Ann, disappointed, thought he was
done. But then she saw that he was still erect. "Turn over," he said
with bated breath. "I wanna take you from behind."

Julie-Ann happily flipped over and got on her hands and knees.
Almost instantly she could feel Chris thrust deep inside her. As
Chris fondled her breasts, Julie-Ann worked her body forward,
then backwards.

"How does this feel?" Chris asked out of breath.

"Oh yes," Julie-Ann replied in heat. "Fuck me."

After Chris came, he and went into the bathroom to remove the condom. As he did, Julie-Ann laid on her back, still naked, trying to catch her breath.

After Chris came out of the bathroom, Julie-Ann grabbed her panties and t-shirt and excused herself to go and cleanup. Before going back into the bedroom, she looked at herself in the mirror. *I can't believe you just did that. You just met this guy at a bar. But it felt so good. It's been way too long. I only wish I could have come.*

Chris and Julie-Ann laid underneath the covers. Chris put on the television. An old episode of the King of Queens was on. Julie-Ann said how funny the show was. Chris said he had never seen it before, so they watched it. After the episode was over, they started fooling around and had sex again.

Between all the alcohol and sex, Julie-Ann fell asleep with her head resting against Chris' bare chest. Not long afterwards, with the TV still on, Chris also fell asleep.

When Julie-Ann woke-up she looked at the clock on Chris' nightstand. It was 8:15 p.m. Chris must have heard or felt her stirring, because he groggily opened his eyes.

"It's eight-fifteen," Julie-Ann said in a sleepy voice.

Chris gingerly lifted his head and looked at the clock. "Wow, yeah. I guess we passed out."

"Maybe I should be going?"

Chris sat up in the bed. "Do you have to go? Why don't you spend the night? We can order some pizza. I'm actually pretty hungry."

"Me too. We did work up quite an appetite," Julie-Ann replied with a sinister grin. "But I don't know if I should spend the night. I mean I don't have any clothes or even a toothbrush."

"Listen, I don't want to pressure you into staying over. I can drive you back to your hotel. But I'd like you to stay."

Julie-Ann looked at Chris. The sex was great, but she also enjoyed just sleeping beside a man, having someone hold her. Truth be told, the main reason she had mentioned going home was because she thought that's what he would have wanted. "Well, pizza and a movie does sound good."

Chris smiled.

While Chris ordered the food, Julie-Ann went into the bathroom and freshened up. She put toothpaste on her index finger and used it to brush her teeth.

When the pizza came they ate it on the couch, in front of the TV. Chris ordered the movie Inception on pay-per-view. After the movie was over, they made love again, in the living room.

Chapter 26

When Julie-Ann woke-up, for a split second, she didn't know where she was. But then everything quickly came back to her. Chris was already out of bed. Sunlight was seeping in through the slits in the blinds. The clock on the nightstand read 10:47 a.m. Julie-Ann lifted her head. She was hung-over but not as bad as she thought she would be.

Julie-Ann had had a great time. The sex was well needed and passionate, and she genuinely liked Chris. But she also felt embarrassed, even guilty. There she was in some guy's bed that she had just met the prior afternoon—at a bar. As she contemplated where she was and what she had done, the unmistakable smell of bacon waft through the air, after stretching, she climbed out of bed and put on her shorts and Chris' t-shirt. She then strolled out into the kitchen, where she found Chris busy cooking breakfast.

"Oh, you're up," he said in a vibrant voice as he flipped a pancake. "Good. I didn't want to wake you, but breakfast is almost ready. I hope you like pancakes and bacon."

"Yes. Thank you. What a pleasant surprise to wake-up to."

Julie-Ann excused herself to go to the restroom. There, she washed her face, used some of Chris' mouthwash, and brushed her teeth with her index finger. When she came back, Chris was already plating the food on his small kitchen table. He told Julie-Ann to take a seat and poured her a glass of orange juice. He then sat down across from her.

"Chris, this is very nice. I certainly wasn't expecting you to cook me breakfast. And I really had a good time yesterday."

Chris put down his glass of juice. "Uh-oh."

Julie-Ann could tell Chris was worried about what was coming next. "No, no. I honestly did have a good time—in many ways," she added with a smile. "And I don't have any regrets. But, well…I…I don't want to sound cliché, but I just want you to know that it's not like I do this sort of thing all the time. I don't want you to think that I'm a…I guess what I'm trying to say…"

"It's okay. I understand, really. And whether you believe me or not, I don't do this sort of thing either. In fact, you're only the second woman I've been with since my wife died."

Julie-Ann put down her fork. "I'm so sorry about your wife. I can't even imagine. Do you mind if I ask how long you were married?"

Chris paused before answering. "Four and a half years," he said in a somber voice. He then let out a breath. "I know I told you that she died in a car accident—and she did—but unfortunately, that's not the whole story. When I was in UCLA, my friend and I started this website. It started off as a list of bars and what each one was like. For instance, if it was a college bar, a dive, a good place to take a date. It told you which bars had drink specials and what nights they were happening, like every Wednesday this place has ladies night. Then we had links to each bar's website—if they had one."

"That sounds pretty cool."

"Yeah. I mean there were other websites that had similar info; even sites like Yelp had reviews on various bars. But week-by-week we expanded the site. People could leave reviews and then we started putting reviews and bios of some of the bartenders, and sometimes even their schedules. It started to really catch on, and people started leaving up-to-the-minute comments, like 'this place is happening now, come down', or 'dead tonight, don't even bother'. That got us thinking. We went to the bars and made an agreement with some of them to let us put live webcam feeds in the bars. This way if you wanted to know if a certain place was happening, you could actually look at it live on our site before you went down there."

"That's an excellent idea."

Chris nodded with a proud smile. "Yeah. At first we just started with local bars, but like I said, it truly caught on. The site even got play in the news and on radio. After that, bars were asking us to be on our site. We started charging a fee for the webcam service. Then advertisers started coming in. Different breweries or companies like Jagermeister paid to have spots on our site. But of course, it was free to users." Chris paused. "Anyway, soon we started doing bars in other areas of California. The money really started to come in. And people started offering to buy the site. This one investor offered us a million dollars." Chris laughed. "No shit. Here we were twenty-three-years old, still in college, and someone was offering us a million dollars for some website we started as fun."

"Did you take the money?"

"No. We both dropped out of UCLA so we could focus on the business fulltime. We figured if someone was offering us a million dollars for it, if we really put all of our effort into it and expanded it, we could make it worth a lot more. So that's what we did. We rented office space and hired several employees. They had great jobs. Most of the time they were going to different bars. Soon, we had fifty bars on our site throughout California, over half of them with live webcam feeds. Then we started expanding to Arizona— Phoenix, Tempe, and Scottsdale. Then Nevada."

"Wow."

"Yeah, it was pretty cool. Anyway, while all this was going on I met Mary. After going out for nine months, we married." Chris paused. "It seemed like I was on top of the world," he continued in a more subdued voice. "I was only twenty-five. I was married and able to buy a nice house. I had money rolling in. Everyone wanted to be my friend. I could go to any of the clubs and drink for free. I thought I had everything. And it only got better. In two-thousand-nine someone made us an offer for the site that we couldn't refuse—seven million dollars. Don't forget, this is right after the financial collapse. Businesses were closing left and right. You were lucky to just have a job."

Julie-Ann finished chewing a piece of pancake. "So you took it?"

"Yep. We split it fifty-fifty. You know, after taxes and the lawyers, my share was closer to two million. But for me it was still a lot of money. Plus I had been saving money all along from our profit distributions. So many people around the country had just lost all their money. I was rolling in it. Then I found out that Mary was pregnant."

Julie-Ann could see in his facial expression and sense in his voice that something bad was coming. She stopped eating.

"I'm sorry, I didn't mean to go off on this long story."

Julie-Ann reached across the small table and put her hand on his. "It's okay."

Chris took a deep breath. "Anyway, Mary liked the good life. She liked to go out partying, do the social circuit. She started drinking a lot and then got into pills. You know, Xanax, Oxys. Once she got pregnant she said she would quit. And it seemed like she did for a while. But then one afternoon I was at home working on a new website I was designing. She had gone shopping. Anyway, when I opened the front door there was a policeman there." Chris stopped and looked away from Julie-Ann.

"It's okay, you don't have to tell me. I didn't mean for you…"

Chris tried to compose himself. "She ran a red light and plowed into the side of a minivan carrying a mother and her two daughters. My wife was killed instantly, and the baby was lost."

"Oh my God Chris, I'm so sorry."

"The woman driving the minivan and her seven-year-old daughter were also killed," he continued in a shaky voice. "The other girl, twelve at the time, was paralyzed from the waist down."

Chris cleared a lump in his throat. "Mary had been drinking and was high on oxycodone."

Julie-Ann felt like bursting into tears. "I am so sorry Chris," she said again, not knowing what else to say.

"The husband of the woman—and father to the girls—sued me."

"But how could that be your fault? I mean you weren't even in the car?"

"Well they couldn't sue my wife since she was dead. The car was registered in my name, the house was in both of our names."

"But still, how are you responsible?"

Chris let out an uncomfortable laugh. "The American legal system is quite amazing," he said sarcastically. "But truth be told, I didn't have the will to fight. I was crushed as you can imagine. Plus I felt so terrible for that family. I mean they were completely innocent. They were just going to the mall or wherever. Just at the wrong place at the wrong time. Anyway, I wound up settling out of court. After the settlement and the lawyers' fees, I was left with about a hundred-fifty thousand dollars to my name. I even lost my house."

"That's awful. And you didn't even do anything wrong."

"After the settlement I just needed to get away. I just needed to try to go somewhere and see if I could start again, somehow move on. That's how I ended up in Wyoming." Chris could see that Julie-Ann was fighting back tears. "I'm, sorry Julie-Ann. I didn't mean to lay all that on you—tell you my whole life story."

Julie-Ann put her hand on his forearm. "No, no. Please don't worry about that."

Chris tried to change to a more lighthearted subject as they finished their breakfast. Afterwards, he told Julie-Ann that she could take a shower, but she said that she would take one back at the hotel. Chris didn't want Julie-Ann to feel like she had to stay any longer, so he offered her a ride back. She accepted his offer, but said she would help him clean up first.

"Please, don't worry about it. It's just a couple of plates and a pan. Just let me put on some shoes."

"Okay. You don't have to rush." Julie-Ann was not sure if Chris had offered to take her back to the hotel because he wanted her to leave, or he thought she wanted to leave.

Before leaving the apartment, Chris and Julie-Ann exchanged numbers and email addresses.

It was only a ten-minute drive to the hotel. On the ride, the atmosphere was light, Julie-Ann and Chris even joked about the bar fight. However, the moment Chris pulled up to the hotel; an uneasy silence overtook the car.

"So, you're leaving in the morning?" Chris asked in a drawn out, hesitant tone as he looked at Julie-Ann.

"Yeah," she replied in a soft voice.

Chris took a breath. "So this is it? I mean I don't want to get all weird or anything, but we're just never going to see each other again?"

Chris' words seemed so final, Julie-Ann looked at him from the passenger seat. "I really like you Chris. And I don't want you to think that it was just some random one-night stand—because it wasn't. But what are we supposed to do? You live here and I live in New York. Maybe you can come out there some time. I would really like that. I really do want to see you again."

Chris nodded in defeat. "I understand. I just wish we had more time. I would really like to get to know you better."

"I know. I want to get to know you better too."

"Why don't you stay for one more day? I mean you don't have any set schedule. I can take you out to dinner." Chris paused. "I'm sorry. Listen to me, trying to talk you into staying. I shouldn't have said that. You…"

Julie-Ann put her index finger over his lip. "Shh. Don't take it back. I'll tell you what, I'm going to see if I can change my reservations and stay another day or two."

Chris wanted Julie-Ann to stay, but didn't want to pressure her into it. "Listen, I don't know what I was thinking. I don't want you to go through a bunch of trouble and change your plans."

"Would you like me to stay and take me out to dinner or not?" Julie-Ann asked with a smile.

"Yes. Yes, I would."

"Then I'll call you later and let you know." With that, Julie-Ann leaned over and gave Chris a quick kiss.

Once Julie-Ann was back in her hotel room, all she wanted to do was take a shower and veg out. She was tired and hung-over. But there were numerous missed calls and texts on her phone.

Two of the missed calls were from her father, so she decided to call him back before taking a shower. She talked to him for a little while, saying she had been out sightseeing. She wasn't about to tell him that she had met some guy at a bar and spent the night with him. She explained that she was supposed to leave for Yellowstone in the morning, but was debating whether or not to extend her stay for a day or two. She said that Cheyenne was beautiful country—which it was. Julie-Ann also asked about things back home. She asked to talk to Theresa, but her father was not with her. It was a casual call that ended with "I love you" and the continuing promise that Julie-Ann would keep her father updated on her whereabouts and wellbeing.

After talking with her father, Julie-Ann replied to some of her texts, including ones from Lisa, Kathy, and Lexi.

Julie-Ann ran the hot water in the shower before getting in, to let the bathroom steam up. After about five minutes, she stepped in and stood naked under the hot stream of water. It felt so soothing and replenishing. She felt as though she could stand there for the rest of the day. But as relaxing as it felt, Julie-Ann soon started thinking about Chris. Despite how their meeting started off, she certainly didn't think of it as just a wild night of sex (though she thoroughly enjoyed the sex). There was something more about him, something there. It was his personality. He was a gentleman, smart and witty. And though the story of how he lost his wife and wealth was so tragic, it brought a human, humble quality to him. Of course, she could also relate to him having to get away from everything he had known, to try and find himself and start anew.

But as it often happens, there were conflicting thoughts. *You're getting carried away,* she told herself as the shower rained down on her. *You just met him. Maybe you're just lonely. But why not stay an-other day or two? It's not like I have a schedule. I'm sure it won't be a problem to change the hotel dates. But what if I spend more time with him and start to fall for him? What then? I can't stay here. Wait. Slow down. No one's talking about getting serious. I haven't been with any-one since Ken. Why not spend another day with Chris and have some fun? There's no commitment. If things turn south for some reason, I'm leaving anyway.*

When Julie-Ann finished with the shower, she put on a robe that the hotel provided and called the front desk to see about being able to stay an extra two days. It was no problem. Then she called the Internet site that she had made the hotel reservation through for Yellowstone to see if she could change those dates from Monday to Thursday, to Wednesday to Saturday. She obviously did not care about any penalties she would have to pay. Unfortunately, Julie-Ann ran into the same problem that she encountered when making the original reservations—the hotel was booked solid on Fridays. The woman on the phone also checked other hotels in the area, but it was the same thing. Summer was peak season for Yellowstone. The best the representative could do was reserve a room through Thurs-day, checking out Friday morning. Julie-Ann had to make a quick decision. She definitely wanted to see Yellowstone. She reserved Tuesday to Friday. She was also able to keep the same one bedroom suite at the Snake River Lodge.

Next, Julie-Ann called Chris and told him that she was able to stay one extra day. Happy, but feeling a little guilty about having her change her plans, he said that he hoped it was not too much trouble. She said it was not. Since Julie-Ann now was leaving early Tuesday morning, Chris figured that she would probably not want to be out late Monday night, so he asked if she instead wanted to go to dinner later on that evening. Julie-Ann was feeling tired, and really just wanted to lounge around. But it was only 2:00 p.m., and the whole reason she had changed her plans was to spend more time with Chris. So she accepted the offer, and they agreed he would pick her up at the hotel at 7:00 p.m.

With her robe still on, Julie-Ann laid on the bed and turned on the TV. After about a half hour, she was fading in and out when her cell phone, which was on the nightstand next to the bed, rang. It was Amber. Julie-Ann picked it up. Amber asked how she was doing and about Wyoming. But Julie-Ann had to tell her all about Chris.

"Good for you Jules," Amber said with excitement. "How long had it been?"

"Since Ken. But it was more than just sex. I mean the sex was great, but he genuinely seems like a nice guy."

"Jules, you just met him yesterday at a bar. Don't get me wrong, if he's a good guy and you really like him that's great. But don't move too fast. And just be careful. I mean you're all alone out there. You have to watch yourself."

Julie-Ann said she appreciated Amber's concern, and that she would be careful, but was not worried about Chris having any nefarious intentions. She told Amber about Chris' story, his Internet company, his late wife, how she died, and how he was sued. Amber seemed interested, but again told Julie-Ann to be vigilant. She also told her to somehow take a picture of Chris and send it to her.

That evening, Julie-Ann met Chris in the hotel lobby at 7:00 p.m. as planned. She had asked him how to dress. His response had been "nothing too fancy", so she was wearing jeans, and a black top. Chris had on designer jeans and a tucked-in black button down shirt.

"You look great," Chris said with a smile.

"Thank you. You look good, too," she replied.

As Chris walked Julie-Ann to the car, for the first time, she started feeling a little awkward. No matter what she had told herself, the truth was that she had just met this guy the previous afternoon, and they had drunk sex. Now she was going out to dinner with him. What if she ran out of things to say? What if he wasn't really as charming as she thought he was? What if there was no connection? But Chris did his best to make her comfortable, keeping the conversation light and flowing. He asked about the hotel. He even joked that hopefully tonight they wouldn't get into a bar fight.

Chris took Julie-Ann to a steakhouse in downtown Cheyenne. It was nice, but not pretentious or too romantic for a casual date. It was lively, but not a hokey chain restaurant. Though a good crowd, Chris had made reservations and they were seated right away. He requested a booth, where they could have some seclusion and hear each other talk.

"They have really good prime rib here," Chris said after they sat down. "But all the steak is good here." Before picking the restaurant, Chris had asked Julie-Ann if she liked steak.

The waiter came over and gave them their menus and told them about a few specials. He then asked what they wanted to drink. Chris asked if Julie-Ann wanted a glass of wine. Still a little hung-over, she hadn't planned on drinking any alcohol. But then she figured one drink might take the edge off. So she said she would have a glass of red. Chris did the ordering, two glasses of Pinot Noir.

"So I was watching the video of the final shuttle launch today," Chris said as he looked over the menu.

"Oh, that was today? I knew it was coming up."

Chris put down his menu. "Yeah. It's kind of sad. I mean you think about the whole space race and Apollo Eleven, us landing on the moon. Then what a big deal the space shuttle was. Now, it's like we don't even have a space program anymore. It's a shame. I know it costs a lot of money and the deficit is out of control, but it just seems un-American, like we're losing our national pride."

Julie-Ann put down her menu. "Do you think America is losing its identity?" She asked in a straightforward tone.

"It sure seems that way. I mean there are still a lot of patriotic people out there, I'm one of them. You think of all those young men and women that joined the military after 9/11. They're out there dying for their country." Chris paused and took a sip of water.

"But when you look at the big picture, America as a whole, it just seems like there's so much discord and corruption. There's definitely a lack of leadership in Washington. Then you have politicians going overseas, basically apologizing for America, appeasing our enemies. I don't want war, believe me. But it just seems like our standing in the world is getting weaker and weaker."

"I agree," Julie-Ann replied. "I'll tell you, one of the things that I treasure the most about my journey thus far is how much I've learned about what's really going on in the country. I guess to truly understand it, you have to experience it—or at least talk with those people who have."

Just then the waiter came by with their wine and took their orders.

Once he left, Chris lifted his glass in the air. "Well, I'm glad you decided to stay an extra day and let me take you out to dinner."

Julie-Ann smiled and raised her glass. "Me too," she replied in a soft voice before touching his glass with hers and taking a drink.

Any fleeting worries Julie-Ann had about how the dinner would go were gone. The atmosphere was relaxed and fun. The conversation flowed without any awkward pauses. Chris didn't bring up anything personal or too serious. Julie-Ann never tried to wonder what he was thinking or what he was getting at.

"So, did it take you a while to get acclimated to living in Cheyenne?" Julie-Ann asked before dunking a crisped piece of bread into the spinach artichoke dip they had ordered as an appetizer.

Chris took a sip of his wine. "Well it's a lot slower pace than Los Angeles, that's for sure. But Cheyenne is a cool place. It's obviously a lot smaller and has a lot less happening than other prominent cities, but it's not some tiny country outpost either. I mean, you see, they have all the chains that Everywhere America has."

"Yeah. I have to say, that does take some of the charm away. Don't get me wrong it's beautiful here. But, I didn't travel a thousand miles to see a Starbucks or Target or Chilis."

Chris laughed. "I know what you mean. I feel like I could go to the North Pole and find a Subway or Best Buy. It's a shame what happened to all the mom-and-pop stores. Like I was saying before, it's like the vanishing of Americana."

Julie-Ann nodded. "Yeah. It must have been something driving through the country forty, fifty years ago."

The waiter came by with their meals; prime rib for Chris and New York strip for Julie-Ann. Like the steakhouse in Nebraska, Julie-Ann was amazed by how delicious the steak was.

For dessert, they shared a crème brulee.

"So, what do you want to do after this?" Chris asked. "You want to go somewhere for a nightcap? The evening is still young."

"How about we go back to your place?" Julie-Ann replied with an alluring smile.

"Sounds good to me."

When the bill came Julie-Ann tried to pay for it, but Chris would not let her.

"Thank you for dinner," Julie-Ann said as they walked out of the restaurant.

"You're welcome. Thank you for the good time." Chris held the door for her as she exited. "Listen, Julie-Ann, I don't mean to be to forward, but I'd love for you to spend the night. I mean you don't have to. I was just asking because if you wanted to we could go by your hotel and pick up anything you need."

"I don't know what you think was going to happen tonight, but…"

Chris turned ashen. "I'm so sorry, he cut her off. "Please, I didn't mean to be presumptuous. I just thought…I mean…God, I can't believe I asked you that…I'm just…"

Julie-Ann laughed. "I'm just kidding. Okay, we can swing by the hotel, and I can grab an overnight bag."

Now Chris turned beet red. "You know you didn't have to let me go on for so long," he said jokingly.

Julie-Ann took Chris up to her hotel room. She was just going to put together an overnight bag while he waited, but they wound up having sex. Afterwards, as they laid naked in the bed, Julie-Ann asked if instead of going back to his place he just wanted to spend the night at the hotel. On cloud nine, he saw no reason to squabble.

Feeling relaxed and satisfied, but awake, Julie-Ann put on her panties on and went over to the minibar and grabbed two Heinekens. Under the covers, with their bodies touching, they drank their beers and turned on the television. Mostly they talked.

Before going to sleep, they made love again.

Julie-Ann and Chris woke-up late the next morning. Julie-Ann suggested they order breakfast up to the room. When the food came, Chris tried paying, but Julie-Ann insisted she put it on her bill. As they ate, they kept the conversation light, but an unsaid feeling, that they may soon never see each other again, hung in the air. It was on both of their minds, but neither one wanted to bring it up.

"Well I guess I should be getting on my way," Chris said after breakfast.

Julie-Ann looked at him. She wanted him to stay, but knew it couldn't go on forever. He had to leave at some point. "Okay," was all she replied in a solemn tone.

Julie-Ann was going to walk Chris down to his car, but he said there was no need. In front of the hotel door, they gave each other a short kiss. Then they paused as they looked into each other's eyes.

Julie-Ann could tell that Chris wanted to say something, but either couldn't find the words or held them back. "Listen, maybe we can meet this evening at the hotel for an early dinner?"

Chris's glum face smiled. "Sure. I would like that."

The rest of the morning and early afternoon Julie-Ann lounged around the hotel room. She watched some TV, went through her emails, and went on Facebook and Twitter. She could not help thinking of Chris. On the one hand, it seemed crazy that she was falling for someone that she had just met two days earlier. But on the other hand, it was hard for her to grasp that she would never seen him again after dinner. Making it worse was knowing that she would be going back to traveling her journey alone. Sure, she had met many great people along the way: Krista, Connie, Michelle, Rory and Kathy, Sergeant Francisco, Lexi and Evan, Lisa and Adele. And the bonds and time she spent with them she would treasure forever. Yet there was still always something missing: the hand of a man's touch; having someone lie next to her in the bed; the intimacy that she had been without for too long. Then she thought about the long drive to Yellowstone that she would be making alone, and another empty hotel bed.

Later on that afternoon, as Julie-Ann started packing some things, her cell phone rang. She could see from the caller ID that it was Adele. Needing a big sister figure to talk to, she happily answered the phone. She told Adele all about Chris, how they met and how she had spent the last two nights with him. Julie-Ann didn't want her to think that she was a slut, but Adele didn't seem like the person to pass judgment. Besides, if she was going to confide in her, what was the point in lying or holding anything back?

"We just click," Julie-Ann said. "I mean there's never any awkward pauses. There's just this connection. I feel like I've known him for a long time." She paused. "I'm being crazy right? I mean I just met this guy. Besides, it's not like I can just stay here in Cheyenne."

"Well it's understandable after what you went through with Ken, breaking off the wedding. And you haven't been with anyone since. It's only natural to fill that void with the first person you felt some connection with. It's kind of like you're still on the rebound. But on the other hand, life does work in mysterious ways. I know you don't want to hear this, especially that you're planning on leaving tomorrow, but you never know when that chance encounter is going to lead to you finding 'the one'. I remember the first time I met Jim. I was eighteen and had just graduated high school. I was living in Omaha with my parents, but that summer I stayed with a friend of mine that had just moved to Hastings. I was just supposed to stay for three weeks, but I met Jim at this horse show. It sounds crazy, but I just knew right away. There was just something I can't explain. He asked me out on a date. After that one date, it was like we were together every day. I wound up going back to

Omaha when I was supposed to, but I just couldn't get him out of my mind. I just couldn't stop wondering if he was the one. Anyway, after being back home for several weeks, communicating with him every day, I wound up moving to Hastings. My parents of course, weren't too happy. But they got over it. Less than a year later we were married."

"Oh, I didn't know that's how you guys met."

"Yeah," Adele replied in a reminiscing voice. "Anyway,

I'm sorry, I probably shouldn't be telling you that. That's the last thing you probably want to hear."

"No, that's okay."

Julie-Ann and Adele talked for a little while longer. Before ending the phone call, Adele told Julie-Ann to be careful and to call or text when she reached Yellowstone, to let her know she arrived okay.

At 6:00 p.m. Julie-Ann met Chris at the hotel restaurant as planned. The Capitol Grille was more upscale, but Julie-Ann had checked beforehand, and it was acceptable to wear jeans, as long as men wore a collared shirt, which Chris was.

Over an excellent meal, Chris and Julie-Ann kept the mood loose, joking around and laughing. Chris purposely didn't want things to get heavy and start talking about how much he would miss Julie-Ann. But then Julie-Ann surprised him.

"Listen Chris," she said in a more serious tone than the conversation had been following, "I know you have a job. And, well this might sound crazy, but how would you like to go to Yellowstone with me for a few days? I mean if you're able to get away."

Chris tried not to overreact and jump for joy. "Are you serious?"

Julie-Ann nodded. "Yeah. I've been thinking about it. I know we just met. And I don't want you to feel obligated. I mean, maybe I'm being too forward, but..."

"I would love to go," Chris cut her off. "And it wouldn't be a problem at all. I' mean I'm working on two websites right now, but I can certainly take off a couple of days. Besides, the great thing about building websites is you can do it from anywhere. All I need is a laptop."

"So we're going to Yellowstone together?"

Chris smiled from ear to ear. "I guess so."

After dinner, which Julie-Ann insisted on paying, instead of going back up to the hotel room, Chris went home so he could pack.

Chapter 27

The alarm clock woke Julie-Ann up at 6:00 a.m. Tuesday morning. With an eight-hour drive ahead, she wanted to be on the road by 7:30 a.m. She had done most of her packing the night before. As she took a shower, she could not help but wonder if she had made a mistake asking Chris to go along. When they were together, everything went so smoothly. But that was a short sampling. She would be spending the next three days with him. What if they got on each other's nerves? They would be stuck together. But it was too late to turn back now. Besides, she told herself, it was only three days.

Julie-Ann picked Chris up at his apartment. He had one suitcase, his laptop bag, and another, large rectangular black canvas case. He explained that it was his drawing supplies, saying how he couldn't go to Yellowstone and not do at least one etching. Julie-Ann was glad he brought it along, wanting to see him in action.

They stopped at a McDonalds in Cheyenne for a quick breakfast and then filled up the tank. Chris wanted to pay for the gas, but Julie-Ann insisted she pay, saying that she had planned on going to Yellowstone before she ever invited him. Chris still couldn't let her pay for all the gas. Finally, for the sake of not having a prolonged debate, they agreed to split the cost. He would pay for this fill up, and she would pay for the next.

If there were any worries that they would run out of things to talk about on such a long drive, they were abated. Whether it was Chris' old website business, his time in Cheyenne, Julie-Ann's journey, her childhood in New York, music, or politics, the conversation flowed uninterrupted. And though sometimes they entered into serious topics, most of the dialogue was blithe. In fact, there was a lot of laughing.

About an hour and a half into the drive, they stopped at their first service station, so Julie-Ann could use the restroom. Chris also took the opportunity to stretch his legs and look around. He said he was going to get some coffee and asked Julie-Ann what she wanted.

Chris gave Julie-Ann her coffee. Before heading back to the car, Julie-Ann stopped in the gift shop and bought some snacks for the ride.

"Why don't you let me drive for a while," Chris said as they walked through the parking lot.

"Sure. Okay."

"Hey, you want to put the top down? I mean a convertible was meant for drives like this—summertime, blue sky, not too hot, the open country."

Julie-Ann smiled. "I'm sold."

Just as they reached the car, Julie-Ann's cellphone rang. She quickly retrieved it from her purse. It was a Jefferson City number. She answered it and tossed the car keys to Chris.

It was Helen Vigman, the woman with the two children at the Center of Hope, to whom Julie-Ann had given $10,000. She was calling to let Julie-Ann know that she had found an apartment and a babysitter and was going to try and find a job. She thanked Julie-Ann profusely for her help and said that without her, she and her kids would still be in the shelter. Julie-Ann said how happy she was that Helen was able to find an apartment and asked that she keep her updated.

Already in the car, as soon as Julie-Ann finished the call, she told Chris about Helen and her story.

"That's so generous of you," he said as they headed out to the highway. "Do you mind if I ask how much you gave her?"

"Ten thousand dollars," she replied without hesitation.

Chris had to focus to keep from crashing. "Ten thousand dollars?"

"Well, I figured what was a thousand dollars going to do? At least ten thousand she might be able to find a temporary place to stay—besides a homeless shelter. I mean, it wasn't just her, it was her two kids. If that money can somehow help her start anew, then it was worth every penny."

Chris was in awe of Julie-Ann's generosity and benevolence. He wondered how much more money she had given away to people that she met along her journey, though he did not ask. However, they did stay on the topic of helping people and different, specific causes. Julie-Ann explained that eventually she wanted to start her own charitable foundation. Chris said that he could build the website for her. In fact, he said he would love to, not only because it would be helping her out, but also he truly wanted to play some part.

They arrived at the Snake River Lodge at 5:50 p.m. It had been a long drive, but the pulchritude of the hotel and surrounding area revitalized them. Resembling a sprawling, wooden ranch, the hotel was nestled in a lush valley, against a backdrop of towering, majestic mountains. There was no town, no houses, just open, breathtaking wilderness.

The inside of the hotel was just as beautiful, and it was clear that considerable attention had been paid to matching the interior with its environment. The expansive lobby had glistening hardwood floors and preserved, decorative tree posts for beams, which met its high ceilings. To the right of the entranceway was a seating area with over-sized cushioned chairs and love seat, in front of a large, stone fireplace. Plenty of windows let in the natural light of day.

While looking around and taking it all in, Julie-Ann and Chris walked up to the front desk, which was a marble counter with a wood base that had carved into it the scene of woods, complete with a bear. As they checked in, the polite gentleman assisting them went over the hotels amenities, including a 17,000 square foot spa, and both an indoor and outdoor pool.

The room, which was located on the third and top floor, had a large balcony, which overlooked the sprawling valley. Inside, it had a private bedroom with a king bed, and a separate living room with a couch, two cushioned chairs, and a gas fireplace. It also had a half bath. In the bedroom was the master bathroom, with marble floors, jet-powered tub, and separate glass-walled shower. There was a large, flat panel television in both the living area and the bedroom.

"This is so cool. They have a fireplace," Julie-Ann said with excitement as she walked over to it. "Oh, that sounds so good tonight, ordering some room service, then sitting by the fire, maybe with a bottle of wine."

"You do realize that it's summer, right," Chris said jokingly.

"I don't care, we're gonna turn on the fireplace. It's romantic."

Chris walked over to Julie-Ann from behind and put his arms around her. "I'm all for being romantic."

"This place is beautiful."

"It sure is." Chris then walked over to the sliding glass door that lead to the balcony. "And speaking of beautiful and romantic," he said as he peered out the door, which had its curtains pushed to one side, "look at this view." He then slid the glass door open and stepped onto the balcony, which had a table and two chairs.

Julie-Ann followed him outside. "It's amazing. You can see forever. Those mountains—they're so gorgeous."

Chris took a deep breath of the fresh Wyoming summer air. "It's like you can forget that it's two-thousand-eleven. It's almost as if

I'm waiting for a wagon train to roll by, or a band of Indians and buffalo."

Chris and Julie-Ann stood out on the balcony for another five minutes or so, just soaking up the wide-open expanse. When they went back inside Chris asked her if she was hungry. Julie-Ann was starving. Since their McDonalds breakfast, they had only snacked on chips and beef jerky during their drive. So they ordered room service.

They ate in front of the television, in the living room. Shortly after they were finished, Chris said he was going to go down to the shop in the lobby to get some bottled water. Julie-Ann pointed out that there was bottled water in the stocked minibar, but he said it would be cheaper just to get a few larger bottles. He also asked if Julie-Ann wanted anything.

As Chris went downstairs, Julie-Ann did some more unpacking and setting up her things in the bathroom. She then changed into a silk nightgown that she had brought with her on the trip, but had not yet worn.

When Chris returned, he had a bag of bottled water, as well as a bottle of red wine. "They actually have a place downstairs where you can buy beer and wine," he said with a smile as he held the bottle up. "I remembered what you said about sitting by the fireplace with some wine."

Julie-Ann smiled. "Why don't you change into something more comfortable?"

"Sounds good."

As Chris went to change, Julie-Ann went into the stocked minibar and took out a box of chocolate and a round package of assorted cheese wedges. She also grabbed two short glasses that were on the counter and brought everything to the small table in front of the couch, by the fireplace.

Chris walked out of the bedroom wearing only boxers. "How's this?" He said, posing with his arms spread open.

"Perfect."

"I was going to hook my iPod up to the radio. You want to listen to anything in particular?"

Julie-Ann let out a long breath as she thought about it for a second. "Yeah. Do you have any blues?"

"Yes I do. I'll put on some Albert King."

Chris put the music on low, so it was easily audible, but blended into the background. He then turned on the fireplace and turned off all the lights in the room. As Julie-Ann waited on the corner of the couch, Chris opened the bottle of Merlot with a corkscrew the hotel provided and poured two glasses.

After sitting on the couch, his bare legs touching Julie-Ann's legs, Chris raised his glass. "Here's to Yellowstone. I'm so glad I came."

"I am too."

They then took a sip of their wine.

"So, what's with the chocolates and cheese?"

Julie-Ann broke off a piece of chocolate, which she had already unwrapped. "Here," she said in a seductive voice as she went to put it Chris' mouth. But as soon as it touched his lips, she pulled it away. Then, she slowly brought it back to his mouth and glided it along his open lips before gently it halfway in his mouth.

Chris took a bite. Then he took hold of Julie-Ann's hand and held it by his mouth. As he ate the rest of the small piece of chocolate, he sucked on her finger.

After a few seconds, he broke off another piece of chocolate and brought it to Julie-Ann's lips. She immediately took a bite, chomping down on the tip of his finger. As she held his finger with her teeth, her tongue massaged the part that was inside her mouth. Then she grabbed his hand and put his entire finger in her mouth and simulated oral sex.

Chris closed his eyes and let her play. After about a minute, he pulled his finger out, grabbed the back of her head with both hands and brought her to his mouth. As the slow blues of Albert King played in the background and the dancing flames of the fire flickered, they kissed.

When they finally separated from each other's lips, Chris climbed off the couch and kneeled on the floor. His head at the level of Julie-Ann's stomach, he pulled down her silk panties.

Julie-Ann knew what was coming next. She closed her eyes, let out a deep breath, and widened her legs. A feeling of bliss washed over her whole body as Chris went to work. His tongue shot tingles up her spine. She closed her eyes and enjoyed the ride. "Oh yes, right there," she moaned. "That's it, just like that. Don't stop." As he listened to her directions, her thighs began to quiver. "Oh yes," she said again as her chest expanded and compressed. Her entire body started to quake. "I'm going to come. I'm almost there. Don't stop. Don't...oh yeah..." As an overwhelming feeling of adrenaline and euphoria shot through her, she climaxed.

Afterwards, she bent down, grabbed Chris' face and brought it up to hers. They kissed unrestrained.

"Do you want to fuck me?"

"Oh yes," Chris replied in the throes of ecstasy.

After they had sex, Chris and Julie-Ann cuddled on the couch in front of the fireplace and had another glass of wine.

Julie-Ann and Chris woke-up at 8:00 a.m. to the annoying, high-pitched beeping of the alarm clock Julie-Ann had set. It was almost an hour drive to Yellowstone, and they wanted to get in a full day.

Though Julie-Ann and Chris had spent the night together before, they had never gotten ready together. Trying to be courteous, and figuring it would take Julie-Ann longer to get ready since she was a woman, Chris let her take a shower first. For most of her life, Julie-Ann had been one of those women who took forever to get ready in the morning, laboring over every detail and making sure she was perfect. But her priorities had changed. Her way of thinking had changed. She still wanted to look good, but she was not going to stress out over it. Of course, it also helped that her hair was so short. In fact, Chris was surprised by how quickly it took her to get ready.

By 9:00 a.m., Julie-Ann and Chris were both showered and dressed. Before hitting the road for hours, they decided to go down to the hotel restaurant and to get a good breakfast.

With a hearty breakfast under their belts, Chris and Julie-Ann waited outside for the valet to get the car. It was a beautiful July day. The sun was bursting through a clear, blue sky. The air was dry and the temperature warm, but not hot. Julie-Ann felt energized. She felt no effects from the two glasses of wine she had consumed the previous night. She was ready to explore Yellowstone and all of its splendor.

Chris brought his drawing case with him, wanting to do at least one etching of the landscape. After all, that's why he had brought it on the trip.

The drive to Yellowstone, which took them through Teton National Park, was breathtaking. Sprawling mountains towered majestically into the air as if they were kissing the heavens. Their valley was lush and capacious, rolling far beyond the eye's sight. Just beyond the road seemed a land untouched by modern times, pure and naturalistic, as if a window into the past.

As they reached the south entrance to Yellowstone, the land opened even wider. Vast woodlands met roving parries, cut by the mighty, winding Snake River. In the background stood prodigious mountain ranges, watching over the land below like mighty guardians. Julie-Ann and Chris drove down the pathway, with eyes in wide wonder, enthralled by the infinite landscape. Observing through the cars' windows was not enough. They began stopping at the many pull-offs and scenic overlooks and in some instances walked around and explore.

Both Julie-Ann and Chris took plenty of pictures. At one point, Julie-Ann asked a woman if she could take a couple of pictures of her and Chris. On the edge of an overlook, with vast valley and winding river to their backs, Julie-Ann and Chris posed for several shots. Chris put his arm around Julie-Ann's shoulders, and she had her arm around his back.

They thanked the woman and then looked at the pictures on Julie-Ann's phone. "That's a great shot," she said with excitement as Chris looked at it over her shoulder. "You can see the whole valley below."

After staying at the overlook a little longer, they went back to the car and headed further down the road. About fifteen minutes later they came to another overlook. Chris, who was driving, pulled over so they could take in the view. It was a rather large area, with plenty of parking. There were a few other cars there already, but what caught Julie-Ann's attention was the row of seven motorcycles parked in one corner of the overlook. Specifically, she took note of the American and black MIA flags that stood on the backs of several of the bikes. Her attention was shifted as Chris, who was already at the edge of the overlook, called for her.

It was a breathtaking sight: columns of towering, carved mountains, protruding from the snaking valley floor, up into the blue sky. Julie-Ann snuggled up to Chris and gazed out into the divine, sprawling landscape. As Julie-Ann turned her head towards the west, she noticed a group of men standing by the motorcycles. Two of them had on shirts with VFW insignia. Then, one of them, probably in his early thirties, with an American flag bandana on his head, approached them.

"Excuse me," he said in a polite voice to both Chris and Julie-Ann, "but I was wondering if you might be able to take a few pictures of me and my buddies?"

"Of course," Julie-Ann answered before Chris could say anything.

The stranger smiled. "Thank you." He then led them back to his group.

"I couldn't help noticing the MIA flags on your bikes and that some of you are wearing VFW shirts," said Julie-Ann.

He went on to explain that he and his buddies were all veterans of either Iraq or Afghanistan. They had been taking an annual ride to Yellowstone for the past three years, as a way of therapy, keeping solidarity, and remembering their fallen brothers. But this was a particularly special trip, he added. A good friend had heard about their trips to Yellowstone, but was unable to go the first two years, because he was still deployed in Afghanistan. However, he was set to come home in June and promised to join their next trip. But two weeks before he was to leave Afghanistan he was killed in a fire-fight. He had never married and had no children. It had been his wish that if he died, to be cremated. The group, along with his brother, who was the only non-veteran, had brought his ashes to Yellowstone to spread them.

Both Julie-Ann and Chris said how sorry they were. Everyone in the group appreciated their condolences, but seemed upbeat for being on such a somber mission. But as one of them put it, they were there to celebrate life, not death. They were all very kind and polite, and their close camaraderie was immediately apparent.

Julie-Ann took numerous pictures, using several of their cameras. The men thanked her and Chris profusely.

"You know, I don't know how much time you guys have," Chris said, "but I do pencil drawings. And if you guys like, I can do one of all of you, maybe by your bikes, with the mountains in the background. I mean I don't want anything for it. I'd just like to do it for you, show some kind of appreciation for your service. I'll try to do it fast—maybe about twenty minutes."

"He's really amazing," added Julie-Ann. "He has his supplies in the car."

The men looked at each other. "That would be great," one of them then said.

Chris went to the car and retrieved his supplies. He unfolded a portable easel and put an 11" x 14" pad of pastel paper on it. He then had the men pose in front of their row of motorcycles. As Chris vigorously etched with his pencil, Julie-Ann, who was off to the side, conversed with the men. Standing in place, they would answer her questions and tell her more about their trip—and the friend they had laid to rest.

After about half an hour, Chris announced he was finished and brought the drawing over so they could see. It was better than any of them had expected. Not only was he able to encapsulate their image with detail, as if taken a penciled photograph, but he was also able to capture the backdrop of the Yellowstone Mountains kissing the sky. The men tried to pay Chris for his time, but he would not take any money. However, one of the men took several pictures with Julie-Ann's camera of her and Chris posing with the rest of the gang. Before leaving, they thanked Chris again, and he and Julie-Ann thanked them for their service.

It was then back into the car and onto the next pull-off. Julie-Ann and Chris were having a great time exploring the park, but they still had another full day. So at 3:00 p.m., Julie-Ann suggested they head back to the hotel and hang out at the pool. It sounded good to Chris.

On the way back to the hotel, they passed a lone diner on the side of the road. "You wanna stop there and grab something to eat?" Julie-Ann asked. "I always wanted to stop at some random diner in the middle of nowhere."

Chris laughed. "Well, if that's on your bucket list. I am pretty hungry anyway."

Chris turned the car around. There were a few cars in the parking lot, including a minivan, so neither Chris nor Julie-Ann thought it was a place they were going to find trouble. Sure enough, inside, were a couple of families, along with some younger couples. Still, the diner had a rustic vibe. They sat down at a booth and ordered a late lunch. Chris had a cheeseburger with fries; Julie-Ann had a turkey club. They both breathed a sigh of relief when the food came, and it was delicious. In fact, Chris made Julie-Ann take a bite of his burger.

By the time they arrived back at the hotel, it was 5:00 p.m. With daylight burning, they went up to the room to change into their bathing suits. Before leaving Cheyenne, Julie-Ann told Chris there was a pool at the hotel and to pack his swimming shorts.

Chris had already put on his shorts and was grabbing a beer out of the minibar when Julie-Ann walked out of the bathroom wearing her black with gold-trim bikini.

"God, you look so sexy," Chris said as he stared her over.

Julie-Ann smiled. "Well thank you."

Chris put down his beer, walked right up to Julie-Ann and put his hands on her upper arms. "I'd love to throw you down on that bed right now and…"

"Shhh," Julie-Ann cut him off. "Don't get me all started. Otherwise, we'll never get down to the pool. There'll be plenty of time to fool around later."

Though Julie-Ann had seen pictures of the pool on the website, she was surprised by how elegant it and the surrounding area looked. One giant pool, it had both an indoor and outdoor area, separated by huge glass-pane door that retracted up and down like a garage. When up, one could swim or wade from indoors to outdoors, where the pool expanded to replicate a natural lake, flowing into different inlets. In one part, there was even a stone grotto, complete with a waterfall. Adjacent to the pool was a small outdoor bar with seating area. The backdrop of the Grand Teton mountain range encircled the entire outside.

After hanging out at the pool for about an hour, Chris and Julie-Ann went inside to soak in one of the hot tubs. A small group of people was just leaving, so they had it all to themselves.

"God this feels so great," Julie-Ann proclaimed as she sat down in the hot, bubbling water.

"Oh yeah. This place must be great in the winter. I can imagine Yellowstone all covered in snow."

"Yeah, that must be so beautiful," Julie-Ann agreed.

"Then coming back to the hotel, going in the heated pool and then the hot tub," Chris added. "I mean don't get me wrong, it's amazing right now."

They stayed in the hot tub for about twenty-five minutes before going back upstairs. Once in the room, Julie-Ann asked Chris if he wanted to take a shower together. They took off their bathing suits and stood under the wide spray of hot water.

"Let me wash you," Chris said.

Julie-Ann turned around so that her back was facing Chris. As steam started to form around them, he worked the soap into a lather. He then gently caressed Julie-Ann's shoulders with the soap, slowly working his way down each arm, then her back. Her head under the streaming water, she took in a deep breath. His hands felt exhilarating on her wet flesh.

"How does that feel," Chris asked as he continued to take his time working down the back of her body.

"Fantastic," Julie-Ann replied with her head tilted towards the floor, letting the beads of water rain down on her head and neck.

Chris's hands then wrapped around her and started massaging the bubbly lather on her front side, starting by her inner thighs. Slowly using the small bar of soap in a circular motion, he glided upwards to her stomach. His other hand massaged the suds on her skin. As he came to her breasts, Julie-Ann could feel her body tingling. Every movement of his hands seemed amplified. Starting to breathe heavily, she reached her hand back and took hold of him and began to stroke until he quickly came to an erection. She then leaned forward and braced herself against the front wall of the shower.

With the hot water beating down on them and steam filling the room, Chris widen her legs and put himself inside of her. As he made love to her, he fondled her wet, lathered breasts.

"Oh God, oh yes," Julie-Ann moaned in ecstasy. "Just like that. Don't stop."

Chris worked in rhythm, slow, then faster. Just as he was about to explode, he quickly pulled all the way out and climaxed.

Julie-Ann turned around, grabbed the back of Chris' head and started ravenously kissing him. His bare body felt so good rubbing up against hers.

"Now let me wash you," she said after finally prying herself from his lips.

By the time they were finished with the shower, it was 7:30 p.m. After a full day, and both were completely content, they decided to stay in the room for the rest of the evening.

As Chris went on his laptop to tend to some emails about the websites he was currently designing, Julie-Ann took the time to go through her emails. Afterwards, she went on Facebook. She had already posted that she was in Yellowstone and numerous people had left comments—including Michelle, Krista, Lisa, and Lexi—and several people had asked for pictures. So Julie-Ann connected her phone up to her computer via Bluetooth and downloaded several pictures into an album. Two of the photos were of her and Chris at the scenic overlook. Underneath one, she put the caption: *Me and Chris. He's a wonderful guy.* Julie-Ann knew she would receive replies asking who the hell was Chris. But at that point she didn't care. She didn't want to keep him a secret. In fact, she wanted to talk about him.

As soon as Julie-Ann turned off her laptop, she saw that she had a new text on her phone. It was from Amber. She apparently had been on Facebook and had already seen the pictures Julie-Ann had posted. *You took him to Yellowstone??? How are things going?* The text read.

Julie-Ann text back. *They're going great. I know, it sounds crazy, seeing how we just met. Maybe I'm moving too fast. But it feels so right. In fact, the more time we spend together the more right it feels.*

Amber immediately replied. *Well I guess if he was some psychopath we would have already chopped you up by now. LOL. But seriously, still be careful. I'm glad that you're happy and with someone. But don't get too attached. What are you going to do when you come back to NY—which will hopefully be soon?*

I don't know. She simply replied. It was something that Julie-Ann didn't even want to think about.

The next morning Chris and Julie-Ann decided to order breakfast in the room as they got ready. They then drove back out to Yellowstone, where they spent the day. They parked the car several times and ventured down walking trails. They took plenty of pictures. Chris also brought his art case with him.

At one point, Chris penciled a drawing of Julie-Ann, standing by the banks of a river, with a towering waterfall behind her. It took about a half hour, but she was glad to stand there.

"It's so beautiful," she declared, looking at the finished product. "I can't believe how you're able to get such detail. And draw it so fast."

"It's easy for me to capture the landscape. The hard part was being able to capture your natural beauty.

Julie-Ann smiled. "You're going to make me blush."

"Really. You're so beautiful. I don't want to sound all sappy, but I can just look at you all day long."

As the day before, Julie-Ann drove to Yellowstone and Chris drove the way back. On the ride to the hotel Julie-Ann's phone rang. It was Theresa. She really didn't want to talk to her in the car, with Chris right there, so she sent her a text saying she would call her back later.

Theresa replied to her text. *OK. Saw your pics on FB. Who's Chris? Don't worry, I didn't show your father.*

It was a conversation Julie-Ann was not particularly looking forward to, but again, she did not want to keep Chris some secret, or feel guilty about what she was doing.

The plan had been to go down to the pool once they got back to the hotel. But when they walked into the lobby, Julie-Ann said she needed to stop in the gift shop and told Chris to go ahead up to the room. Chris didn't question it. He figured she had to buy some feminine product or make a phone call. He told her to take her time.

In the lobby's seating area, Julie-Ann called Theresa back. She told her the truth about Chris, how they met and his story. She explained that she was a grown woman and was not ashamed or was not going to be made to feel guilty. There was nothing for Theresa to talk Julie-Ann out of. She had already slept with him and had taken him to Yellowstone. She just told her stepdaughter to be careful and that she would not tell her father about it—though he might find out anyway.

"I really don't care if he finds out," Julie-Ann said in a calm, but firm tone. "I'm twenty-five-years old, soon to be twenty-six. I don't want to start an argument with him, but this is my life. It's my life more than it's ever been. And I'm loving it."

Julie-Ann and Theresa ended on a lighter note as Theresa asked her about Yellowstone National Park. Julie-Ann also told her about the veterans they had met and their story.

Julie-Ann then went upstairs and changed into her bathing suit.

It was already 5:45 p.m. and Chris and Julie-Ann had not had any lunch, so they decided to eat something at the bar by the pool. They also had a few drinks. They then went in the water for a while, with beers in hand. Afterwards, they went back into the hot tub.

"I can't believe we have to leave tomorrow," Chris said over the jets of the tub. "I could stay here for another week."

Julie-Ann let out a deep breath. "I know, so can I. In fact, while you were in the shower this morning I called the front desk to see if anyone cancelled their reservations and we can stay for another night."

Chris' steamed face lit up.

"But they still had no availabilities," Julie-Ann replied in a defeated voice.

Chris moved closer to Julie-Ann. "I don't mean to get all serious and bring down the mood, but what's going to happen to us? I mean are we going to drive back to Cheyenne tomorrow morning, you drop me off at my apartment and then be on your way? Am I never going to see you again?"

Julie-Ann looked at Chris with melancholy eyes.

"Wait, before you answer that, there's something I have to tell you."

"What is it?" Julie-Ann asked, puzzled.

Chris paused. "I love you, Julie-Ann. I know we've been together such a short time, but I can't help how I feel. And if we were to part ways without me ever telling you, I know I would always regret it. It's just…"

Julie-Ann put her wet index finger over Chris' lips. "I love you, too." Even as she said it, a part of her thought it was crazy. But it was true. She had fallen in love with Chris.

"You do?"

Julie-Ann gave a seductive smile. "Yes, I do."

"So what are we going to do about it?"

Julie-Ann let out an uncomfortable laugh. "I don't know. How about from here we go somewhere else?" She said on the fly.

"Come with me to my next destination—wherever that is. Then we'll just see how it goes. Maybe by that time we'll get so sick of each other we'll be dying to part ways," she jokingly added.

"If you're serious, I would love to."

That night, Julie-Ann and Chris sat on the couch in front of the fireplace and looked at Julie-Ann's laptop, trying to figure out their next destination.

"What about Idaho?" Chris asked as they looked at a map of the northwestern United States.

Julie-Ann gave him a puzzled look. "What's in Idaho?"

"Exactly. I thought you want to go places that you would never normally go to. Well, have you ever been to Idaho? I mean what's even in Idaho?" He asked jokingly. "It's like a mystery."

"You're absolutely right. Let's go to Idaho."

They pulled up a map of Idaho and did some quick research on several locations. On one hand, they didn't want to stay in some big, homogenized city where it looked like every-town America. But on the other hand, they didn't want to get stuck in a motel room in some small town where there was nothing to do. Ultimately, they settled on Idaho Falls, which was only a two-hour drive. They then went on Expedia and reserved three nights at a place called Le Ritz Hotel & Suites. Beyond that, they made no plans, just deciding to play it by ear.

Chapter 28

With Idaho Falls being less than a three-hour drive, Julie-Ann and Chris took their time getting ready Friday morning and went downstairs to have a sit-down breakfast.

When they arrived in Idaho Falls, they were both happy to see that it was beautiful country, with a backdrop of green roving mountains, snaking rivers, and wide open spaces. The hotel was also alluring, both its inside and location, which was set on the banks of the Snake River, the same river their previous hotel was named after. However, it was also close to town. Though not as extravagant as the Snake River Lodge, it had a pool and hot tub.

That afternoon, having originally packed for only three days, Chris bought some extra clothes at a mall in town. Julie-Ann also bought a few items. She also used the hotel's laundry service to wash some of her other clothes. After the mall, they walked around the town and went to the Museum of Idaho, which had different historic exhibits, including one dedicated to Lewis and Clark.

Julie-Ann had looked on the Internet and found a local homeless shelter, called The Haven, and on Saturday morning, she and

Chris went there. They talked to some of the staff and were given an overview and even a brief tour of the facilities. Julie-Ann donated $7,000 to the shelter. Chris did not have that kind of money to give away, but felt compelled to help in any way he could, and donated $300.

After leaving the shelter, Julie-Ann and Chris walked around Idaho Falls and discovered there was a county fair going on. They walked the two miles to the fairgrounds, which was on a vast, grassy field, on the outskirt of town. There were rides and rows of carnival games and concession stands. People of all ages were walking around, kids, teenagers, families. But it was not too crowded as there was plenty of space. Though it had rained for about an hour earlier that morning, the sky had turned blue, and it was about eighty degrees.

Julie-Ann and Chris were like a couple of kids. They went on a small rollercoaster and the Ferris wheel. Chris even talked her into riding the bumper cars. He also won Julie-Ann a large stuffed bear, spending about twenty minutes playing knock the bowling pins down with a baseball. They partook is some of the customary fair food, including a corn dog and funnel cake.

At one point, as Julie-Ann was walking through an open area, holding Chris' hand, she thought back to the dream she had after her operation, about strolling through a fair, holding some unknown person's hand. She had not thought about the dream since a few days after having it. But now, she remembered the powerful feeling of the dream, the feeling of peace and serenity. Could it be, she wondered? Could that dream really have been some prophetic foreshadowing? Julie-Ann had never seriously believed in premonitions or the supernatural. However, walking through the fair, holding Chris' hand, and feeling such contentment, she could not help but think of the dream and see it as some kind of sign. Though she never mentioned it to Chris.

That evening, while Chris was doing some work on his laptop, Julie-Ann went downstairs to the lobby and called her father. She told him about Chris. She figured why prolong something that was probably going to come out anyway? Besides, like Julie-Ann had told Theresa, she was not going to feel ashamed or guilty for being with him. She told her father how Chris had stuck up for her and that one thing just led to another. She told him about his story, about his late wife. Julie-Ann did not tell her father that she had fallen in love with Chris, but Mr. Crown knew that she would not be telling him about Chris unless she had strong feelings for him. Her father was not pleased, but not wanting to get in a big fight, bit his tongue. He knew she was an adult and was going to do whatever she wanted anyway. Besides, Julie-Ann seemed so genuinely happy. He just told her to be careful.

Not having to adhere to any schedules, Julie-Ann and Chris moved at a leisurely pace, taking their time sightseeing, eating, and even going in the pool. In one sense, the days were long and had multiple chapters to them. But in another sense, their time in Idaho Falls went by with the blink of an eye. During their last afternoon, they went out to a late lunch at an American bistro in the small downtown area. There, they finally had the conversation that had been staved off since they arrived in Idaho—what were they going to do next? What were they going to do about their relationship?

Julie-Ann could not imagine just taking Chris back to Cheyenne and then never seeing him again. Chris felt the same way. They also both knew that agreeing to some cross-country relationship where they "might" see each other a couple of times a year was the same as saying goodbye.

"Listen, I know this sounds crazy, because we've only been together such a short time," Chris said across the table, "but I can't just walk away from you. I mean, if that's what you want, than I'll respect that. But I love you and I know I'll regret it for the rest of my life if we just go our separate ways."

"I feel the same way," Julie-Ann said, nearly in tears. "I have to be honest, a small part of me was almost hoping that we would come to Idaho, and we'd argue or just realize that we're just having fun, and it'd be easier to go our own ways. But it had the opposite effect. Spending more time with you just made me realize that I really do love you, and I want you in my life."

Chris leaned across the table. "I don't care what I have to do. I'll move to New York. I'll do my website business from there."

"You would do that for me? Leave Wyoming and move to New York just to be with me?"

"In a heartbeat," he replied without hesitation.

Julie-Ann and Chris finally decided that they would drive back to Cheyenne. Julie-Ann would spend a few days there and then go back to New York. Not wanting to drive all the way across the country again, she would leave her car with Chris and fly to New York. She would then have her car shipped. Once Julie-Ann was back in New York, the separation would give them a few days, or even a few weeks, to think about their relationship. If they still felt the same way and wanted to be together, Chris would move out to New York.

The next morning, Julie-Ann and Chris headed back to Cheyenne, which was just over five hundred miles away. At one of the service stations they stopped at, Julie-Ann took the opportunity to call her father. She told him that she would be flying back to New York in several days and having the car shipped. Though Mr. crown had come to understand and respect his daughter's journey, he was overly relieved to hear that she would finally be coming back home. He also missed her very much. Julie-Ann explained that she was still with Chris, but did not tell her father about the possibility of him moving to New York. She figured she would cross that bridge if and when it came, and it would be in person.

Julie-Ann's father said he would send his leer jet to fly her back to New York, but she insisted on taking a commercial flight. That evening she went on line and booked a flight—that had a stopover in Denver—for that coming Saturday and emailed her father the itinerary.

Julie-Ann spent four days in Cheyenne, at Chris' apartment. By the time it was ready for her to leave, the idea of Chris moving to New York seemed set in stone. With each passing day they had talked more about it, even discussing where they would look for a place and how Chris would drum up his website business there. Julie-Ann talked about telling her father and Theresa. The plan was that once back in New York, Julie-Ann would start looking for an apartment and Chris would begin readying to move. Though there was no set timeframe, they talked about him hopefully coming out by the beginning of September.

It was Saturday, July 21st. It had been fifty-one days since Julie-Ann had left New York (though it felt even longer). That morning, Chris drove her to the Cheyenne Regional Airport for her flight home.

Julie-Ann and Chris hugged and kissed each other and promised that they would be together again soon. However, as Julie-Ann waited at the gate for her flight, she already started to miss him. She hoped it would not take long for him to come to New York, and prayed that for whatever reason he would not change his mind. When Julie-Ann boarded the plane, her thoughts turned to home and seeing her father and Theresa.

On the flight from Denver to New York, Julie-Ann was able to sleep for a couple of hours.

"Ladies and Gentleman, we are about to make our initial approach into John F. Kennedy International Airport," the Captain's voice rang over the intercom, waking Julie-Ann from her sleep. "We should be landing in about ten to fifteen minutes. The local time in New York is 5:12 p.m. We ask that you now make sure your seats and trays are in the upright position and that you turn off any electronic devices."

Julie-Ann, who was sitting in a window seat, peered out the small, oblong shaped window. But the only thing she could see was the ocean, appearing transiently through breaks in the low cloud coverage. It was raining, and there was precipitation on the window. However, after about five more minutes, as the plane descended, she could see intermittent views of Queens. She was back in New York.

By the time the plane landed and pulled up to the gate, Julie-Ann was wide-awake. In fact, though it had been a long flight, with a change of planes, she was pulsing with energy. As Julie-Ann made her way through the corridor, towards the baggage claim area, she could see Theresa and her father standing on the other side of the security checkpoint. Theresa spotted Julie-Ann and waved to her. Julie-Ann stepped up her pace as a smile grew from ear-to-ear. It seemed like a year since she had seen them.

As Julie-Ann passed the security checkpoint, Theresa ran to her and gave her a loving hug. "Oh, Jules, it's so good to have you back. I missed you so much."

"I missed you, too," Julie-Ann replied as she squeezed her.

Next it was her father's turn. James Crown was usually reserved, but he hugged his daughter so tight that he nearly lifted her off the ground. "Julie-Ann, it feels seems like I haven't seen you in forever."

"I know. I know."

After they were done with their greetings, they went over to the baggage claim to wait for Julie-Ann's luggage. Julie-Ann often thought about her father and stepmother on her journey, but it was not until she was standing there next to them that she realized just how much she missed them.

After getting her bags, they went outside to the curb, where her father had a limousine waiting. It was dark and rainy, and Theresa nestled Julie-Ann under her umbrella. The chauffeur quickly opened the back door for them and put the suitcases in the trunk.

"It's been raining for the last two days," Theresa said as she sat down.

"I have to say, I was pretty lucky with the weather on my trip," Julie-Ann replied.

Mr. Crown was sitting facing his daughter. "So, you had quite a trip," he said as the limousine pulled away. "You traveled across the whole country, you made friends, and you met a man."

"Dad, it was so much more than that," she replied as her face lit up. "I feel like I lived more, experience more, in these past two months than I had the whole rest of my life. I learned so much—not just about myself and life, but also about the country."

"And what did you learn about the country?" Theresa asked.

"I learned that most Americans are decent, hardworking people. I know there are a lot of people with bad intentions out there, but you'd be amazed at how many good people there are. People who love their community and their family and would do anything to help out someone in need—even a perfect stranger. And they're a resilient people, not easily knocked down, and even harder to keep down."

"I have to say, I've never seen you so passionate," her father said.

Julie-Ann smiled. "There's so much to be passionate about."

As the limousine exited onto the Belt Parkway, it immediately hit bumper-to-bumper traffic.

"Wow," Julie-Ann said as she looked out the back window.

"What's that?" Asked Theresa.

"It's been a while since I've seen this much traffic. I've gotten so used to wide-open roads. I almost forgot what gridlock looks like."

It took them an hour to get to their Midtown penthouse. When they walked in, Julie-Ann was overjoyed to see Rita there. They embraced in a long, tight hug. Julie-Ann wanted to fill her in on her journey, but Rita had made dinner for them, and it was ready.

"Rita, why don't you sit down and eat with us?" Julie-Ann asked.

"Oh, thank you, but I shouldn't," Rita replied in an apprehensive voice. In her years with the Crowns, she had never sat down and shared a meal with them."

"Come on, it's okay," Julie-Ann said. "You made the food. We can all sit down together, and I can tell everyone more about my journey."

Theresa and James looked at each other. "Yes, sit down with us," Theresa said.

"I don't know," Rita replied as she glanced at Mr. Crown.

"Yes, sit down and eat with us," he said. "It's a special occasion."

Though uncomfortable at first, Rita sat at the dining room table and had dinner with them. Over lamb chops and roasted potatoes, Julie-Ann talked about Yellowstone and Idaho Falls. She also talked about her desire to start a foundation to help people in need. Eventually, her father asked more about Chris, and she replied truthfully. However, she still did not mention about his plans to come to New York and for them to move in together. She was going to break the news soon, but not that first night, while they were all sitting down for dinner together.

That evening, after talking to Chris for a while, Julie-Ann laid in her bed with the television off. Exhausted from a long day, she looked around her sprawling bedroom. It was nice to be back. However, a part of her could not help but feel as though she had somehow out grown it—not physically of course, but rather mentally, spiritually.

Chapter 29

The morning after arriving back in New York, Julie-Ann finally scheduled her follow-up appointment for an MRI and blood work. Several days later, it was time for her appointment. Her father wanted to go with her, but she assured him there was no need.

"Dad, you know what Dr. Libowitz said, though there's a chance of the tumor re-growing, it usually doesn't happen for a while. Besides, I feel fine."

Figuring it *was* just a routine follow-up; her father relented. However, Theresa went with her. Julie-Ann had an MRI and blood drawn. Everything seemed to be routine, and she was out of there in less than an hour. Afterwards, she and Theresa went for lunch.

The next morning Julie-Ann was home when Dr. Libowitz called on the house phone.

"Hi doctor," she said in an upbeat voice. "I didn't realize you would be calling so soon with the results. I figured it would take a couple of days."

"Yes, well I got them yesterday and analyzed them. I'd like to make an appointment with you today or tomorrow to discuss the results."

A cold chill ran through Julie-Ann's body. She knew that something was wrong. If the MRI didn't show anything than why wouldn't he just come out and say it, there would be no need for a sit-down. And the fact that he wanted to see her that day made it that much more troubling. "Do...doc...did...did you find something? Is my tumor back?"

"I'd rather you just come in, and I can explain it to you."

When your neurosurgeon tells you that he would like to see you that afternoon, you do not put it off. Julie-Ann wanted to go to his office right then. Nevertheless, she had to wait until 3:00 p.m.

Her father was already at work, but Theresa was home and happened to catch Julie-Ann just as she was hanging up. Theresa could tell that something was wrong. Tears were starting to swell in Julie-Ann's eyes. She told Theresa. Theresa tried her hardest to keep her composure for her stepdaughter's sake and comfort her by telling her not to jump to any conclusions. But it was evident that something was not right. The only question was: How bad was it?

Theresa talked Julie-Ann into telling her father so that he could go with her to the appointment. He also told his daughter not to jump to any conclusions.

Mr. Crown came home early and went with his daughter and Theresa to the appointment. By that time, Julie-Ann had hours to ponder what she might hear. She hoped that it was that the tumor was returning, but they would just need to monitor it, which was the most likely scenario. After all, she had learned that meningioma was rarely fatal. Still, she tried to prepare herself for anything.

Dr. Libowitz brought Julie-Ann, her father, and Theresa into his office. After a somewhat somber hello, he swiveled a flat-panel monitor that was on his desk so that they could see it. He then brought up a large, detailed image of Julie-Ann's scan and pointed to a spot on Julie-Ann's brain. "As you can see here, the tumor has returned."

"I don't understand," Julie-Ann said in a distressed voice. "I feel fine. I haven't had any headaches or anything."

"Usually, such symptoms are caused by the placement and size of the tumor. At this point, this tumor is still relatively small."

Mr. Crown let out a sigh of relief. "Well thank God for that."

"But that doesn't exactly mean that it's good news," Dr. Libowitz said in a matter-of-fact tone. "As I previously told you, it is not uncommon for atypical tumors to grow back eventually. However, it's rare that they grow back so fast."

"What does that mean?" Mr. Crown asked in a rare, shaky voice.

Dr. Libowitz paused before answering. "For a tumor to grow this fast—it usually means that it's become malignant."

James jumped up from his seat. "What? What do you mean?"

"It could be cancerous. With meningioma, it's extremely rare. Maybe five percent of atypical tumors that have been surgically removed come back as malignant. And probably even less than five percent would grow back this fast."

"So what do we do?" Julie-Ann asked in a surprisingly calm voice.

"Well, for a tumor of this rapid growth, I would definitely recommend surgery."

"And will you be able to get it out?" Her father asked.

"It's impossible to know until we get in there. Of course, we can go in, take a biopsy and find out that it's not cancerous. Julie-Ann, I have to be straight with you, in my experience, that's highly unlikely. Though we'll try to remove the tumor, there's no guarantee. Of course, as I went over with you before your first surgery, there are always risks when operating on the brain." Dr. Libowitz paused. "But I don't honestly see an alternative. Even if it turns out to be non-cancerous, if the tumor keeps growing at this rate and is not removed, it will not take long before it impedes on some of the brain's functions."

Julie-Ann agreed to the surgery. She actually did not see that she had a choice. Dr. Libowitz said he would try to schedule something as soon as possible and would let them know of a date.

On the car ride home, both James and Theresa fought to keep their own fears and anguish in check and to be strong for Julie-Ann. For her part, Julie-Ann sat there and said little but was engulfed in a deluge of thoughts. Her whole life flashed before her eyes, but the vast majority of it was of the last several months. She thought about her journey, the phenomenal people she had met, the friends she had made. She thought about her spiritual awakening. She thought about Chris.

"It's okay," she said to Theresa and her father. "I don't want you guys worrying about me. Whatever happens, I'll be okay."

Theresa and her father each thought that Julie-Ann was in shock, not able to process and deal with the news she had just received. They could not have been further from the truth.

When Julie-Ann arrived back home, she went to her room to call Chris. It was not a conversation to which she was looking forward. Yet it had to be done, and there was no point putting it off. Although she had only known Chris a short time, he had his moments of romance and sensitivity. For the most part, she knew him to be strong. She never saw him whine or get down. But when she told him the news, she could tell he was crying. He wanted to console Julie-Ann, but in the end, it was her consoling him, telling him that everything would be okay. She told him that though the operation had not yet been scheduled, it would probably be soon. Chris said he was going to fly out on the next available flight.

A half hour later, Chris called Julie-Ann back to tell her he had booked a flight early the next morning. Julie-Ann told her father that Chris was coming out. It was not the way Mr. Crown intended to meet him, but he understood and respected that he wanted to be there for the operation. In fact, he even told Julie-Ann that Chris could stay in the penthouse. Out of respect, Chris politely declined the offer, and insisted on staying in a hotel.

Julie-Ann also told Amber that night. Amber came right over. In Julie-Ann's room, the two best friends from childhood talked. Amber had expected Julie-Ann to break down in tears, but she never did. In fact, she could not believe how calm and accepting Julie-

Ann was. Like Theresa and Mr. Crown, Amber thought that perhaps Julie-Ann was in shock, or had suppressed her true emotions. Nevertheless, Amber told her that she was there for her, no matter what she needed, no matter what time of day or night. That was the only time Julie-Ann's eyes started to swell with tears.

Julie-Ann didn't post anything about her condition or pending surgery on Facebook or Twitter. However, over the next few days, she did call Rory and Kathy, Sergeant Francisco, Lisa and Adele, and Lexi. She was not looking for any pity, but thought just in case something went wrong in the surgery, and she didn't make it, she should let them know. Naturally, they were all devastated. They also all told her that their prayers were with her. Rory and Kathy said they would go to church that night and pray for her. Of course, they also told her that they were sure everything would work out.

All the conversations Julie-Ann had with the friends she had made on her journey were heartfelt and emotional. They also all gave Julie-Ann great solace. But of all the phone calls she made, it was the one to Lisa that stuck with her the most. If anyone could understand her predicament, understand the word "cancer" it was Lisa. Yet it was more than that. The two had forged a special bond. Fifteen-year-old Lisa had taught Julie-Ann more about life than she had ever known.

The next morning Julie-Ann took a chauffeured car to pick Chris up from the airport and bring him to his hotel. She stayed with him there for a while. It was the first time since hearing the news that Julie-Ann cried. Both of them tried to be upbeat—at least in their words.

Chris' hotel was in Manhattan and cost $320 a night—$410 on the weekend. Julie-Ann wanted to pay for it, but Chris would not let her. Julie-Ann knew that Chris didn't have a lot of money, and she could not let him spend so much just because he wanted to be there for her. So unbeknownst to him, Julie-Ann charged the room to her card, with instructions to have an open tab. Chris found out after a few days, when he checked on his running bill. Not wanting to argue or stress Julie-Ann out in any way, he never brought it up to her.

A week and a half after Julie-Ann's appointment with Dr. Libowitz, she entered Sloan Kettering Hospital for her operation. Chris, who had met her father and Theresa, waited with them. Amber and her father were also there, as was James' brother. Even Rita was there.

There were also two other visitors waiting at the hospital that day. Two days earlier, knowing the date of the operation, Rory and Kathy McAlister came to New York. They did not tell Julie-Ann that they were coming, but called her the afternoon they arrived. Julie-Ann invited them over that evening to meet her father and Theresa. The McAlister's did not want to intrude, especially at such a critical and personal time for the family, but they did want to see Julie-Ann before the operation. By this time, James and Theresa had heard many stories about the McAlister's. They welcomed them as if they were family and thanked them for coming, as well as for everything they did for Julie-Ann while she was on her journey.

Now at the hospital, they waited along with Julie-Ann's father and stepmother. It was also the first time they had met Chris, though they had heard so much about each other through Julie-Ann. It was a long, nerve-racking wait. As not to take up the entire waiting room, and also to keep from going crazy, everyone took turns walking around and going outside. At one point, Rory and Chris went out together and had a long talk, of course, about Julie-Ann. Then Kathy, Theresa, and Rita took a stroll together.

Finally, after five hours, Dr. Libowitz came out to the waiting room and announced that the surgery was over, but everyone instantly feared by his demeanor that something was not right. He took James and Theresa aside, into an unoccupied room, and broke the news. The tumor was cancerous. Worse, it was an unusually aggressive cancer and had already spread to the region just outside the tumor. Not only was he unable to remove all the affected area just outside the growth, but because of its proximity to vital regions of the brain; Dr. Libowitz was not even able to remove the entire tumor.

As James and Theresa stood there trembling, tears flowing from their eyes, Dr. Libowitz went on to explain that Julie-Ann would have to undergo a rigorous radiation and chemotherapy treatment. And that was not even the worst of it.

"We'll schedule a follow-up appointment as soon as we can so we can sit down, and I can go over everything with you and Julie-Ann in detail," he said in a slow, methodical voice. "But I have to tell you and be honest with you, even with the chemo and radiation, the prognosis isn't good at all."

"Wha…what do you mean?" James asked in a quivering voice, afraid of the answer.

"Well, she might have a year, maybe even less."

"What?" James cried out.

Theresa's knees buckled and Dr. Libowitz had to catch her before she fell to the floor. He quickly sat her down on a chair while calling for a nurse to get her some water.

Before leaving, Dr. Libowitz explained that Julie-Ann was still under and had not yet learned of her condition.

James took it upon himself to break the news to everyone. Understandably, there was a lot of crying and disbelief. They all told James and Theresa that they were there for them whatever they needed—but in reality, there was nothing anyone could do. Everyone wanted to be supportive, but also wanted to give the family some space.

Kathy, Rory, and Rita went down to the hospital's chapel to pray. Chris also went with them. He was inconsolable. He could not believe what was happening. He had lost his wife, and now, he was going to lose Julie-Ann. He had finally found his soul mate, finally found love again, and with the blink of an eye, as quickly as they had said hello, they would have to say goodbye. Chris also felt for Julie-Ann herself, as well as her father and Theresa. *Why is it always the good people,* he angrily prayed to God in the chapel? *Why her? It's not her time.*

Julie-Ann's father and Theresa were by her bedside the next morning when Dr. Libowitz came by and finally broke the news to her. Tears swelled in her eyes, but it was not the reaction that they had expected. James and Theresa thought she would become hysterical. Once again, they thought she might be in shock.

As soon as Dr. Libowitz left the room, Julie-Ann took a deep breath. "I prepared myself for this," she said in a rather stoic voice. She then put her hand on her father's. "I want both of you to know that I'm at peace with this. I don't want either of you to worry about me or drive yourselves crazy over this."

"This stupid tumor," her father cried out. "Less than five-percent chance of it becoming malignant my ass. I mean, why you? Of all the people in the world..."

"It's okay Dad," Julie-Ann said in a weak, but calm voice. "I don't want to die, believe me. I want to live to be a hundred. But—and I know this is going to sound crazy—if I had to go back in time and never have gotten this tumor in the first place and live the rest of my life like I was doing, I wouldn't. Don't get me wrong, I had an extraordinary life, and you were both always so good to me. But getting that tumor, realizing how fragile life truly is, is what made me go on my journey. Otherwise, I would have never met the people I did, never experienced what I experienced, never learned what I learned. And that—I wouldn't trade that for all the time in the world."

Julie-Ann was in the hospital for the next five days. Her room had become overfilled with flowers and cards. She also had constant visitors, including of course, Amber. Naturally, Chris was also at Julie-Ann's side for hours at a time, but wanted to be respectful and give her time alone with her father and Theresa. However, they were often there at the same time and quickly formed a bond.

A week after her operation, Julie-Ann began a rigorous radiation and chemotherapy regimen. The cocktail of drugs that she was taking made her constantly sick, sometimes leaving her bedridden.

What strength the chemo didn't take from her, the radiation did, leaving her perpetually lethargic.

Chris moved to New York early that September to be with Julie-Ann. They moved into an apartment together in SoHo. He was able to continue to work on his website business, but most of his time was spent taking care of Julie-Ann, making sure she was comfortable, taking her to treatment, and being there for her when she was sick. Seeing how Chris treated Julie-Ann, and how much he loved her, adorned him to her father and Theresa. In fact, it was not long before they considered him like a son.

Chris had thought about asking Julie-Ann to marry him, but he never did. Only because he was afraid how it would look to her father. Chris was not interested in Julie-Ann's money and did not want there to be a perception that he was, even if he gladly would have signed a prenuptial agreement.

Amber also visited Julie-Ann often. She still could not believe that her best friend, whom she had known since grade school, was actually dying. Dying! Amber felt guilty for not understanding Julie-Ann's journey at first, and the rift that had formed between them—even though it was now water under the bridge. It all seemed insignificant. Most of all, Amber felt angry. How could God take Julie-Ann away, such a loving, caring person—and so young? It was not fair at all. She tried to hide her despair and bitterness from Julie-Ann and to put on a strong front. But Julie-Ann knew her friend too well and would tell Amber not to feel bad or sorry for her.

Julie-Ann, of course, wanted to spend as much time with Chris, her father, Theresa, and the rest of her family and friends as possible. However, she devoted much of the time she had left to becoming a philanthropist. With the help of her father, she started The Helping Road Foundation, which catered to myriad of causes. Chris, who designed and maintained the website, also helped with the foundation's work, as did Theresa. People could contact the foundation with their stories and ask for assistance. However, most of the time it was Julie-Ann that sought out an individual or family that needed help and contacted them. She might hear about their situation from a news story, or from a friend or family member. Of course, Lisa Hendricks always knew someone that needed help and was always in close contact with Julie-Ann, not just to help with the foundation, but also as a friend. Amber assisted as well, and in doing so, it lessened her anger towards the cruel hands of fate.

Despite her condition, Julie-Ann worked tirelessly with the foundation that she had started. No matter how she felt physically, knowing that she had helped someone through a difficult time or get back on their feet brought her joy and peace of mind. She always took extra comfort any time she was able to help a child or a veteran.

Julie-Ann's condition continued to deteriorate. It seemed all the chemotherapy and radiation was doing was making her sick and taking away what strength the cancer had left her. In December of 2011, in consultation with Dr. Libowitz, with the inevitable approaching, Julie-Ann stopped all treatment.

Chris had talked to Adele and Lisa on the phone many times. Adele had mentioned that they wanted to come to New York and see Julie-Ann. Not knowing how much time she had left, and figuring Lisa would be on break from school, Chris suggested that they visit that Christmas. They agreed not to tell Julie-Ann and surprise her. Afterwards, Chris began to worry that Mr. Crown would be upset.

Not that he wouldn't want her to see Adele and Lisa, but only because it would be the holidays and he had limited time to spend with his daughter. However, when Chris called him, Mr. Crown thought it was a great idea. He knew how much both Adele and Lisa meant to Julie-Ann. In fact, he insisted on flying them out on his private jet and putting them up in a hotel.

They arrived in New York the night before Christmas Eve. However, Julie-Ann still didn't know that they had come. Instead, Theresa had picked them up from their hotel on Christmas Eve and brought them to the penthouse. When Chris brought Julie-Ann over later that day, she instantly broke down in tears—but they were tears of joy. She said it was the best Christmas present she could have received.

Adele and Lisa were in New York for four days, and during that time, it was as if Julie-Ann found hidden strength. She actually took them sightseeing around the city. They went to see the tree at Rockefeller Center and even the Rockettes. Though they sometimes talked about the foundation and the excellent work it was doing, most of the time they tried to keep things upbeat.

As it always does, time went fast, and before any of them knew it, they were at the airport saying their goodbyes. Though they dared not say it, they all understood that it could very well be goodbye forever. Julie-Ann had been somehow able to keep it together. Even though Adele's eyes could not help swell with tears, she smiled, hugged Julie-Ann and said that they would come out again, maybe during Lisa's spring break. However, it was Lisa, always strong and positive that could not help but break down as she threw her arms around Julie-Ann. As tears flowed down her face, the sixteen-year-old cried unrestrainedly.

"I love you so much," she sobbed into Julie-Ann's shoulder. There was more she wanted to say but refrained. However, there were no other words that mattered.

"I love you, too," Julie-Ann replied, unable to stop herself from crying. "And I'll see you again."

Not long after Adele and Lisa left, Julie-Ann started to deteriorate. The cancer was beginning to take over her brain and metastasize. Her speech was impeded, and then her short-term memory began to flicker. Eventually, even her motor skills were affected.

One day in April, while spending the afternoon with her father, Julie-Ann seemed to be having a particularly lucid day. He was taking her for a walk in Central Park, just as he had done when she was a child. He wanted so much to be upbeat and just enjoy their day together. Overwhelmed by the memory, he stopped walking, went over to a nearby rock, and sat down.

Though he tried to wipe them away inconspicuously, Julie-Ann could see tears in her father's eyes. "What's wrong Dad?" She asked in a slightly slurred voice.

"I'm sorry sweetie. I don't mean to ruin our time together, but it's just not fair."

Julie-Ann sat down on the rock next to her father. "Don't cry Dad."

Her father wiped away more tears. "It's just that it seems like just yesterday that I would take you to Central Park as a little girl. I can still see you, so tiny and smiling. What happened to the time? And why is the time you have ahead being stolen from you? You're only twenty-six. You should have forty, fifty years ahead of you."

Julie-Ann put her arm around her father's shoulder. "It's not about how much we have dad; it's about what we do with that time."

On June 11, 2012, while at her apartment with Chris, Julie-Ann Dyanna Crown suffered a massive stroke. She was pronounced dead at the hospital. She was only twenty-six-years-old.

Four days later Julie-Ann's funeral was held. Adele and Lisa came to New York to attend, as did Rory and Kathy, Connie and her husband Frank, Michelle, Sgt. Francisco, Lester, Helen Vigman, and Lexi and Evan.

Though Julie-Ann had died, her memory and work lived on, not only in the hearts and minds of those that had known her, but also in The Helping Road Foundation. In her will, which she had created after learning her prognosis, Julie-Ann left nearly all of her estate to the foundation. Her father, who had already donated several million dollars to the foundation, would wind up giving over $100 million of his own money to The Helping Road.

Also in her will, Julie-Ann requested that Chris stay on as the chairman of the foundation. Over the years, he worked relentlessly making sure that the foundation's money went to appropriate causes, helping countless individuals and families in need. He also enlisted the help of Lisa Hendricks, putting her to work fulltime in The Helping Road. Amber would also volunteer much of her time and money.

Chris did not stop there. He started a blog, writing about injustices that were going on around the country, but were rarely mentioned by the mainstream media. However, he would also write about different stories of selfless deeds, patriotism, perseverance, and hope.

In Cedar Grove Cemetery in Queens, New York, Julie-Ann was buried next to her natural mother. On her headstone read:

Julie-Ann Dyanna Crown
1986 – 2012
Though Her Time On This Earth
May Have Been Short,
The Mark She Left On It
Will Live Forever